For the Nethansons

Thanks to Sandy
for making this all
possible

Norman Gaub

Turner's Wife

Norman Garbo

Turner's Wife

W · W · NORTON & COMPANY
New York   London

Published simultaneously in Canada by George J. McLeod Limited, Toronto.
Printed in the United States of America.

The text of this book is composed in Baskerville. Composition by New England
Typographic Service, Inc. Printing and binding by The Haddon Craftsmen, Inc.

First Edition

Library of Congress Cataloging in Publication Data

Garbo, Norman.
    Turner's wife.

    I. Title.
PS3557.A65T8 1983   813'.54   82–14221

ISBN 0-393-01521-1

W. W. Norton & Company, Inc., 500 Fifth Avenue, New York, N. Y. 10110
W. W. Norton & Company, Ltd., 37 Great Russell Street, London WC1B 3NU

1 2 3 4 5 6 7 8 9 0

For Rhoda . . .
Garbo's Wife.

Turner's Wife

ONE

The Present

Paul Turner came up out of sleep slowly, like a diver, pausing at each successive level. Not quite awake, he reached for his wife and touched only a pillow. He opened his eyes, wondering when he would stop doing that.

Then he remembered what day this was.

"Well," he said and lit a cigarette, virtuously promising himself not to smoke another until midmorning and not to have his third until noon. Terrific: He could be dead in twenty-four hours, and he was still protecting his lungs. Turner, the exemplary corpse.

He rose slowly and painfully from the bed, a tall, lean, still young man with the scars of seventeen battle wounds making a welted map of his torso and thighs. Half-bent, naked, he limped about the room in irregular circles, gradually working his body straighter until he was walking fully erect and with no limp at all. It was a daily ceremony, longer on some mornings than on others, depending upon the weather and other variables, but as much a part of his waking as the opening of his eyes. Today, because the air was clear and without humidity, it took a bit less time. When the ritual was done, when he considered himself straight enough to deal with the world and the particular day that lay ahead, Turner went in to shower.

He was not normally fussy about his clothes, but this morning he dressed with care . . . even to the point of changing his underwear twice because there were slight tears in the shorts he had chosen, and torn underwear had always bothered his wife. So what was he doing today? Dressing for Maria? Why not? he thought and went a step further by putting on the navy jacket, blue oxford shirt, rep tie, and gray whipcord slacks that had been her favorite outfit. At one moment, dressing, he almost began to feel like an aging matador going through his ritual preparations to face a final edition of death in the afternoon. Except that in this case there was neither the history nor the tradition of the bullring, only the threat.

Turner was not especially hungry, but he had his usual breakfast of orange juice, toast, and coffee. He thought it a good idea not to change anything today. It was not superstition. It was just that he was a great believer in the efficacy of routine, in the power of a regular, disciplined approach to see you through the worst of times and situations. If you did what you had to, if you met all your hourly, daily, and weekly contracts and obligations, the rest would somehow take care of itself. Or so he had always believed.

The telephone rang as he was finishing his coffee, and he automatically rose to answer it. Then he stopped and returned to his chair. The phone kept ringing, going on and on, as if the caller knew Turner was there and refused to accept the fiction of his absence. Turner felt himself start to sweat. It was very hard for him not to pick up a ringing telephone. An irrepressible optimist, he was convinced that every call that came in was sure to change his life for the better. But not this one, he thought. This one would just mean more conversation. And there had already been too much of that. The time for talking was over. Still, the tension did not leave until the ringing had stopped.

There was a dishwasher, but he washed and dried the few utensils by hand. Then he went into the bedroom to pack. He was taking very little, just a Samsonite one-suiter with changes of linen and another sport jacket and pair of slacks. He rarely wore a suit and could not remember the last time he had bought one. He took a revolver from a drawer, broke it open, and loaded all six chambers from a box of .38-caliber cartridges. He started to take along a few extra rounds, but he changed his mind and put them back into the box and the box back into the drawer. Six would be enough. If not, neither would sixty.

He tucked the revolver inside his belt and buttoned his jacket over it. The weapon pressed against his stomach, making him suck in an already flat gut. He found a silencer in his handkerchief drawer and slipped it into a breast pocket. It bulged. He stood there, feeling ridiculous: Wyatt Earp, off to the O.K. Corral.

Then he remembered airport security, with its electronic gates and buzzers, and he transferred the revolver and silencer to his suitcase. Lovely. Imagine if he had not remembered in time and had just walked into the waiting arms of the machine. Go and explain that one to the FBI. Truly, gentlemen, it was not my intention to hijack the airplane. Consider: Why would I have needed a silencer for *that?* Turner smiled, but he had the feeling the FBI might have been less amused.

He spent almost an hour on two lengthy notes that he wrote at his desk in the study and that he left there sealed in separate envelopes. The first was to his editor, detailing pretty much how he felt the final chapters of his unfinished novel should go and assuring her that he had absolute confidence in her ability to complete the manuscript as well as, if not better than, he could. He also thanked her for her encouragement and help in turning out his previous books and credited her with being largely responsible for their success. Turner apologized for not having been able to get very much writing done during the past months, but circumstances had simply not allowed it. He had always been a gut writer rather than a cerebral one, and unfortunately most of his gut had been taken up elsewhere. Finally, he hoped that Peggy's congenital Wasp reticence would not be too greatly compromised if he dedicated this, his last published work, to her with his deepest respect and affection. He had briefly considered substituting *love* for the *affection,* but thought better of it. What would be the point? Turner left the note on top of the nearly five hundred pages of manuscript that he was sure Peggy would very quickly cut down by 20 percent.

The second note was addressed to Turner's lawyer and concerned several details of his will. Turner regretted not having been able to compose his last testament himself. Instead, it was written in dry legalese, peppered with dozens of *whereases* and *in the events of.* This was not how he would have chosen to be remembered. He felt a last will and testament should be warm, simple, and personal, representative of the man or woman whose final wishes were being carried out by it. But, of course, it was foolish of him to be concerned about something like that when his books were all still out there, very much in print. Whatever he was, whatever he thought, felt, and believed, was in one way or another reflected in his published works. Not many had the chance to leave behind so complete a record. He was one of the lucky ones. He, at least, had been a writer. My God, he thought, I'm using the past tense.

He took a last look around. He had left lights on in one of the hallways and the bathroom, and he switched them off. There still seemed to be a faint scent of perfume in the bathroom, and he stood there for a moment breathing it in. He went into his bedroom, saw that the bed was unmade, and carefully straightened the sheets and blankets. Although he hardly ever bothered with the bedspread, he somehow felt the need to put it on today. Maria's photograph was on a bureau, and he glanced at it in passing, seeing a lovely, fair-haired woman with an incredible smile, caught and held forever in the brightness of a summer day.

Turner picked up his suitcase, left the apartment, and locked the door behind him.

The Past

On another morning, some months earlier, Paul Turner awoke to the sound of rain and looked at his wife in the gray dawn light. Her face was turned toward him on the pillow, soft and vulnerable in sleep, trusting, a child's face. Maria, he thought . . . Maruschka. He wished he had known her as a little girl, wished he had seen her walking through the streets of the small New Jersey town where she had grown up. She must have had that same happy, eager look even then, as though there were only good surprises waiting ahead and nothing and no one would ever make her believe otherwise. She probably had had lots of friends, girls and boys who would have been drawn to her without understanding why, but who knew they felt just a little better when she was with them and not nearly as good when she was gone.

How different from him. While he was fighting to survive the streets of New York, ducking fists, bottles, and knives, an urban cat with nine lives, had she been planting flowers and cutting dress patterns? If there was any sort of scheme to the ways things worked, they had been getting ready to spend their lives together even then. That is, if you believed in such a notion. Sometimes the idea seemed ridiculous. Other times Turner found it impossible to consider his life as just a series of insane accidents. There had to be an overall plan. Because

13

if there wasn't, any number of other men could be lying beside his wife at this moment, looking into her face, and feeling an equal joy and wonder in loving her. And this was something he was simply not prepared to accept.

Maria stirred, and her eyes fluttered open as she came awake. Seeing Turner, she pulled the blanket over her face. "You know I hate you to watch me sleep."

"Would you deny me one of my least offensive pleasures?"

"But I look so awful."

"You look like a little girl, all soft, pink, and blonde."

"I don't," she said from under the blanket. "I look like a thirty-four-year-old bag with her mouth open and a dopey expression on her aging face."

He drew back the blanket and kissed her eyes. "Some aging face."

"I've even started to think about having some plastic surgery done."

"You're out of your head. You look eighteen years old."

"Not to the camera. My publicity shots need more and more retouching."

"Screw the camera."

She considered it. "For that, I think I prefer you."

"Okay," he said happily and gathered her to him.

"What time is it?"

"Great. Now you've gone and wired it to a clock."

"It's going to be one of those wild mornings. I don't know what to do first."

"I'll show you."

In time, they were content, and he lay like a wounded soldier on her breast. "Such a mechanism," he breathed, awed, as always, by the recurring miracle.

She smiled, holding him. A gust of wind drove the rain against the window, and they lay listening to its sound. The east side of New York had not yet come fully awake, but the traffic was beginning to build and squeal. Steel and glass monsters in an asphalt cage. Still, it was mostly the rain they heard.

14

"It will be eight years next week," he said. "Isn't it time I started getting a little bored with you?"

"Men never get bored with Ukrainian women. We're trained to give pleasure. The geishas of the western world."

"The closest you've ever been to the Ukraine is West Patterson, New Jersey."

"That doesn't matter. My mother was a superb teacher. 'Maruschka,' she used to say, 'one day you will drive your husband wild.' "

Ukrainians, Turner thought. A rare breed . . . tough, strong, clannish, jealously proud of their history and traditions. Even as immigrants, they remained a group apart. Visiting Maria's parents for the first time, Turner had been fascinated by the transplanted culture their little colony managed to preserve in their own corner of New Jersey. Above all, they were survivors. Czars and dictators came and went, along with their bloody wars, purges, and *gulags.* These people sent down new roots in a new land and lived on. Maria, conceived behind barbed wire somewhere in Poland, born near the Garden State Parkway, had done more than just survive. She had prevailed.

"I have an idea," he whispered to her breast. "Let's not go tonight. I'll send a telegram to the British ambassador. I'll say I have to go in for an emergency lobotomy. A small one."

"Darling, we've been through all that."

"They'll never miss us."

"Paul, you can't just turn down an invitation to something like this."

"Why not? It's an invitation, not a command. And you know how I hate these big mob scenes."

Maria disengaged herself and slid out of bed. "What about me? The invitation happens to have been addressed to both of us."

"You can go without me." He watched her put on her robe. "We never stay together at these things anyway."

"Paul!"

His name, so spoken, meant it was serious. "It's really that important to you?"

"Paul, you're being honored. I've heard that even the president may put in an appearance." She walked toward the bathroom, slender, long-necked, a lily. "Besides, it can be very useful to me. I can probably pick up bushels of world-class guests for the show."

"You're a shameless opportunist."

"That's the best kind to be ... shameless." She disappeared and Turner heard the shower start. But an instant later she stuck her head into the room and made a face at him. "It's also why I'm such a big success, you ape," she said and vanished once more.

Turner smiled and lay there, savoring the moment. Then, with a sigh, he pushed himself out of bed and began his morning circling. Today, because of the rain and the exertions of love-making, he knew it was going to take longer than usual to get himself straightened out. He caught a glimpse of himself in the closet mirror, bent, twisted, limping along like a latter-day Quasimodo. Then he thought, stop bitching. At least you're alive. A lot of good ones aren't.

Maria left for the studio at nine, and Turner stayed at his typewriter for most of the morning despite a stream of interruptions. Maria and he occupied the entire top floor of an old, converted limestone mansion on East Sixty-third Street, a former robber baron's home, in which something always seemed to be going wrong with either the plumbing or the electricity. This morning a circuit breaker kept going off, and the janitor was in and out half a dozen times before he was able to diagnose the problem. But Turner was working well, and when he was going like that no intrusion could bother him. He was on the final novel of his Vietnam trilogy, with the battered remnants of his platoon coming home to almost as much pain and frustration as they had suffered in the line, and he was wallowing in it right along with them. Writing about the war could come very close to living it again for him

. . . at least, when he was writing well. At such times he felt it as a tide of pure physical energy that rose in his chest and flowed out from there. These strange creative victories. There could be true literary exaltation in him. Still, at other times, he found it hard to believe he was really a writer, thinking himself presumptuous to even dare place words on paper and send them naked into the world. God knows, he was no intellectual. He was not even an especially original thinker. What he did have, however, was a good solid depth of feeling and enough perception to let him cut through to the heart of things. And when he was at his best, and a little lucky besides, he was able to make others know it.

The phone rang and he picked it up. "How about breaking away from that miserable typewriter and taking me to lunch?"

Turner glanced at his watch. "You're on the air in exactly eight minutes."

"So?"

"So that's all you have on your mind? Me and food?"

"Yes, but not in that order."

"Just keep talking like that. You'll end up fat and alone."

"Come on, Paul."

He pulled thoughtfully at an ear.

"You do have to eat," she said.

"Yes, but not your two-hours' worth." He usually gulped a sandwich as he worked. "And I'm hot right now."

"Stop being such a time miser. Remember what Hemingway said."

What Hemingway had said was that he usually found it best to quit while the juices were flowing. "Who's Hemingway?"

"Will you pick me up at the studio?"

"Will it help our marriage?"

"Definitely."

"Okay."

"Look nice," she said and hung up before he could change his mind.

17

Looking nice meant shaving and wearing something other than his usual turtleneck, jeans, and sneakers. Turner put the receiver down slowly, thinking about his wife. Then he finished the scene he had been working on, made a few penciled notes about what was to follow, and went to shave.

It had stopped raining and the sun was out by the time Turner reached the street. Starting uptown, he suddenly felt lightfooted and free, his home and work in order and safely locked behind him. Maria's studio was just five blocks away, on East Sixty-eighth Street, a pleasant walk on a day like this. He gazed warmly at the hurrying lunch hour crowds on Lexington Avenue, like a farmer with a good day's work under his belt strolling over his rich acreage. Recalling a similar noontime stroll in Saigon years before, he thought of a possible Vietcong grenade or rocket exploding on the sidewalk between Sixty-fourth and Sixty-fifth streets, and he stared curiously at those passing by on the avenue. Grenades, rockets, and bombs might explode in Beirut, Jerusalem, Kabul, Belfast, Saigon, or Hanoi, but life would never render itself so cruelly insane as to shatter a single pane of glass in Bloomingdale's windows.

Turner entered a soaring steel and glass tower, took an express elevator to the thirty-fifth floor, and came out onto the opulent red carpeting of the Continental Broadcasting Network. The receptionist flashed him her most dazzling smile and glanced at a wallclock. "Maria still has another twelve minutes to go, Mr. Turner. Why don't you wait in the control room. It's Studio Ten, same as always."

Typical. Maria was Maria and he was Mr. Turner. But at least it was better than being called Mr. Monroe, which was his wife's professional name. He followed the red carpeting between framed portraits of the network's stars, then stopped in front of Maria's. Underneath the picture was written, *Maria Monroe, Star of "Maria at Noon," Radio's Most Talked-about Talk Show.* There was also a long list of distinguished people who had appeared as guests on the show over the years. Three presidents were among them, including the present one. Turner was not on the list, although he had been on the show more than a few times. He had teased Maria about it. "Are you ashamed of me or is it just that the network frowns on nepotism?"

He had met her at his first appearance on "Maria at Noon." Turner had been a nervous, tongue-tied, neophyte author, who was being pushed to promote his new book and failing miserably until Maria put him at ease and uncorked him. She claimed he fell in love with her out of sheer gratitude. Not true. He fell in love with her because she made him feel he was more than he knew himself to be. No mean feat. He also fell in love with her (he decided long after the fact) because she was probably the kindest person he had ever known. That tiny hard core of pettiness that occasionally surfaced in almost everyone was simply not in her.

Turner continued on down the corridor to Studio Ten and entered the control room. It was a live broadcast, and the show's producer-director, Henry Walton, was seated beside an earphoned engineer at a large control panel. They nodded to Turner, and Walton waved him into a seat. "Sit down, sit down. You're just in time to hear her really give it to this joker." The producer chuckled softly. "What a job she's been doing on him. Devastating."

Turner peered through the soundproof glass at Maria and her guest, a sleek, dark-eyed, swarthy man wearing a frozen smile. They were seated at a table before separate microphones. "Who is he?"

"Abu Zuhair. The Kuwaitian oil minister. He's also this year's head of OPEC."

Turner sat down and listened.

". . . And the truth of it is, Mr. Zuhair," Maria was saying gently, "that the only motivation I can see behind OPEC's pricing policy these past years is simple, naked greed. While the rest of the world strangles on the inflationary spiral that the cost of your oil is feeding, you people clap your hands with joy and claim you're just getting even for your years of exploitation. Well, let me tell you something, sir. If it wasn't

19

for those so-called years of exploitation, most of your people would still be sitting on their buried resources, as hungry, illiterate, and diseased as they've been for the past thousand years. And how do you show your gratitude? By putting a knife at our throats and treating us as your enemies instead of as your benefactors. Do you think that's fair?"

The man opened his mouth to reply, but Maria did not give him the chance. "No, it's not," she said. "And America, for one, is running out of patience. This country is not going to just stand around indefinitely with a sharpened blade at its jugular. Not when its economic survival is at stake. You would do well to remember that at your upcoming pricing session."

Zuhair began what was obviously one of his stock retorts, but Walton was not interested. "What do you think of that?" the producer asked Turner.

"Pretty strong stuff. Can she really get away with that kind of saber rattling?"

"Why not? Maria is a private citizen. She can say what she pleases." Walton leaned closer. "But I'll tell you this. She doesn't always operate off the cuff. Someone from the State Department did actually call her this morning. He knew Zuhair was going to be on today's show and was interested in Maria's approach. I didn't hear the conversation, but it wouldn't surprise me if he asked Maria to say some of the things she said. There's a lot that Washington can't say officially that it likes to get across in other ways."

Walton held up three warning fingers and waited for Maria to notice. Without breaking the cadence of her delivery, she lifted a hand to acknowledge the signal. A moment later Walton held up one finger to indicate the wrap-up, and Maria concluded her last thought, thanked a no-longer-smiling Abu Zuhair for appearing on her show and finished with her usual closing line. "This is 'Maria at Noon,' hoping you have a wonderful rest of the day."

The engineer twisted several dials, the show's theme swelled, and an announcer's voice praised the sponsor's product generously. Then the engineer twisted another dial, and an almost shocking silence settled over the control room. Turner stood up, and Maria waved to him through the glass.

They had lunch at La Boite, a small French restaurant on East Sixty-fourth Street with a narrow bar near the window and old-fashioned maps of the wine sections of France hung around soothingly dark walls. It was a place they had started coming to when they first met, and although it had changed hands several times over the years and Turner was no longer especially fond of French cooking, he still enjoyed looking at his wife across one of La Boite's ridiculously tiny tables, enjoyed the quiet softness of her face, the bouncy way she wore her hair, the casual elegance of her clothes. A young woman at a nearby table came over to have her menu autographed, and Maria talked to her for a few moments. It did not happen often enough to be an annoyance. Radio personalities were rarely recognized by even their more devoted fans.

The waiter brought their food and fussed over them, smiling with a French fondness for prosperous diners who ate expensive lunches and were celebrities besides. When he left, all but bowing and scraping, Turner said, "You were kind of rough on that poor little Arab today, weren't you?"

"Some poor little Arab. Four wives, three Mercedes and two Rolls, a roughly estimated income of fifty million a year, and a thief besides. I swear they're all thieves. I wouldn't trust the best of them with a dying goat."

"Careful. You're starting to sound like a Jew."

"I *am* a Jew, you pumpkinhead."

"I keep forgetting." It was a private joke. Maria was one of those rarities, Jew by conversion.

"Do you think I came on too strong?"

"Not for me. But I doubt that you picked up many new friends among the oil-producing countries of the world."

"That wasn't my purpose."

"So I understand. Henry said you had a call from the State Department this morning."

"Henry sometimes talks too much."

21

"It was only to me."

"I know, darling. But it isn't always only to you."

Turner watched the delicate way she used her knife and fork on the veal. "So what did the State Department want?"

"The usual. They just wanted to touch base when they saw I was having Zuhair on." She smiled. "They rather hoped I might run him over the coals a bit."

"You sure did that."

She looked at him. "It bothers you, doesn't it?"

"What?"

"My singeing Zuhair's tail feathers."

"Why should it bother me?"

"Because you happen to be a nice man who hates to see anyone at all take a beating. And also because it offends your incredibly idealized image of me as a sweet, gracious type."

"You make me sound like an absolute ass."

Maria laughed. "But such a lovely, romantic one."

"And this is what I'm losing two hours of work to hear?"

"Don't sulk. Why do you think I fell in love with you?"

"Because I'm such a lovely romantic ass?"

"Because you're one of the last of that marvelous vanishing breed that still believes in the perfection of his woman, the righteousness of his country, and the infallability of his God."

"That just makes me sound like a naïve ass."

She touched his hand. "Not to me. I adore it. At least you're a believer. I'm so tired of the cynical and resigned, the poetic despairers who never have anything decent or hopeful to say about anything. They've made this a sour time to live. You make it a little sweeter."

"Okay," Turner said, embarrassed because he knew she meant every word and he was not quite certain he was able to handle it. Yet he loved the straight way she could come out with something like that, and he suddenly wished he could preserve the moment in bronze, like a pair of baby's shoes, to be taken out and held to the light at odd, lonely moments during the years ahead. "Okay. You've redeemed yourself.

22

No separate checks. Lunch is on me."

At 10:35 that evening, Turner, stiff and uncomfortable in dinner clothes, lifted a glass of champagne (his sixth) from a passing tray and gazed almost benignly about him at the sparkling scene. A large, multi-stringed orchestra was playing, beautiful women were laughing, distinguished men in dinner clothes and dress uniforms were speaking in confident voices, and Turner had the feeling he had seen all this before in a whole series of old and not very good movies. Looking around, he guessed there must be at least a dozen generals present. Astounding. Two full years of combat in the cities and jungles of Southeast Asia and he could remember seeing no more than a single general officer . . . and that one on a parade ground at a distance of two hundred yards. Now, standing and sipping vintage champagne in the Sybaritic elegance of the Sixty-sixth Street residence of the British ambassador to the UN, generals were clustered about him like ants. Turner was certain there was a significant moral judgment to be drawn from this somewhere, but he had no interest at all in figuring it out.

The crowd in front of him shifted at that moment, and he caught a glimpse of Maria. She was standing beside a full-length portrait of the queen of England, talking and laughing with the chief Soviet delegate to the United Nations and two stolid-looking Russian generals. Without being able to hear a word of their conversation, Turner was sure it was in Russian, which Maria spoke fluently and never missed a chance to use. It always intrigued Turner to hear her. It made him feel he was listening to a complete stranger who somehow was managing to speak with his wife's voice from his wife's body.

The British ambassador approached the group, stood chatting for a moment, then escorted Maria over to where his own wife was talking to a pair of celebrated Southern playwrights and a Nobel Prize–winning poet. Earlier, Turner had been able to pick out a veritable gaggle of Pulitzers and at

23

least half a dozen English literary lights whose names were famous enough to impress even a functioning illiterate. The reception was being held as a tribute to the English-speaking literary community, and there were indeed some outstanding people present. Which merely added to Turner's general discomfort. He was an English-speaking writer, truly enough, but a writer with a very small "w," while most of these others were highly capitalized. Still, his invitation had been the same as theirs, and Maria appeared to be having a fine time. The odds favored his surviving the evening.

It was his father who really would have enjoyed seeing him here with these people, he thought. God, the *naches* he would have felt. Imagine. His son, the writer, being honored in the home of the British ambassador to the United Nations. And a *Jewish* writer, besides. Only in America. Turner's father had been born in this country, but his father's parents had not, and it evidently took more than a single generation to erase the stamp of Russian ghettos. So Turner had always been a *Jewish* writer to his father, although his themes were never specifically those of the Jewish experience, and it was his father himself who had Americanized Turnovsky into Turner. "Not from shame," explained the new Max Turner. "God should strike me dead if I should ever be ashamed to be called a Jew. It just sounds more American."

Nevertheless, the name change was part of the greenhorn mentality, the reverse side of the American dream. Assimilation was a desperately needed nipple that the immigrant fought to suckle. Better a Yankee than a *greener*. Also, Max had lived out his life as a traveling salesman, and more hardware could be sold in Fargo, Terra Haute, and Cheyenne by a Turner than by a Turnovsky. Or so Max had believed. His poor father, Turner thought, had traded in his *kishkas* for a crack at Mount Rushmore and had been sadly short-changed. The only Cadillac in his future had turned out to be a black one, rented to carry him to his grave in a style to which he had never had the chance to become accustomed. But at least he had been around to see his son presented with no less a distinction than the Medal of Honor. Riddled with lymphomata and down to 111 pounds, Max Turner, nee Turnovsky, had sat straight as a West Pointer in the East Room of the White House and watched with drowning eyes as the president of the United States hung America's highest military decoration around Paul's neck and shook his hand. Afterward, Max had only two things to say: "Momma should only have been alive to see," and "That'll show those *goyim*." He died exactly nineteen days later, never knowing that his son would soon fall in love with and marry one of them.

Dimly, Turner became aware that Maria was now part of another group, this one boasting the president himself as its centerpiece. True to advance notices, the chief executive had indeed stopped by earlier, enunciated a few suitably laudatory words to the literary figures being honored, and was now doing his obligatory socializing. Which he did well, Turner thought, carrying off the chore with an easy style that made it appear as though there was nothing in the world he would rather be doing at that moment. President Woodruff was a man of medium height and build, with a face that Turner had long ago decided was not an especially good face for a president. It looked too much like the face of a prosperous business man . . . a little too soft, a little too pleased with itself, a little too absorbed with beating last year's figures. Still, it was the face of the president of the United States, and no one said it had to come out of a political casting office.

Turner sipped his champagne and established a new and better protected position in a corner. Axiom: Always keep your rear and flanks protected and you'll be safe from surprise attack. In situations like this, you also had to keep your mobility. Sit down, and you could be hopelessly trapped.

"Hello," someone said.

Turner found himself looking at a slender, dark-haired young woman with big, curious eyes and an open face. "Hi," he said cautiously.

"I don't believe we've met. I'm Fran."

"Paul."

"Paul who?"

"Turner."

"Should I know who you are?"

"Not really."

"Aren't you famous?"

"No."

"Then why were you invited here tonight with all these famous people?"

Turner laughed. Her eyes, besides being big and curious, were rather impudent. "Why were you?"

"Because my father is famous."

"Who is your father?"

"The president."

"Jesus Christ," said Turner.

"No . . . just the president," said the girl sweetly and moved off through the crowd.

She returned a short while later. "I've found out all about you," she reported, "and you are, too, famous."

"Someone has been lying to you."

"Are you calling the president of the United States a liar?"

"No offense to your father, but I'm afraid the Oval Office has never carried very much immunity in that area."

"I think you've just said something insulting."

"It was meant to be only factual."

"My father has read your books. He said no one since Stephen Crane has written more honestly about war and those who fight it. He also said you were a genuine war hero."

Turner said nothing. In spite of a hard-earned cynicism about such things, he felt pleased. The president was still, after all, the president.

"How did you get to be a hero?"

"By sheer accident," said Turner and found a refuge of sorts in his champagne.

"Am I embarrassing you?"

"A little."

"Good, I'm glad I'm able to at least do *something* to you."

26

He looked at her without comprehension.

"I've been watching you," she said. "You're separate from the world. Everyone else mingles. Everyone else talks to people. Everyone else makes an effort to be sociable. While you just stand here like a solitary fortress, mysterious and impenetrable."

"I don't mean to be mysterious and impenetrable."

"Well, you are."

"Then I am," he said agreeably, not looking for any arguments with a member of the First Family. "But I can't see why or how that should affect you in any way."

"I guess I just hate feeling shut out by anyone that completely."

"Why? Because you're the president's daughter?"

"No. Because I'm me," she said and left.

What a strange girl, Turner thought. He glanced at his watch and found, sadly, that it was only 11:10. A stately and beautiful woman walked by with enough bosom showing to power a sloop in a fair wind, and Turner watched her with mild interest.

"Stop drooling," said Maria, coming up behind him. "You happen to be a happily married man."

"Not at all my type. Much too obvious."

"Ha. Your eyes almost rolled out after her."

"Looking is something else."

"We once had a presidential candidate who admitted to the same sort of visual lust."

"Yes, and look what happened to him."

"What?"

"He became president."

"But not a very good one." She kissed him and started to leave. "See you around."

Turner caught her hand. "What are you up to now?"

"I have to line up a few more guests for the show. This place is turning into a bonanza. I've already gotten commitments from an ambassador, two generals, a Nobel laureate, and the next prime minister of England."

He nibbled at her with his eyes. "Let's go home and screw."

"Paul!"

"It's okay. I hear even the British sometimes do it."

"Yes, but they don't make public announcements," she said and blew him a kiss as she walked off.

Standing alone once again, Turner felt even more the specter at the feast. He had never been very good at parties and seemed to be getting worse as he grew older. If he was not bored, he was irritated. But mostly, he was finding it increasingly difficult, even impossible, to appear fascinated by things that did not interest him. Drifting among the chattering guests, he reached one of several bars and exchanged his now empty champagne glass for a full one of bourbon. There were two young women beside him with the gaunt, pretty, and rather barren faces of models, who were drinking straight vodka out of highball glasses. "Has he asked you to marry him?" Turner heard one of them saying.

"No," the other girl said and shook back long, sleek, dark hair. "But he will."

"How do you know?"

"He's Jewish."

Both women stared gravely at their vodka. Then they walked off together, graceful and predatory as two cougars on a mountain. Turner smiled faintly at their backs. Of course. But the poor girl might find herself disappointed. Jewish men were not nearly what they used to be. Five thousand years of morality and guilt were being assimilated right out of them, along with their names, noses, and traditional disdain for alcohol. It would soon be impossible to tell a Jew from a Gentile without an identifying stamp. Somewhere in the fires of Hell, Adolph Hitler would be pleased. The final solution he had failed to achieve was being accomplished forty years later by the Jews themselves.

Still, there remained small pockets of resistance. Maria, with no true religious convictions of her own, had converted to Judaism and been married to Turner by a rabbi. She had made the offer, and Turner, to his own surprise, had been pleased to accept. He had not prayed in a synagogue since he was thirteen, but evidently blood was blood and something remained. If he himself had not been smart enough to know this, Maria had. Never mind that his father had turned him into a Turner. Inside, he remained a Turnovsky.

He carried his bourbon away from the swirling activity of the bar and discovered a sanctuary of sorts in a small Victorian lounge off the main entrance hall. He was quietly sitting there about half an hour later, when a tall, resplendently uniformed British army officer with a chest full of ribbons peered at him. "I beg your pardon, sir, but would you by any chance be Mr. Paul Turner?"

Feeling himself caught in some sort of shameful act, Turner nodded. "Yes. I'm Turner."

"I say . . . I've been looking all over creation for you. I'm General Strickland."

Turner waited.

"Would you mind coming with me, please?"

"Why? Am I going to be court-martialed?"

General Strickland failed to smile. He looked, to Turner, as though he had no idea how. "Lord Hutchins would like to see you in his study."

"The ambassador?"

"Yes, sir."

Turner did not move. He had been introduced to his host earlier in the evening and had been graced with the customary receiving-line handshake and platitudes, but that had been the extent of their relationship. Why would the man want to see *him*? Had he somehow offended the president's undeniably strange daughter? "Are you sure it's me that Lord Hutchins wants to see?"

"If you are Mr. Turner."

"Sometimes I'm Turnovsky."

"I beg your pardon?"

"Just a bad joke." Turner stood up. "Lead on, General."

Turner accompanied Strickland across the entrance hall

29

and up a flight of stairs. The general made no attempt at conversation. He was clearly not one to waste time on pleasantries. At the far end of the second-floor corridor, he opened a door without knocking, and Turner entered a book-lined study. Lord Hutchins was seated there along with a heavy-set man whom Turner did not know. They both rose, and Lord Hutchins shook Turner's hand for the second time that evening and introduced the other man as Dr. Lederer. "Please sit down, Mr. Turner," said the ambassador.

Turner settled into a straight chair. He noted that General Strickland had closed the door and now stood with his back to it and his arms folded. Turner began to feel a familiar coldness run through his stomach. It was much the same sensation he used to feel during an obviously bad combat briefing, with the captain doing his best to break it easy, but the whole company knowing they were about to be blown away.

"It is your wife," said the ambassador, speaking evenly but with obvious effort. "She was suddenly taken ill. Dr. Lederer tells me it was evidently a heart attack. A massive one."

Turner sat there dumbly, looking at him. His entire body was now packed in ice. All sensation was frozen. Somehow, he managed to stand. "Where is she?"

"She was taken to an emergency medical facility just down the hall."

Turner started toward the door. The general still stood there. He did not move.

"Mr. Turner!" Lord Hutchins's voice was agitated. "Please. Just one moment."

Turner swung around to face him.

"There is no way in the world for me to say this easily . . . and I wish to God I did not have to say it at all . . . but I am afraid that your wife is dead."

Turner heard, yet he had not heard. There suddenly were spots in front of his eyes, and something heavy and hard was pounding the back of his head.

"I am so sorry," said the ambassador, almost whispering now. "Dr. Lederer is a guest, but he was kind enough to re-

30

spond the moment your wife was found. Unfortunately, she was already gone. There was no use in even calling the hospital. She was long past any hope of resuscitation."

Turner stared hard at Lord Hutchins's long, bony face. At this moment it looked weary and slightly desperate. Indeed, it was a face that showed genuine pain. Turner found a kind of voice. "What in God's name are you talking about? I saw my wife less than an hour ago. She was fine. Where is she, goddamn it? I want to see her. I want to see my wife."

The three men looked at him, but no one answered. They were mourners with no visible body to grieve over.

"I want to see my wife," Turner said.

The ambassador's shoulders drooped beneath the exquisitely tailored lines of his dinner jacket. "I'm so sorry," he whispered, and he nodded to Strickland.

The general opened the door and led Turner to the opposite end of the corridor. Strickland marched rigidly, as though at the head of the queen's own guards. Turner saw only the back of his neck.

Maria lay on a gleaming, metal examining table in an antiseptically white room. Her eyes were closed and she seemed to be asleep. A single lamp was on in a corner, and splinters of light fell on her face, on the high, almost childish brow, on the short blonde hair, on the cheekbones, broad like an Indian's. She looked beautiful and incredibly young to Turner . . . flawless. He touched her cheek with the back of his hand, and it felt sort of cool. He took her wrist and searched for a pulse. There was none.

"Leave me alone," he told Strickland.

"Lord Hutchins would rather I stay with you."

Turner faced him. "I said leave me alone."

The general, a big-chested man with a tough, soldier's face who had taken thirty-six years to bully his way to the top and who had learned a great deal about men along the way, studied him silently.

"You just get the hell out of here," said Turner.

The general went.

31

But after he was gone, Turner did not know what to do. He stared for a long time at Maria's face, feature by feature, and tried vainly to believe she was gone. Ah, love.

Closing his eyes, he forced himself to think of her as she had been, with her quick movements and easy laugh, walking confidently into crowded rooms, her eyes bright and searching. Maruschka. How far she had come, how much she had done to end up in this sterile, white room in the house of an English lord. Did this mean she would not be going home with him later?

Turner opened his eyes and noticed the stain on her dress. Something had spilled, perhaps some food or drink when she was stricken. It was only a small stain, but it was in the exact center of her bosom, and it did not seem right to Turner that his wife should have to lie there like that. She had always been so clean, so neat, so thoroughly meticulous about herself.

He reached for his handkerchief and tried to rub out the stain. It did not budge. He rubbed harder, but the stain remained. He soaked his handkerchief with water from a faucet and attacked the spot anew. It only spread and became worse.

Turner stepped back, away from the table. He was breathing heavily, and there was a harsh sound deep in his throat. The entire front of his wife's dress was soiled, a sodden mass. His lovely, his immaculate, Maruschka.

Finally, he wept.

THREE

The Past

If Turner had indulged his own feelings, he would have kept the funeral small and private. Maria's parents were dead, she had no brothers or sisters, and Turner was afraid of the occasion being turned into a spectacle by her fans. But he knew his wife would have preferred it otherwise. For Maria, it was always the more the merrier. She would have said that if people cared enough to want to pay their last respects, why not let them? Turner had rarely argued with his wife when she was alive. Dead, he did not even try. So it was a spectacle.

Hundreds of mourners filled Temple Emanu-El, and the overflow spilled out onto Fifth Avenue, where police lines had been set up and news photographers lay in wait for celebrities. Henry Walton had offered to handle all the arrangements, and Turner had been just as pleased to let him. Why not? Walton had produced and directed all of Maria's other shows. It seemed only fitting that he should handle the final one. And in the truest sense it was, of course, a show. In fact, with the help of the media, Walton was able to develop it into one of the more successful public affairs of the season. The fact that Maria had been a convert to Judaism seemed to add an extra dimension to the proceedings, with the rabbi taking particular note of this in his eulogy and praising both her devotion to her adopted religion and the pride she felt in being called a Jew. The rabbi himself was deep-voiced and impressive, and he had sharp, pale eyes that missed no one of importance among the mourners. When he spoke of Maria's career, of her association with the great and near great, Turner had the feeling he was jealous. The rabbi had talked privately with him before the ceremony, wanting to know if there were any personal thoughts he cared to have included in the eulogy. Turner was polite, but gave him nothing. As if he could share what he felt with battalions of strangers.

At the gravesite, among the converted potato fields of Long Island, Turner stood beneath a gray winter sky and watched the springtime of his life being lowered into the earth.

The rabbi, doing his prescribed job, recited the mourner's *Kaddish*—"*Yisgadal v'yiskadash sh'meh rabbo . . .*"—and Turner repeated it after him, a five-thousand-year-old prayer for a thirty-four-year-old apostate Russian Orthodox woman turned Jew by act of love. Turner guessed it was about as good a prayer as any and better than most. At least it was still going strong after five millenia, and how many prayers had been able to manage that? Nevertheless, Turner thought there should be something more definitive to be said about his wife. But what? How? What could you say about a woman who had been as much a part of you as your flesh and who, without warning or logical reason, was suddenly gone? If only there was a reason. He deserved at least that. And what sort of reasons were they peddling these days for premature coronaries? Whatever they were, he was not buying, anyway. What good were reasons? With or without them, she was gone. He was torn and torn again. Some lived long, full lives, sickened, hung on for years, and finally, almost as a blessing, were released from pain. Others were simply cut down.

"May the father of peace send peace to all who mourn," chanted the highest-paid rabbi in New York, "and comfort all the bereaved among us."

34

The Past

"Amen," whispered Turner, but expected neither peace nor comfort.

He had dreaded going back to the apartment. He had known it would be bad. And it was. Yet at first he actually had welcomed the silence. He sat alone in rooms once shared, thoughts drifting, searching, hands touching the fabric of chairs and couches. But then the quiet became dark and ominous, and he put on the radio to break it with sound. He spent hours staring down at the streets below. He watched cars and delivery trucks arrive and depart. He saw people walking dogs and scooping up their droppings with great care. He learned to recognize the houses that various tenants went into, although he had lived here for years without any such knowledge. From his rear windows, he looked down at tiny patches of bleak winter garden where, during the spring and summer ahead, people would putter among the plants during the day and sit drinking and laughing when evening came. Turner opened his wife's closets and drawers, touched her things, breathed the ghosts of her fragrance. He prepared endless pots of coffee and slowly drank cup after cup.

At night he walked from one room to another, switching lights on and off. Looking for what? He went in and out of the bedroom, seeing the perfume still on the dresser, the pillow beside his own, and the formal shoes she had tried on, changed her mind about, and left in corner before going to the reception. He passed through the living room, the dining room, the kitchen, the study where he worked . . . a man in transit with no place to light. He had never watered a plant in his life, but at three o'clock in the morning he found himself watering Maria's plants near to drowning. And insanely, for him who was normally a stranger to orthodox Jewish rituals of any kind, he hung bedsheets over every mirror in the apartment for the protection of his wife's immortal soul.

For a few hours at a time, each night, he lay stiffly in the

35

middle of the big double bed. By morning an unbearable fatigue filled him. Sometimes he just lay there, not getting up until noon although he had always been a compulsive early riser. Through long days and evenings, he heard his telephone and doorbell ring and was not even tempted to answer. Sometimes he sat at his typewriter, wrote words and sentences he did not believe. And he swore, not at anyone or anything in particular, but with a cold fury that left him spent.

Late in the afternoon of the eighth day, the downstairs buzzer sounded and kept going. Turner gazed blankly at a wall until it stopped. But moments later his doorbell rang insistently, and a familiar voice called his name. With something near to a groan, he went to the door and opened it.

"Paul, for God sake!"

"Hello, Peggy." A rush of feeling caught him as he embraced the tall, slender woman who stood in the doorway. With great effort, he controlled it. He had to watch himself. If he was not careful he was going to drown in a tub of self-pity.

"I flew into Kennedy less than two hours ago. I took a cab straight here. My God, I'm sorry, Paul."

He saw her valise on the hall carpet and remembered that she had been to some sort of publishing meeting in Frankfurt. "Hell, come on in. You may be just in time. I think I was starting to go stir-crazy."

Some bourbon helped ease them into it. Peggy knew just the bare facts. She had seen no newspapers in Germany and had only learned of Maria's death from a copy of *Time* on the flight home. Her dark eyes were black, carrying their own shades of mourning. Seeing what was there, Turner realized how much he had missed her this past week. Besides being a friend, Peggy Larsen had been Turner's editor from the day his first oversized manuscript was dumped on her desk because no one else in her office wanted to read still another first novel about the Vietnam war. And the only reason she herself had bothered to read it (she admitted later) was because she had never before seen so much pure anguish concentrated in an opening paragraph and absolutely had to find out whether things were going to get better or worse. Much later, when she and Turner had become friends, she confessed that she had also read the manuscript because she had lost her husband in an accident a month before, and anguish had suddenly become her medium. Misery not only loved company, it required it.

She shook her head helplessly. "I think I'm still in shock. I can't believe it. It's too crazy. Women aren't supposed to die of heart attacks. That's for you guys, not us."

"You know Maria. Equal rights all the way."

Peggy sat brooding over her drink. She had known Maria longer than Turner had known her. She had, in fact, been the one responsible for arranging Turner's first appearance on Maria's show. "What did the doctor say?" she asked.

"He said she was dead." Turner sighed. "He called it a myocardial infarction. And inasmuch as I've since been told he's a big heart man at Columbia Presbyterian, I guess he knows what he's talking about."

"Wasn't there an autopsy?"

"No."

"Why not?"

"Because I didn't want any."

"But isn't there usually?"

"I don't care about usually. I just didn't want any goddamn autopsy. Okay?"

Peggy looked hurt.

"I'm sorry," he said. "I have to practice talking to people. You're really my first." He drank some bourbon and felt the warmth going down. "The doctor did suggest an autopsy, but I said no. Maria was gone. No autopsy was going to bring her back. And I didn't really give a damn whether it was her heart, brain, liver, or pancreas that took her. But mostly, I guess I just couldn't stand the idea of them picking at her with knives."

37

They sat in silence.

"I'm just angry," he said.

"I know. I felt the same way when that drunk's car jumped the divider and landed in my poor David's lap. You feel it's such a senseless waste. I wanted to kill that sauced-up moron with my bare hands."

Turner had forgotten about her husband. "I wish I had someone to want to kill."

"Save your wishes. It's no help." She stared at the covered mirrors. "What's with the bedsheets?"

"An old Jewish custom. It's supposed to protect Maria's immortal soul." He shrugged. "What the hell. It can't hurt."

They sat with their bourbon and ghosts.

Peggy finished her drink and rose to leave. "Just remember, I'm here."

Turner nodded, but his eyes were off somewhere.

"I guess you haven't felt much like working."

"You guess right."

"You should try."

"I did."

"I'll call you."

"I haven't been answering the phone."

She kissed him. "I'll call anyway."

Turner barely slept that night. When he did manage to doze, he was haunted by nightmares. Awake, lying in the dark, it was worse. His army dead began coming back to him . . . some alive and whole . . . others in bloody pieces . . . still others in their green body bags. He saw faces he thought he had forgotten, heard their cries, heard the machine guns and mortars, heard the roar of the choppers and felt their blast. It had not been this bad for years, not since he had left the last of his hospitals behind him. And none of the dead was Maria. He looked, but he was unable to find her. He was not even able to picture her face, and this was what frightened him most.

He went through the stacks of condolence cards and let-

38

ters that were piling up and learned again and again how highly his wife had been regarded. There was a note from the British ambassador and his wife and, surprisingly, one from the president's daughter, Fran Woodruff, whose name, taken out of context, Turner did not even recognize at first. Another letter was from an uncle that Turner had not seen or heard from in years.

Dear Pauly,

You have my deepest sympathy. Losing a loved one is surely like losing a part of yourself. Although I never had the pleasure of meeting your wife personally, I did listen to her program for years and almost felt as though I knew her. She was a fighter, and her causes were always just. My heart goes out to you in your grief.

With love,
Uncle Herschel

The letterhead bore the name of Herschel Turnovsky and showed the Waldorf Towers as his address.

My God, thought Turner, Herschel the *Gonif*, which meant Herschel the Thief and was the only way Turner could remember his father ever having referred to his older brother, whom he had stubbornly refused to speak to for the last twenty-five years of his life. To Max Turner, his brother Herschel had never been anything but a crook and a hoodlum and a disgrace to the Jews of America. Max had believed it was necessary for every Jew to be absolutely perfect. He had believed any deviation would reflect on all Jews everywhere and thereby justify two thousand years of anti-Semitism. As if such insanity required a logical base. Turner had received a handwritten note of congratulations from his Uncle Herschel when he was awarded the Medal of Honor, but he had never acknowledged it. His father was dying at the time, and it would not have seemed right. This one, however, he would answer.

The fact was that Turner found himself curiously touched by his uncle's letter. It carried a surprising warmth and sensitivity for someone he remembered only as the family thief. And when was the last time anyone had called Turner Pauly? But, of course, to currently think of Herschel Turnovsky as the family thief was a little like thinking of the Pope as a parish priest. Uncle Herschel had moved on a bit since his street gangster days. He had, in fact, evolved into a kind of mythical, high level, career criminal who, as far as Turner knew, had never been indicted for a single crime—an emperor whose empire was neither visible nor acknowledged. He led a quiet, discreet life, scrupulously free of publicity or contact with unsavory types. Turner had occasionally seen news photos of Turnovsky at concerts, at the theatre and opera, and at charity affairs where he was invariably accompanied by an attractive, much younger woman who was identified simply as his longtime companion. Seeing these pictures of his uncle as an apparent star of the *haute monde* of the arts always amused Turner . . . though he felt perhaps a trifle sad as he remembered his father's lifetime of rigidly honest striving and failure. Evidently the wages of sin were wealth, beautiful women, and universal respect.

Turner's reaction to his uncle's note was wholly positive. It gave him a sense of family that he had not felt since the death of his father. He supposed that mourning made you vulnerable to such things. He was also beginning to feel that mourning could be pushed to the point of absurdity. And which philosopher was it who had said, and to whom, "Grief, sir, is a species of idleness"?

He wrote a careful answer to his uncle's letter. He hoped it would accurately reflect his feelings. It was the first more than idle act he had performed since Maria's death.

His second such act was to finally leave his apartment and walk over to the Continental Broadcasting Network. It felt strange to get out. He looked at people and things closely, as though making new discoveries. Incredibly, there was still a world out here, moving serenely along, totally unaffected by his loss.

At the studio, Henry Walton clutched Turner's hand, em-

40

braced him, and regarded him with large misty eyes. "Where have you been? I thought you'd left the country. I've written you, called you on the phone. I even went over and rang your bell a few times."

"I'm sorry. I just wasn't up to seeing anyone."

The producer nodded in commiseration, his plump, handsome face reflecting all he felt. He shut his office door as though fearful that Turner might again disappear. Then he quietly delivered his own eulogy, a requiem for ten years of "Maria at Noon." It was Walton's personal paean to a woman who had taken simple conversation and honed it into a unique and glittering art form. "And all she did was talk to people," he mourned. "No cheap sensationalism, no phony razzle-dazzle. Just good solid talk that people were happy to welcome into their homes week after week, year after year. Even overseas. Did you know the Armed Forces Network was short-waving Maria into twelve countries on three continents? Our servicemen adored her. She was their Main Street, apple pie, and Statue of Liberty rolled into one. She was the best I ever had or ever will have again. I don't know what I'm going to do without her." Walton caught himself. "I must be out of my cottonpicking head. Look whom I'm telling this to."

They sat together in silence. Death apparently had its own rules, thought Turner. He suddenly felt closer to Walton than he ever had before. At times, he had not even liked the producer, had considered him opinionated, bossy, and too talkative. A state of mourning quickly rearranged your values, returned you to basics. The man had cared about Maria. He felt her death. There was a bond simply in that.

Turner said, "Henry, I'd like to go through Maria's desk and files. There are some things I may want to take. Would it be convenient?"

"Sure. Only I think we gave just about everything to your people."

"What people?"

"Those movers you sent. They took Maria's desk, file cabinets, books, everything."

"I never sent any movers, Henry."

"What do you mean?"

"Just what I said. I never sent anyone for Maria's things."

The producer stared at him. "Then who did, for God sake?"

"I don't know. Did you see the movers yourself?"

"Of course I saw them."

"Did they wear company uniforms with a name on them?"

"I don't remember. But they must have left a receipt," said Walton and went to check with his secretary. He was back in a moment with a dated and signed receipt under the letterhead of the Pilgrim Moving and Storage Company of Brooklyn, New York. But when he called the company office and spoke to everyone from the chief dispatcher on up to the president himself, nothing could be found in their records to indicate that any such pickup had been made at the offices of the Continental Broadcasting Network on that or any other date. Walton called the police.

Leaving the studio, Turner felt little more than mild curiosity mixed with relief. He had not been looking forward to going through Maria's office effects. He had enough such reminders at home to be disposed of. In fact, if he knew who the enterprising thieves were, he might have invited them over to clear out his apartment as well.

He stopped at a Second Avenue market to pick up some cans for his dwindling food supply and started home with them. Now that he was out, he hated the thought of going back. He walked slowly, pausing to look at window displays he cared nothing about, but hoping to kill an extra few minutes. A new building was going up on his corner, and he stood watching the big cranes at work. He felt the vibration of heavy machinery under his feet and wondered how any recognizable form was ever going to evolve from such a maze of confusion. Then a battery of rivet guns began sounding just a bit too much like .50-calibers, and he hurried away. The rattling and banging followed him down the block, into his house, and up the three flights of stairs to his door. He opened the lock and leaned against the jamb with his eyes closed. The machine guns echoed. Standing there, he waited for the mortar rounds to start coming in. But it was something else that he heard. Metal on metal. Moving silently on the thick carpeting, he walked through the living room and into the library.

He saw the man.

Two seconds later, the man saw him and almost instantly had a pistol in his hand. He's going to kill me, thought Turner with vague surprise, and left his feet in a flat-out dive. In midair, he heard the soft *whoosh* of a silenced shot and felt the shock of it on his left side. Then his body hit the man and took him down, still holding on to the pistol. Turner went for his wrist with his right hand, grabbed it, and twisted. His left hand was not reacting. They rolled on the floor, and Turner saw his blood on Maria's white rug. He was going to have to do something fast. His lungs were flaming.

They lay squirming together like two lovers, their faces inches apart. The man's eyes were golden yellow, an animal's eyes. Turner spat straight into them. The man blinked, and Turner lifted a knee into his groin. Then he drove the knee in again. Pressure was building behind his neck, and all he could feel was a brain full of blood. The man was young and strong and obviously too much for him. I'm not used to this stuff, Turner thought dully. All I do is sit on my ass and write all day. Now I'm goddamn going to die from it.

The man heaved upward with all his strength, rolled, and was on top of him. But Turner still held his wrist, and they hung there in delicate balance. Then the gun muzzle slowly came down until it was almost at Turner's head. Turner gasped for air and had a sudden vision of jeweled cities. Do something, he told himself. Your head is about to be blown off. *Think,* for God sake!

Suddenly, he let go of the man's wrist. The move was unexpected. With all counterpressure gone, the hand and the gun in it slammed past Turner's head and into the floor. As the man fell, Turner was around and on him. Anger passed through

43

him in waves, nine days of it, and rot and illness as well. A pestilence. He drew back his good arm and swung with the hard edge of his hand, swung with everything he had, at the back of the man's neck, swung knowing this was going to be his one chance. As if from a long way off, he heard his own voice cry out, heard the awful crack of bone. He struck again to be sure. The man went limp and Turner rolled him over. He was dead.

Turner sat on the blood-stained rug, struggling to breathe. He felt a terrible fatigue, and his flesh seemed old. The army had taught him how to kill with his hands, but this was the first time he had ever tried it. The army was right. A hand could be a lethal weapon. He looked at his left arm and found it still dripping blood. The bullet had caught him in the heavy muscle below his shoulder, but it seemed to have missed the bone and gone out. He tried to raise the arm and it responded. That part was apparently all right. He carefully worked his way out of his jacket and shirt and examined the wound. The flesh around it was already turning blue from bruising. And he had thought he was through with all this.

He took care of the wound first. He washed it with peroxide and tightened a clean handkerchief over it, using his belt, his teeth, and his good hand. The pressure seemed to stop the bleeding. He was an exceptionally good clotter anyway. An army doctor had once called him the best clotter in the battalion. He said it had probably saved his life.

Okay, the next thing.

Turner approached the dead man. He looked to have been under thirty, with the blond, sun-streaked hair, tanned skin, and even, stock features of a California athlete. Well, no more tennis and surfing for this one. Then, anticipating what he was about to be sucked into, he reminded himself that this man had violated the sanctity of his home, had put a bullet into him, and undoubtedly would have killed him with his next shot. With the threat of foolish sentiment out of the way, Turner set about the business of finding out who the unsuccessful burglar was.

44

But when he had emptied the man's pockets, all he had in front of him was a neatly folded handkerchief, a comb, an elaborate set of lock-picking tools, and $37.86. There was no wallet, no driver's license, no credit cards, no identification of any kind. And whatever labels might once have been attached to his clothing had all been removed. Whoever the man was, he was obviously someone who went about prepared to die in anonymity.

For the first time, Turner became conscious of the condition of the room. Furniture was drawn away from the walls, drawers were open, and books were out of the bookcases and stacked in neat piles on the floor. If nothing else, the man had been orderly and systematic in his searching. Then Turner saw the open panel. It was in the wall, between two of the emptied bookshelves, and was of the same walnut-stained material as the bookcase itself. Closed, it must have been almost invisible. Now open, it exposed a wall safe, although on closer examination it seemed to be less a wall safe than a metal strongbox that had been set into the wall. There were no combination tumblers or dial, only a conventional, key-operated lock from which a skeleton key, attached to a ring of similar keys, protruded. The man had obviously been in the process of opening the lock when he was interrupted.

Turner stood considering the box. He had lived in this apartment for eight years with Maria and had never even known it was there. Had Maria known? Or had it been installed by a previous tenant and remained undiscovered until this burglar had blundered over it? Then Turner quit asking himself unanswerable questions and opened the box. Inside, was a thick brown envelope and a small notebook. Turner inspected the envelope first and found it stuffed with crisp thousand-dollar bills. He was so startled that he promptly dropped the money all over the floor. Scooping the bills up, he counted roughly two hundred thousand dollars. He had never seen this much cash in one place in his life. Nervously, he stuffed it all back into the envelope. Then he looked at the notebook, which was narrow and thin and bound in black leather. A great many numbers and letters were written inside, all in Maria's neat, graceful script, and none of it made the slightest sense to him. Clustered in groups and sequences, the numbers and letters looked as though they might be part of a code of some sort. Slowly, Turner sat down.

He sat without moving for ten minutes. At the end of that time he still understood nothing, but he felt composed enough to pick up the phone and call the police. Then he returned the envelope of money and the notebook to the safe, closed the wood panel over it, put back the books in that particular area, and waited.

The police arrived quickly, first one squad car, then two more. They were soon all over the apartment. Other than for the wall safe and its contents, Turner told everything exactly as it had happened. The police were brisk, efficient, and reasonably sympathetic. There had apparently been a rash of similar break-ins in that part of town during the past several months, but only Turner had walked in while the burglary was actually in progress. A pleasant young doctor from the coroner's office treated his wound, gave him some antibiotics to take, and said he was very lucky. Maybe so. But somehow, Turner did not feel very lucky.

Later that evening, when the police had cleared out and Turner was on his third brandy, he tried to think it all through once more. The intruder was finally just a dead burglar and would probably be identified easily enough by his fingerprints. But what about the money and the notebook? If it were not for the fact of Maria's handwriting, Turner would have been as ready as not to believe that the safe and its contents had belonged to a previous tenant who had somehow died without having the chance to reveal his secret cache to anyone. Maria had simply not been the type to keep large amounts of cash and mysterious ciphers hidden about. Yet there was no mistaking her handwriting. And if it was her handwriting, it was also her money. He went to bed more confused than ever.

Then, waking at first light, something additionally strange

46

occurred to him. The silenced bullet that had passed through his arm had been fired from a revolver without a silencer attached.

Turner went through the newspapers anxiously the next day. He was eager to see whether the police had been able to identify the dead intruder. But there was no mention of either the break-in or the killing, which Turner found rather odd since there were detailed reports of other less dramatic incidents from the police blotter. Nor was there any notice of it the following day or the day after that. What Turner did read, however, was a report of the death, in the crash of a private plane, of Dr. Henry Lederer, the cardiologist who had attended Maria at the reception. It was a long, two-column obituary that included a photograph of the doctor as well as a list of his professional achievements. Turner read the obituary twice. Then he cut it out of the newspaper and read it several times more that evening.

In the morning, he called Ralph Yurick, an internist and friend who had, from time to time, treated Maria for minor ailments and had her medical records on file. "I have a few questions, Ralph," Turner said when the regrets and condolences were out of the way. "Can you spare me a minute?"

"Sure. What is it?"

"It's about Maria. Her death was the result of a massive coronary. I suppose you read that in the papers."

"Yes, Paul."

"Did it surprise you? I mean, from what you know of Maria's medical history, would you have expected her to die of a heart attack at age thirty-four?"

"No, I can't say I'd have expected it. But the more I practice medicine, the more accustomed I get to the unexpected happening."

"What kind of odds would you quote on this happening to Maria?"

"You can't make book on these things, Paul."

"Still, you'd have to call it a pretty long shot, wouldn't you?"

"I suppose I would."

"But it could happen?"

"What are you talking about? It *did* happen."

"I know," Turner said softly.

"I'm afraid I don't understand what you're getting at, Paul."

"Neither do I. Forget it. My head is just full of soup these days."

"It's a rough time for you. Let's get together soon. Okay?"

"Okay," said Turner.

He dreamed of Maria that night. But when he lifted his hand to touch her, she was gone. Still, it was her presence that had wakened him, setting loose a hundred trivialities—a wisp of hair, an off-key whistle, her voice from another room. Sensations returned—the feel of her flesh, the soft warmth within her, the touch of her lips. Deep glimpses into her eyes came back to punish him. Painfully, he made his decision.

It was midmorning when he put through the call to Herschel Turnovsky. A Waldorf operator answered.

"Mr. Turnovsky, please," said Turner.

"Who's calling?"

"Paul Turner."

"Could you tell me what this is in reference to?"

"It's personal."

"Perhaps I can help you."

"Would you please tell Mr. Turnovsky it's his nephew."

It took several moments. Then a man said, "Pauly? Is that you, Pauly?"

"Hello, Uncle Herschel." Turner found himself grinning at the Pauly. "Have I caught you at a bad time?"

"What bad time? I haven't heard your voice since your bar mitzvah speech."

"I guess it's changed a little."

"I'm sorry about your lady. A terrible thing. You okay?"

48

"Sure. I'm fine. I appreciated your note. It meant a lot."
Turner's lips were suddenly dry. "Uncle Herschel, there's
something I'd like to talk to you about. I wonder if I could
come up to see you?"

"Anytime. It would be my pleasure."

"Would this evening be convenient?"

"Why not?"

Turnovsky asked him to come for dinner, but Turner
made the appointment for later, at nine. He did not expect to
have much of an appetite for food that evening. When he
hung up the phone he found, without surprise, that his hand
was shaking.

FOUR

The Present

He came out of his house into the morning sun, glanced at his watch and found it was 11:23. Which meant nothing. His checking of the time was simply a conditioned reflex. He no longer felt subject to schedules. What he had to do now could be done at his own pace, as slowly or as quickly as he pleased. He put down the suitcase he carried, lit a cigarette, and stood savoring it without the slightest concern for his lungs. Then he picked up his bag and headed for Fifth Avenue.

He walked slowly, casually, enjoying his new disregard for time and lungs, but basking also in a heightened awareness of the cloudless new day about him. And all because of a loaded pistol, he thought. The possible closeness of death could do that. You tended to look at things very carefully when you knew you might not see them again. Although the sensation was not really all that new to him. It was much the same as going into combat. Only then, he had not been alone. Which made a difference. Going in with a squad, platoon, or company you knew that some were going to get it, but felt it would always be others, never you. Except, of course, for the first time. Which was the exception and which, for him, had been in a chopper, with his squad huddled close about him and the certainty clotted deep in his throat that he, of all of them, would soon be dead. He remembered staring down at the trees and silently praying for some sort of mechanical trouble, but the kind that would send them back to the base for repairs and not crashing into the jungle. He had been afraid and had not yet understood how to handle fear. Did you share it or lock it away inside? What he had done was to chew on a Hershey bar and try not to look at anyone's eyes. The candy had reminded him of home, of Saturday movies and playing ball and dancing and chasing girls. Scattered fire had been coming up from the jungle, and everyone had been sitting on their helmets and worrying about catching one in the balls. Jesus, was that what a warrior was supposed to be thinking about, going into battle? He had no idea. At that point he had been only a paper warrior who had yet to fire a shot at anything but paper targets. What the hell am I doing here? he had asked himself.

It was a purely rhetorical question. He had known very well what he had been doing there. He was fulfilling his obligation to his country. Never mind that the war was not a popular one. Never mind that there were those who burned their draft cards, or who became instant conscientious objectors, or who ran off to Canada or Sweden. He had his own lights to follow. If America had a war to fight, and if you were male, healthy, and of the proper age, you fought it. As his father before him had fought it, crawling and bleeding through the mud of France and Germany because he would have found it unthinkable for a Jew to be called upon and do otherwise. To his father, everything finally came down to the fact of being a Jew. And to be an American and a Jew carried obligations as great as its privileges. So that Max Turner, a man who wept unashamedly at the playing of "The Star Spangled Banner," would have been proud to pay with blood for the matchless blessings of American citizenship.

Not so Max's wife, Turner's mother, who was not nearly so cavalier about offering up her son's blood. Fanny Turner had nothing against America. She found it a lovely place to live in spite of its 99 percent Christian population, most of whom you only had to scratch a little to find out what they really thought of the few Jews they graciously allowed to dwell among them. But war was war, crippled was crippled, dead was dead, and it was all just another gentile insanity. So above everything else you preserved your loved ones. You did not kiss your only son goodbye and send him off to be blown apart in this recurring *goyish* madness. It was the only issue over which Turner could remember his parents every really fighting. "For shame!" Max roared at his wife. "You want your son, a Jew, to hide under the bed while others do the fighting?" Fanny's response was less thunderous but just as firm: "I want my son, a Jew, to live and be well and in one piece." Still, it was Max the patriot and World War II veteran who did the weeping when he kissed his son goodbye. Fanny's eyes were dry. Whatever tears she shed were inside. Although she never saw her son again. She died quietly in her sleep while Turner was finishing his basic training in North Carolina. When Turner returned for the funeral, his father clutched him fiercely. "Now I have only you. Don't make me sorry we won over Momma. I want no dead heroes. Come back nice, without damage. You hear me?"

Turner heard him. And he did come back. But not really so nice or without damage. And a hero besides.

Turner had his own theories about heroes. It was all circumstance, reflex, and luck. No one ever knew in advance how they were going to react. But in his particular case, it was also desperation. The thing was, he had had no choice. He had just made sergeant the week before and was taking out his first patrol when they were caught right smack in the middle of a goddamned clearing. Later, it was easy enough to think that maybe he should have sent them across one at a time, but anyone could be smart with hindsight. So there they were, all ten of them out in the open when the first shots exploded. "Hit it!" he yelled and sent them running for the protection of the jungle. He himself dropped flat, spraying the green wall with his submachine gun, doing his best to cover them, but seeing only foliage and trees. A bullet caught Warneke in the neck, angled upward, and exploded the side of his face. Lewis dashed past him toward the jungle, tripped a mine, and went up in a bundle of yellow smoke. The others were yelling, firing, running, and falling. Turner felt his own gun kicking, but there were no targets, and it was impossible to kill jungle with bullets. Suddenly, grenades filled the air and exploded like black baseballs. Turner was lifted, breathed cordite, and came down with a crash. Somehow, he was still gripping his weapon. He was covered with blood, but was unaware of pain. The earth grumbled and growled. Turner lay flat in the tall grass, oozing blood from seventeen separate places, struggling to reload. Everything was quiet.

Then he saw them coming out of the trees. Incredibly, there were only seven of them, all dressed in their baggy black pajamas. They held burp guns and pistols and carried satchels of grenades. They came slowly, carefully, prepared to finish off survivors. They had smooth, egg-shaped faces, one-third of which was forehead. Moving in a loose line, they watched the high grass, guns ready. They reached Lewis's body, and one of them fired into it in case life remained. Turner sighted along the blued steel of his gun, feeling the barrel slippery with blood. He had to get all seven with a single burst or he and any other of his surviving wounded would be dead. They were probably dead anyway, but why make it easy for the VC? He placed his front sight on the chest of the first man on the left. Then, very gently, he squeezed the trigger. He felt the quick, spastic lurching of the gun against his cheek and saw the man's body pop like a large black balloon. Still squeezing the trigger, he eased his sights to the right across the six others. They seemed to go up, then down, in puffs of brown smoke. Turner passed out.

He lay in the grass with the sun on his back, slipping in and out of consciousness. How easy it was to kill. You just had to point a gun and squeeze the trigger. Anyone could be taught to do it. But they should have taught him sooner. At the age of six he should have been put into the army instead of into school. By now he might have learned enough about killing to have kept his men alive.

53

Another patrol from their company found them several hours later. There were four survivors. Turner was out of his head for almost a week, but two of the others were able to give lucid, detailed accounts of what had happened. On the basis of their reports, Turner was recommended for and received the congressional Medal of Honor. He was surprised. He should have been court-martialed.

But that was almost twelve years ago. Now the dead in that jungle clearing were long buried, and he was carrying another gun (though this time a pistol in a suitcase) through the late winter sunshine of New York.

He reached Fifth Avenue and walked downtown, toward the stores. He still strolled casually. He might have been a tourist just arrived in town, enjoying the sights of the most dazzling city on earth. *His* city, he thought. Which his grandfather had once crossed a continent and an ocean to reach because the land and the people were free and the streets were supposed to be paved with gold. His grandfather's name was Duvid, and he was a thin, stripped-down man with a softness in his eyes that Turner had inherited. Turner remembered him mostly as an old man who gave him nickels and told stories about what it was like for a Jew to live in Russia under the bestial czarist maniacs. He told Turner he was a lucky *boychikel* to be born in a country where a Jew could come and go as he pleased and not have to worry about looking at the bottom of a Cossack horseshoe. Turner last saw his grandfather in Bellevue Hospital, where he was dying of emphysema. His hands and face were gaunt, and there was a gray mist over his once beautiful eyes. But he smiled at Turner and pressed into his hand the old pocket watch that he had carried every day of his life since his thirteenth birthday, when his own grandfather had given it to him. "You keep it for me, *boychikel*," he whispered. And Turner had kept

54

it. He kept it even after a grenade fragment tore it apart in that same jungle clearing. One of the medics said it had probably saved his life, and Turner was pleased to believe it. He wondered if perhaps he should have taken it with him today.

At Rockefeller Center he turned in toward the plaza and stopped to watch the skaters. It was one of the milder days of the season, and the rink was crowded and bright with color. Once, a day like this would have sent him dashing for his fielder's mitt. A hundred years ago? Not really. It was just that so much had happened in between. Famous and infamous men had made speeches. Guns had sounded. Sirens had wailed. People had died. Yet the first vague promise of spring felt as warm and filled with hope as ever.

He watched a graceful, dark-haired girl in a blue skating costume move across the ice like a dream. She was tall, young, and lovely, with the kind of long, sculptured legs that seemed to go on forever. She glanced up and smiled as she caught his eye, and Turner smiled back, feeling something pleasant inside. She was not his, this stranger, but she was there, a female animal of his own species who flew as though on wings and further blessed the day with her flesh.

Then he turned away, walked back to Fifth Avenue, and hailed a cab. "La Guardia Airport," he told the driver.

FIVE

The Past

The air in the Waldorf had the vacant force of a bank vault or perhaps a tomb. . . . Obvious luxury embarrassed Turner.

He gave his uncle's name and his own to a desk clerk and waited while the man spoke softly into a house phone. Then, having received the necessary clearance, Turner was directed to a private elevator at the rear of the lobby and rocketed toward the thirty-third floor. Shooting upward, he had the feeling that something of substance was leaving him forever. Whether this was good or bad, he had no idea. But the fact that the new bullet wound in his arm suddenly ached as the elevator whipped to a halt was not a happy sign.

Two oversized men with the cold, measuring eyes of headwaiters met him in a carpeted vestibule. "Mr. Turner?" said one.

"Yes."

"Would you raise your arms, please?"

Turner looked at his jacket and saw the unmistakable bulge of a shoulder holster. "I'm Mr. Turnovsky's nephew."

"Yes, sir," said the man and waited.

Turner raised his arms. The man went over his body lightly but thoroughly and then led him to the nearer of two doors and rapped three times with a brass knocker. A woman opened the door and offered Turner her hand. "Good evening. I'm Hank Adams."

Some Hank, thought Turner. Straight, wheat-colored hair framed one of those perfect Anglo-Saxon faces—a cool, Back Bay Boston face with the sort of clean, spare features you saw in portraits by Stuart and Copley. It was also the face Turner had seen beside his uncle's in news photos. Except that it looked younger in the flesh and somehow better, with a quiet, remote air that no camera would ever capture.

"Please come in," she said. "Herschel had to take a call. He'll be with you in a moment."

Turner followed her down the hall of the suite to a huge sitting room that seemed to be an omnibus library and art gallery. There had also been paintings out in the vestibule and along the hallway. Some of the paintings looked familiar to Turner, and he suddenly realized why. They were the originals of Renoirs, Monets, and Van Goghs, reproductions of which he had been seeing since his first art appreciation course in high school.

"I was just fixing myself some brandy," Hank said. "Will you join me?"

"Please."

There was a fire going, and they sat facing one another in its glow. Softly, a violin concerto that Turner did not recognize drifted in silvery strains from invisible speakers. Bravo, Uncle Herschel. Hank looked at him with blue New England eyes. "I'm sorry about your wife. I was a longtime fan."

"Thank you." Turner was beginning to find that mourning gave you a unique and separate status. He wondered what people had talked to him about before.

"And I'm also a fan of yours. I found your books quite moving."

He looked at her.

"You seem surprised."

"I guess I'm always surprised when someone other than my editor has actually read something I've written."

She smiled. It softened her eyes.

"Besides, my books are mostly about war. I wouldn't have expected them to have much appeal to you."

"Unfortunately, war is a fact of life. You can't hide from it. And I wouldn't want to if I could."

Herschel Turnovsky came into the room. "Pauly!"

Turner rose to greet him and found himself locked in an embrace, a powerful, confusing bearhug that gripped him with some deep authority of emotion for which he was utterly unprepared. He felt the beat of his uncle's heart and breathed his shaving lotion.

"Pauly, Pauly," said Turnovsky in a husky voice and let his nephew go. There were tears in his eyes, and, looking at him, Turner found there were tears in his own. For his uncle had a great deal of his father's face—the wide, full mouth, the dark Tartar eyes, the noble brow with its etched lines—and it all came flooding back.

Turnovsky stepped back and wiped the tears from his eyes with one swift, impatient pass of his hand. "An indulgence of creeping age." He grimaced. "Hank, be a sweetheart and pour me a spot of that Napoleon."

Turner cleared his own eyes with a handkerchief. He was vulnerable to emotion these days, but there was no denying Turnovksy's effect on him. "It's good to see you, Uncle Herschel," he said and meant it. Still shocked at the intensity of his reaction, he stood considering his father's older brother as though searching for hidden reasons in his flesh. Nearing the age of sixty-eight, Herschel Turnovsky remained a powerfully built man with a headful of iron gray hair that he wore full at the sides in the manner of symphony conductors and fashion conscious younger men. Although not overly tall, he was physically impressive, radiating the kind of energetic good humor that is described as star presence in the entertainment field and is often found in successful politicians, publishers, and statesmen. Right now, he appeared all softness and light, but Turner could easily imagine him at other times, with those same Tartar eyes able to close you out and blow you away without even blinking. Turner had read about him

58

over the years, read of some of the less than compassionate things of which he had been suspected. None had ever been proved, but Turner somehow felt (if a bit guiltily) that it would have taken a minimum amount of evidence to convince him of their truth.

Now Turnovsky said, "I hate to think how many years it's been. What's wrong with us, Pauly? We're all the blood, all the *mishpocheh* we have left. How do we let a lifetime go by without a word? Even the animals don't walk away from their own."

He reached for the brandy that Hank had poured, and Turner saw the small black skullcap on the back of his head, almost lost in the grizzled mass of hair. Had it been a bishop's miter, Turner could not have been more astonished. His uncle saw his expression and smiled. "The *yarmulkah* is a shock, huh? Well, it's harmless enough. Some men reach for a favorite pipe or slippers at home. I put on my *yarmulkah*." He sat down on the couch beside Hank and absently took her hand. "I guess it also helps tie me to my father. I seem to need more and more of that lately. Do you remember your grandpa at all?"

"Of course. I still carry his watch." Turner took out the battered old timepiece and showed it to his uncle. "It stopped a chunk of grenade for me in Nam. A medic said it saved my life."

"I'm not surprised. Your *zayde* is keeping a close eye on you. And don't think it was just a crazy accident. There's a certain order to these things, Pauly."

Turner sipped his brandy. Herschel the mystic. There was a mood to this whole scene that was as confusing as it was unexpected. The warmth and sentiment, the *yarmulkah,* the two lovebirds (surely thirty-five years apart in age) holding hands on the couch, the French impressionist masterpieces on the walls, and the music on the stereo (which he had moments before thought might possibly be Brahms) were all very lovely, but had nothing to do with why he was here. Still, it was obvious that his uncle had his own needs.

True. It was as though Turner's sudden entrance into his life had infected Turnovsky with instant nostalgia, with a compulsion to touch, to remember, to go back and explain. Pressed roses of a melting pot. Kids ran in packs like wolves. Blood covered the stoops and dripped from fire escapes. The *micks* went after you with clubs, the *jigs* with razors, the *wops* with knives. Survival was a daily battle, and he, a *sheeney* who never knew when to quit, had survived. He had made sure, too, that his brother, Maxie, survived. Except that his poor *shnook* of a brother refused to learn. To the end, Max had tried to make everyone, even the Jew-haters, love him . . . had believed that by changing his name to Turner and smiling as he ate shit, he could get rid of the little Yiddish lox peddler in his belly and be welcomed into the American dream. "He wouldn't learn," mourned Turnovsky to his dead brother's son. "I'd have been happy to die teaching him, but he absolutely refused to learn. All I ever did was love and try to help that poor *shlemiel,* and he was never anything but ashamed of me. I swear to Christ . . . *Herschel the Gonif* was one word to him till the day they put a stone on his head."

The pain was still there. Turner saw it. He was being offered a rare peek into the Talmud of his uncle's carefully preserved nightmares. Turnovsky had fought the deadly pushcart wars. He had discovered at an early age that he was going to be violated and must violate in return. The only way to beat the system was to beat hell out of anyone who tried to enforce it. He found that his parents had taught Max and him the wrong things. They had been scrubbed, shined, and sent out to bow and scrape. If they were neat, clean, obedient, and good, they would be accepted into the gentile world. If not, they would never be anything but dirty Jews. His parents— they should only rest in peace—had been sadly deceived. They had ridden a beast all their lives and never really understood the kind of perch they were on. After two thousand years of wandering, of being driven from one swamp to the next, they believed they were finally on solid ground. As Maxie had believed. "This very minute," declared Turnovsky, bitterness and love glittering from his eyes, "my brother—your father—is probably floating in some eternal sea of crap, still bellowing his beloved 'Star Spangled Banner.' "

By the time his uncle seemed to have exorcised the last of his ghosts, Turner felt like a reluctant scholar who, without officially enrolling, had been thrust into an intensive postgraduate course in the dialectics of Jews, survival, and brotherly love.

Pausing for more brandy, Turnovsky laughed softly. "Some *geschichte.* But you must understand. I've been waiting more than twenty years to unload." He refilled all three glasses. "So what is it, Pauly? You said on the phone there was something you wanted to talk about, and I have a feeling it wasn't just me and my tics. So tell me." When Turner appeared to hesitate, he added, "If you're worried about Hank, there's no need. What I know, she knows. And a lot more besides."

Hank started to rise. "Perhaps Paul would be more comfortable if I . . ."

"No, no. Please." Turner waved her back. "It has to do with my wife's death. Some things have happened lately, and they've begun to bother me."

The first words were difficult, as though the act of sharing itself constituted a breach of trust. But this passed quickly as the pressure broke. He addressed himself to both of them, consciously including Hank and telling it just as it had happened—the disappearance of Maria's office files, the killing of the intruder, the discovery of the wall safe and its contents, the news blackout on the incident, the plane-crash death of the cardiologist, and, finally, the statistical unlikelihood that someone with Maria's medical history would suddenly drop dead of a heart attack.

Hank and Turnovsky listened without comment or visible reaction. Yet Turner had the feeling that every word he spoke was being gobbled up, chewed to its core, and sucked dry of meaning. When he finished, they sat in silence while

61

the Brahms soared and the fire crackled. Then Turnovsky
said, "So what do you think, Pauly?"

"I don't know. Except that I'm beginning to wonder
whether my wife really did die of a heart attack."

"There was no autopsy?"

"No. I didn't want one."

"But you want one now?"

Turner nodded. "Only it can't be an official one. If something is wrong here, it would just be covered up. That's why I
came to you, Uncle Herschel. I was hoping you might be able
to help me out."

"With an illegal exhumation and autopsy? You think I run
some kind of fancy grave-robbing service?"

"No. I . . ."

Turnovsky laughed. "To my brother's son, I'm still Herschel the *Gonif.*" He saw Turner's face. "I'm sorry, Pauly. It
just struck me funny. You did right coming to me. Who
should you go to, some strange gangster? Better to keep such
things in the family." He turned to Hank. "How should we
handle this?"

She thought for a moment. "What about Artie Frankel?"

"All right. But he'll need help and a place to work."

Hank asked Turner, "Where is your wife buried?"

"Zion Hills Cemetery. It's out on Long Island."

"Sol Immerman's place is in that area," Hank said.

"Fine," said Turnovsky. "Call them both. Have them take
care of it as quickly as possible. Tell them I'll appreciate it."

Hank made the calls from the phone at the far end of the
room, but spoke so softly that Turner heard nothing but the
music. Returning, she said, "No problems. It's all arranged
for tomorrow night."

"But I'm not even sure of the plot number," Turner said.

"Sol has your wife's name. He'll find it."

Turner sat looking at them both. Hank was seated beside
his uncle once more. Just like that, he thought. "Thank you.
But I'd like to go along also."

"You don't have to," said Turnovsky.

"Yes, I do."

Turnovsky did not push it. Hank made another call to set up the meeting.

They rendezvoused in a motel parking lot just off exit 41-S of the Long Island Expressway. Hank had arranged the details with a quiet efficiency that Turner had already begun to take for granted in her. She was not your average, run-of-the-mill, sleep-in companion. Besides being a singularly smashing-looking dish, Hank had also turned out to be a Harvard Doctor of Law, as well as part of the same Adams line that had produced the second and sixth presidents of the United States. Both of which facts Turnovsky had revealed with a pride that Turner might have thought understandable enough in someone else, but which he found surprising in his uncle. It was as though Turnovsky, with all he had achieved, remained inherently the poor, immigrant dropout, naïvely impressed with the trappings of education and lineage. Look, declared those dark Tartar eyes, I may be an old East Side street gangster who never finished school, but this is the sort of woman who loves and does for me. Not bad, huh?

Turner and Frankel left their respective cars in the motel parking lot and joined Immerman in his mortuary van for the drive to the cemetery. Both men were young, had never met before this evening, and (Turner quickly learned) shared a mutual bond of indebtedness to his uncle. Frankel—fair, slender, prematurely balding, and wearing steel-rimmed glasses—was a resident in pathology at the New York University Medical Center whom Turnovsky had put through medical school because his father had taken a bullet in the head while in Turnovsky's employ. As for Immerman, he was a deep-chested man with a tough face who had been a promising welterweight before an eye injury turned him into a mortician. Having owned a piece of Immerman as a fighter, Turnovsky had generously extended his guardianship by helping to launch him as a funeral director. Both men apparently had a good schooling in gratitude, thought Turner. They were risking not only their careers but stiff jail sentences as well to do what they were doing for him tonight. Or did they really have a choice?

Seated between them in the van, Turner had his own batch of poems to recite, but held them in check. It would be better if no one knew more than was necessary. Mostly silent, he rode through the Long Island darkness in a shiningly clean mortuary wagon that still smelled strongly of disinfectant and something else that no amount of scrubbing would ever remove. Silhouettes of scrub pine and oak rose on either side, and sometimes they passed the lights of a house. They had started out early, soon after dark, because everything had to be finished before daybreak and there was no certainty of how much time would be needed. Then they were there. The place did not seem like a real cemetery to Turner, but rather like an empty field that stretched, vast and treeless, to the horizon. There were no headstones, only flat, bronze markers set in the earth. A real cemetery would have looked like the one in Maspeth where his parents and grandparents were buried, with its forests of monuments, its perpetually cared-for ivy, and its collections of small stones left by families and friends to show that their dead were not forgotten. But there had been no room for Maria there. The earlier Turnovskys had failed to plan this far ahead. Every inch of earth was already occupied. Turner was glad his family was unable to see what he was about to do. To dig up his blessed wife, a Jewish soul. Perhaps not born a Jew, but a Jew by choice, by act of love. The best kind. How long his parents had been gone. Both had died on rainy days. They said if you died on a rainy day, it meant you were a good person. It had rained only on the morning of Maria's death. But it was not her goodness that was in question, just the way she had died.

They searched for and found the proper marker. Then they unloaded shovels, pulleys, stakes, cables, and a portable motor for the lifting. "You're sure there are no watchmen?" asked Turner.

64

The Past   "They don't waste money on watchmen out
here," Immerman told him. "There's nothing to steal or des-
ecrate." He looked closely at Turner. "You okay?"

"No."

"Why don't you wait in the van?"

"Come on. Let's dig."

The ground was still soft, not yet impacted, so the digging
was easy. Then Turner's shovel hit wood. "Oh Christ," he
said and had to go off for a while.

The digging was finished when he returned. "We can handle the hoist without you," said Immerman.

"Like hell," Turner told him and raged at his own weakness. She was still his. Whatever needed to be done, he would
somehow do. "I'll be all right now." And to a certain point
he was.

Perhaps, along with the worst of what he was feeling, he
had an intimation of Maria's presence. Did you lift after death
like a leaf in a breeze, or did you remain with those you
loved? For one brief moment, Turner had the sense he had
been touched on the back, there at the exact place where she
used to hold him in sleep. Or was he simply going a little
nuts? No matter. For there was suddenly a bit less ache in his
chest, and expectation came to life in him. It was the first
such feeling he had known since Maria had been gone. He
had no idea what it meant.

The motor hummed softly, and the hoist lifted the casket
out of the ground. They brushed it free of earth, swung it
onto a wheeled stretcher, and slid it into the back of the van.
Then, leaving the grave open, a black wound in the darkness,
they drove away.

It was a twenty-minute ride to Immerman's funeral home
in Brentwood, and they did it without conversation. Nor did
anyone speak as they rolled the smooth, mahogany box
through the garage entrance and into the mortuary basement.
Then Immerman said, "Paul, you'd better wait upstairs."

Turner climbed a single flight of steps and sat down in
one of the mourning rooms, which was airless behind velvet

drapes. His stomach was caught in a wringer, and there was no way to free it. He tried not to think about what was happening downstairs, but it leaked into his brain like some eternal seepage of waste. That once lovely, once beloved body. Sitting there, smoking endless cigarettes, his nerves spoke in separate broken bits. They told him he was dead, in the first circle of hell.

A lifetime later, Frankel came upstairs alone. He appeared hollow. His cheeks were gray and drawn, and behind his lenses blue bags hung under his eyes. He looked, thought Turner, like Woody Allen after still another failure at love. Turner offered him a cigarette and he absentmindedly took it. Then he handed it back. "I don't smoke."

He sat down and stared tiredly at Turner. "What did they say your wife died of?"

"A heart attack."

"Who made the diagnosis?"

"A Dr. Lederer. He happened to be there when it happened."

Frankel nodded. "I read where he was killed in a plane crash the other day. I've heard him lecture. He was good. But he was wrong about your wife. She didn't die of any heart attack. She died of acute cyanide poisoning."

Turner felt as though his soul, if he indeed had one, was at that moment trying to lift itself free of his body. "What are you telling me? That Maria . . . that my wife was murdered?"

"I'm not a detective, Paul. I'm a pathologist. All I'm telling you is that she died of cyanide poisoning. How, why, and by who it was administered is a whole different ball game."

"You couldn't have made a mistake?"

"Not in this."

"Dr. Lederer made a mistake. Why couldn't you?"

"Because I performed an autopsy. Lederer didn't. And without a postmortem, the symptoms of a coronary thrombosis and those of cyanide poisoning can appear very similar."

Turner withdrew into himself.

Immerman drove more quickly on the return trip to the

cemetery. He was anxious to finish up. Occasionally a car passed, going the other way, a single pair of eyes in the darkness. But the road was empty most of the time and the night unbroken. A light mist had begun to fall, and Turner stared off through the drizzle. Suddenly, he was no longer able to rail against the fates, against what had seemed a reasonless act of God. Now there was a human factor involved. He was finding it hard to adjust.

Returning to the open grave, they replaced the casket. Turner had to steel himself against the final shoveling. She was twice dead. Then, having made certain that everything at the site was exactly as they had found it, they drove back to the motel parking lot for the other cars. Turner shook hands with the two men and thanked them. But when he offered them payment, they looked at him as though he were mad. He was Herschel Turnovsky's *mishpocheh*. To even mention money was an insult. Turner apologized.

He slid into bed as the sky was turning gray. It was someplace to go. He did not expect to do any sleeping. He heard the rumble and sigh of plumbing between the walls and the faint wail of a siren in the distance. He lay there, discovering lumps in the mattress he had not known about before. Hollow, he waited for rage to fill the void. When it finally came, when he was able to feel it thick and solid in his chest, he embraced it.

Turner did not immediately consider himself ready to see his uncle again. He had to prepare himself. He had to feel sure of certain things. He did make a formal call of appreciation to Hank, but the postmortem itself was not mentioned. Turner assumed, in any case, that his uncle had received a full report from Frankel. Meanwhile, as Turner did his preparing, Peggy Larsen called three times—twice to find out how he was doing and once to invite him to dinner. Turner said he guessed he was doing okay, but was not quite ready for such things as dinner. The editor wanted to know what the hell that meant, and Turner told her it meant he would be lousy company. "Who cares?" she asked, and Turner said that he did. "I'm going to keep pestering you, you know," she promised. "I hope you will," he said.

When Turner did return to the Waldorf several days later, it was in the early afternoon, and he again raised his arms for the ritual inspection, heard the brass knocker fall three times, and was let in by Hank. She smiled at him with the perfect American teeth of a beauty queen. "Herschel is waiting for you in the study." Turner followed her past approximately two million dollars worth of paintings, but allowed himself a moment of respectful appreciation for her behind, which, having nothing to do with the cool elegance of her face, moved to a lusty beat of its own. It was a very round, practical, no-nonsense type of behind, with a clear understanding of life's more important priorities, and Turner felt pleased for his uncle.

Turnovsky was working at a carved desk in the room that served as his office, an oversized paneled chamber with oriental rugs on the floor, walnut cabinets, a Dow Jones teletype, an omnipotent-looking computer, and a battery of colored phones. "Pauly," he said and was on Turner with all the warmth and gusto of his earlier greeting, a man given to the dialectics of touch. "Sit down, sit down. That's a good comfortable chair over there. Straight. Good for the back. Some of the chairs these *faygelehs* design today can make you a cripple. You want something to drink? Coffee? Whiskey? A soft drink?"

"No thanks. Nothing."

Turnovsky opened a humidor. "A cigar? Real Havana."

Turner shook his head and took out his cigarettes. He offered the pack to Hank, who had sat down beside him. "I gave it up years ago," she said. "Herschel told me I was beginning to smell like an ash tray."

Which pretty much took care of the amenities.

Turner began: "I guess Artie Frankel told you about the autopsy."

His uncle selected a cigar and carefully bit off the tip. He nodded, his normally expressive face showing nothing.

68

"It's taken me a few days to adjust. Now I want to do something about it."

Turnovsky lit his cigar and waited.

"The thing is, I don't even know where to begin. Do I go to the police, or what?"

"Well, let's see. Hank, who's the precinct captain in Pauly's area?"

"Frank McKinley."

"Be a doll and get him for me."

Hank moved her chair closer to the bank of phones, dialed a number, and spoke softly for a moment. Then she nodded to Turnovsky, who picked up a red receiver. "Hello, Frank. Fine. It's been a while. Just a small point of information, Frank. There was an attempted burglary on East Sixty-third Street last week. The intruder was killed. You know the one? Yeah. There was no media mention. What's the story on it?" Turnovsky listened. "That's all? Okay. I appreciate it."

He hung up and studied the tip of his cigar. When he faced Turner, his eyes were blank. "Is there anything about your wife you haven't told me?"

"What do you mean?"

"Anything dangerous she was fooling with?"

Turner frowned. He shook his head.

"What about her politics?"

"She voted straight Democratic. Why? Are they poisoning people for that now?"

"The police captain I just spoke to said there was pressure to bury any sign or mention of that intruder you killed. And his body was taken from the morgue an hour after it arrived. That kind of pressure never has a name, but usually has a national security label on it."

"What does that mean?"

"That it's high level and nothing has to be explained."

"But what in Christ's name would any of that have to do with Maria?"

"You tell *me*. What about that code book and cash in the safe?"

69

Turner stared helplessly at him.

"How long were you two married, Pauly?"

"Eight years."

"You were close?"

Turner nodded.

"And none of this makes any sense to you?"

"The whole damn thing is crazy."

"It only looks that way." Turnovsky chewed at his cigar. "Hank, does Tom Coleman still head the FAA's northeastern division?"

"They moved him to Washington about six months ago. He's assistant director now."

"Even better. Call him. Tell him we're interested in the crash of a small private plane in Connecticut five or six days ago. A Doctor Something-or-other . . ."

"Lederer," said Turner.

"A Dr. Lederer was killed in it. Find out what he knows."

Hank was looking up the number on a Rolodex before Turnovsky finished speaking. Turner watched her put though the call on a green phone, then listened to one end of a cryptic dialogue that was mostly questions. She hung up and said flatly, "Guess what?"

"More pressure?" said Turnovsky.

"Exactly. They were told not to waste time on it. Just clean up the mess and mark it pilot error."

Turnovsky rocked gently in his chair, the cigar and *yarmulkah* giving him the look of an old orthodox Jew in violation of the smoking ban on the Day of Atonement. He sighed. "Well, Pauly, it looks like you've got yourself a little problem."

Along with everything else, Turner was beginning to feel like a fool. How could he have lived a heartbeat away from this woman for eight years and not have even suspected she was involved in something hazardous enough to get her killed? "I don't understand any of it."

"You can thank God for that. And they must know it. If they didn't, you'd by lying with your Maria right now."

70

"They. Who the hell are *they?*"

"You're lucky you don't know that either."

"Lucky, shit."

They sat in cold silence.

"So what do I do now?" Turner said.

"You're asking my advice?"

"Yes."

"Go home and write another book."

Turner's palms were clammy. "My wife was murdered, Uncle Herschel."

"I feel for you. But it looks like your Maria was playing at some kind of hanky-panky. She must have known the risks."

Hanky-panky. Who else but his uncle, thought Turner, would use an expression like that to describe a reason for murder? "So that means I'm supposed to just forget it?"

"You're an intelligent man, Pauly. A writer of books. Use your writer's head. You've just heard us talk on the phone. There's weight on this. That doctor was killed because he was there and might have asked the wrong questions. You yourself had to kill a man to stay alive. You can't go crying to the cops. They've already clamped a lid on it. And if you try making any kind of fuss, how long do you think you'll last?"

Turner ground out his cigarette. "I can't just do nothing."

"What do you think you're going to do?" asked Hank.

Turner was surprised when he looked at her. Her face was as lovely, as smoothly well bred as ever, but her eyes glinted like dirty river ice. Along with the two presidents, there must have been a few Boston pistols in her bloodline.

"You were smart enough to go to Herschel instead of to the police for an autopsy," she said. "What's suddenly happened to your brains?"

Turner held back an angry reply. These people had, after all, done him favors. Why take out his frustrations on them? "I appreciate all you've done," he told them stiffly and rose to go. "Thank you very much."

His uncle saw him to the door. "We're not unfeeling. We

71

know how it is for you. But getting yourself closed out isn't going to help your lady any." Turnovsky held him close. "Don't be a stranger, Pauly."

He had no idea of what time it had been when he left the Waldorf, but he must have been walking for several hours because it was well past six when he came out of Central Park at the Seventy-second Street access and found himself in front of Peggy Larsen's house. He stood there. Why not? he thought. The doorman greeted him by name and saw him to the elevator. On the eleventh floor, Peggy opened the door, stared at him, and went pale. "What is it? What's happened?"

"Nothing. I just came to dinner. You invited me."

"Not for tonight. All I have is tuna fish."

"I love tuna fish."

"You hate it."

He closed the door behind him. "I've changed."

"I wanted to make something special when you finally came."

"You sound just like a woman."

She kissed his cheek. "Thanks for noticing."

She had just come out of a tub and smelled of baby powder and soap. Her hair was in soft, damp ringlets, and she wore a long, white terry robe. Barefoot, she was almost as tall as him, and he was an inch over six feet. Breathing her clean freshness, Turner felt something cold and dark drain out of him. He was glad he was there.

"Make us enough to drink," she said, "and I might let you stay."

He mixed a sizable pitcher of martinis while she bustled about the kitchen and set things up in a dining area. She chattered happily as she worked . . . news of the office, the return of an author whose writing she liked, an exciting paperback deal in the offing, a hint that she might be made executive editor before the end of the year, her ongoing battle for more ad money for deserving books. Turner let her pleasant midwestern voice wash comfortably over him. It was better than silence. It was infinitely better than his own thoughts. The apartment itself added familiar warmth. Books and manuscripts lay everywhere, a loving, literary grab bag. A polished baby grand carried family history in frames . . . mother, father, sisters, brothers, all still happily alive back in Minot, North Dakota ("Why not Minot?" asked a lacquered lapel button). A picture of Peggy's late husband was also there, a dark-eyed, smiling engineer who looked to Turner as though he had been easy, relaxed, and the possessor of unlimited reserves of understanding. This woman, this Peggy, had been widowed for almost nine years, and she was not yet thirty-six. Turner felt like a newcomer to a very old club.

They dined beside a window that brought the park into the room along with the distant lights of Fifth Avenue. Peggy had tossed a large salad to go with the tuna and heated some frozen crepes. They drank their martinis instead of wine and agreed, by their third, that ninety proof gin had it all over the grape. Outside, on the window ledge, pigeons strutted, made cooing sounds, and then went to sleep. Earlier Peggy had started to go to her room to dress, but Turner stopped her, swearing that for him, no greater turn on existed than a terry robe and baby powder after a bath. "Keep talking like that," she said, "and I just may never put clothes on again."

After coffee, they finished the last of the martinis in the living room, which finally was enough to press the heart to fulfillment, even to truth. "I must tell you something," he said. And with his tongue only the slightest bit unwieldy, he told her all of it. He told her because she was there and caring and he trusted her. But he especially told her because the thought of keeping it locked inside him like a flowering malignancy was suddenly intolerable. Why else was he here?

"Oh, Paul." Tears slid unnoticed down her cheeks. "But who? Why?"

73

"I don't know."

"What are you going to do?"

He shrugged. "Something."

"But they said you couldn't."

"Take a good look at me. Do I really look like a man who can be told his wife was murdered and be able to just forget it?"

"No. That's what frightens me."

All at once they were cold sober. The pigeons on the window ledge awoke and made soft, oddly human sounds.

She knuckled her eyes dry like a child. "You want to know something? The truth? When I learned Maria was gone, I had two immediate thoughts. Ah, poor Maria, was one. Ah, Paul is free, was the other. And I swear to God I'm not even sure which came first."

Turner said nothing.

"Does that make you uncomfortable?"

"It does surprise me a little."

"You never knew how I felt?"

"I guess I never thought about it. I was always pretty much a one-woman guy and I already had my woman. Besides, you were always going with somebody or other."

"David has been dead a long time."

"Yet you never remarried."

"It's not that simple. In my age bracket most of the good ones are already taken. The rest usually come with problems, strings, and losses." She looked at him straight on. "Besides, I suppose in my mind there was always you out there."

"I'm really not that great a bargain."

"I know what you are and aren't. I've been your editor for nine years. Remember? And a writer is still very much what he writes."

Slowly, deliberately, her eyes still locked into his, she stood up, unbelted her robe, and let it fall to the carpet. She was naked underneath. "Maria is gone. Sooner or later you're going to want me or some other woman. Given the choice, I'd rather it be sooner and me."

The Past

Her body had a golden glow in the lamplight. Her breasts were like a young girl's—high, pink-nippled, saucy—her thighs surprisingly voluptuous, her stomach flat and unmarked above the pelvic darkness. She stood motionless, hands at her sides, letting him take inventory.

"Funny," he said. "You don't *look* like an editor."

"If you dare make jokes," she said fiercely, "I'll strangle you."

He stood up and kissed her mouth, tasting the remains of the coffee and gin along with a warm sweetness that had nothing to do with either one. Her flesh, under his hands, was silky and cool, a prize, and he felt himself reacting so quickly that it stunned him. There was evidently no prescribed period of mourning down there.

She led him to the bedroom and turned on a lamp. "Now you. I want to look at you."

"My body is not like yours."

"Thank God."

"It's a mess, a battleground."

"Please. I've thought about this for so long."

"Can't we turn out the light? I feel like a bride."

"I warned you. No jokes."

He took off his clothes and looked down at his damaged flesh, seeing the fine tracings of the surgical scars, the crazy, formless patterns of the bone fragment scars, the red, wizened burn marks from pieces of hot grenade that made him look as though someone had been holding lighted matches to his ribs. With the best of intentions a corpsman had almost cost him his right arm by leaving a tourniquet on too long, and a deadened ring of skin still marked the spot. This, plus the gougings of needles and catheters, blue, black, and green, that seemed to dance across his skin like a chorus of carpenter ants. And to top it all off, the new and still raw bullet wound in his upper arm.

"Mr. Universe," he said.

But she was not listening. She was on her knees before him, as if trying to heal, to render him perfect with her

75

mouth. She had a savant's lips, full and knowing, and the miracle of the rising began in him again. Yet he found something sad in her virtuosity. She was too expert, too knowing. He had had only one woman in eight years, but how many men had she had since the smiling engineer on the piano? Turner felt their presence, imagined himself competing in some sort of grand sexual round robin, and went soft.

Eyes puzzled, she looked up from her labors. Turner gently disengaged her, lifted her, and took her to the bed. He went for his cigarettes, came back, and lay down beside her. "Just give me a minute."

"Did I do something wrong?"

"Hell, no. You're a real expert."

She was sensitive enough to understand. "Would you rather I was shy, clumsy, and hiding under the sheets?"

"I'm sorry. I've been with one woman too long."

"While I've been with the army, navy, and marines?"

He hid behind his cigarette.

"I'm not especially proud of the past nine years, Paul, but neither am I ashamed of them. I'm not a solitary animal. I'm human. And the men I went to bed with were human too." She smiled but it was sad. "My husband was the only man I ever had until I lost him. Then, after a year of living like a nun, I found it was possible for me to actually enjoy sex without love. The same as a man. But you evidently haven't granted us that much liberation yet."

"You think I'm that bad?"

"The quintessential male chauvinist, darling."

He had not meant to hurt her. "Peggy . . ."

"It's true. It's even in your response to Maria's murder. The lone avenger. You're positively archaic. Straight out of King Arthur. Except that you'll die with a bullet in you rather than a lance."

They lay there, together but apart.

What's wrong with me, he thought. And he put out his cigarette and gathered her up, all sweet balm to his flesh. It was better this time, and afloat in this nonsolitary woman with

76

the golden skin, this book editor who knew all about him and had been his wife's friend, something sweet took root in him again and he accepted it without threat.

SIX

The Past

On a dark street of single-family houses in Little Neck, Queens, Turner sat in an aging green Mustang and waited for Captain McKinley to come home from his late night at the Sixth Precinct. Turner had a carefully worked out plan in his head and a loaded .38-caliber Smith & Wesson in his pocket. Although he had no intention of using the gun, it was nevertheless an integral part of his plan.

It had been a tense, frustrating week. Committed to taking action, Turner had found himself without any idea of what action to take. Eventually, he had tried to make a beginning of sorts with the codebook he had found in the wall safe. At least he assumed it to be a codebook. But since he had never actually seen one, he went to the library, checked though several volumes of cryptology, and found that indeed it seemed to be a book of codes. Fine. So what then? The book's cryptic jottings meant nothing unless there were messages to be decoded, and Turner had no messages. In addition, the subject of cryptology itself proved to be so vast that it embraced such broadly divergent areas as the military, the diplomatic, the political, the scientific, the industrial, and innumerable phases of the commercial. Turner even came across categories such as lovers' codes, religious codes, literary codes (were there really ciphers scattered throughout Shakespeare?), and a chapter on how cryptoanalysis led to the execution of Mary Queen of Scots. Undoubtedly fascinating, but of no practical help at all. So he had been forced to follow up on his only other visible lead—the precinct captain he had heard his uncle call and speak to and who, Turner felt, probably knew a lot more than he had been willing to reveal in a casual telephone conversation.

It was past midnight and, except for a scattering of parked cars, the block was empty. The neighborhood itself was a good one, middle-class and pleasant, with scrupulously well cared-for homes and lawns. Yet the longer Turner sat there waiting, the more menacing it seemed to become. Until he finally began to wonder what he was doing there at all. Even his carefully considered plan suddenly struck him as incredibly dangerous and foolish. How the devil could he have ever imagined such a scheme would work? It was a form of action, rightly enough, but it was action being taken more out of desperation, more out of a growing fear of not doing anything at all, than out of any true conviction that it would really succeed. Still, because he did not know what else to do, he remained committed. And when he saw that it was approaching the time to get into position, he left the car, slipped through some bushes, and circled behind the garage at the rear of the police captain's house.

He stood in the shadows. He was not quite certain if he was a hound after a fox or the fox itself, caught in a bog. He fingered the revolver in his pocket for reassurance, but it only made him more nervous. Regardless of intentions, a gun was never anything but a gun and its purpose was to kill. Besides, motivation was not always pure. He was an angry, frustrated man, which in itself was dangerous. It happened often in combat. Magic, dread, and the fascination of death became incentives of their own. Often, the worst of discoveries was made: There was release in violence. Not that you could live with it for long. The tension would sicken you after a while. But for brief periods, there was a frightening exhilaration in it.

79

He heard a stirring in the darkness behind him, and he whirled around, gun in hand and the safety off. A cat's eyes shone. Mystic green jewels. "Scat," he hissed, and the eyes went away. He put the gun back in his pocket, almost wishing he had kept the cat for company. It was a lonely time. A moment later he heard the cat once more. He turned to welcome it. Something exploded in the back of his head. Dimly, he saw lightning flashes. Then nothing.

He grew conscious of an aching head, a steady rocking motion, and an inability to see. I'm blind, he thought. He tried to touch his eyes and found that his hands were tied behind his back. He also discovered that he was blindfolded and half-lying, half-sitting on what felt like the back seat of a moving car. Beside him, a man's voice said, "Don't talk and don't cry out. If you do, we'll have to gag you."

Turner swayed as the car went around a corner. So it had not been the cat after all. Some plan. He felt nothing, only the ache in his head and a slight nausea. Curiously, he was not even very concerned. If they had wanted to kill him, he would already be dead. And there was a relief of sorts in not having to think about what to do next. That was out of his hands now. He estimated two men in the car, one driving and the other in the rear with him. He breathed the scent of lilac after shave lotion and the slightly sour smell of beer. Cops. McKinley had spotted him during the past few days and put a pair of detectives on his tail. Yet why would cops have had to knock him out and blindfold him?

"How about a cigarette?" he said.

"I told you no talking."

But a moment later Turner had a lighted cigarette pressed between his lips . . . his own brand. He considered it a good sign. Then he concentrated on figuring out where they were from the traffic noises, from their speed, and from the feel of the roadway under them. It was a futile exercise. Still, he did manage to pick up the distinctive hum of the iron grating on the Fifty-ninth Street Bridge and knew they were headed back to Manhattan. He next recognized the nonstop pace of the East River Drive. Then they were off it, slowing, and finally parked.

Turner was led by the arm into a building that echoed to their steps and smelled like a warehouse of some sort. It definitely was not a police station. A chair was shoved against the back of his legs and he sat down. "Just sit nice and quiet." The man put a freshly lighted cigarette between his lips. The other man dialed a number and spoke softly into a telephone. Turner strained to hear, but he could make out nothing. Not too far away, a ship's horn sounded on the East River.

The cigarette was burning very close to his lips when he heard a door open and close. The butt was taken from his mouth and footsteps moved away. The door opened and closed once more, and other footsteps approached. No one had spoken. Turner breathed perfume and cigar smoke. The perfume grew stronger. Turner's hands were cut loose from behind his back, and his blindfold was removed. He blinked against the glare of a naked bulb and looked into Hank Adams's face, then past Hank at his uncle. Dressed in evening clothes, they had evidently just left a formal party. Hank's pale eyes were cold, her mouth set in a tight angry line. Turnovsky stood contemplating Turner over his cigar. The two anonymous men were gone. Turner sat rubbing his wrists, trying to restore circulation. He touched the back of his head and felt a crust of dried blood.

Turnovsky took some ice from a machine, wrapped it in a handkerchief, and handed it to Turner. His movements and manner were relaxed, almost casual. In contrast to Hank's obvious irritation, he seemed faintly amused. "I had a feeling you'd try something *meshuggener.*" He shook his head. "Tell me, Pauly. I'm curious. Exactly what did you hope to accomplish out there tonight?"

"I just thought I might get some more answers out of McKinley."

"How? By blowing his head off?"

"I didn't expect to use the gun."

"You didn't expect? That's why you loaded it with six bullets?"

Turner pressed the ice to the back of his head and said nothing. Rockets were going off.

"You can take my word," said Turnovsky. "McKinley doesn't know anything more. If he did, he would have told me." He held out his hand, palm up. In it were Turner's revolver and the knitted ski mask he had intended to wear as a disguise. "What kind of foolishness is this for a man like you? The greenest *paisano* off the boat would know better. You want to kill yourself? For suicide you need only one bullet, not six."

"Herschel, save your breath," said Hank. "You're wasting your time and energy. He's not even listening."

Turnovsky smiled, a silver-maned lion in impeccable dinner clothes. "You hear her, Pauly? She's an angry lady, my Hank. All week long she's been on me about you acting like such a *schlimazel*. So what are we going to do with you?"

"I'll tell you what we'll do," said Hank. She snatched the gun and mask from Turnovsky's hand and dumped them in Turner's lap. "Here are your toys back. Shoot anyone you please. Just leave Herschel out of it."

"I didn't ask him to get involved."

"There's more than one way to ask," Hank said flatly. "You're not stupid. You knew he wouldn't let you blunder around until they finally put you away."

"You're wrong. I don't think like that."

Turnovsky waved his cigar impatiently. "Enough, enough. I want this settled. Pauly, once and for all . . . are you going to be sensible? Are you going to leave this craziness alone and get on with your life? You're a young man yet. You have a priceless gift, a talent not given to many. So you had a tragedy. It's over. I beg you not to make it worse. I beg you to forget it."

Turner was silent.

"Well? Are you going to be smart about this?"

82

"I can't, Uncle Herschel."

"You mean you won't," said Hank.

"Can't, won't, what's the difference?" said Turnovsky. It's all the same. Does an addict want to be an addict? The man can't help himself."

"That's *his* problem," said Hank. "Not yours."

Turnovsky looked at her. "It's so hard for you to understand how he feels? You think if someone deep-sixed you, I'd just tip my hat and walk away?"

The warehouse was quiet around them. Outside, on the East River Drive, traffic hummed.

"So what do you want, Pauly? You want to be an instant detective? You want to find out who took away your lady? Okay. So you find out. So what happens then?"

"I'll worry about that when the time comes."

Turnovksy paced between stacks of what appeared to be boxed chemicals. He seemed to be studying the warehouse floor. "All right," he said, coming back. "I'll make you a proposition."

"Herschel!" said Hank. "Please. Don't get involved."

"What are you talking? I'm already involved. He's my brother's son."

"Your brother who called you a thief?"

"So what else am I?" He shrugged. "Here's my proposition, Pauly. I'll do what I can. I have a little muscle here and there. I'll push, squeeze, press. I'll pray. I'll *daven minchah* and *mairev* for you. I'll try to get you your answers. But only on one condition. That you do nothing on your own. That you do nothing without consulting me first. I don't ever want to see something like tonight again. If I do, I'm through, finished." He paused, a man whose life had been built on deals. "Well? What do you say?"

"Are you serious?"

"Do I look like I'm joking?"

"But why would you do this?"

"Because you won't leave it alone. Because it's the only way I know to keep you from being dead in a week." The

83

dark Tartar eyes took silent inventory. They added, subtracted, struck balances. "Besides, I've been thinking. Someone like you . . . you've paid a lot of dues. More than most. I figure you deserve better than you're getting."

Turner glanced at Hank. Though still beautiful, her face was hard now. New England hard. And it had closed him out. "I'm afraid Hank doesn't agree. And she's probably right as far as you're concerned. You don't really need this kind of trouble."

"I'll tell you something about my high class *shiksa*. She's a worrier. She worries enough to be Jewish. But you'll see. When the time comes, she'll do more than both of us together." Turnovsky put out his hand. "So, Pauly? We're in business?"

Turner felt his uncle's hand, strong and firm in his. "God yes. And I thank you."

"Well, let's wait."

Turner saw no need for waiting. Things were already far better than he had dared hope for ten minutes ago. This man, this elegantly dressed thief, was his father's brother. They shared the same blood, and there was feeling. For now, that was enough.

SEVEN

The Present

Turner first noticed the blue sedan when he heard the squeal of brakes behind his cab and turned to see it beat the light across Madison Avenue. When the car remained in sight as they headed uptown on Third Avenue, he told the cabby to pull over. He got out and bought a newspaper at a corner stand. Returning, he noted that the sedan had parked about fifty feet down the block. There were two men in it. Turner paid the cab driver, reached for his suitcase, and walked uptown until he came to a pay phone on Fifty-eighth Street. Pretending to make a call, he saw that the blue car was now parked between Fifty-seventh and Fifty-eighth streets and that one of the men had gotten out and was walking in his direction. He was a tall man, big through the chest and going to paunch. He passed Turner, then stopped to examine some books in a window. If there were these two, thought Turner, and they were this clumsy, then there were probably more.

Still feigning conversation, he picked out a black Chevrolet parked across the avenue with two men in it and another man reading a newspaper at a bus stop. They apparently had a fair-sized operation going. He hung up the receiver, left the booth, and walked crosstown to Bloomingdale's.

The store was crowded with midday shoppers. Turner worked his way through the aisles and took an escalator to the third floor. He looked for a door leading to an emergency stairs. Finding one, he pushed through. Then he put down his valise, pressed flat against a wall, and waited to see who would follow him.

It was the tall man from the blue car. He came through the door quickly, without proper caution. Turner caught him with a hard right to his paunch, then cold-chopped him as he doubled over. The man dropped with a soft grunt and lay there. When no one else appeared, Turner ran down the stairs, smashed through a fire door, and came out on Sixty-first Street. He walked to Lexington Avenue and picked up another cab. "La Guardia Airport," he said for the second time in half an hour. "And you've got yourself an extra twenty if you make us hard to follow."

The driver grinned at him in the rearview mirror, white teeth in a black pirate's beard. "Just hold on real good, man."

It was a wild ride—East River Drive to Harlem to the edge of the Bronx to the Triborough Bridge to Grand Central Parkway and finally to La Guardia. Diego Jiminez (said his license) had earned his extra money. Turner was sure they had not been followed. Which he knew meant little. He was a man carrying a suitcase. They had only to watch the airline, train, and bus terminals. Still, it would not be that easy for them.

Using three different names at three different airline counters and paying cash, he bought one-way tickets to Richmond, Virginia, and to Baltimore and Hagerstown, Maryland. All three flights were scheduled to leave within the next three-quarters of an hour. In fifteen minutes, he would decide which one to be on. Keeping his bag with him, he wandered through the terminal. He still watched his back but saw nothing.

He found a seat overlooking the runways. A steady stream of jets landed and took off, each one graceful, swift, and certain. He suddenly envied the pilots, envied their skill and confidence, envied the panels of instruments they had to guide them. He himself had never been guided by anything

86

but his own brain, senses, and intuition, and these had proven less than adequate. Or perhaps he had just lacked the necessary faith. Unlike Maria, he thought. For his wife had come to him with her own laws of faith, grace, and dealing with the hand of God. While he had grown up in a world bounded solely by the covers of *Newsweek*—politics, the arts, finance, the planet's family of nations. What he could not see or touch, what could not be explained in rational terms, had not existed for him. Still, he had tried to change. And at times he had succeeded. At times Maria's insights had brought him closer than he was willing to admit to understanding the incomprehensible. They had certainly helped him in dealing with the mystic wonder of his survival in that jungle clearing. Because by every law of military action and logic, he should have died there with the others. Yet he had not. And it was no longer enough for him to credit dumb luck for his durability. On occasion he had bolted awake in the night, a smothering pressure on his chest, the stink of death in his nostrils, and Maria's eyes glowing anxiously above him in the dark. His only visible link to sanity. Then her voice and touch would bring him back. Often, she would drive off the demons with her body. She could do that. Making love, with a sense of awe, their bodies were the ultimate miracle. What better evidence of God's hand? Naked, she had once pulled him from bed to stand before a mirror. "Look at us." He looked but failed to see what she saw. She reached between his legs, touched him, watched the wonder of his rising. Transfiguration!

On a night almost nine years ago, making love for the first time, she had looked up at him dreamily and whispered, "I think I've just begun falling in love with you."

"It's only lust."

"No. The lust is over."

"Not permanently, I hope."

But she was serious and thinking carefully. There was a full moon, and it was shining through the window, throwing the shadows of the square panes onto the floor. Her face was silver. "Do you love me?"

"My God, yes."

They soared.

"Isn't it a shame we can't feel this way forever?" she said.

"Maybe we can."

"They say people finally become bored with each other."

He considered it. "Not us."

"Or die."

"It's only hearsay."

"Everyone eventually does."

"I believe that in our particular case an exception will be made."

"What a lovely thought." He smile was beatific. "Please arrange it."

"I will," he promised.

Now it was time to choose one of the three flights on which he had booked space. He picked Richmond and checked his valise through at the baggage counter. Then he walked through the electronic security checkpoint and boarded the flight to Baltimore. Just as the flight attendants were about to close the hatch, he dashed off the plane and waited to see if anyone would follow him off. When no one did, he walked to the far end of the gate area and boarded his Richmond flight just four minutes before take-off time. He chose a seat near the tail of the 727 and watched the forward entrance hatch. Only two passengers came on board after he did: an elderly woman carrying an armful of packages and a young man in a sweater and jeans with a load of books. Neither one looked like a surveillance artist. Then the hatch was closed, and the plane pulled away from the terminal. Turner leaned back in his seat and closed his eyes. He could not imagine anyone having been able to follow him onto that flight.

Still, with the engines pulling, he could almost taste the tension in his mouth. He was at home, out of uniform, in a nation nominally at peace, yet he might just as well have been back in Southeast Asia and at war. It was that same kind of taste and feeling, with him and all those other poor, shit-faced grunts sitting around some miserable front-line bunker, trying to get themselves good and pissed off at *Charlie,* because if you were angry enough at the enemy, you were less likely to be wet and sick with fear. To this end, they told horror stories, told of decapitated grunts' heads black with ants. They called the VC dirty, fucking butchers. They said they would shoot the balls off every one of the little, motherfucking commie bastards. They said they were not even human, that they were the enemies of mankind. They recited the right answers without even being asked the questions. They wanted their kids (unborn, of course) to live in a free world. They gave proper lip service to the domino theory. If the fucking Reds weren't stopped here, they'd never be stopped anywhere. This was America's piss-assed crusade for freedom and someone had to fight it. Freedom was worth dying for, right? If they couldn't believe that, then what the fuck did they have? Many of them had died, all right. Turner had not. But what had suddenly happened to his freedom?

"Would you care for something to drink, sir?" asked the stewardess, smiling. "A cocktail?"

"Why the fuck not?" said Turner and was as startled as the girl.

EIGHT

The Past

It was Turner's first outright act of breaking and entering. Although he guessed that like everyone else he had been born more thief than not. The urge to simply reach out and take what you wanted came naturally enough. Later, of course, it was conditioned out of you by fear of punishment and what you acquired instead, called morality. His companion in crime, Mutsie by name, suffered no such false conditioning. A slight, bald, meticulous man who wore expensive rep ties and banker's gray suits and had his nails manicured every week, he was a professional burglar, the best in the business according to Herschel Turnovsky, who knew about such things. Mutsie was classy. A scientist. If awards were given for excellence in that particular area, Turnovsky was sure Mutsie would have been a Nobel laureate. Why not? He had a good Jewish head on his shoulders. Which he carried with the quiet confidence of a surgeon.

Turner, being the apprentice, just did as he was told, kept his mouth shut, and observed the master. Fascinating. Nothing was left to chance. It was all in the preparation, Mutsie had explained. House records were thoroughly checked, wiring and electrical plans studied, security systems analyzed, occupants' habits and schedules pinpointed. All of these elements had to be coordinated and favorable before a break-

90

The Pastin was even considered. Such finally being the case with the house of the British ambassador to the United Nations, Turner and Mutsie made entry at 9:35 P.M. on a night when the ambassador and his wife were above the Atlantic on their way to London, when their house couple was making happy use of the fourth-row-center tickets to a hit show that Lady Hutchins had considerately left behind, and when the security guards, on twenty-four-hour duty when the ambassador was in residence, were off.

Mutsie deactivated the alarm system at its source box buried in the rear garden. Then he picked open the lock on a service door in exactly fifty seconds, and they walked in upright, like gentlemen. To Mutsie, the entire operation was what he described as a piece of cake, hardly even worthy of his sophisticated talents. But if Herschel Turnovsky considered it important enough to have called him in, Mutsie was not about to question it. Carrying tiny, pinpoint flashes for guidance and wearing thin, latex gloves to avoid leaving prints, they walked through the big rooms where the reception had been held and then upstairs to the ambassador's office suite. I'm back where she died, Turner thought. As with the exhumation, he had found it necessary to be there personally. The need came with the rest of the obsession. His uncle had tried, briefly, to dissuade him from going along, but understood his compulsion. He was not so different himself, he confessed. In certain areas he was also a little bit crazy. His own wife (Turner warmly remembered Aunt Daisy) had died twenty-two years ago, and Turnovsky had put on *tvillen* and *tallis* and prayed each morning and night ever since. He had made a deal. When his wife was given no more than a year to live, he had pleaded with his previously unacknowledged God to at least extend it to three. Not unreasonable. Not piggish. Just three good years for his Daisy. Miraculously granted his plea, he had been paying off with his daily devotions for twenty-two years without evasion or regret. When it came to wives, Turnovsky conceded, each of them was evidently a *bissel meshuggener.*

Turner discovered what they needed in a row of file cabinets labeled "Publicity and Protocol." He found an official reception guest list, head photographs that allowed the delegation staff to recognize the guests and know what titles or positions they held, and three large reels of sixteen-millimeter motion picture film that had been used to record the reception itself.

"That's all?" Mutsie asked. "You got everything?"

Turner nodded.

"Good. Now we confuse them a little."

Confusing them a little meant not letting them know the true purpose of the break-in. They emptied cabinets, desks, and bookcases onto the floor. They unwound dozens of reels of film and scattered files everywhere. Mutsie opened a safe and took out several thousand dollars and a dozen sealed folders marked with Special Registry labels. He put the folders, the cash, and about a dozen reels of haphazardly chosen film in a large canvas bag that he had worn folded under his jacket.

They took a last look around. Turner spotted a framed photograph of the ambassador's wife and two children on the floor, half buried under the debris. Almost absentmindedly, he bent, picked it up, and put it back on Lord Hutchins's desk. Mutsie looked at him curiously. Moments later they were out of the house.

There was Maria. Turner was watching her. She walked, talked, laughed, smiled. She moved gracefully among the assembled guests, a bright, spirited racing yacht among lumbering merchantmen. She brushed her hair back from her forehead with the same impatient gesture Turner had seen countless times before. She made the president of the United States laugh like a schoolboy. She scowled and waved her arms at a pair of lumpy Russian generals weighted with medals. There were several hundred other people also on camera, including, from time to time, Turner himself, but the only one he really noticed at the beginning was his wife. Which was foolish. Because this was not the purpose for which the film had been stolen. Nor was it why it was being shown.

Later, he managed to do better, and along with Hank and his uncle was able to pick out, identify, and write down the name of every guest that Maria could be seen speaking to during the evening. The screening was being held in Turnovsky's library, with Hank running the projector and stopping the action at key moments so that particular faces could be identified from the headshots marked with their names and titles. All of which seemed rather futile to Turner. But his uncle felt they had to start somewhere, and whoever it was that they were looking for was, after all, going to be someplace up there on that screen. True enough. And indeed, once underway, Turnovsky seemed to be enjoying himself like a kid with an exciting new mystery game. At his age, thought Turner. As for Hank, she worked with exactly the kind of quiet, efficient energy that Turnovsky had prophesied she would show once the whole idea of the hunt was accepted and put in motion. Which did not fool Turner one bit. Her resentment was still there. It ran like a current between them.

At the end of the screening, when the three separately compiled lists were picked through and correlated, they had the names of sixty-three guests on a master sheet. Forty-one of these had been observed speaking with Maria once, twelve had spoken with her twice, six were with her three times, two others four times, one, five times and one more, six. The grand winner was none other than the president himself. The runner-up was the Russian delegate to the United Nations, and numbers three and four were a British Nobel Prize–winning poet and a famous Southern playwright. The list, Turner realized, did not mark the president as the prime suspect, with the others following him in descending order depending on how many times each had spoken with her. It meant, rather, that these were the people she was anxious to have as guests on her show, that she was having difficulty

93

selling them on the idea, and that she was stubbornly doing her best to convince them. Bearing this out, the film did show that in all these cases Maria was the aggressor, that she was actually the one who came over and initiated the conversations. Refusing to take no for an answer, she simply kept coming back. "Maybe that's why she was poisoned," Hank said dryly.

Turner was not amused.

His uncle said, "In a de Maupassant story, a suspicious husband once found out who his wife's lover was by seeing which of the suspects didn't speak to her during a dinner party."

It was at a ball, thought Turner, recalling the story, and the secret lover was the only man who didn't ask the wife to dance.

"On that basis," said Hank, "we'd be left with exactly three hundred and fourteen suspects."

"Well, I think we can shave that figure a little," Turnovsky said and looked at Turner. "Do you remember what you said about that intruder's gun having no silencer, yet you heard no explosion when you were shot?"

"Yes?"

"I've done some checking. There happens to be a new type of silent bullet that's been patented. And the CIA and FBI are the only security outfits using it right now. Which fits in with the pressure on the local police. So I'd guess we can narrow our candidates to them."

Hank was going over the guest list. "Officially, they had four people there . . . the FBI director himself, the deputy director of the CIA, and the regional heads of both agencies. Unofficially, there could have been a dozen or more. With that many Russians loose in one place, they're always paranoid." She spoke to Turner: "Your wife was Russian, wasn't she?"

"Maria was born in this country." He said it almost defensively. "Her parents were Ukrainian."

"That's not Russian?"

"Not to a Ukrainian."

"But she did speak Russian, didn't she?"

"Fluently. So what? Is that supposed to have made her a Russian agent?"

"You'd better keep an open mind," said Turnovsky quietly. "It's not so impossible."

"If you had known Maria at all, you wouldn't say that. She despised Russia and everthing Russian. I wasn't fooling about Ukrainians. They're a special breed. The Red Army never really trusted them during the war and burned them out. Maria had two sisters she never knew. They went up in smoke with their house. Her parents never let her forget."

"Who told you that?" asked Hank.

"Maria."

There was silence.

"I'd swear on it," Turner said.

Turnovsky leaned over and touched his shoulder. "Don't swear so fast, Pauly. We're just beginning."

Later, a sleek, nervous ferret of a man appeared. Turnovsky called him Jake. He was a science professor at CCNY and had served a term as advisor on cryptography to the National Security Agency. He spent about five minutes studying Maria's code book. Turner had brought it with him for that purpose. Then he spoke briefly to Turnovsky in the foyer and left.

Turnovsky came back into the library. His face showed nothing. "It's a code used by the CIA."

It was really not too great a surprise, yet Turner felt himself shaken. "Which means what?"

"That's what we have to find out."

Turner was still at the Waldorf as dawn neared. He marveled at his uncle's energy. Hank had gone to bed, exhausted, at about two o'clock, and Turner's own eyes were glazed with fatigue, yet Turnovsky was as fresh as he had been when they started almost eight hours before. The CIA's now certain involvement seemed to have tapped fresh reserves of energy for him. Ground rules were gone over. Most importantly, Turner

95

must never give the slightest hint that he considered his wife's death to have been anything but natural. He must also operate on the assumption that his telephone and apartment could be bugged at any time and he himself placed under surveillance. None of these things had yet taken place, Turnovsky told him, but they remained distinct possibilities. Alarmed, Turner asked, "How can you be so sure they haven't been done?"

"Because I've been having your place checked and you followed." Turnovsky showed white, even teeth that were entirely his own. "And, incidentally, your seeing this lady editor of yours is all to the good. It creates exactly the impression we want—that you've gotten on with your life and aren't just brooding and poking around."

"You amaze me, Uncle Herschel."

"Don't be so amazed. In my lifestyle, survival is an infinite capacity for suspicion. You think I've stayed alive and out of jail all these years from dumb luck?"

Turner had no clear idea *what* he thought. But he was gradually learning about this man whom his father had so cavalierly dismissed as Herschel the *Gonif*. In fact, it was becoming increasingly difficult to remember a time when his uncle had not played an active and important part in his life, when he had not been there to question, to seek advice from, and to simply sit and listen to. With no family of his own, Turnovsky seemed to take particular delight in sharing thoughts and ideas with his newly discovered *mishpocheh*. Almost entirely self-educated, he had read more than most people could read in two lifetimes and enjoyed talking to Turner in an easy, rambling way about music, painting, books, politics, religion. He had traveled extensively on every continent, knew people everywhere, and had his own unique theories on everything. He was an absolute pragmatist who believed fully and without apology in his chosen way of life, and who was certain that the ethics of worldwide organized crime (a shining example of a cohesive, functioning system) were no worse than those of any legally constituted government and might

96

even be better, less amoral, than most. Since, at this stage of the planet's existence, illegal activity of one form or another had to be regarded as an inescapable constant of daily living, how much more sensible to keep it out of the hands of the crazies and make a safe, practical business of it. No jokes. He meant every word. "Seriously, Pauly . . . if we'd had a nice, smooth operation going in the Weimar Republic in the early thirties, we would have taken care of crazy Adolph before that dirty little *putz* took care of six million of our *landsleit* and half the world."

To Turnovsky, Adolph Hitler was the century's prime example of a true crazy in government, an unsafe, impractical, unregulated madman who destroyed cities, nations, and millions of innocent lives because other legally constituted governments tremblingly granted him a free hand until it was too late to do much more than send out burying parties to gather up the remains. Today's world-class syndicate operation would have eliminated him early on as a threat to their functioning system and to that system's profits. "If the truth could be made public and appreciated," said Turnovsky, "our current syndicate system would be hailed as the world's first working model of a pure universalist philosophy in action. National prejudices, hostility, petty hatreds would be stamped out for the best of all possible reasons—mutual profit. And with war's destruction as the single greatest threat to our earnings, that scourge would be ended once and for all."

To Turner, listening, it actually made a cynical kind of sense. Which, in itself, was troubling.

Now, as the sky started to lighten behind the East River's lacy steel bridges, Turnovsky poured them each a full measure of brandy as an eye opener. Not that he himself appeared to need it. His color was high, his eyes sparkled, and he had never seemed more like a big, healthy animal. "In thinking it through, Pauly, there couldn't have been any advance planning to their killing your Maria. The need was probably sudden, unexpected. Otherwise, why would they have done it at a reception for almost four hundred high-level guests that included even the president. Had they planned it, they also would never have used cyanide, which shows up in autopsy. Not when there are newer drugs around that can't be traced. I figure they used the cyanide because it was all they happened to have when the need arose, and they couldn't wait."

"You still keep saying *they*."

"After Jake's confirmation of the code, I'm willing to settle for the CIA." He threw Turner a look behind which seemed to be unseen pressures. "Think hard, Pauly. Your Maria never said anything at all . . . not that night, not before, that might give us some idea what it was all about?"

Turner slowly shook his head. "I feel like a damn fool. I mean she was my wife, but I can't think of a thing." His mind felt sluggish, dull. "You think Maria was working for the CIA?"

"For . . . against . . . who knows?"

"Not against. Never that. My wife loved this country, Uncle Herschel."

"So what's that got to do with the price of oranges?"

"What do you mean?"

"Please, Pauly. Do me a favor. No more 'Oh say can you see . . .' No more wrapping your lady in the Stars and Stripes. Okay? It wastes good time. Worse, it confuses things. We all love this country. It's a nice place to live. Better than most. But it's still only a country, right?"

Turner stared at him without comprehension.

"Maybe it's time for a little practical lesson in patriotism."

Turnovsky left the room and returned a moment later with a reel of 16-millimeter film. The projector and screen were still set up from before, and he inserted the film and switched off the lights. The reel ran for about fifteen minutes and showed Turnovsky alone in the company of four different men in four different hotel rooms. Two of the men were United States senators, from New Jersey and Pennsylvania, respectively. The third man was the assistant attorney general of the United States. And the fourth man was the lieutenant-governor of Nevada. It was a sound-synchronized film—the dialogue was clearly audible and little explanation was required. In short, Herschel Turnovsky was paying off for services rendered. The payments ran into many thousands of dollars and were all made in cash and on camera. One payment was related to a gambling casino license, another to a plea bargaining arrangement in a multimillion-dollar tax fraud case, a third to the settlement of an antitrust suit, and the fourth to the sponsoring of legislation favorable to the future of a major financial institution. All of the conversations were affable and seemed to constitute little more than regularly scheduled meetings between old friends. In every case it was Turnovsky who appeared to be fawned upon, who was the one whose favor was being curried.

Turnovsky switched the lights back on. "Those men love this country too, Pauly. Their families have probably loved it for generations. They've fought in its wars and bled for it. But, as I said, it's still only a country. One way or another it goes on. People don't. So if they're smart, they take care of their own needs first."

"Maria had more money than she could use. She didn't need any more, Uncle Herschel."

"There are other needs."

"Like what?"

Turnovsky shrugged. "I never had the pleasure of knowing your lady, Pauly. But I know this—there's usually something."

With most of the city still asleep, Turner walked home through the gray dawn light. He felt tired and depressed because he had not slept for almost twenty-four hours and it had been a confusing, unsettling night. He had sworn to Maria's love for her country, and his uncle had given him a short, cynical, utterly irrelevent lesson in pragmatic patriotism. Yet what could he say? That he knew better? Suddenly, he was not at all sure that he did know better. Everything he thought he knew was being turned upside-down. Though not really everything. Some things had to stay right side up, no

99

matter what. Some things were so deeply ingrained they were unalterable. And the way Maria felt about Russia surely had to be one of them.

Once, in speaking of world peace in his usual role as a knee-jerk liberal, he had said that a certain amount of trust would finally be needed to achieve true détente with Russia, and Maria's reaction had been so violent, so bitter and angry, that he had never forgotten it. "Good God, Paul!" she had exploded. "You talk like a child. Don't you know anything at all about communism? It's *founded* on a lack of trust. Russia's leaders will say and do anything as long as it suits their purposes. They've lied to and murdered millions of their own people and put millions more into camps to preserve their sacred vision of revolution. What makes you think they'd treat their enemies any better?" Her eyes had blazed furiously at him. "They write their history in blood. The best of human traits—conscience, honor, pity, atonement—are the worst of sins to them. God himself had to be stamped out because he stood in the way of mass murder. And these are the animals you expect to trust? Just hearing you say it makes me shiver."

No, he thought. He'd be damned if all of that could have been merely a performance.

The thunder came just as he thrust into her, its timing perfect, as if the explosion was part of the act itself and not out of the heavens. Maybe no fireworks, as there had once been for Grace Kelly and Cary Grant, but a flash of genuine, nonmovie lightning did stab into the room and turn Peggy's face blue-white beneath him and widen her eyes with shock. For it had all begun to come together for them then, and they were like a wild, two-humped beast with no part of it tender and neither of them wanting it to be. He looked down at her, and her irises were turned up into her head, unseeing. She cried out, a cry not freely given but ripped loose. In response, his breath tore out of his throat so fast that it burned.

100

Her body lurched, arched upward as if convulsed by unseen currents. And he came to meet her, tuned high, all pure spirits, readying for the miracle. In all that violence he could not have moved better, could not have made a mistake. Yet nothing was loving in him. Nor was there any visible hint of love in her. Then the thunder came again and they along with it.

Their bodies changed in tone. They might have been dead. Sweat joined them along with their other juices . . . cheek to cheek, breasts to chest, belly to belly. Turner felt his heart going. It was hopping around inside him like some crazy little animal. Gasping, they hung onto each other, two shipwrecked sailors who had barely managed to make it to shore.

Other than for their breathing, they were silent. She usually spoke first, but not this time. "Hey," he said softly.

"Hey, yourself."

"You all right?"

She did not answer.

"What is it?"

"I don't know." Her voice sounded as though it were coming from farther away than just beside him in bed. "I guess I'm just scared."

Earlier, he had brought her up to date. She had asked, so he had told her. But it had been as much for his own needs as for hers. There had to be someone he could talk freely to, confide in. He had his uncle, of course, but his uncle had never known and cared about Maria as Peggy had. Somehow, this made a difference. "Maybe I shouldn't have told you anything."

"That would have been worse."

"Stop worrying. Uncle Herschel is all-powerful."

She stared up at the ceiling, her profile a cameo lit by a flash of lightning. Seconds later, the thunder came rolling in.

"I've been tearing my brains apart," he said. "I knew her for nine years, and now I seem to have known nothing."

"I knew her for twelve, Paul."

101

"Then maybe *you* can think of something."

"Like what?"

"Whatever might make sense of this. Who knows? Maybe something to connect her with the CIA. Which is where Uncle Herschel thinks the threads seem to lead."

"My God, he thinks Maria was a goddamn spy?"

"He never said spy, exactly."

"What then?"

"It's just that the codebook seems to say CIA and so does the silent bullet I took in the arm."

"But it all sounds so crazy."

"It's all we have, Peggy."

The sound of traffic rose from Central Park West, and they floated above it, their minds controlled, but cluttered with doubts.

"I don't understand," said Peggy. "Whatever she was involved in, how could she have shut you out like that? I mean, not a word, not a hint, nothing. I know she loved you, but what kind of love is that?"

Turner was not about to fool with that one.

"I could never have done it," she said. "Not in a million years. Could you?"

"I don't know. I never did. But then I never really had anything much to hide."

"I don't think you could have hidden it even if you did. You're just not that cold-blooded."

"And Maria was?"

"It's beginning to look that way." Peggy shook her head in sudden disgust. "Jesus, that sounds awful. Heaven help me, I think I'm getting jealous."

"Of a dead woman?"

"Maria won't be dead until you bury her, Paul. And the way things are going, God only knows when that will be." She smiled sadly. "So you see? You've already given her a kind of immortality."

They lay in separate cages of silence. Maria lay between them.

"Of course, there was once Handy," Peggy said slowly,

out of nowhere. "But even that was way back, maybe ten or eleven years ago. It was nothing much then and couldn't really mean anything now."

"Who's Handy?"

"A man Maria occasionally saw before she met you. She never mentioned him?"

"No. What about him."

"Well, you asked if I knew of anything that might have connected Maria to the CIA, and Handy just crossed my mind."

"Was he CIA?"

"I don't know what he was. But Maria did once say that he did some sort of intelligence work for one of our national security agencies. As a matter of fact, she used to laugh about it. He apparently took himself very seriously. A real Ivy League type. Wore cordovan brogues and smoked a pipe. I never met him, but he didn't sound very appealing." Peggy leaned over and licked his ear. A warm, affectionate cat. "Not the least bit like you."

Turner frowned. "Handy?"

"That was just what she called him. I suppose it was a kind of nickname."

"What was his real name?"

"I'm not sure I even remember." She thought through a lightning flash and a clap of thunder. "It was short for something."

"Like what?"

She shrugged. "Maybe like Handel . . . or Handelling . . . or Handelberg. I don't know. It was about eleven years ago. I have trouble remembering the names of people I met yesterday."

"How about Handley?"

"Could be. As a matter of fact, I think that's what it was. Handley . . . Handley . . ." She tried it a few times. "By George, I think you've got it."

Turner was up on one elbow. "Could it have been *Wendell* Handley?"

"As a matter of fact, yes." Her eyes had gone wide.

103

"Don't tell me you actually know him."

"No. But his name did happen to be on the guest list for the reception that night."

"Are you kidding me?"

He shook his head.

"Who is he?"

"The deputy director of the CIA."

Herschel Turnovsky had a complete and detailed report in his hands within forty-eight hours.

Wendell C. Handley was forty-three years old and had been born and raised in Ann Arbor, Michigan, the eldest of four children, two of whom had died in an automobile accident twenty-five years ago in which Wendell had been the driver. His father was chairman of the political science department at the University of Michigan; his mother was active in the Ann Arbor Women's and Garden clubs and in church-related charities; and his surviving brother was assistant secretary of state for Middle Eastern affairs. He had Bachelor of Arts and Doctor of Law degrees from Yale University, had been in private law practice in Washington, D. C. for two years, and had worked for the Central Intelligence Agency for sixteen. He had been officially posted, at various times, in London, Paris, and Berlin. But he had also been involved in covert operations in Budapest, Prague, Warsaw, and Moscow. He had been appointed deputy director three years before and was certain to succeed the agency's current head in another two. There were memos in the report attesting to Handley's ambition, excellent work habits, and superior performance under the most difficult and dangerous of conditions. There were also personal commendations from three presidents, two secretaries of state, and five senior senators. For the past eight years he had been married to the daughter of a former governor of Texas. They had a pair of six-year-old girl twins and lived in the Georgetown section of Washington D. C.

There were half a dozen photographs of Handley attached

to the report, some old and some very recent. They showed a lean, coldly handsome man who looked younger than his forty-three years and who had an air of quiet confidence about him that seemed to fit him perfectly for the often trying, often unpredictable demands of intelligence work. Taken altogether, Wendell C. Handley appeared to be a man whom Turner did not expect to like very much. Still, he was not so prejudiced that he was unable to see where women would very likely find him attractive. Once, a long time ago, Maria apparently had. Or had it also been more recently? If not, why had she never mentioned anything about him?

Then de Maupassant's suspicious husband also began to gnaw. According to the film, they had not spoken to one another once during the entire reception.

NINE

The Past

Turner came home from dinner and a movie with Peggy, approached his door, and found that someone was either inside his apartment at that moment or else had been there and left. Here we go again, he thought, and swore silently.

Moving quietly on the vestibule carpeting, he pressed an ear to the door and listened. He heard nothing. At that instant, he was perhaps less startled by the fact that someone had once again broken into his apartment than by the fact that his scheme to detect it had worked. Having read about the tactic in an intelligence training manual, he had taken to placing a tiny sliver of wood inside his door jamb whenever he went out. And tonight, for the first time, the marker had fallen to the floor.

So what did he do now?

His first instinct was to rush over and tell his uncle. Then he realized that Turnovsky and Hank had left two days ago on a trip to London, Paris, and Rome, and that for the next few weeks he was going to be very much on his own. The abrupt awareness of this made him feel helpless, like a man without resources. Which, in turn, angered him. He had not been this dependent on anyone since he was a child, and he hated the feeling. Still, he had accepted his dependency as the price of the deal with his uncle and had considered the cost

106

cheap for what he was getting. Nothing alone, Pauly, Turnovsky had reminded him before he left. They would look into this whole Wendell Handley business when he returned. What was the rush? Sadly, his Maria was going to be dead a long time. She would not mind waiting an extra few weeks for her retribution. Remember, Pauly, nothing alone.

Yet he now stood about as alone as he had ever been. He felt the tension in his body and was acutely aware of a sense of imminent danger. Foolish, he thought. He was not even sure anyone was inside. They might have entered and left during the five or six hours he had been gone. And there was always the possibility that the sliver of wood had fallen by itself. Heavy construction was still going on up the block, and vibrations could have shaken the splinter loose. Which, as he thought it through, was probably what had happened. Yet the memory of his last intruder was still strong enough to make him wary. Bullet holes, even nice, clean, fast-healing ones, had a way of lingering. So he stood against his door, waited and listened. When he heard nothing for fifteen minutes, he opened up and went in.

Moving quietly from one room to another, he found no one. But the apartment had been thoroughly gone over. Not that there was anything like the mess of last time. Nothing had been scattered about. In fact, the search seemed to have been rather orderly, as if the intruder or intruders were sensitive to the trauma that such a violation might cause and had considerately done their best to minimize the damage. Nevertheless, the search had been exhaustive. Nothing appeared to have been overlooked, not even the wall safe, although Turner had long ago emptied it. Nor, as far as he could tell, had anything been taken. Which again eliminated any possibility of the break-in having been an ordinary burglary.

He poured himself half a tumbler of bourbon and sat down to think. He assumed, wryly, that even the deal with his uncle would allow him to do this much alone. And one of the things he thought was that Maria must have left something damned important behind if they were still pushing to find it.

107

And since the first intruder had actually gone so far as to try to kill for it, and had himself died in the attempt, it had to be more important than just a codebook and some money. So maybe there was something else. And maybe, too, they had not been able to find it.

He started his own search early the next morning. Maybe it was a completely wild idea, but it was at least something to do and he did it eagerly. He had no way of guessing at the silly actions to which anger, frustration, and an overwhelming feeling of helplessness could drive even the most sensible of men. He went through drawers, clothing, closets, and shelves. He searched every book in the apartment, page by page. He tapped on walls, floors, and ceilings, listening for he knew not what. He took apart appliances and lamps and was unable to put three of them together again. He lifted rugs and carpeting and rooted about in years of accumulated dust. He probed mattresses, couches, pillows, and upholstered chairs with needles and fine wires. He dug behind pictures and frames. He poked in and around sinks, bathtubs, medicine cabinets, toilets, and drains. He loosened baseboards and moldings. For sixteen hours he looked everwhere he could think of and found nothing.

Then he sat down and thought some more. And this time it occurred to him to call a professional.

Mutsie arrived the following evening in his banker's gray suit and a twenty-dollar rep tie. He carried a small black leather bag of the type that doctors once carried when they made house calls. He listened gravely as Turner briefed him, the specialist preparing himself with his patient's history.

"Exactly what are you looking for?" he asked.

"I don't really know. It could be anything. It could also be nothing."

"Tell me where you've already looked."

Turner told him. When he finished, Mutsie walked slowly about the apartment. His eyes were X-ray machines. They missed nothing. "Did your wife ever work at home?" he asked.

"Sometimes."

"Show me where."

Turner took him to a graceful French Provincial desk in the spare bedroom. "I've already gone over it," he said. "Top to bottom."

Mutsie sat down at the desk, hands folded in front of him. His manicured nails gleamed. "A beautiful piece of furniture. A work of art. I must say I admire your wife's taste." He caressed the wood, fingers drifting lovingly over each curve. "I've been looking for such a piece for a long time. This kind of quality isn't easy to find."

"Find me something, Mutsie, and it's yours."

"You shouldn't make such rash statements."

"I mean it."

"I could never accept such a gift."

"It's only a piece of wood."

Mutsie sighed. "Ah, but such a piece."

He opened his doctor's bag, laid out an assortment of fine, polished steel tools, and went to work. He took off every piece of hardware—every hinge, bolt, screw, and plate. He did it with care and affection, scratching no surface. When everything that would come off had been removed, he examined each piece with a large magnifying glass. Then he pried apart a pair of decorative brass knobs that did not look as though they came apart at all. He looked inside them. Using a miniature tweezers, he removed two tiny rolls of what appeared to be a celluloidlike material.

"Jesus, what's that?" said Turner.

"Microfilm."

Turner had the desk delivered to Mutsie's apartment the following morning.

He remembered that his uncle had called the cryptographer Jake and that he was a professor of science at City College. So Turner put a call through to the Convent Avenue campus of the college, was connected with the science department, and asked an administrative assistant if she would please be kind enough to read him the names of all the full professors on the department's roster. When the woman became unpleasant, he told her he was an editor for the *New York Times* weekly science section and that they were compiling a list of distinguished people in that area to whom they might offer writing assignments. At which point the woman reluctantly gave him five names. One of them was a Dr. Jacob Holtzman.

Turner found Holtzman's address in the Manhattan telephone directory and went to his home that same night without calling. He lived in a narrow brownstone on West Eighty-ninth Street, just off Central Park West. Frail, recently planted sycamores fought for survival in the polluted air. Turner doubted that they would make it. He saw the name beside the bell for the ground floor apartment and pressed the button.

"Who's there?" said a man's voice through the intercom.

"Paul Turner."

"Who?"

"Herschel's nephew."

"You must have the wrong apartment."

The line went dead.

Turner stood staring at the receiver. God, I'm stupid, he thought.

He called the professor's number five minutes later from a booth on Columbus Avenue.

"Hello?" said Jake.

"I'm sorry. I wasn't thinking."

"You'd damn well better start." The voice was cold, unforgiving. "Where are you calling from now?"

"A booth on Columbus Avenue."

There was no response.

"I wasn't followed," said Turner. "I watched. I saw no one."

"You never do. Not if they're any good. Did Turnovsky tell you to come to me?"

"No. He's in Europe. But I found something last night, and I think it may be important."

110

"Maybe to you. I couldn't care less what you found. I finished with all this nonsense when I finished with those madmen at the National Security Agency. Now I just teach nice, illiterate dunces. So leave me alone."

"It's microfilm."

"Who asked you?" Jake said furiously. "Did I ask you what it was? Do me a big favor. Don't tell me what I don't want to know."

"There's no one else I can go to."

"That's your problem. I owed Turnovsky and I paid him. Now we're finished. Goodbye and good luck."

He hung up.

Turner called him back immediately. "Do you want me following you around? Do you want me camping outside your door?"

There was heavy silence. "You'd do that to me?"

"Only if I have to."

"I should have known what to expect. Why not? You've got Turnovsky's blood. You're a bandit, too." Jake swore softly. "All right. Listen to me. Pay careful attention. You have cigarettes?"

"Cigarettes? Why cigarettes?"

"Don't ask me questions. Just answer me."

"Yes. I have cigarettes."

"Empty the package, crumple it up, and put the microfilm in it. Then, in exactly ten minutes, take a walk beside the wall that runs outside Central Park. Halfway between Eighty-ninth and Ninetieth streets, make sure no one is watching and drop the package against the base of the wall. I'll pick it up there."

"And I'll just keep walking?"

"No. You'll stay and do the cha cha with me."

Turner grinned. "Be patient, Professor. I'm new at this."

"And you'll never get old at it. Call me tomorrow night at this time. From a public phone." He paused. "You're sure you have everything straight now?"

"Yes."

"Congratulations."

111

Turner followed his instructions. It was nearly 11:00 P.M., and there were few pedestrians alongside the park. He dropped the cigarette package at the designated spot and kept on walking. The way things were going, he half expected to be arrested as a litterbug. As he crossed Central Park West, he glanced back. Jake's nervous, quick-moving figure was bending to make the pickup.

He tried desperately to work all the next day, but his mind was mostly on the film, and he ended up with less than a single manuscript page, edited half to death. Which depressed him. As usual at such moments, he wondered if he would ever be able to write anything worthwhile again.

At 10:00 P.M. he went out to a phone on Third Avenue to make the call. Jake answered on the seventh ring, just as Turner was beginning to worry.

"It's me," said Turner.

"Of course it's you. Who else would call in the middle of the best crap I've had in a month?"

Turner wondered if he was supposed to apologize for that, too. "What did you find on the film?"

"What I found on the film," said the professor, suddenly sounding less sardonic, "is not something I'm going to even try to tell you over the telephone."

They met an hour later among the neo-Gothic spires of CCNY's uptown campus, where Jake was able to observe Turner's approach through high-powered night glasses from his fourth floor office in the science building. It was the only way he could be certain no one was behind Turner. The building was locked for the night, but Jake had his own key and came down to let Turner in. The professor said he often worked late, sometimes till dawn, so there was nothing unusual about his light being on. The office itself was a mammoth clutter of dust, papers, and books that had overflowed shelves and desk and, like creeping vines, had taken over even the chairs and a cracked leather couch. Turner cleared himself a place to sit. Then he lit a cigarette to rescue his nose from the dust.

Jake leaned against his desk, opened a folder, and shuffled through some papers. "This is a blowup and printout of what was on the film you gave me." He paused to glance through the papers, frowning slightly as he read again what he had read before. "Tell me," he said, "exactly what is it you think your wife was doing?"

"I don't know."

"I know you don't know. That's not what I asked. I asked what you *think* she was doing?"

Turner was beginning to feel like one of the professor's more backward dunces. "Something for the CIA?"

"Why do you think that?"

"You identified that code I found as one of theirs."

"And that's all you think?"

"What else is there?"

Jake looked at him with his black, ferret eyes. He shrugged. "All I can tell you is what's in these papers. After that you're on your own. You can look at it yourself, of course, but some of it is in Russian, and most of the rest is so highly technical that it won't mean anything to you."

"May I see it?"

Jake handed him the folder. There were twenty-eight closely printed pages inside, many of which contained detailed drawings and diagrams. The language used was almost equally divided between English and Russian. The idea of Maria being associated with any of this was about as alien to Turner as the material itself. As if fearing contamination, he dropped the folder on the professor's desk. "You know Russian?"

"My grandparents spoke it. For some reason, they thought it necessary to teach me."

"Okay. What's it all about?"

"You gave me two separate rolls of film," said Jake. "One printed out in Russian, the other, in English. The Russian segment contained technical specifications on several newly developed Soviet tanks, as well as detailed orders of battle data and tables of equipment for Soviet mechanized and infantry divisions. It also included a description of the latest Soviet army tactics in the use of atomic weapons."

Jake picked up the folder and flipped through it once more to jog his memory. "Oh, yes. And there's an explanation of a brand new Soviet tactical missile system. It's perfect. Complete. Not a punctuation mark is missing." He turned several pages. "And the English printout seems just as impressive, just as highly classified. There are comprehensive details on American medium range missiles and thorough particulars on our antimissile systems and their locations. Included, too, are valuable comments by senior American generals on our strategic offensive and defensive capabilities."

Turner lit another cigarette. His hands were steady, but it took effort. "Is that it?"

"Except for about half a dozen names and telephone numbers. But these are in a separate list. Handwritten. And there are code designations of some sort beside each one. Offhand, I couldn't say what they meant."

Jake opened the folder to the page and showed Turner the names. They were in Maria's handwriting. They meant nothing to him.

Other than for the ticking of a stained-faced clock, the office was quiet.

"All right?" said Jake. "I gave you what you wanted?"

"Yes. Thanks."

"You can keep your thanks. You had me by the throat. You and your Yiddish mafioso uncle." He seemed to be angry all over again. "You really want to thank me? Forget I'm alive."

Turner picked up the folder. "Where's the microfilm?"

Jake dug the two minute rolls out of a pocket and gave them to him. He sighed with more than tiredness. "If you're smart, you'll light a match to the whole business before you walk out of here."

"It's too late for me to be smart."

He spent the next day reading and rereading the material that was in English. He also brooded over the handwritten list of names. According to the telephone area codes, they were in New London, Boston, Washington, D. C., Houston, Seattle, and Oakland. That evening, his pockets heavy with quarters, he found a reasonably comfortable pay phone in a Lexington Avenue drugstore and settled in. I'm wasting my prime in public phone booths, he thought.

He started off by dialing the New London number, for no better reason than that it was at the top of the list. A child's voice, a boy's, answered.

"Is your daddy home?" said Turner.

"No."

"Is he coming home soon?"

"My daddy's not coming home anymore. He's dead."

Turner heard a woman's voice in the background. Then the phone was taken from the child. "Hello? Who is this, please?"

"Is this Mrs. Benton?"

"Yes?"

"I'm sorry to disturb you. The little boy . . . your son, said that Mr. Benton was dead. Surely that isn't true."

"I'm afraid it is." The woman's voice was controlled, yet it caught a little. It was evidently recent. "What is it you wanted with my husband? Who are you?"

"My name is Connally . . . Frank Connally. My God, I'm shocked to hear about Tom. We knew one another through business. I'm from Chicago and just passing through. Thought I'd call to say hello. I'm so sorry, Mrs. Benton. Honestly, I can't believe it."

"Neither can we."

"But how did it happen? When? Tom seemed so strong, so vital."

The line was silent.

"Forgive me," said Turner. "This must be very painful

115

for you. And you don't even know me."

"No, no. It's quite all right. I must start dealing with this. Tom knew so many people. He was such an outgoing person. You have no idea how many people have called. People I've never even met. They've all been so kind."

Turner sat in the airless booth. He felt like the meanest man in the world.

"It was an accident," she said. "Tom was driving alone, at night. The police said he must have fallen asleep at the wheel. He missed a turn and went into a tree. They said he died instantly." She took a long, deep breath. "It was on March sixteenth. My son's birthday. Isn't that a lovely gift for a three-year-old boy? Imagine. On his birthday."

Turner listened as it poured out. Then he again expressed his shock, commiserated with the widow, and hoped her little boy would know only good things in the years ahead. He hung up and sat staring at nothing. Maria had died on March 15, one night before Benton.

Turner called the remaining five on Maria's list (two of whom were women) and learned without surprise that they were dead. All had died on either March 16 or 17. Two had been killed instantly in single-car crashes, one had drowned in a boating accident, and the remaining two had died from lethal combinations of drugs and alcohol.

It was all very neat and thorough.

Things were suddenly happening too fast. Wanting to slow himself down before he did something foolish and blew the whole thing, he pushed himself to write. Which was about the only way he knew to break free for awhile. He was writing now. And curiously enough, he was doing well, with the thoughts and images crowding and the words rushing to keep up. It was the best way for him. Controlled spontaneity. When he fooled around too much with advance planning, the results often felt labored and forced. He was a mood writer. He had to feel things first. Everything had to soar, full-blown, from his gut. And happily, the writing seemed to be doing that now.

Yet even so, even at this moment, there were still doubts. And he wondered if he was really breaking his feelings through to the reader, really making them intelligible to someone who had never been there and experienced what he had, who had never lived in the oozing green, in the rain and mud like an animal, who had never slept in holes, never stepped on some poor dying grunt's open belly in the dark and heard the scream that came out of him. The thing was, all he had to work with were words. Yet what more was there, other than the murderous pictures inside his brain? So all he could do was try to tear these loose and throw them in, too. And maybe then, if he was lucky and the writing was going well besides, he might make someone feel just a fraction of what it was like to have a rocket go off in the earth right near you and the concussion alone like a mountain come down on your head . . . or how the silver napalm cans came tumbling out of the sky, end over end, setting off walls of flame, the VC wildly tearing out of the bush, all afire, blind, torched bugs at a barbecue. And they all had those little boy faces with the bulging foreheads and the dark, shiny eyes.

He scraped the deadly images out of his head and waited for a sign of blood. None came.

Still dripping sweat, he ran to Peggy with the dozen pages. Approval was needed. Reassurance. Was it really that good? Smoking nervously, he sat watching her face as she read. His eyes dug for hints, signs, anything. It was too much for her. "Get out of here. I don't know what I'm reading with you watching me like that."

He went into the bedroom and stretched out on the bed. When did you get over it? When did you build up a small backlog of security? When did you stop feeling no better than your last five pages? He had to talk to other writers. Did they all feel the same, or was he unique?

Peggy came in. "It hits like an iron fist. It's as strong as anything you've done."

"That's straight?"

"Have I ever lied about your writing?"

"It's a little different now."

"I'm still your editor."

"Yes, but you're also my something else."

"See that you remember that."

"If I don't, you'll remind me."

And she would. She was open. What she felt, she said. How clear, bright, and simple. Exactly what he needed right now. He was beginning to feel like a small, nervous animal burrowing through dark places. She let in light and air. She helped him breathe.

Peggy leaned over and kissed him. "I'm so happy you're writing again."

"Twelve pages, anyway." He was still cautious about it. He had not yet told her the real reason, that this was strictly *Rest and Recreation* before his all-out offensive. She thought that with Turnovsky away, Maria's ghost was granting him a brief holiday.

"Let's celebrate," she said.

Which meant, Turner knew, making love. He was finding that most things with Peggy ended up in making love. It was her ever available opiate. It relaxed strained nerves, chased fears, broke the barriers of loneliness, and was balm to all ailments. It also cured colds, chased depression, promoted confidence, eased tension, and made death and dying seem exclusively for others. Peggy Larsen, his tall, cool-looking editor from Minot, North Dakota, carried the gift of immortality between her legs.

She undressed him, which was part of the ritual. Then he lay back like a king lion as she romped. She brought riches to his soul that he chased in all the wrong places (her accusation was tacit but there). She restored order to his brooding, troubled life. See? said her flesh, pressing him with its message, this is what life and living are all about. Come fly with me and bury your ghost. Yet even here, in bed, his ghost remained, making them a curious *menage à trois*. Comparisons were inev-

118

itable. Love making had never been like this with Maria. It
had been good, the best (he had always believed), but different. In bed, his wife had never been the aggressor. Although
she had never refused an advance, had indeed given herself
fully and with evident pleasure to all such festivities, she had
never initiated them. It was almost as though she were following an archaic code of conduct that considered it unfitting for
a woman to make the first move sexually. When he had
wanted her, he had had her. Yet the thought had occasionally
nagged. Despite compliance, did *she* really want *him?*

With Peggy, there was no such doubt. Man, did she ever
want him. She wanted him on beds, chairs, floors, couches,
window-sills, and once, in a rare burst of creative passion, on
a bathroom sink that threatened to pull away from the wall
under stress for which it had never been intended. She
wanted him lying, standing, sitting, kneeling, and in varying
combinations that left him gasping in wonder. She sought joy
and salvation through sex, and Turner was her willing disciple. To be less would be to give in to the malignancies of sorrow and age. Or so she said. More often than not, Turner
was content to believe her.

He believed her now. She loved him. She gave him love.
Or sex. Or varying portions of both. Or whatever it was you
chose to call it. She was a conservatively brought up girl from
the Midwest who had traveled east, married, been widowed,
and, in the course of time and events, become less conservative. They sank lost into the bed's breadth.

Then Turner heard a siren wailing somewhere, and he
could almost sniff out the blood in the streets. Right then, his
holiday was over. He knew there were riddles out there to
which he might never be able to find solutions. And he had a
sudden hatred of all mystery, an instant when he wanted his
days returned to things simple enough for him to understand.
Lord, why couldn't he just lie in bed with a woman, with no
thought reaching past her and the four walls of the room?

Peggy had felt it almost as soon as he had. "Well, it was
lovely while it lasted, wasn't it?"

119

"Yes."

"All right. What's happened?"

He did not answer.

"Well?" she pressed.

"You're sure you want to know?"

"No. But as I've said, it's worse when I imagine."

He told her, starting with the microfilm and ending with the telephone calls.

"I was wrong," she whispered. "I don't think I could have imagined anything this bad. My God, six more dead. Where does it end?"

"That's what I'm going to find out."

Naked, she sat up in bed. Her small breasts, their nipples pale and hard-tipped, seemed to point accusingly. "You promised your uncle you'd do nothing alone."

"I know."

"But you're going to anyway?"

"I've been doing it."

"Why?"

"I've never really felt comfortable being led around. It's not me, not my style. Besides, this is still pretty much my monkey. It's not my Uncle Herschel's."

"But you made a deal."

"Yes. And in all good faith. But I'm breaking it."

It was nearly 3:00 A.M. when a cab dropped him in front of his house, but he felt an odd horror of climbing his own stairs and entering his own apartment, and he started to walk instead. He walked over to Sutton Place, where there were some benches overlooking the river, and he sat and watched the water slide darkly past. Closer, a few cars still rushed home along the drive. This was the United States of America, he thought. It was not perfect, but neither was it a place where people could simply be blown away. Or was he being as naïve about this as he was turning out to have been about other things? No. He could not afford to think that way. Yet could he afford not to?

He sensed movement behind him and turned. A bulky man was approaching from the shadows of a building. Turner stood up. There was no one else in sight, and the windows of the surrounding apartment houses were dark, the residents of Sutton Place all safely asleep behind their doormen, closed circuit TVs, and double-locked doors. The man came in a straight line. He wore a black raincoat, and his hands were in the pockets. So now it's my turn, thought Turner coldly. I'm going to die right here. He felt nothing, only a mild curiosity as to the reason. Then he thought of Peggy, his uncle, and Hank, in that order, and the possible response of each to his death. Peggy would weep over the loss of his talent, his unfinished novel, and, undoubtedly, his cock. His uncle would sit *shiva*, mourn the passing of his bloodline, and posthumously berate him for breaking their deal. While Hank would discreetly celebrate with brandy, grateful that her Herschel would be freed of his nephew's dangerous obsessions.

Which was a fair amount to consider in the time it took the man to close the distance between them and finally stop four feet away. But Turner thought it all, his sense of time stretched out like that instant of hesitation before an air drop. Then the man took his right hand out of his pocket and a switchblade opened from his palm like a snake. "Hand it over," he said.

Turner felt weirdly disapointed. After all that, it was only a mugging. "Hand what over?"

"Don't smartass me, yuh sonofabitch. And make it fast or I'll slice yuh just for fun."

Turner looked at him: He was a big, sloppy man with pale eyes, a two-day growth of beard, and an unwashed body that fouled the air. "You want my money? Okay. Give me your blade and you can have it."

The man stood there. "Yuh crazy or somethin'?"

"Nothing for nothing." Turner took out his wallet, removed fifty-three dollars in bills—all the cash he had—and placed the money on the bench. "There it is. Hand over your

121

knife and you can have it."

"I'll hand shit over."

Turner smiled. "Then come and take it, fatso. But you're going to have to climb over me first."

Their eyes met and stayed together. A feeling of joy came up in Turner, the way the suddenly remembered lyric of a song might remind a dying man of what it had once been like to feel young, loved, and immortal. Come on, he thought, come and take it, just come on and try.

The man's eyes blinked and wavered. He was confused. There was something wrong here. The guy was either crazy or he had a gun on him somewhere. Either way, he wanted no part of it. Cursing under his breath, he hurried off.

Wearily, Turner picked up his fifty-three dollars. Then, bereft of joy, he walked home through the early morning streets of the city.

It seemed strange that the actual making of the call should be so ordinary, so matter-of-fact, so lacking in drama. He had simply asked information for the Central Intelligence Agency's number in Langley, Virginia, dialed it direct, and told a switchboard operator that he wanted to speak to Wendell Handley, the deputy director. A moment later a woman asked who was calling, and Turner gave her his name.

"Could you tell me what this is about, Mr. Turner?"

"I'll tell that to Mr. Handley."

"I screen all of the deputy director's calls."

"I'm quite happy for you, but would you just give Mr. Handley my name, please."

Turner waited for several moments.

Then a man's voice said, "Handley speaking."

"This is Paul Turner."

There was a pause. "The writer?"

"Yes."

"I've read your books, Mr. Turner. I almost felt I deserved combat pay when I finished."

"Good. I felt pretty much the same way writing them." That's it, Turner thought, cool and easy.

122

They both waited. It was Handley who spoke first. "How can I help you, Mr. Turner?"

"Something has come up. It may involve your agency. And it's important enough for me to want to talk with you about it."

"With me specifically?"

"Yes."

There was silence.

"It has to do with my late wife," said Turner. "I don't know whether you're aware of it, but I was married to Maria Monroe."

"Yes. I know that."

"I've come across some things that belonged to Maria, things I never even knew existed. They seem significant. But I don't think I'd like to discuss it on the telephone."

"Why don't we arrange a meeting? Are you calling from the Washington area?"

"No. I'm in New York. But I'd be willing to come down at your convenience."

There was another period of silence, longer than the last. "That won't be necessary. I expect to be in New York myself within the next day or two. Suppose I call you. We can set something up then."

Turner gave Handley his number, and they said goodbye.

It was done.

Two nights later, Turner shuddered awake to the ringing of the telephone. He groped for a lamp switch. It was 2:10 A.M. There was no possible way that this could be anything good, he thought. Then he picked up the receiver.

"Mr. Turner?"

"Yes."

"This is Wendell Handley. I know this is an unholy hour to call, but I'm going to have less time in New York than I thought, and I wondered if we could talk tonight."

"You mean *now?*"

"Yes. If possible."

"Where are you?"

"Right downstairs. Parked in front of your house."

Turner shook his head to clear it. He felt unprepared, shaky, at a disadvantage. "Okay. Come on up."

"If you don't mind, I'd feel more comfortable if you came down."

"Just give me a minute to get some clothes on."

He lit a cigarette and sat on the edge of the bed, smoking. When his nerves had quieted, he got up and started to dress. He dressed slowly, using the time to put his thoughts in order. He had to be sharp for this, and he felt anything but sharp right now. Which was undoubtedly why Handley had chosen to wake him in the middle of the night. The man had probably never made an unplanned move in his life. Even his refusal to come upstairs had been thought out. The apartment might be bugged. Wearing jeans and a sweater and moving with unaccustomed deliberateness, Turner went downstairs.

Handley was parked at the curb in a black sedan with New York plates. The car had a high antenna in back, but was otherwise undistinguished. The deputy director sat behind the wheel in dinner clothes, smoking a pipe, looking as though this was precisely what he was accustomed to doing at two-thirty in the morning. A streetlight was close by, and Turner was able to recognize him from his photographs. But he was even better looking in person, bigger and more physically impressive, with the kind of cold blue eyes that seemed to live for a contest.

"Forgive the jeans," said Turner and slid in beside him. "You never told me we were dressing."

Handley smiled. His teeth seemed perfect, too. "One of our less publicized occupational hazards. Dull, endless, official dinners. I should have been a writer."

They shook hands and looked at one another. Turner felt a mild shock, the kind you feel upon meeting for the first time someone whom you have previously only heard about or

124

known via the telephone. In his mind, he tried to relate Maria to this man whose hand he now gripped and felt something akin to jealousy. What woman wouldn't be attracted to him? It took an effort to remind himself that his wife was dead.

Handley started the motor. "Would you object to taking a drive as we talk?"

"Where?" Turner was instantly cautious. Or was it the beginning of paranoia?

"Nowhere, really. Just a short ride. Two-thirty in the morning happens to be about the only sensible time to drive a car in New York, and I thought I might as well take advantage of the opportunity." Handley laughed, and it had a warm, relaxed sound. "Besides, my analyst says I'm dangerously hyper, that if I were ever forced to do only one thing at a time, like just sit and talk, I'd fly into a million pieces."

"It's your gas," said Turner, but knew it was nothing but tradecraft. Handley was just making certain he was not being set up. Moving, he would be able to watch his back. In fact he might even have arranged for some of his own people to be following them. Nothing was simple anymore.

They drove crosstown to the FDR Drive and headed north at a leisurely pace. A full moon hung over the river, the night was clear, and Handley drove as though the act of driving was pleasurable to him. Turner glanced at the side-view mirror, but the angle was wrong, and it was impossible to tell whether they were being followed. He felt a strong sense of anticipation, but none of his earlier nervousness. He looked at the intelligence agent's hands on the wheel. They were large and muscular, a worker's hands. They did not seem to go with the lean, patrician face above them. Nor did the pipe. Yet judging from the well-chewed look of the stem, Handley was not often without it.

"I'm all yours, Mr. Turner. I'm anxious to hear what this is all about."

Off to the right, Turner saw the lights of Roosevelt Island drifting behind them. "As I told you, it has to do with my wife." He paused, sighted, and gently squeezed off his opening burst. "Exactly how well did you know Maria?"

Handley's vaguely bemused expression did not change. "Why do you ask?"

"Because only a few weeks ago I was surprised to discover that you had known her at all."

"That surprised you?"

"Very much."

"Why?"

"Because it seemed odd that Maria should have known you yet never have said anything about it. It certainly wasn't typical of her. She went out with a fair number of men before we met and at one time or another mentioned them all. Her never having said a word about you immediately robbed any relationship between you of its possible innocence."

"Do you think I was having an affair with your wife?"

Turner laughed.

"That amuses you?"

"You answer every question with another question. You haven't told me a thing yet."

"Let me hear the rest. Then we'll talk."

"After Maria died, I stumbled across some things she had hidden in the apartment. There was a lot of cash, a codebook, and some microfilm."

"Where are these things now?" Handley cut in.

"Put away. I wanted them safe until I figured out what they meant."

"And have you figured it out?"

Turner did not answer. He gazed past Handley's face at the river, which was on their left now as they drove north on the Major Deegan. He saw Coogan's Bluff, where the old Polo Grounds had once stood and which now held only high-rise housing. When the silence had stretched thin, he said, "That's where you suddenly seemed to fit in. That's where it began to make a crazy kind of sense—Maria's never mentioning anything about you. At that point, I figured she might have been secretly working for the CIA and didn't want any visible connection between you."

Handley chewed on his pipe. "And that's when you called me?"

"I was beginning to worry about the stuff I'd found."

"Who told you I'd known Maria?"

"What's the difference? I was told."

Handley drove without speaking, his features blue ice in the glow of the dashboard. A glacier, thought Turner, and I'm trying to melt him down with candles.

"Well, whoever it was," Handley said, "told you the truth. I did know Maria. In fact we go back quite a long way. Let me tell you. It does make for a story."

Turner's pulse took a quantum leap. A dozen questions formed. He smothered them. It was time to listen.

"I guess it was about ten or eleven years ago that I first met her. And it was an odd sort of meeting, although I was vain enough to accept it without question at the time. But the fact is Maria literally picked me up at a large UN press party. It was like an adolescent's fantasy. With all those world class heavyweights around, it was me, a low level agency hack, that this beautiful, young media personality seemed to find irresistible." Handley shook his head at the memory. "I swear I couldn't believe my luck. Anyway, I accepted it. I thought I had something very lovely going. And for a few weeks I did. Maria was adoring, enchanting, superb. Until I made the mistake of taking her to a party and introducing her to Charlie Cochrane." He glanced at Turner as he drove. "I don't suppose you remember Big C, do you?"

"You mean the football player?"

"All-American three years running and a Rhodes Scholar, besides. But at the time Maria met him he was assistant director of our Office of Strategic Research and, compared to me at that point, a very important man in The Company. Well, as far as Maria was concerned, I didn't exist from that night on. It was all Charlie after that . . . Big C, the dashing superspy, James Bond incarnate, who dealt with strategic military thinking on a global scale. Unfortunately, he died in his bathtub a few months later." Handley chuckled softly. "The poor bastard was listening to the radio, and the bloody thing fell into the water and zonked him out. At least that was what the official coroner's report and the newspapers said. The Company's own report said something else."

"What do you mean?"

Handley shrugged. "We tend to take a dim view of fatal accidents in our line of work. Intelligence agents are usually very careful people. By nature as well as training. When one of us dies in an alleged accident, we do a lot of sniffing around. And in most instances the accident doesn't turn out to be nearly as accidental as it at first seemed. In Charlie's case, the radio itself offered some evidence. It had been given to him as a gift only the week before. And when the local stores were thoroughly checked out, Maria was fairly well identified as the purchaser."

Turner could feel his heart suddenly banging against his chest. He pressed it with both hands. Gradually, it quieted.

"Of course, this was hardly proof of murder," Handley continued. "Five million women a year give men radios without tossing them into their bath water. But remember. I was a used and jilted lover, so it was enough to set me wondering. Also in my mind somewhere was the fact of Maria's Russian background. It was all just too neat, too coincidental. That is, her aggressively making a play for a Company man, using him to meet a much higher ranking agent, and then this man, in turn, dying accidentally by reason of *her* gift. So what I did was bug her apartment and put her under surveillance. And in less than a month, I didn't have to wonder anymore. I had evidence."

"Are you telling me that Maria murdered Cochrane?"

"Relax, Paul," said Handley, sliding them smoothly and naturally onto a first name basis. Why not? Confidences were being exchanged, old secrets shared. However briefly, this man had also been Maria's lover. They were no longer strangers. "All this was a very long time ago," Handley went on. "Cochrane himself is no longer relevant. He may or may not have died accidentally. His death is important only insofar as it set off my investigation and because of what that investigation revealed." He squinted into the glare of a car's high beams. "And, to put it as simply as possible, what it revealed was that Maria was doing some extremely high level intelligence work for the Soviet Committee for State Security. The KGB."

Turner remained silent. He had no choice. Handley did not even bother to glance at him. Above his pipe, his eyes remained fixed on the road ahead, straight and shining in the car's headlights. "I'm sure this isn't easy for you," he said quietly. "I know how you feel about this country, and I know how you felt about your wife." He paused. "You probably think I'm out of my head, don't you?"

Turner did not answer.

They were on the New York State Thruway now. Handley drove into a service area and parked. "I expected this, so I've brought you proof. It's all documented." He switched on the dome light. Then he reached back for a tan leather attaché case, opened it, and took out a manila folder.

"You can shove your proof." Turner's voice was hoarse, not his own. "My wife was not a Russian agent."

"Please. I'm not an animal. I wouldn't be doing this to you if it wasn't urgent. Just take a minute to look at this."

Turner sat there, unmoving. Then, reluctantly, he accepted the folder, opened it, and looked at the first page. The words swam. With effort, he focused his eyes. There were pictures as well as written material. A high-powered telescopic lens had been used to photograph Maria in apparently clandestine meetings with a variety of men and women who were later identified as either Russian agents in place or high level members of the United States defense and scientific communities. The identification was supported by additional photographs and detailed evidence describing their professional specialties and areas of involvement. These included individuals with a knowledge of America's strategic offensive and defensive capabilities as well as experts on nuclear tactical warfare. Still others were shown, through their job descrip-

129

tions, as being in positions to furnish the latest data on anti-missile systems and their locations.

There were also photographs of Maria depositing and picking up envelopes in what were called dead-drops in Company jargon and shots of some of her contacts doing the same. The dead-drops were in such places as airport and bus terminal lockers, post office boxes, and occasionally even in openings in walls and trees. There were short excerpts, copied in Maria's handwriting, taken out of the President's Intelligence Checklist (PICKLE), which was a report put out daily by the CIA's Office of Current Intelligence and delivered each morning to the Oval Office. There were three series of photographs of Maria, taken on three separate occasions, showing her sitting in different airport waiting areas. In each series she was sitting alone, reading a newspaper, until a man appeared and sat down beside her. It was the same man each time. A blowup showed his face in clear detail—large black eyes, a broad nose, and a strong, clefted chin. They neither spoke nor otherwise acknowledged one another's presence. Then Maria rose and walked away, leaving the newspaper behind on her seat. Another photograph was of the man picking the paper up and putting it in an attaché case. The following sequence of shots showed what was obviously the same man, although several years younger. In these photographs he wore the uniform of a Russian Army officer and stood in the reviewing stand of a May Day parade in Moscow's Red Square. A brief biography identified him as Igor Koznitaya, a colonel of military intelligence who had allegedly retired some years before but who was now known to be working for the KGB.

There was a great deal of additional material, all in chronological order, all meticulously detailed, and all irrefutable evidence that Maria had indeed been working undercover for the Russians. Turner closed the folder and handed it back.

"I'm sorry," said Handley.

"How long have you people known about this?"

130

"Since Cochrane died in his tub. Which makes it about ten years."

"And you just let her go on with it?"

"Not quite. Once we knew about her, she became very valuable to us. We fed her whatever disinformation we wanted the KGB to have."

"How could she not have caught on?"

"We're not that simple. We threw in a lot of good stuff, too. But nothing truly damaging. And often it was material that the Russians already had from another source. We saved the disinformation for key strategic areas."

Turner stared broodingly out the window. There were mostly trucks parked in the service area, huge tractor-trailers, many of the drivers of which lay asleep in their cabs. He envied them all. "Maria is dead," he said flatly. "Why did you tell me this now?"

"It wasn't maliciousness, believe me. I have only respect for you. But it's important that I have that material you found. And I knew of no quicker way of getting it than by telling you the truth."

"If it was so damned important, why did you wait this long?"

"I didn't know you had anything until you called the other day. And even then I didn't know for certain until you described it to me a moment ago." Handley fussed with and relit his pipe. "Maria's death was so godawful sudden. We had no way of knowing what she might have left behind or with whom. We did check out all her known drops and contacts, and we did pick up some material. But there was no way to be sure we had flushed out everything."

An alarm went off somewhere in Turner's brain. Much of this was undoubtedly true, but how much? And Handley had thus far avoided all mention of Maria's death. Which instantly lent a false note to the whole tune. "Then it was you people," he said slowly, as if just now working it through, "who stole everything from Maria's office."

"I'm afraid it was."

"And that intruder I caught in my apartment? He was also one of yours?"

"You weren't expected back so soon."

"The sonofabitch tried to kill me."

"He was new and nervous. He must have panicked when you walked in on him."

"My God, what kind of people are you?" There was also Maria and the six additional dead listed on the microfilm. "You're no better than the KGB."

"Are we supposed to be?"

"This is America!"

"Yes, and we're trying to keep it that way." Handley's voice was still soft, but it had taken on an edge. "Tell me. Why do you think we're in this? Why do you think we're doing the kind of work you say makes us no better than the KGB?"

Turner remained silent.

"Are we getting rich on it? No. Any one of us could make far more money in the commercial area or practicing law. Is it for honor and glory?" Handley laughed coldly. "We're all but spat upon in the streets. Is it for personal power? The lowliest political hack enjoys more of that. Is it a sadistic need to cause suffering? Hardly. We and our families are most often the true victims." He made a stiff awkward gesture with his pipe. "So what are we in it for?"

Turner again offered no answer.

"I'll tell you," said Handley, a lecturer to an audience of one. "It comes down to what most decent citizens would consider the ultimate horror, the single thing they absolutely couldn't stand to believe—that we're in this not for ourselves, but to preserve a way of life that may not be exactly utopian, but is still pretty much the best around."

Turner looked at him dimly, as if Handley were off in the darkness somewhere. Altruism, he thought . . . everyone so sure of his sacrifices, so certain of his intentions, so convinced of his commitment to the greater good. And all while how

132

many bodies were being piled up? And how many freedoms
sacrificed?

They sat without speaking. The big rigs arrived and de-
parted in gusts of poisoned air. Turner waited. Would Handley throw in the truth about Maria's death as further evidence
of his sincerity? Not a chance. Regardless of reasons, you'd
have to be an utter fool to tell a man you had poisoned his
wife. And Handley was a long way from being a fool. Unless
—and the thought occurred as suddenly as that—unless
Handley himself was unaware of the true facts. Why not?
Wasn't it possible that he had been taken in by the heart attack story along with everyone else? Considering all that he
had just revealed, it certainly seemed to make sense. Why
suddenly kill a valuable uncovered agent of ten years' dura-
tion? And at an embassy reception, of all places. Especially if
her sudden death would leave him with obviously important
material unaccounted for. The thought took hold.

"I need those things, Paul."

Handley's voice brought him back. "Of course."

"When?"

Somehow, caution flags were still flying. "What about all
that cash?"

It was only for a barely perceptible instant, but Handley
hesitated. "It's probably KGB money that Maria used for
buying information. Technically, it becomes impounded by us
with the rest of the stuff. You'll get a receipt for it."

"Give me a few days."

"Why so long?"

"It's cached some distance away. I didn't want to take any
chances. Will you be going back to Langley?"

"Yes."

"I'll call you as soon as I have it."

They drove back to the city in tobacco smoke and silence.
Turner's face was dark. Appearing sensitive to his mood,
Handley left him to his thoughts. As Turner saw it, the deputy director had just told a man who had fought heroically
for his country, who had bled and almost died for it, that his

133

wife had spent much of her life betraying it. What was there to say to him after that?

Still, letting Turner out in front of his house, Handley did say quietly, "For whatever it's worth, Maria had a thousand years of Russian blood in her veins. You don't drain that off easily. She did only as she believed. Like the rest of us. She lost no honor, Paul."

It was an unsolicited testimonial from the opposition and surprisingly kind. But it provided little comfort.

Turner stood at the curb, looking after the black sedan. Its antenna waved over it like a whip. It was after four o'clock, and the street was deserted. He turned and crossed the sidewalk. Reflected in the glass of his front door, he thought he saw a hint of movement behind him. He stopped, groped through his pockets for a cigarette, and took his time lighting it. Unless it was his imagination, the movement had been in the almost opaque darkness of an alley across the street. Turner abruptly left his doorway and started walking east. He walked slowly, smoking, a man apparently deciding to take a predawn stroll on a clear, star-filled night before going to bed. He heard no footsteps behind him, yet he sensed that he was being followed. And if he was, he felt sure that this time it was not going to be by any would-be mugger.

He turned downtown on York Avenue. Rounding the corner, he glimpsed a solitary figure about a hundred yards back. A patrol car drove by, not even slowing as it passed. The New York City police took a practical view of lone nocturnal strollers. If they were ignorant enough to challenge the empty streets of the city, no working cop was going to educate them. The Queensborough Bridge loomed over Fifty-ninth Street, and Turner entered its massive shadow, turned left under the lower roadway, and walked toward the river. He breathed a whiff of brackish water and saw the man still behind him, still keeping his hundred-yard distance. Turner stepped behind a stone abutment, crushed out his cigarette, and waited. He heard the man's footsteps approaching. He bent, groped around, and picked up a rock. The footsteps slowed, then stopped. He had fooled no one.

"Take it easy, Turner," said a voice. "I just want to talk."

Turner's breath whistled through his throat. "Who are you?"

"I knew your wife."

Jesus Christ, thought Turner, who didn't?

"Listen," said the man. "I think we can help each other."

He came around so that Turner could see him. He was wide-shouldered and thick through the chest, looking to be in his middle to late thirties, and had the hard, tight-skinned face and strong bones of a professional athlete. He held his hands low and hanging loose at his sides where they could be seen. "I'm Peter Konrad." He waited for a possible reaction. "I don't suppose Maria ever mentioned my name."

Turner shook his head. Still gripping the rock, he felt caught up in a fine madness. If he had indeed entered such a realm, it was beginning to seem almost natural.

"We grew up together in south Jersey. The same nutty bunch of Ukrainians. Our parents were friends. We were close. Like cousins." He spoke quickly, in short gasps, as though fearful of running out of time. "You're sure Maria never mentioned me?"

Turner was tired of the whole game. "What do you want? Why are you following me out of alleys in the middle of the night?"

"I didn't know if you were being watched. I couldn't take chances. Those CIA goons are all over the place. I saw one of them take you for a ride tonight. Handley, wasn't it?"

Turner looked at him curiously. "How long have you been watching my house?"

"Off and on, about seventy-two hours. I've been out of the country. Got back less than a week ago. I didn't even know Maria was dead." Konrad shook his head back and forth like a bear. Astonished, Turner saw the glint of tears. "Shit. That was some girl you had there. They broke the mold after that one. Christ, could I tell stories."

Turner lit a fresh cigarette. He had heard enough stories

135

for one night. His fingers let go of the rock, and it fell with a thud. "What did you mean about our being able to help each other?"

Half lost in shadow, the tough face turned crafty. "What do you think I meant?"

Turner abruptly walked away.

Konrad caught up. "Hey, what's with you?"

"No games. You've got something to say to me? Say it. Otherwise crawl back in your alley."

Konrad grinned. He had two broken teeth in front. "You Irish or something? I've got to be careful. I'm still not all that sure where you stand in this."

"Where I stand in *what?*"

"In what Maria was doing," said Konrad uncomfortably, still being cautious. "Come on. Give me a break."

"You're talking riddles. You came after *me*. Remember?"

Konrad had the look of a man with conflicting problems who was trying to decide which one to worry about first. "Okay. What the hell. Maria lived a lot of years with you. You were real close. She was crazy about you. So I figure you've got to know things, right?"

But Turner was learning the value of silence. He offered nothing. He was also beginning to sniff out something that smelled vaguely like opportunity.

"From what I've heard," said Konrad, "Maria died suddenly. She wasn't even sick. She had no warning, no time to prepare. So there had to be loose ends." He looked at Turner with golden eyes, like an animal's. "That's what I'm looking for."

"What kind of loose ends?"

They had come back to York Avenue, and Konrad stopped walking. Turner stopped with him. The bridge roadway was directly overhead, black against a graying sky. On the river, the lights of a tug and some barges worked slowly upstream. "Some rolls of microfilm," said Konrad.

Turner started to walk again.

"Those Company head-hunters are looking for the same

136

thing," said Konrad, keeping pace. "But I'm sure you know that by now."

"I don't think you're sure of anything," Turner said.

Konrad showed his broken teeth. "You're right. Maria left me in a hell of a spot."

"How many rolls of film?"

"Four."

"Are you sure about *that?*"

"Yeah. There should be four."

Turner walked, looking straight ahead. He was still too new at this to trust his eyes. So there were two additional rolls of film somewhere. He felt himself caught up in it.

"Well?" said Konrad. "What about it? Do you have the stuff?"

Turner studied the tip of his cigarette. "All you've told me so far is how *I* can help *you*. Now let's hear what *you* can do for *me*."

"Hell, man, I can get those Ivy League hounds off your back. If you don't throw them some bones, they'll be nipping at you for the next twenty years. I know things. I can tell you what to tell them. I can fix it so they'd be satisfied and you wouldn't be hurt."

"Why do I need you? Why couldn't I just give them what they're looking for? Assuming I have it, of course."

A sanitation truck rattled by on the way to work, and Konrad stared after it. "It's not that simple. There's too much there. They couldn't just leave you walking around, knowing that much. Besides, war hero or not, they'd never believe you weren't in it with Maria. You'd be finished."

"Then why couldn't I just plead innocence and give them nothing?"

"Because they wouldn't be happy with it. You've got to understand CIA mentality. It's important for them to think they're getting *something*. It doesn't have to be much. Just as long as they feel you're cooperating. Believe me. I know these bastards. You can't frustrate them."

Turner kept walking. The logic of the insane. Worst of

all, it was starting to make a terrible kind of sense. "How did you know they were onto Maria? You said you were out of the country."

"I've been back almost a week." Head lowered, he regarded Turner from under thick, dark brows. "The whole network was blown, wiped out. Everyone. Four men, two women. All dead. I don't understand it. It's not normal Company procedure. Why not just picked up, arrested? Why a fucking massacre?"

The tough face suddenly seemed vulnerable. A couple approached, walking quickly and arguing. Turner waited until they had passed, the woman trailing perfume. "How do you stand in this?"

"Not as bad as you think. There was nothing to connect me to the others."

Turner remembered. There had been no Peter Konrad anywhere on the film where the other six names had appeared.

Konrad stopped at Sixty-second Street. "Well, what about it?"

"I need time to think."

The golden eyes ran him up and down. "Do you have the stuff?"

"Part. Not all."

"You know how Maria felt." It was Konrad's ultimate argument.

"Yes."

"Please. Not too long. Neither of us has that much time."

"How can I reach you?"

"You can't. I'll reach you." His eyes shone. "Listen. I'm sorry as hell about Maria. For both of us."

They shook hands, and Turner stood watching him walk off, spraddle-legged and rolling slightly. The surviving gladiator leaving the carnage of the arena. For once, Turner made no judgments.

138

The Present

The 727 dropped, held, shuddered, and climbed as it tore through mountains of cloud. Off to the east, there were jagged blue flashes of lightning. The seat belt sign had been on for the past five minutes, and several passengers were showing signs of sickness. There was little conversation in the plane.

Turner stared out through the rain-splattered window. Lightning streaked off the tip of a wing. A moment later thunder exploded like a stick of bombs, and a child started to cry. How simple everything would be if the plane suddenly dissolved, how conclusive. There was something sickly appealing in the thought. So much so, it made Turner smile. Hank, of course, would call it his congenital death wish, and maybe she'd be right. He had evidently reached the point where he was willing to concede such things. Lately, he found he was becoming more tolerant of views that differed from his own. Blacks and whites were increasingly shading off toward the grays. No one seemed to be totally right or wrong anymore. Or was that simply weakness, a poor coward's attempt at rationalization? Was he just trying to fool himself about that, too? He hoped not. Because somewhere beneath him in the baggage hold, he had a gun riding in his suitcase. And few things required as much certainty of purpose as a loaded .38.

139

Turner's Wife

The slow, painful education of Paul (Turnovsky) Turner. If all of life was just one long learning experience, what stage was he in right now? And how much had he ever really learned? Pressed, he would have been willing to swear he had learned nothing. He had not always felt this way. When he was very young he had believed that learning was indeed a steady progression; that if you lived, if you experienced, if you paid careful attention to what was happening to yourself and to those around you, you couldn't help but grow wiser. Time had proven him wrong.

Once, near the beginning of his tour in Vietnam, when he still had the idea he was fighting an ordinary kind of war in which the enemy was armed and obviously the enemy and that he would try to kill you and you would try to kill him, he had made a mistake. On patrol one day, along a red dirt trail that ran alongside a rice paddy, there were three of them strung out single file, and he was the last in line. He saw a farmer. The man was old. His hair was white, and he had a small, scraggly beard that was white, too. He stood up to his thighs in the water of the paddy. He was friendly. He smiled and waved at the three soldiers as they went by. Turner was the only one who waved back. To the others, he was invisible. They were there to save his country, but he was no more to them than a tree. Turner remembered thinking that the old man should be on social security, playing shuffleboard in Florida. A moment later they had passed him. Turner heard a soft splash, no more than a twig hitting the water. The others, in front, either did not hear the sound or else paid it no attention. Turner glanced back. Then he yelled and dived for the ground just as the machine gun went off. He fired twice from the dirt and blew the old man away. The two soldiers were dead. Turner had no idea how the old man had kept the gun hidden. He had been stupid. But he had been a split second less stupid than his two buddies so he was alive. Also, he had learned. Trust no one and nothing. It was kill or be killed. The enemy was a chameleon. He would not be fooled again.

140

The Present

Another time, he was returning alone from an Intelligence and Reconaissance patrol. It had been a night recon, and he had become separated from the others and had been lost for awhile. It was daylight before he found his bearings. Cresting a hill in an open area, he saw a file of black pajamas coming up a path toward him. Quickly, he ducked behind some boulders. As they came closer, he saw that there were four of them, all men and all young. This was Vietcong territory so they had to be VC. They were not carrying rifles or machine guns, but they had packs on their backs, and the packs bulged with what was probably hand grenades, pistols, and ammunition. He had seen those packs before on dead VC. He had also been warned by training films, lectures, and, more recently and practically, by that innocent-looking old farmer in the rice paddy. They might not look like soldiers, but they were soldiers. They were worse than soldiers, more treacherous and deadly.They looked like civilians and shot you in the back. He crouched behind the line of boulders and decided. It was open country. If he tried to leave his position, they would see him, finish him, cut off his head, and put it on a stake. Not appealing. He prepared a cluster of grenades on the ground beside him. Then he checked the full clip in his rifle, released the safety, and waited. When the line of VC was no more than thirty feet away, he began pulling the pins on the grenades, counting, and lobbing. The explosions shook the earth, blotting out all other sound. He heard no cries or screams. When the smoke began to clear, he emptied his rifle into the scattered bodies. Then he put in another full clip, left his position, and approached the path, his rifle leveled and ready. VC died hard. He was taking no chances. But they were all quite dead. They lay like bundles of dirty rags in puddles of blood. *Better them than him. Kill or be killed. War is hell.* The tired clichés ran through his head in a reassuring stream. Curious, he dug into one of the packs. It held only food and clothes. He tried another. It was the same. In sudden panic, he ripped through blood and bits of torn flesh to get at the remaining two packs. More clothes and food. And

141

that was all. No guns, no grenades, no ammunition. He dropped to his knees. Then he was sick. His platoon welcomed him back joyously. They had not expected to see him again. He never told a soul what had happened.

So what did you finally learn? That people were either quick or dead, with very few in between? Maybe not even that. Every minute was new. And they threw you in and let you figure it out for yourself or die trying.

But that was a long time ago. Now he was tearing through mountains of clouds at six hundred miles an hour while thunder roared and bolts of lightning were hurled at his head like spears. Why did he keep going back in his thoughts? The past either mattered or it didn't matter. Despite everything, he evidently still thought it did. It all depended upon what you carried in your heart. His heart was loaded and heavy. The lightning made it no lighter.

Then the plane broke out of the clouds into clear sky and sunlight. The seat belt sign went off, and the stewardesses began serving drinks. Turner ordered bourbon and water and drank gratefully as the 727 swept smoothly southward. He watched passengers move up and down the aisles. They looked relieved and tired, like soldiers after a firefight. He saw the young man in sweater and jeans who had boarded after him. He was standing and talking to a stewardess up forward. The stewardess shook her head, and the young man took out his wallet and showed it to her. Then she went into the cockpit and came out a moment later with the pilot. He also looked at the young man's wallet. Then he let his glance travel casually back over the plane as they talked. After the pilot had returned to the cockpit, the young man sat down and opened one of the books he had carried on board. He read without looking up.

Turner smiled dimly. The small charade had not been difficult to figure out. The young man had managed to follow him onto the plane, but he had evidently not had time to call ahead for additional surveillance at the Richmond airport. Identifying himself, he had asked the pilot to radio ahead.

Turner guessed him to be a New York cop. Had he been FBI or CIA, he would have shown better tradecraft than to carry on his conversations up front where Turner could see what was happening. Still, the kid had been the only one smart enough to end up on the same plane with him. But how well would he be able to handle things in Richmond?

Turner finished his drink and signaled a stewardess for another. Sipping bourbon, he sat staring at the back of the young detective's head. Nice looking kid. He had fair, rather long hair that he wore layered and fashionably full over the ears, and he was good looking enough to be an actor or a model. On impulse, Turner rose, carried his drink down the aisle, and sat down in the empty seat beside him.

"Hi," he said and offered his best smile to remove any possible doubt as to his intentions. "Some storm back there."

The young man instinctively started to rise. Then he settled back. Where could he go? "Okay, how did I blow it?" he sighed.

"Other than for that old lady, you were the only one who boarded after me. And that whole business with the stewardess and pilot wasn't exactly brilliant."

"Shit. The girl wouldn't believe I was a goddamn cop."

"New York Police?"

"Yeah."

"And you had the pilot radio Richmond?"

The detective looked disgusted. "Terrific, huh? I feel like a real ass."

"At least you stayed with me." Turner offered him a cigarette and they sat smoking. "Cheer up. I won't give you away in Richmond."

The young man grinned and held out his hand. "Jim Lewicki. And I'm in no mood for any lousy Polish jokes right now."

"Paul Turner."

"As if I didn't know." Lewicki closed his book. "What do they want with you, anyway?"

"What do your orders say?"

143

"Nothing. That is, nothing but surveillance. We're just supposed to watch and let the Feds know what you're up to."

"Which Feds?"

Lewicki shrugged. "CIA . . . FBI . . . Internal Revenue . . . Military . . . Who knows? They don't make us partners. The word just comes down. And we don't ask questions."

"I don't ask questions either."

"Sure. I'll bet." Lewicki looked at him curiously. "Aren't you the guy who was married to Maria Monroe?"

"That's me."

"Hey, I liked your wife a lot."

"Me too." The great fraternity of Maria's fans. It still pleased him each time someone remembered. How nice if there happened to be some way for her to know. Even unspoken, the sentiment embarrassed him.

The seat belt sign lit up moments later, and they were told to prepare for landing. Turner rose.

"I'm sorry," said Lewicki, "but I'm going to have to ride your tail."

"I wish you luck."

Turner returned to his own seat.

The plane landed smoothly at Richmond's Municipal Airport, and Turner followed the other passengers into the terminal. He waited for his suitcase at the baggage carousel and saw Lewicki, off at a distance, standing and reading one of his books. Waiting, Turner picked out three possible watchers in various parts of the terminal. When his bag came through, he went over to the Hertz counter and rented a medium-sized Chevrolet. He used his own name and credit card. Then he drove toward Richmond at a steady forty-five miles an hour. He was not trying to lose anyone at this point. Knowing that Lewicki and others were probably strung out in convoy somewhere behind him, he began to feel less lonely.

ELEVEN

The Past

How lonely it must have been for her, he thought.

Once, in the night, he had felt Maria awake beside him. She was silent, barely stirring, but awake. "What is it?" he asked. "Are you all right?"

She pressed against him, her body chilled, like river ice. "Hold me. Please. Just hold me."

He did. But it was like holding someone near death. It frightened him.

"Harder," she pleaded.

They suddenly seemed to be drowning together.

"What is it?"

"Just hold me."

He sank into her terror. Through the darkness, he caught glimpses of hidden pain, lost reason. There was no air worth breathing. Her arms pressed his ribs, wanting whatever warmth was in him. Finally, she fell asleep that way. In the morning she said she didn't really remember much about it, that it had probably just been a bad dream. It was perhaps the closest she had ever come to telling him.

Maruschka, why didn't you?

And if she had? What then? Could he have lived with it? Would he have cherished her less? Handley had said she did only as she believed, that she had lost no honor. Would her

145

husband have shown her less compassion, less understanding than her enemy? What sort of man was he to even ask the question? Sleepless, in the pink dawn light, lingering over the remains of a full pot of coffee, he looked around his living room. There was a time not so long ago when these walls and furnishings had reassured him of the substance of his life, had convinced him of the magic of his continuing existence. No more. The room seemed a very ordinary place now. It might have been anywhere and have belonged to anyone. If it disappeared under the wrecker's ball tomorrow, it would leave no void behind. Its value had been only in sharing it with Maria. It was a sufficient answer.

Altogether, it had not been the best of nights. And now, four hours after the fact, he could almost hear Turnovsky saying, "Well, Pauly, so now you have it." His uncle had tried to prepare him, but how could you prepare anyone for this? And what did he really have? He still had no idea who had killed Maria, nor did he have the reason. It was simply not enough that she had been working for the KGB. According to Handley, the CIA had known about that for ten years. In fact, her death had caused them nothing but trouble. So why would they have killed her? And why, too, would they have wiped out her entire network? Not even Konrad could understand that part, and he had been one of them. Why not just arrested? With all Turner had learned this night, he seemed to have ended up with as many questions as answers.

When the sun was fully up, slanting between the buildings and adding its patch of early brilliance to a faded living room rug, he picked up the phone and called Mutsie.

The slender, meticulously dressed thief arrived at exactly 9:00 A.M., carrying his little black bag. Turner shook his hand. "Thanks for coming."

Mutsie's shrug was pure noblesse oblige. "You must see your wife's desk. It's perfect in my living room. It was most generous of you." This was the fifth time he had thanked Turner. Gifts of any sort embarrassed him. He had never learned to deal with generosity. From the age of eleven on, he had lived believing that what you couldn't steal, you were better off paying for. Anything free came with a rattlesnake under it. "So what are we looking for today?"

"Two more rolls of microfilm."

Mutsie took off his jacket and draped it carefully over a hanger. Then he removed a pair of amethyst cuff links, rolled up his shirtsleeves, and went to work.

But it was different from last time. Six hours later, he sat limply in a chair, gulping coffee. Small beads of perspiration dotted his forehead and upper lip. His dark eyes were red-rimmed and moist, as though he had been weeping. "Are you sure it's here?"

"I thought I was sure," said Turner. "Now I'm not so sure."

"Microfilm can be a bitch. I was just lucky last time. You can spend days picking apart this many rooms and still not find something that small." Mutsie rose, stretched, and moved about to loosen his muscles. "You're going to have to help me. I want you to tell me about your wife. I want to know her habits at home, everything she did from the minute she got up in the morning. I want to see her living in every foot of every room in this place."

Turner put up a fresh pot of coffee and began. It was not easy. He seemed to have no clear focus on his wife anymore. It was as if he was suddenly talking about someone else, a stranger who had shared his bed, board, and life for eight years and then walked away without saying goodbye. He talked, telling Mutsie what he wanted to know—what she had done, where she had done it, even why and when—but his thoughts were on less tangible things. There had been so much joy and passion, and now there was none. He had retreated into a kind of deadness in his attitude toward his memories, and he wanted to stay that way. It hurt less.

"Let's hear that again," said Mutsie.

"What?"

"About the geraniums."

Turner had been describing Maria's involvement with her

147

plants, a continuum of watering, feeding, pruning, and love that was as much a part of her daily routine as brushing her teeth. "I guess the geraniums were her favorite. She used to call them her happy weeds . . . unsophisticated, simple, and basic. She grew up with them at home."

"You said she kept moving them?"

"Geraniums need sun, and we get very little in the apartment. So she used to keep putting them in the best spots. It depended on the time of year. Sometimes she'd even call during the day to remind me. Since I worked at home, it was my job to move them to a bedroom window in the afternoon. Funny. With all Maria had on her mind, she never forgot those geraniums. I once asked why she didn't take them to bed instead of me."

Mutsie was examining a geranium on an end table in the only sunny place in the room. "What did she say?"

"That I was sexier."

Mutsie carried the geranium into the kitchen and removed the plant and its clay pot from the brass receptacle in which it rested. Then he began probing the soil with a long needlelike instrument.

"Why do you think it's in there?" said Turner.

"There's a certain psychology in how people hide valuables. If they don't use a safe, they usually keep them nearby, in something they feel an attachment for." Mutsie seemed to be listening as he probed. "Freud would have called it proof of our need to return to the womb."

But despite his applied psychology, Mutsie's probing was without success. As was his finally emptying the clay pot into old newspapers and combing through the soil. Frowning, he considered the decorative brass container in which the pot had stood. It was molded in the form of a duck, with an opening in its back for the flowerpot. Mutsie examined it with his magnifying glass, then with the tips of his fingers. Lightly, he felt the brass duck's head, neck, and bill. He applied pressure at a point where the bill joined the head. The bill slid free in his hand. Mutsie grinned, a man fortunate enough to find pleasure in his work. The duck's bill was hollow. Inside were three tiny metal containers. Each one held an even tinier roll of microfilm.

"There were only supposed to be two," said Turner.

"You can put one back."

Turner called Professor Holtzman that evening from an outside phone. "I'm sorry, but it's me again."

"*Vay iz mir,*" said Jake, which meant "woe is me" and was probably the first time he had lapsed into the purity of Yiddish anguish since the death of his grandmother.

"I have some more business for you."

"Lovely. Exactly what I needed."

"Should we use the same spot beside the park wall?"

"I was sure you'd be dead by now," Jake sighed.

"I'll drop it there in a cigarette pack at eleven tonight," said Turner and hung up.

It was getting easier.

Once more he cleared a place for himself among the papers, books, and general litter on Jake's cracked leather Except that this time he felt much more comfortable. In fact, there was something almost appealing about sitting with the professor in his small island of light. At 1:30 in the morning, the science office, surrounded by the dark vastness of the City College campus, seemed to project the curiously comforting isolation of a ship at sea. And there was at least the promise of progress.

Jake sat studying Turner from behind his desk. He, too, seemed more relaxed tonight, as if he had finally resigned himself to his appointed role in Turner's affairs and was making the best of it. Moments before, he had unlocked the downstairs entrance for Turner and led him to his office with an almost cheerful expression on his usually dour face. Now he abruptly produced a fifth of Canadian Club and two glasses, poured generous measures, and pushed one across the

149

desk. For the first time he seemed to have a true awareness of Turner. It was as if some instinct in him had been reached and he was not displeased. Turner could sense all this but had not yet figured out what it meant.

Jake half raised his glass. "Up the Jews."

It seemed an oddly mocking and irrelevant toast, but Turner drank with him and felt the whiskey burn its way down.

"Exactly how many more of these little cellulose gems do you have lying around?" Jake said.

"As far as I know, these are the last. Did you find out what's on them?" It was twenty-six hours since he had delivered the three rolls to the professor, and he was anxious about the printout.

"Before I go into that, I want to know about your wife."

"The other day you said you didn't want to know."

"That was the other day. Now I have no choice. Now I have to protect myself."

"Why now?"

"Because of what's in the material you gave me. And also because someone seems to have followed you here."

Turner found his mouth open. "I was careful. I didn't see anyone."

"I've told you. You don't see them if they're any good."

"Then how did you?"

Jake smiled for the first time. "I'm better."

Turner went to the window and looked out over the campus. The Gothic buildings facing the quadrangle were dark. A few street lamps glowed along the walkways. He saw no one. "Why did you let me in?"

"Any fool would have been able to figure out where you were going. Besides, I want to know what you've found out about your wife."

"Who said I found out anything?"

Jake just looked at him.

"Okay." Turner gulped some whiskey. "It seems she was working for the KGB," he said and went on to describe everything he had learned during the past few days. A tiny, newly acquired nerve tried to warn him it was always best to keep something in reserve, but he brushed it aside. It was he who needed Jake.

"How have you taken all this?" the professor finally asked.

"Badly."

"But not badly enough to make you forget the whole thing?"

"How do you forget someone murdered your wife?"

Jake drank his whiskey and said nothing. His face seemed to hold several layers of expressions, one behind the other. But it was the last one that puzzled Turner. It showed genuine interest.

"Was your wife Jewish?"

"Yes. But not by birth. She converted after we were married."

"Did you know of her involvement with Soviet Jewry?"

"Come on, Professor. I didn't know of her involvement with *anything.*"

"Remarkable," said Jake. "The printout from one of those films puts her smack in the middle of the whole Russian-Jewish battleground. And I mean all of it . . . all the suppression and persecution, the denial of exit visas, everything. It's all there and all documented . . . names, dates, places, a detailed record of Soviet Jews jailed, exiled, murdered, or simply vanished. Also, details of a functioning underground, with the names and addresses of sympathizers, Jewish and non-Jewish, who have helped and continue to help Jews trying to leave the country."

The whiskey felt about to curdle in Turner's stomach. "What's the matter with you? She was probably just handing all that over to the KGB."

"Not so. I know many of the people listed. They're still active, still part of the movement. Whatever else your wife was doing for the Russians, betraying their Jews wasn't part of it." Jake took a folder out of a drawer and placed it on the desk in front of him. "In fact, there's even evidence here that she did a great deal to help them. I'd forgive her a lot for that."

151

"How do you know so much about Russian Jewry?"

"I've been working to get them out of there for twenty years. That's the only reason I hired on with the National Security Agency in the first place. It gave me all the information I needed in that area."

Which explained his abrupt change in attitude. But at that moment Turner failed to share his absorption with the oppressed Jews of Russia. "What else did you find on the film?"

Jake reluctantly left his Jews. "Several months ago there were reports of thousands dying of an outbreak of anthrax in Sverdlovsk, a Soviet city in the Urals, east of Moscow. The official Russian explanation was that the disease was caused by contaminated meat. Do you remember reading about it?"

"Vaguely."

"Well, your wife's film carries evidence that the death were caused not by contaminated meat, but by an explosion at a nearby biological warfare facility, identified as Military Compound Sixteen, that released anthrax spores into the atmosphere. It proves that Moscow has been in violation of the 1975 biological weapons pact that expressly forbids production of biological agents such as anthrax. If Washington ever saw this all hell could break loose."

"It's written in Russian?"

"Photographed straight from official Soviet documentation."

"And the evidence about the Jews?"

"That, too."

Turner poured himself another drink from Jake's bottle. "I don't understand. What was Maria doing with all this? It could only damage the Russians."

"It was probably her insurance. There are power struggles in Moscow like anywhere else. People fall in and out of grace. Policies change. Smart agents always put a little something aside for their own protection. And your wife was smart."

"Not smart enough to stay alive. What about the rest of the material?"

Jake opened the folder and flipped through several pages.

"More dynamite. Would you believe two planned CIA assassinations? One in Afghanistan, the other in Libya." Jake smiled
coldly. "This could hardly be part of Handley's disinformation. Your wife must have dug these up on her own. And I'll
tell you something else. KGB or no KGB, I'm enormously
impressed with what she was doing for Russia's Jews. Although that doesn't seem to mean much to you."

"I have other things on my mind."

"Who hasn't? But to a Jew, worrying about all Jews should
be a constant. Our survival depends on it. If we don't stand
together when any one of us is threatened, they'll bury us
separately. And this time they'll finish the job because a prec-
edent has been set."

Turner said nothing. He had met these Jewish paranoiacs
before. They saw gas jets in every shower room.

Jake nailed him with his eyes. "Your uncle is a crook and
a corruptionist, and I despise everything he stands for. But at
least he understands about the Jews. He'll never turn from
one of his own in trouble. That's the single purity in his
blood." He leaned back in his chair, suddenly tired. "Now
listen to me. As I see it . . ."

He stopped. His eyes were focused somewhere above and
beyond Turner's right shoulder. Turner swung around. Peter
Konrad stood in the open doorway. He had a pistol in his
hand with a silencer attached. He held the weapon almost casually, its muzzle pointing at the floor.

"Konrad!" Turner made it seem an involuntary cry of
surprise, but it was to let Jake know who he was.

The professor nodded to acknowledge the introduction.
"Have a drink," he said and moved to offer the bottle.

There was a sound, a soft *whoosh*, no more. Jake jerked
back. At the same instant, his hand came up from below the
desk with an automatic in it. There was another *whoosh*. Bits
of red and gray spattered the wall behind him, and Turner
saw that part of his head was gone. Then he fell forward
across his desk, knocking over the whiskey bottle and sending
it rolling across the floor. Konrad picked it up. His eyes

153

showed nothing. The bones pressed against the thin flesh of his face. He walked across the room with his rolling walk and put the bottle back on the desk.

Turner sat staring at what remained of Jake's head, his responses not yet caught up with events. The sensation was not new to him. In a free fire zone, you could be talking to a buddy one minute and looking at his corpse the next. But you never got used to it. There was always the same stunned disbelief. "You didn't have to do that."

"Like hell I didn't."

That much was true. A split second later and Konrad himself would have been dead. Jake had proved surprisingly fast. Turner had barely noticed him move and the automatic was in his hand. Nothing had changed. It was still the quick and the dead.

"Where's the microfilm?" Konrad said.

"Up your ass."

Konrad looked at him with a hunter's eyes. "I told you before, we haven't much time. Now we have even less. Where's the goddamned film?"

"Why don't you blow my head off, too? Maybe that's where it is."

"Hey, come on, buddy. We're on the same side, remember?"

"Sure. Is that why you followed me up here and blasted someone doing me a favor?"

"He never should have gone for his gun."

"What about you tailing me?"

"I was just keeping a friendly eye on you."

Turner glanced at the silenced pistol in his hand. "Some friendly eye."

Konrad tucked the weapon inside his belt and offered his most disarming grin. "Nothing personal." He nodded toward Jake. "What kind of favor was he doing you?"

Turner considered lying. But that was one duck that never got off the ground. The folder was right there on the desk, half under Jake's chest. "I wanted to know what was on the

154

film. Jake was getting me a printout."

"Bullshit. You expect me to believe you brought Maria's prime stuff to a fucking NSA cryptographer?"

"Jake quit the National Security Agency a long time ago."

"Like hell he did. He hasn't been off their goddamned payroll in twenty years. Don't you think I know Jake Holtzman? Why would a college professor keep a gun in his desk drawer? And why would he have gone for it the minute I walked in?"

"You're wrong. I had to force him to look at the film. The only reason he saw me at all was because he owed my uncle a favor."

Konrad walked around behind Jake's body, lifted him from the desk and let him slump back in his chair. He found a wallet in his pocket, picked apart the stitching with a pen-knife, and slid a green card from between two pieces of leather. He tossed the card in Turner's lap. It was an NSA identification card, bearing the agency's seal and issued in the name of Jacob Holtzman. The date said it was currently in effect.

Konrad had seen the printout folder. Then, going through a desk drawer, he also found the microfilm. Turner sat brooding in his chair, hands deep in his pockets. He watched as Konrad read through the sheets of printout. Maria's partner, he thought.

"What's all this Jewish shit?" Konrad said. "I never even knew Maria had it."

"Neither did I."

Konrad's golden eyes were cold. They swung back and forth between Turner and Holtzman. Two Jews . . . one alive, the other dead. You never knew about Jews. "I don't think that's Maria's film."

"Whose then?"

"Yours."

Turner suddenly found himself looking straight into the silencer. He was careful not to move.

"What kind of deal did you have going with Holtzman?"

155

"You're crazy. I told you the truth."

Konrad shook his head in disgust. "I should have known better than to trust you. The day after Maria died you went and sold out all six of our people, the whole goddamned network. Jesus! The next fucking day! Couldn't you even goddamned wait?"

"No. It's not . . ."

Konrad hit him. Watching the gun, Turner had not even seen the left hand coming. The blow caught him on the side of the jaw and half swung him around in his chair.

"What did Holtzman promise? That he'd help get some of your Russian Yids out to Israel? Was that it? Was that what you buried six good agents for? A bunch of kikes?"

Turner swallowed blood and saw dancing white spots. Somehow, everything always seemed to end up with the Jews. Moving deliberately, he picked up his glass and sloshed some whiskey around the inside of his mouth. Konrad watched him. He appeared to be trying to decide whether to shoot him right away or get some answers out of him first.

"Was Handley in on it too, or was this an all-Jewish operation?" Konrad's voice was calmer. He had evidently chosen to go for answers. But the gun remained pointed at Turner's head.

"Do you want the truth?" Turner said, "or are you just interested in punching me around and asking unanswerable questions?"

"Go ahead. Talk. But it damn well better be good."

Turner could feel the pent-up violence in the room. A hurricane was about to rise from a swamp. He decided right then. "The truth is," he began slowly, "that Maria didn't really die of a heart attack. She was murdered. Poisoned. And the only reason I'm into this whole mess at all is to find out who killed her. In fact, it wasn't until Maria died that I discovered she was working for the Russians. I never even suspected. She kept it from me for eight years. Then certain things started to happen, and I . . ." He stopped.

Konrad was laughing. He laughed loudly and harshly, the sound rising from deep in his chest. Turner watched him. He

156

doesn't believe me, he thought. I'm telling the absolute truth for the first time, and he thinks I'm making it all up.

"Turner, I swear you're too much. Nobody but a damn writer could even think up a story like that."

Turner finished his drink in one long swallow and put down his glass. He shivered slightly, shoulders hunched, hands burrowing into his jacket pockets for warmth. Lights danced in Konrad's eyes. His good humor had been restored. Turner himself felt cold all the way through, as if even his re-actions had been packed away in ice. He looked at Konrad's gun. It was no longer aimed at his head, but was pointed off to one side. Looking at that gun was like standing at the edge of a mountain, feeling the fall.

"You know, you're not a bad guy for a Jew," Konrad said softly. "It's just that I can't trust you worth a shit. Besides, how can I let you get away with blowing the whole fucking network?"

He swung the pistol back toward Turner's head, slowly, taking his time because there was really no rush. Then Turner could see his finger tightening on the trigger.

Whoosh.

But Turner had pushed off to the right and fired through his pocket. He got off three shots from Jake's automatic be-fore he hit the floor. Their sound was a single explosion. Konrad slammed back against the wall as if knocked there by a car. The .45-caliber slugs carried a ton of weight. All three were in a tight pattern in Konrad's chest. He grabbed at Jake's body, dragged him from his chair, and was dead when he fell. They lay together.

Turner got up and went to the window. About once an hour an elderly guard shuffled across the quadrangle, but he was nowhere in sight. Turner went back and looked at Konrad. His yellow animal eyes stared at the ceiling. They were glazed, paler than they had ever been alive, but Konrad's face remained as hard and tough as ever. My grand-father would have called it an *anti-Semiten,* Cossack's face, Turner thought. He lit a cigarette and went through

157

Konrad's pockets, taking out the microfilm, a wallet, and some keys and papers. He dragged him around the desk and left him sitting propped against a wall, facing Jake. Konrad still held his gun. Then he wiped the automatic free of his own prints and placed it in Jake's hand. He took a last look around. Two dead men and a lot of dust, papers, and books. Sorry, Jake. He took the folder of printout and left.

He had the keys to Peggy's apartment, and he went there instead of to his own. She was a pure, untroubled sleeper and did not awake until he lay naked beside her. His hand cupping a breast, he felt her heart.

"Who is it?" she whispered.

"Robert Redford."

"What's wrong?"

"Not a thing."

She turned and welcomed him.

He was weighted with blood, and she restored him with love. He felt no guilt in using her. It was her own treatment, freely offered, no prescription required. He was simply there to accept it. Half an hour later he was soothed.

The curtains at the window were silver. The moon was a cold stone over Central Park. A clock with luminous hands placed the time near four. No siren wailed, no child cried. It was a world at peace.

"Are you able to tell me now?" she said.

He told her, of course. Why else was he there?

She said nothing for awhile. Then, "I'm getting better, aren't I?"

"Much better."

"I don't even nag you to stop anymore, do I?"

"No."

"Do you know why?"

He shook his head.

"Three reasons: I know you'll do as you please anyway; I'm afraid I might sound like a wife; and I don't want you to start keeping things from me."

Along with the moon, they floated motionless above the park.

"Do you know what I sometimes wonder?" she said.

He waited.

"Whether Maria ever really knew how much you loved her."

He was in his own apartment that morning in time to hear the ten o'clock news. There were few details, but the double killing on CCNY's campus was the lead item. The newscaster said that Dr. Jacob Holtzman, a science professor, had died of gunshot wounds inflicted by an as yet unidentified male visitor, who had himself been shot by Holtzman. A cleaning woman had discovered the bodies and called the police. Since there were no signs of forced entry, the police believed the two men had known one another. Possible motives would have to await identification of the second body as well as further investigation.

Turner switched off the radio, put up some coffee, and emptied his pockets onto the kitchen table. He had Jake's National Security Agency card, the papers, wallet, and keys he had taken from Konrad, and the three containers of microfilm. He also had the folder of printout, part in Russian and part in English. Konrad's papers showed him to have been licensed as a private investigator under the name of Peter Cranston with a New York address and telephone number. Turner called the number and found it to be an answering service. The address was on West Forty-sixth Street. Turner considered going there, then realized that by now the police had probably identified Konrad as Cranston from his fingerprints and would be there themselves. The time to have gone was six hours ago, before the bodies were discovered.

159

Instead, he had gone to Peggy.

He stood thinking about it. Then he went downstairs to a cellar storage room, unlocked the door, and switched on a bare bulb. An assembly of roaches scattered. Cartons and suitcases were piled on top of one another, along with stacks of books, a folding bed, bicycles, golf bags, and tennis rackets. Turner emptied the clubs from one of the bags. In a brown paper sack at the bottom was the cash and codebook from Maria's wall safe, as well as the two rolls of microfilm discovered earlier and the printout of them. Despite Mutsie's theory, he was aware of no emotional attachment for the golf bag. He put everything in a briefcase and carried it upstairs. Then he poured coffee, lit a cigarette, and settled down to consider what he had.

He sat alone two days later in a rented Chevrolet, off a sun-dappled country trail in Fairfax County, Virginia. To get there he had flown down on Eastern Airline's 12:30 P.M. shuttle flight from La Guardia, picked up the car at Washington's National Airport, driven northwest on the George Washington Memorial Parkway to Route 695, and then gone a mile and a half south to the burned-out remains of a barn. From there, he had followed a dirt road for two hundred yards to the place, beside a stream, where he was now parked. He had watched his back carefully all the way and had seen no one. He had learned to doubt, but with his growing experience in such things he felt reasonably certain he had not been followed.

Twenty-four hours earlier, he had called Wendell Handley, told him he had his material and asked if he wanted it brought to his office at the agency's Langley headquarters. "No," said Handley and went on to explain exactly where, when, and how he felt it best for them to meet. Apparently, no one in this business ever met normally.

Shortly after three o'clock, a gray Pontiac with Virginia plates and the inevitable high antenna pulled up behind the Chevrolet. Turner took his briefcase and went back to where Handley stood lighting his pipe. They shook hands, walked

160

over to a stretch of rock beside the stream, and sat down in the sun. The water was running fast and high after several days of rain, and they heard the calls of birds in the upper branches of trees and the slight rustle of leaves. High up, they saw a plane begin its descent toward Washington, but it was too far off to hear.

Turner worked the lock on his briefcase, and it opened with the smooth metallic sound of a bullet sliding into a firing chamber. He took out Maria's codebook and two large envelopes stuffed with thousand dollar bills. Then he removed three metal microfilm containers and arranged everything neatly on the rock beside him. He moved things several times, as though trying to please a finely tuned sense of design. Handley sucked at his pipe and watched. It might have been an outdoor religious ceremony.

"Here's what you wanted," Turner said. "Codebook, cash, and microfilm containers. You can check them out."

Handley briefly examined each item. "Fine. Everything seems in order."

"How do you know? You haven't even opened the containers."

"There's little point in looking at microfilm without a printout. If you found them in your apartment, I'm sure they're what I'm looking for."

"Open a container."

Handley looked at him.

"Go ahead. Open one."

Handley picked up a container and took off its cap. He glanced inside. Then he shook it over his palm. Nothing came out.

"Now open the others."

Handley repeated the process twice more. The other containers were also empty. "I don't understand. You said you'd found film, not empty containers."

"I did."

Handley was suddenly staring at Turner with intense interest. He removed his pipe and pursed his mouth as though

161

adding up an expensive bill. "You surprise me, Paul."

There was a flicker in the branches above them, and they both snapped their heads up sharply. But it was only a bird, swinging on the tip of a branch. It called down to the shadows under the trees.

"What do you want?" said Handley.

"The truth about Maria's death."

Handley sat unmoving. He took a long, deep breath. "What's that supposed to mean?"

"Maria died of cyanide poisoning. There was no heart attack."

"Who said so?"

"A pathologist. I had an autopsy performed. Unofficially."

"And you're sure of the findings?"

"Absolutely sure."

"You're full of surprises today, aren't you?" He sucked at his pipe. "But why come to me?"

"You've known Maria for eleven years, everything she was doing, everything about her. If you don't actually know the truth yourself, you'll know where to look for it."

"You credit me with too much."

"I don't think so."

"Assuming I could find out, why would I bother?"

"For your precious film."

"I'm not even sure what Maria had on those rolls. It could be nothing, just a lot of innocuous material."

Turner took a folder of printout from his briefcase and gave it to Handley. It contained the section written in English and covered the two planned CIA assassinations along with the details on American missiles and antimissile systems. Nothing in Russian was included. The deputy director read through the printout. The sun glinted on his hair, thick and full with golden highlights. There was a steady drone of insects and a frog's boom downstream.

Handley finished reading, closed the folder, and knocked out his pipe on a rock. "What if I say this isn't really important, that it's worthless to me?"

"Then I'll take it to the Russians. Maybe they can help."

"You would do that?"

"Damned right I would. I've made my contribution. More than most. Now I'm collecting."

Handley reached inside his jacket, took out a revolver, and aimed it at Turner's chest. "And if I killed you right here?"

"Then I'd be dead. But exactly two weeks from today, both the Russian ambassador and the editor of the *New York Times* would receive identical copies of everything you've just read, plus a lot more."

"You're learning fast." Handley put away his gun. "And if you do find out the truth about Maria's death? What then? An eye for an eye? *Bang,* you're dead?"

Turner hesitated. "It depends."

"On what?"

"Reasons. I'm not nearly the hero I was when I started out. And Maria turns out to have been a lot less than innocent. Right now I just want to know who did it and why. Then I'll decide."

The agent said nothing. Other than for the soft sounds of the woods, they sat in silence. Turner could feel Handley's pulse as if it were his own, and there was a curious heat between them. They might have been in bed at that moment, sharing Maria.

"All right," Handley murmured, his voice so low it seemed to come from somewhere in his gut. "I don't even know why I should be surprised. I had a feeling it might finally come to this. And, in a way, it almost has nothing to do with the film."

Turner felt a sudden fear. He tasted it.

"I don't know whether you're lucky or unlucky, but you've sure stumbled into the right pile of manure."

"What are you telling me? That you actually *know?*"

"I wish to God I didn't, but I'm afraid I do."

They were like two hunters resting in a jungle. In a moment they would pick up their guns, and the killing would begin.

Handley looked at Turner with something close to pity. "This is going to put an awful weight on you. Are you sure you want to hear?"

A vein pulsed wildly in Turner's temple. It was his only answer.

"Of course you want to hear. You've risked everything for this, haven't you?" Handley filled and lit his pipe, letting the smoke enclose them. "But first, you're going to have to listen to the whole story because that's part of it, too. And it's a devil's own bitter tale."

He paused, a seasoned storyteller, building suspense in his audience.

"Well," he began with a profound sigh, "as I told you, Maria's value to us was in our being able to feed her the kind of disinformation we knew she'd pass on to the KGB. It was all high level material and all personally handled by me and a few of my own people in The Company. And it went on for years without Maria suspecting a thing. She even set up her own network around the country, six strategically placed KGB agents whom we were also able to feed disinformation and monitor. It was the broadest, most productive operation of its kind we've ever run. And, quite frankly, it had more than a little to do with my own rapid advancement up the Company ladder." He shook his head sadly. "I tell you I sometimes have the unpleasant feeling I made my climb on Maria's poor back."

Turner nervously lit a cigarette. Handley was telling the truth so far, he thought, about Maria's six agents.

"Unfortunately," Handley went on, "the thing you always fear most in an operation like this, the thing you never stop having nightmares about, actually happened the night of the British reception. There was a foul-up. I swear to Christ I'm still not sure how it happened. We take endless precautions. We check and double check. We go through continuous drills. We have long lists of safeguards. But there's always the human factor, and they don't make safeguards against that. An agent can be overworked and tired. He can have an ounce

164

too much to drink. He can be suffering severe personal problems. He can be emotionally or sexually repressed and God only knows what else. The possible distractions from the required concentration are infinite. But whatever the cause, a deadly error was made that night. And instead of our carefully rigged disinformation being passed to Maria, she was given something else, something potentially disastrous for us."

Handley pursed his lips and stared off across the stream. His eyes were clouded. "Understand. There are all kinds of mistakes. Some can be corrected easily, some with difficulty, some not at all. They also vary in their cost. This one happened to be one of the worst. Extremely expensive. At the very least, eight lives." He stopped. "Do you understand what I'm saying?"

Turner nodded.

"If you remember, there were Russians all over the place that night . . . diplomats, military personnel, and a fair sprinkling of wolves in KGB clothing. Maria had to do nothing more than pass her information on to any one of them and eight of our people in Poland and Czechoslovakia, all nationals . . . and possibly their families as well, would be dead. Easier yet, she had only to pick up a phone."

Handley stopped. He seemed to be out of breath.

His pipe had died in his hand, and he looked down at it. "There's something I must tell you," he said in a different voice. "I knew this woman, Maria, your wife, for eleven years, and in all that time there was not a day that I didn't think about, love, and want her." His eyes found Turner's, and there was a needle's point of such pure anguish at their core that Turner had to look away. "Consider this. I have a wife and two daughters at home to whom I'm everything, the center of the universe, and whom I care for deeply. Yet given the chance, I think I'd have turned my back on them in a minute if Maria had so much as crooked her finger at me."

He stopped, his throat clotted with blood and pain. The clot broke. "And it was I . . . no one else . . . *I* . . . who had to give her the cyanide."

165

Turner sat gazing at the base of a tree. He felt he had blundered through some sort of terminal barrier and was floating free.

"There was no chance, no chance," Handley mourned, rocking gently. "I wanted to tear Rawson, the man, to bits. Later, I almost did. I had to be dragged off the sonofabitch. A man made a mistake, and I went crazy and almost blew everything. Within hours, I'd had him shipped to the worst part of Africa I could think of. I'll bury him there. I never want to have to look at his face again." He sighed. "Still, I was the one who killed her."

Turner was still gazing at the tree. He was afraid of what he might do if he stopped. Then a squirrel appeared, and he watched intently as it climbed up and down the trunk and sped along the branches.

"Here," said Handley in a muffled voice.

Turner managed to focus on him. Handley was offering a gift, his revolver, butt forward. "If you want to make payment, do it now and get it over with. I don't want to walk around waiting for a bullet in the back."

In a single whipping motion, Turner grabbed the gun and swung. The barrel hit high on Handley's cheek, tearing flesh. He rolled down the bank and half into the stream. Turner followed. He drew back his arm to hit him again, but it fell of its own weight. If he hit him again, he would not be able to stop. He threw the gun as far as he could among the trees. Then he scrambled up the bank and tore off in the rented Chevrolet.

The blessings of confession. No wonder the Catholics did so well. Confess, win absolution, and walk forever in grace.

The Present

Turner had decided to spend the night in Richmond. Why not? What was his rush? Whatever he had waiting for him would wait. Which, for a congenital time miser, was a dramatic change in attitude. Or was it mostly the lassitude of fear?

Driving into the city from the airport, with Lewicki and the local police somewhere at his back, he passed the white frame church on Broad Street where Patrick Henry had made his liberty-or-death speech to the Second Virginia Convention. And how would old Patrick have reacted to the state of liberty here this afternoon?

He checked into the Hotel John Marshall because he had once spent a pleasant night there with Maria and remembered it warmly. The hotel was one of those old, graceful, high-ceilinged antiques that were being torn down all over the country, but which Turner still preferred to the plastic boxes that were replacing them. Maria had felt the same way. She had come down to Richmond with him for a book and author luncheon, and they had made a brief holiday of it. Which was a novelty for them. They had taken few vacations together. Maria was always on a rigid broadcast schedule, and Turner had evolved into a chronic workaholic, fearful that any break in his writing routine would destroy all hope of his ever pick-

167

ing it up again. As if it mattered that much. As if the literary world would sicken and die without regular doses of his prose. Their five-day honeymoon had turned out to be the longest they were ever away together, a frail, hastily erected barricade against time and obligation. Behind the closed door of their ocean-view room, Turner had watched his brand new wife unpack, loving her swift, efficient movements as she put away their things. When she was through, she sealed both their watches in an envelope and had it locked in the hotel safe. "I don't want to even think about time for as long as we're here." And for five days they were joyously unaware of more than each other. At the end of that time, they collected their watches and left the cocoon forever.

Now I have plenty of time, he thought. Now I have more time than I know what to do with. Axiom—stay away from places where you have known joy.

He took a cold shower to help him stay alert. He had begun to feel as if his eyes were fractionally slow in keeping up with the movements of his head. He had room service send up a double bourbon and was in a better mood and better condition by the time he had shaved and dressed. Switching on the TV, he tried to concentrate on the evening news. The prime minister of Iran and fourteen members of his government had been killed in a bomb blast. South Africa's soldiers had shot three Soviet army officers in an attack against Angola's black nationalist guerrillas. The United States was protesting North Korea's firing of a missile at one of its reconaissance planes. Soviet exit visas for Jews were reported to be at a five-year low. The army had toppled the leader of the Central African Republic. Eleven American-owned cars were set afire in West Germany in incidents that investigators said had a clearly anti-American flavor.

Very perceptive investigators, he thought, and turned off the set. Then he took the revolver out of his suitcase, settled it inside his belt, and buttoned his jacket over it. The silencer, he put in an inside breast pocket. He would have preferred leaving the gun where it was, but expected his room to be searched the moment he went out.

He saw Lewicki as he stepped out of the elevator. The New York detective was sitting in the lobby, pretending to read. He looked up at Turner, and his eyes carried a message. Then he glanced casually around and tilted his head at two separate points. Turner paused to light a cigarette, seeing the two watchers Lewicki had indicated, solidly built men with blank eyes whom he had already picked out at the airport. But how nice to have a friend in town, he thought, and proceeded across the lobby to the grill for dinner.

He had another bourbon, then ordered broiled flounder, feeling the same virtuousness he always felt when he chose fish over meat. Eat fish and you'll live to a hundred, Maria had promised him. Memory was a wolf at his back. Nothing was lonelier than eating by oneself in a restaurant, and he gazed jealously at the couples and groups at other tables. He wished he could have asked Lewicki to join him, but knew the young detective would only be humiliated in the presence of the two local watchers. A third drink with the fish helped make the meal bearable.

Needing movement and air, he decided to go for a walk. This time he saw none of his watchers as he went out through the lobby. He strolled through the downtown area, past shops, movie theatres, honky-tonk joints, and people with closed faces. The night was soft, maternal, and carried the promise of summer, but no one seemed to care. The place was a belt of apathy through which people moved wearily, worrying about food and rent. Farther on was a restored area with well-kept Federalist houses and date signs that carried them back to the 1700s. There were few pedestrians, and the atmosphere of the time when the houses were built seemed to have been sustained. Turner breathed the air of another century. Soft, yellow lights brightened some windows, and people could be seen inside the rooms. If the sidewalk opened, swallowed me up, and closed over my head, thought Turner, who would know the difference? I wouldn't leave a ripple.

The lights faded behind him, and he entered an urban

park. There were magnolias and dogwood, and a fragment of moon peeked through lacy branches. Benches were spaced at regular intervals, but no one was using them. There were muggers in Richmond, too. Walking, he felt his pistol pressing against his stomach and suddenly found it reassuring. The walkway abutted a winding road, but little traffic passed. Then a car pulled up a few feet ahead of him, and two men got out.

"Mr. Turner?"

The soft tidewater accent was in marked contrast to the chipped granite face that had produced it. Turner recognized the two locals from the hotel lobby. They stood blocking the path like a pair of tackles. He nodded.

"I'm Lieutenant Taylor." He held out a shield as identification. "Richmond Police Department. This is Sergeant Byrd."

"What can I do for you, Lieutenant?"

"Would you mind coming with us, please?"

"Where?"

"Downtown police headquarters."

"Why?"

"Just routine questioning."

Turner stood unmoving. What worried him was the pistol in his belt. It was unlicensed, and he had no idea what the laws were in Virginia. "Routine questioning about what?"

"I couldn't say, sir."

"Am I under suspicion for something?"

"I can't answer that, sir."

"How do you know who I am?"

"We received orders to keep you under surveillance."

"Orders from whom?"

Sergeant Byrd cut in. "We're not here to answer questions. Just get in the car."

"I think I'd rather talk to Lieutenant Taylor."

Byrd took out a snub-nosed .38 and pointed it at Turner's stomach. He rested the gun in the crook of his elbow where only the muzzle was visible. "The talking is over. Now get in the car."

170

The Present

Turner looked at the two men, then at the automobile, a dark, unmarked sedan with a short-wave antenna. He had the feeling that if he ever did get into it, he was going to have to be carried out. Something was suddenly coming off the magnolias like gas out of a swamp, and it smelled lethal. "There's an old army saying: Never point a gun at a man unless you're ready to kill him." Turner dropped his voice to a murmur. "Are you really ready to kill me, Sergeant?"

Byrd grinned, and Turner watched his eyes. They were near to the required madness.

"Take it easy, Andy," said Taylor. "We don't want anything here."

"Hell, it's as good here as anywhere."

Lieutenant Taylor spoke to Turner. "I really think you'd better do like he says, sir."

Turner measured his chances of charging the gun or going for his own. They were nil. "What's happening here? I don't understand any of this."

"You don't have to understand it," said Byrd. "Long as *we* understand it." He had begun to enjoy himself, and it made him expansive. "You're a real big man. We figure if we stay nice and close, some of it might just rub off."

"Shut up, Andy," said the lieutenant.

"What's the difference?"

"I said shut up." Lieutenant Taylor was getting edgy. "I hate to tell you this, Mr. Turner, but if you don't get in the car this minute, Sergeant Byrd is liable to shoot you right here for resisting police officers in the performance of their duty."

Turner had pretty well put it together by now. He was their chance to make names for themselves. Each would be a witness for the other. And when they found the gun on him, it would be even easier—self defense. America's free enterprise system. Everyone in business for himself. It was almost funny. After all his careful planning, he had to run into two rednecks looking for a quick score. Moving very slowly, he started toward the car.

None of them saw Lewicki until he had the muzzle of his

171

service revolver pressed to the back of Sergeant Byrd's skull. "Drop the gun."

Byrd froze. So did Lieutenant Taylor. Turner stared at Lewicki. Even in the darkness, his face looked pale.

"I said drop it. I'm very nervous."

The sergeant dropped the gun. Turner picked it up and pointed it at the lieutenant. The four of them stood like figures in a tableau.

"Jesus, what do we do now?" said Lewicki.

Turner fought off an urge to hug him. "Take them back into the woods a little."

"You dumb, fucking Polack," said Byrd. "You don't even know what the hell you're doing. This'll be your goddamned ass."

Turner motioned with the revolver. "Walk."

About a hundred yards in from the road, they positioned the two men on opposite sides of a large tree, extended their arms about the trunk, and manacled them to one another with their own handcuffs.

"Just tell me this," said Turner. He spoke softly, but anger burned with a white heat in him, and he had only a thin edge of control. "Do you two have something against me? Have I ever hurt or offended you in some way?"

Neither police officer answered.

"Christ, you don't even *know* me."

They said nothing. Sergeant Byrd spit.

"Yet you were ready to shoot me like some kind of animal and drag in my carcass as a trophy."

In the moonlit darkness, they embraced the tree like two lovers. Passing cars sounded faintly from the road. Lewicki stood silently to one side.

Turner shook his head in disgust. "You sons of bitches. You think a cop's badge is a goddamned hunting license?"

"Go screw," said the sergeant.

Turner abruptly tossed the gun into the brush. Then he took out his own revolver, attached the silencer, released the safety, and drew a bead on the sergeant's right eye. Slowly, he squeezed the trigger. *Whoosh!* But at the last instant he had moved the gun barrel a hair to the left. A small black hole showed in the tree beside Byrd's ear. The sergeant's eyes were wide.

"Let's get out of here," Turner said to Lewicki.

"We'd better gag them first."

Moments later they walked off through the dark. Turner felt the heat go out of him, but there was something worse in its place. He had never come this close before. He had done a lot during the war, but never that, never killing cold, on impulse. Many had. And worse. There had been all kinds, and apart from their particular oddities, they had conducted themselves with decency. But what oddities! There had been the ear collectors, the rapers, the eye shooters, the scalpers, and God only knew what else. At first you regarded yourself as apart and superior. But then, if you were there long enough and if it became bad enough, there would always come a moment of fear or frustration or anger or just the beginnings of madness, when you knew that under certain conditions you finally would be capable of anything.

"Thanks," he said.

Lewicki looked young and embarrassed.

"What made you follow them?" asked Turner.

"I wasn't following *them.* I was following *you.* I told you I was going to ride your tail."

"I'm glad you're conscientious."

They reached the police car. The keys were in the ignition, and they drove it to within a block of the John Marshall and left it on the street.

"You'd better get out of Richmond fast," said Lewicki.

"You, too."

"Don't worry. Where you go, I go."

"I'm beginning to count on it."

THIRTEEN

The Past

My eyes were too blind, thought Turner, my brain too limited, my instincts too trusting. Yet even now he found it hard to believe. So stubborn was human foolishness.

Turnovsky sat regarding him with his brooding Tartar's eyes. It was the same way his father used to look when he wanted to both punish and console him at the same time. Hank, being of a different background, showed nothing. They were at home, back from Europe, and Turner had just finished telling them everything that had happened during their absence. It was straight, unemotional reportage, in itself a small victory. It was also part apology, something he felt he owed them. He had made a deal, and he had broken it. His only excuse was that the deal was wrong to begin with and should never have been made. Maria could not be shared or assigned away. He finally knew that.

Turnovsky reached over and touched and patted his hand. The gesture was instinctive. This, too, reminded Turner of his father. "You've really had a time of it, eh, Pauly?"

They sat drinking before the fireplace. A Chopin étude came softly over the stereo, and the Renoirs and Van Goghs glowed under their separate lights. You could get used to this, thought Turner. He glanced at Hank and felt an almost

174

physical reaction. A pleasant one. She could carry that much impact. The trip seemed to have relaxed and softened her, and there was an edge of pure silver to the shadows in her face. She even seemed pleased to see him. Or was it just that he and his vendetta had stopped being a threat to Herschel?

"I'm sorry it had to turn out this way," said Turnovsky. "But at least you've found out. At least you know."

Turner warmed his brandy between both palms. "Not everything."

"What else is there?" said Hank.

"For one thing, I don't know why Maria's whole network was burned. Why weren't they simply arrested? Which is how these things are usually handled. Or, better still, why weren't they just left in place and fed more disinformation?"

Hank shrugged. "What's the difference? None of that concerns you. But if you're that interested in reasons, why don't you ask Handley? He seems to have been honest enough so far."

Turner drank his brandy.

"Okay," said his uncle, "so what else bothers you?"

"Maria's Russian film. All that documentation of Jewish repression. All that Soviet military information. I still have no idea what any of it means, and Handley never mentioned it. So either he doesn't know it exists, or else he'd rather not have me know. Which in itself makes me curious."

Turnovsky waved his cigar impatiently. "What kind of curious? You've suddenly turned into an intelligence expert? Who knows what goes on in the heads of those *meshuggeneh* spies? And who even cares? You wanted to find out why your Maria was killed? Okay. You found out. You wanted to know who killed her? You know that, too. Maybe you got a few people burned along the way, but thank God you got out of it in one piece. A lucky Jew. The rest of this *cockamamy* business has nothing to do with you. That's for the crazies. For you, it's finished."

Hank laughed. Turnovsky looked at her. "I said something funny?"

175

"Ask your nephew."

"*You're* laughing and I should ask Pauly?"

"Go ahead, Paul. Tell your Uncle Herschel what's funny. I love him, but sometimes he's not too bright. It takes him a little while to catch on to things."

Turner got up and studied the brilliant yellow fields and cerulean skies of a late Van Gogh.

"Coward," said Hank.

"In exactly thirty seconds," said Turnovsky, "I'm going to knock both your heads together."

"For Paul," Hank told him, "it's not finished."

"What do you mean not finished?"

"Just what I said. Not finished. Not over. Not ended. Not completed. It seems your nephew is suffering from one of the oldest of all insanities. It's called faith, and it commonly affects children, fools, religious zealots, and those in love." Hank smiled. It was a sad smile, perhaps even a trifle wistful. "I don't know what we can do for him now, Herschel. He's obviously beyond rational persuasion. But I suppose there's always prayer."

Turner faced her. "You really do make it sound crazy."

"So make it sound better," said Turnovsky.

"I can live with what Maria was and did. I can't change that. I can even understand and accept what Handley had to do. What I can't live with is not knowing the rest of it."

"Try," said Turnovsky.

There was something else, but he could share this only with Peggy. "I've been wondering about Maria and Handley," he told her.

"What about them?" She was fresh out of a shower and curled on the couch in her terry robe. Her hair, still wet, lay in dark tendrils against her face and neck, and she dried it gently with a towel.

"Handley doesn't strike me as the kind of man to brood silently over an unrequited love for eleven years."

"You mean you think he may have been sticking it to her?"

Turner made a face. "You're a high class literary type, a senior editor."

"What's the matter, darling? Is the image too clear for you?"

"Probably."

"Either you want to talk about it or you don't."

He looked at her.

"I'm going to tell you something. Do you know what the weakest part of your writing is? Your women. And do you know why? Because you glorify them too much. A reader could never possibly imagine one of your fictional women saying 'fuck,' or going to the bathroom, or even giving off an unpleasant odor."

"God forbid."

"I'm serious. They're all half saint, half goddess, and a perfect reflection of how you regard women in life. It's certainly how you've always regarded Maria and obviously still do." Toweling her hair, her touch was no longer quite so gentle. "Do you really want to know what I think about Handley and her?"

He shook his head. "Definitely not."

"Well, I'm going to tell you anyway. And don't give me that hurt puppy look that tears my heart out."

"I probably will."

"I think Handley was making it with her for years," she said, hurling the words like stones. "I think he had a perfect three-way deal going. A woman he genuinely cared about, a beautiful mistress, and a top KGB agent he was using to further his career. My God, how could he do better?"

Turner sat staring at Peggy's two walls of unframed paintings by undiscovered artists. He had always hated the collection, hated the harsh, raw colors, the total abstraction, the lack of discipline and craft. He thought the pictures a pretentious mess, full of wads and drippings, signifying nothing. Yet now he suddenly found himself seeing all sorts of dark meanings in them, and he cared even less for this than for his previous disdain. "Do you think she cared about him?" He was absolutely unable to use the word love.

Peggy considered it. "I don't know. She was obviously willing to use herself on him. Whatever that means."

Turner went on staring at the pictures.

"She was no saint, Paul. Who is? What do you want from her, for God sake?"

He had no answer.

Later, they made passionate, sadly skillful love, but it seemed to have nothing to do with anything.

It had been a bad night for him, and the morning was worse. He was trying desperately to get some writing done, passages dealing mostly with the dead . . . the ones he had seen, and the ones he still imagined. There were friends he had loved, and there were strangers—dark, quiet images in a green landscape. He, the living, moved among them. It was not enough just to look. He had to look closely, had to lower his head near the ground so that nothing would be missed. Some had been blown out of their uniforms, others lay like bundles of rags, and still others looked like nothing you could name. Most were stained with dust and blood. One of the VC was skinned. Some of the guys had gotten stoned one night and had a little fun. Hell, he was dead anyway, wasn't he? For many of them, the living, it was a collective nervous breakdown. They had not come here that way. They had been born pure and raised under the same human principles. If you remembered how to cry, you could cry as much for them as for the dead.

By noon, it had become too much. He had to shower, change his clothes, and leave not only the typewriter, but the apartment. It was that real. Walking, he found himself across from La Boite. What the devil, he thought, and went in for lunch. The restaurant was crowded at this hour, and he ordered a martini and waited at the bar for a table. He had not been there since that last day with Maria, and he wondered what he was doing there now. As if he didn't know.

He was halfway through his first drink when a waiter came over and said a lady wanted to speak to him.

"Who?"

"The lady back there, sir." The waiter indicated a dark-haired young woman sitting alone against a far wall.

Turner went over.

"You don't remember me," she said.

Big eyes and a pretty, impish face were only vaguely familiar. "I'm sorry."

"Fran Woodruff. We met at a literary reception. What's the matter with you? I'm the president's daughter."

He laughed. "How could I forget?"

"Apparently with great ease. Are you waiting for someone?"

"No."

"Then why don't you join me?"

He stood looking at her. There were purple shadows edging her cheeks, her eyes were solemn, and she looked more attractive and not nearly as young as he remembered. Still, he hesitated.

"Separate checks," she told him.

"In that case . . ." He sat down. A waiter took his order and left. "I appreciated your condolence note. That was kind of you."

"It was all so terribly sad. I didn't know what to say. I always feel so stupid in the presence of tragedy. You go to school and learn a lot of useless things, but somehow they never teach you anything about tact and humanity."

Turner had become aware of two dark-suited men watching him from a rear table. He stared back, and one of them, a broad, fair-haired man with steady eyes, smiled and nodded. His companion, who looked enough like him to be his brother, just sipped his coffee and went on with his watching.

"That's Tony and Frank," she said. "They keep me safe from tigers."

Of course. Secret Service. The things you normally didn't think of. "How do they know I'm not a tiger?"

"Tony recognized you when you came in. He used to be assigned to my father, and my father got him to read your books. Now he's a real fan. In fact, since we last met, I've also read you. I guess I was curious. It's strange, reading an author you've met and spoken to. You keep looking for the man in the book."

"Did you find me?"

"I wouldn't presume to know. Not on one meeting."

The waiter brought their food, and Turner ate without tasting anything. He noted the quiet, unobtrusive way the Secret Service men watched everyone in the dimly lit room and everyone entering it. What a job. Any crazy with a gun and an imagined grievance could take a shot at this girl, and there was little that these two men could do to prevent it. Then he thought of how it must feel to be the target oneself, and at that moment he felt not one presence in Fran Woodruff, but two—one an attractive young woman with bold eyes and cool lavender shadows and the other blood kin to the single most powerful political leader in the world, potential victim of fanatics and madmen, a princess guarded by goblins.

"Are you in New York for a visit," he said, "or just passing through?"

"Neither. I live and work here. I'm with a design house on Fifty-seventh Street. Crown Interiors."

"How is it for you? Being God's daughter and all."

"Good and bad. It gets you noticed, but you're also judged hard. Which means they expect you to be twice as good as anyone else. I guess I'm the ultimate minority worker . . . one."

He found it an intriguing concept. What a curiously candid girl, he thought, and remembered thinking pretty much the same thing at their only other meeting. "You're my first president's daughter. Give me some help. What should I know about you?"

"What do you want to know?"

180

The Past

"Whatever you feel like telling me."

"Will it be in your next book?"

"Every word."

"Terrific. I'll be immortal."

In the seemingly guileless, matter-of-fact way he had already come to expect of her, she told him she was twenty-six years old and had been raised in Pittsburgh and Boston, the youngest of two daughters born to the Woodruffs, but the only surviving child—her sister had died in a plane crash twelve years ago. She had a bachelor and a master of arts from the University of Pennsylvania, had been working for Crown Interiors for more than two years, and was growing bored with her job. Her family's religion was Episcopalian, but she never attended church and had little tolerance for formal religion of any kind. She did believe in God, however. How could so beautiful and intricately woven a tapestry as life be without a designer? She was an ardent supporter of the arts, equal rights for women, and any minority group you could name. She also continually embarrassed her father with her uniquely ingenuous statements on controversial issues. She had undergone intensive psychotherapy between the ages of fourteen and eighteen, spoke freely about it, and considered the period one of the more positive in her life. In short, she seemed very much her own woman. To Turner, after a less than joyous night, she was breath of clean air.

As they were leaving the restaurant later, Tony came over and shook Turner's hand. "Hey, keep those books coming. You've made me a believer. Anything new in the works?"

"Yes, but it's getting harder."

The security man nodded. He seemed reluctant to pull himself away. "Listen, I'm sorry about your wife. That was real heavy."

"Thank you."

"I happened to be there that night. I was with the Chief. He took it very hard. I mean he was really upset."

Turner looked at this big man with the curiously boyish face. Maria had done a number of interviews with Woodruff

181

over the years, but that hardly seemed enough to send the chief executive into mourning. "I never realized the president knew my wife that well."

"I guess he's that kind of man."

It seemed an odd response. It was also several beats late.

The other Secret Service man stood off to one side, watching in all directions. Fran extended her hand, and Turner felt delicate bones in smooth flesh. "I'm unlisted," she said. "So just in case the urge to call becomes more than you can bear, it may be a good idea to take my number."

He called two days later. "You were absolutely right," he said. "It became more than I could bear."

She chose to have dinner at home, a comfortably furnished cluster of rooms on Fifth Avenue almost directly across the park from Peggy's place. Tony sat reading in a small vestibule outside her apartment door, and Frank was unseen but present in the only other suite on the floor. She had prepared the table before leaving for work that morning, and there were freshly cut flowers and flickering yellow candles. Debussy drifted softly from hidden speakers. The dinner and wine, like everything else, were perfect.

Turner said, "How can you work all day and still manage to come up with something like this at night?"

"By not sleeping for thirty-six hours."

"I think the whole thing is a trap."

"I never said it wasn't."

They had left the dining area. Now they sat side-by-side on a bright couch. The drapes were drawn, rain drummed against the windows, and from twenty-four stories up the city seemed at rest.

"What do you want from me?" he said.

"I'm not that complicated. You're an attractive, interesting, reasonably famous, curiously self-contained man who—

182

happy days—doesn't even come near to boring me." Her eyes were solemn, unblinking. "I think the more logical question should be, what do *you* want from *me?*"

She took a cigarette from his pack without asking, and he lit it for her. "And before you give me any cute, facetious answers," she went on, "I think I'd better tell you a few things. I may make jokes about being the president's daughter, but nobody else does. Everybody else takes it very seriously. And the Federal Government takes it most seriously of all. Along with my parents, I'm considered a national treasure on a par with Fort Knox, and I'm kept under the same sort of twenty-four-hour surveillance. It's a continuing horror, but as long as my father sits in the Oval Office, there's nothing I can do about it. Tony and Frank are never far away, my phone calls are monitored, and although it's been officially denied, I'm sure that every inch of this apartment is bugged."

"Well, it's been nice knowing you."

Her laugh was a bit forced. "Also, the moment anyone shows the slightest interest in me, or I in them, an in-depth security check is automatically initiated. Which is exactly what happened with you after our luncheon at La Boite the other day."

"How did I come out?"

She rose and turned up the music so that it was loud enough to drown out ordinary conversation. "Badly. In fact, so badly that I was told to avoid all further contact with you."

Turner studied her face to see if she was serious. She was. He lit a fresh cigarette and waited.

"Do you know what I'm talking about?"

"It's your story," he said flatly. "Get on with it."

She looked unhappy. "Please don't be angry. Maybe I shouldn't be telling you this, but I hate hiding anything. Besides, I'm terrible at it." She sighed the way an adult might while lecturing a child. "Understand. It wasn't you yourself. You're clean. Pure as a baby. Very patriotic. So were your parents and grandparents. Not the slightest taint to any of you." She stopped and shook her head. "Ah, this is disgust-

183

ing. The whole thing makes me so ashamed."

Turner made it no easier for her. He remained silent. Wonderful. Three generations of Turners and Turnovskys officially adjudged loyal. Wherever they were, he hoped they were properly grateful.

"Of course, your uncle is a crook from way back, but he's evidently a big enough crook to have achieved respectability. Anyway, he's not the problem. It's your wife. It seems she was working for the Russians."

Turner said nothing.

"Did you know that?"

"Only after she had died."

Fran looked at him through a haze of conflicting emotions. "It must have been awful for you."

"It had to be a lot worse for her."

"You're very forgiving."

"Hell, it's easy to forgive the dead."

They sat with the music blasting.

"So what happened?" he said. "I suppose the computer marked me guilty by reason of sexual intercourse?"

"More than sex is usually shared in a marriage."

"Tell me about it."

"God, what I sound like. I don't know what's wrong with me. I must be more nervous than I thought." She ground out her cigarette in disgust. "Anyway, you're here. So I guess I did something right."

"What did you do?"

"I called my father."

"You mean I'm here by presidential dispensation?"

"Thank God he outranks the computer."

"Your father doesn't believe in guilt through marriage?"

"Despite the fact that he's president, my father happens to be a decent, sensitive man with good instincts."

Turner laughed.

"You're not angry anymore?"

"What's the point?"

"You have every right to be." In the dimly lighted room,

184

she glowed with righteous indignation. "You've more than paid for that right. And in blood."

"If you think about it coldly, I suppose you really can't blame them. I lived with a KGB agent for eight years. Who would believe I never knew what she was doing?"

"Obviously the president."

Shortly before midnight, he took a cab across the park on the Sixty-sixth Street transverse, found Peggy awake working on a manuscript, and told her all about Fran Woodruff. The first thing she did was pour fresh coffee. That done, she bent close and sniffed his neck. "Did you go to bed with her?"

"What do you think?"

"I smell her on you, but I think not. Even if she were willing, you wouldn't. Not on the first date. Not Sir Lancelot."

"I did with you."

"That was different. You'd known me for ten years. Besides, I took off my clothes and threw myself at you. How could you reject me?"

Carrying her coffee, she paced as she spoke. Only a single lamp was on, and he seemed to see her in fragments—the flash of an eye, her nose in profile, the curve of her cheek. She wore tight, narrow jeans, and her legs appeared to go on forever. Then he saw her mouth.

"What's the matter?"

She stopped walking. "I'm faced with this terrible dilemma. I can't decide whether you're naïve or just plain stupid."

He laughed.

"I've just insulted you, damn it. Why are you laughing?"

"Because you're a very funny lady." He took her hand and drew her to the couch. "Hey, come on. If I thought you'd behave like a jealous wife, I'd never have told you."

"How did you expect me to behave when you walked in here smelling of another woman?"

185

"She's not another woman. She's the president's daughter."

"Of course. And with nothing between her legs but the presidential seal."

He sighed.

"Never mind the long-suffering sighs. I still don't understand why you saw her in the first place."

"It was accidental."

"I don't mean at the restaurant. I mean tonight."

"I told you. It was a feeling I had, something one of the Secret Service men said about Woodruff's reaction to Maria's death." He shrugged. "Anyway, I thought it worth following up. Do you think I'm getting a little paranoiac, doctor?"

"I think you're looking for an excuse to fool around with the president's daughter."

"If that were so, why would I rush right over here and tell you about it?"

"Because you're too honest to do anything else." She drank her coffee without pleasure. "Jesus, spare me from compulsively honest men. They do more damage than the worst liars."

"No one is damaging you. And what ever happened to all your gloriously liberated ideas about sex? You keep saying a man is a man, a woman is a woman, and the earth doesn't fall out of orbit just because small areas of each are briefly joined. You've lectured me on it a hundred times. So what's suddenly so bloody important about what I might do with that miserable little thing of mine?"

Peggy sat brooding. "I don't know. Maybe it's just that it's not always so miserable and little."

He had begun to feel a need to talk to Wendell Handley. It hit him at odd moments during the day and sometimes even at night. When it grew to the point where he could think of little else, he called CIA headquarters in Langley, Virginia, and gave his name to the deputy director's secre-

186

tary. This time he was put through without delay. "I've found some more material," he said. "What arrangements would you like to make?"

Handley took a moment to respond. "I'm on rather a tight schedule. Would you mind coming down this way again?"

"No problem."

"How would one o'clock tomorrow be?"

"Same place?"

"If that's all right."

"Why not?"

He was up half the night in anticipation. He might have been on his way to meet a new and exciting lover. It was almost that kind of erotic fever. He wondered about it. Why was it so near to being pleasurable? He obviously had some sort of further need for this man. At the very least, he was not ready to let him go.

He was on the ten-thirty shuttle from La Guardia the next morning. He sat among the regular rows of business types, the men in their dark three-piece suits, the women looking just a bit tougher than they had to. At Washington's National Airport, he again rented a Chevrolet and followed the same route to the same dirt trail beside the same stream where he had met Handley previously. But this time the deputy director was there ahead of him, sitting very still in the gray Pontiac, smoking his pipe and waiting. When he saw the Chevrolet pull up behind him he got out, looking elegant in a navy blue pinstripe. He approached Turner cautiously. His face was blank, free of all expression, as if awaiting a signal before committing itself to anything. Then, seeing Turner's hand extended, much of the tension went out of him.

They shook hands, and Turner saw the new scar, high on his cheek, where he had hit him with the gun. Handley probed it with a finger. "I'm told it adds character."

As if by mutual agreement, they started to walk, following a path alongside the stream. Off to their right was forest, mostly pine and maple, trunks dark against the pale green of

187

new foliage. Sun flickered through in patches, and birds called from hidden branches. Neither man seemed anxious to intrude.

Finally, the deputy director began. "Your call surprised me. I never expected to hear from you again." He smiled and once more touched his cheek. It seemed to have become a tic. "Or maybe I just hoped I wouldn't."

"I came across another roll of microfilm. But I'd have called anyway. I felt we should talk. Last time was a nightmare. It was unfair to us both."

Another layer of blankness lifted from Handley's face. There was still caution underneath.

"Since then I've had time to think," said Turner. "So I've thought. Of you. Of Maria. Of myself. We've all paid heavily in this. Maria is dead. I've lost a wife. And you have to walk around remembering what you did." He paused to light a cigarette. "Christ, I still don't know how you were able to do it."

"I had no choice."

"There's always a choice."

"I couldn't let eight of our people die. Could you?"

Turner had no answer. They walked, hearing the sound of their thin city soles on the dirt path.

"You were a soldier," said Handley. "Would you have let your whole squad be wasted rather than sacrifice one man?"

"Probably. That's why I was never an officer. I knew I'd never be able to weigh human lives like vegetables."

"That's fine for you, but someone has to do it. And any kind of sentiment—love, compassion, grief, the very things that make us human—only clouds the issue."

"So, of course, you stop being human."

Handley sucked at his pipe as if the heart of his emotions was rooted in the bowl. "How easily I say these things. But I'll be honest with you. There was a moment back there that night when I was ready to toss it all to hell and let those eight people die rather than hurt her. I swear to Christ I was this close." He held up a thumb and forefinger, and they almost touched. "This close."

188

"What do you mean?"

"The whole thing was so insane, so desperate, so terribly quick. I had to move the moment I learned of the blunder. I had to keep her from reaching a phone or any Russian in the place. So I got her off into an empty room as fast as I could and . . ."

"How did you manage that?" Turner cut in.

"Manage what?"

"Get her to go off with you like that."

"I just said there was something I had to discuss with her. That part was no problem."

"You had that close a relationship?"

"You forget. We had known one another for eleven years."

"That's not what I asked."

Handley stopped walking, and Turner suddenly thought he heard movement in the brush. Had he allowed himself to be led into a trap? Were they going to bury him right here in Virginia? Then a rabbit appeared, stayed frozen for a moment in the grass, and bounded out of sight.

"I've told you how I felt about Maria," Handley said. "There's nothing new about that."

"Yes. But you never told me how *she* felt about *you.*"

Handley began walking again.

"I've already accepted your having killed her," said Turner. "Do you really think your having slept with her would be worse?"

"The world is full of men who would rather see their wives dead than unfaithful."

"I'm not one of them. Besides too many other things have happened for it to matter that much anymore."

"I'm not naïve enough to believe that."

"Maria shut me out of half her life," said Turner quietly. "I was married eight years to a woman I now find I never really knew. Compared to that kind of deception, how important could a casual affair be?"

Handley gazed off at an abandoned shack, gray and sadly

189

lifeless among the trees. "For me, it was never casual."

"And for her?"

"I never fooled myself about that. I knew she was just using me. Or thought she was. She ignored me for years until I moved far enough up in The Company to carry real weight. When I reached deputy director, she discovered me all over again." His eyes, catching the light, gave a hint of bitter amusement. "Maria and I both seemed to be getting what we wanted, yet neither of us ever really did. I know it can only be of small comfort to you now, but she never stopped caring for you."

"You don't have to throw me any bones."

"It's no bone. You and I go back a long way together. Until a few weeks ago you never even knew I existed, yet I've known about you from the first day you walked into Maria's life." He paused, radiating something curiously near to benevolence. "I've studied you, been jealous of you, hated you, and admired you. You've played a continuously important part in my life for more than eight years. You were the one man Maria had chosen to marry, and I don't think I ever stopped wondering why. It was a neverending puzzle to me. With all the important men available to her, heavyweights from every field, why had she married a patched-together ex-soldier?"

Turner smiled without a trace of amusement. "Thanks."

"Consider," said Handley. "I knew Maria pretty well by the time you appeared on the scene. She was no starry-eyed romantic. She was a pragmatic and certifiably dangerous foreign agent who had already used me to reach someone higher up in The Company and who had, in turn, used and wasted him. Whatever she did was for a purpose. At first I thought you might have been with the KGB too and that she perhaps needed one of her own to come in from the cold to at night. When that didn't check out, when it became clear you knew absolutely nothing about that part of her life, I thought she might have chosen to marry you to ward off possible future suspicion. After all, who would suspect the wife of a celebrated war hero and patriot, a Medal of Honor holder, of being a KGB agent? But that theory didn't hold up either. Because the more I learned about you, the more I realized that in any real crisis you'd probably be less of a help to her than you would be an additional threat, that your continuing presence was in itself a potential danger. So I eventually had to settle for the least likely answer of all—that despite everything I knew about Maria, she had remained enough of a schoolgirl to have married you for as insanely impractical a reason as romantic love."

Handley's eyes were self-mocking, as if even to express so simplistic a theory was an embarrassment for him. "Although that particular side of her did neither of us very much good that last night. I started to tell you," he said and paused briefly to rekindle his pipe. "I had her off alone in a small, out-of-the-way room at the rear of the house. I had two glasses of champagne already poured. The cyanide was in one. Then I looked at her and was utterly unable to go through with it. After ten years, I blew it all. I told her I knew she was KGB, that I'd known all along, and that I was ready to make a deal with her. I said I just wanted to save our people in Poland and Czecho. I needed three days to get them out. I told her if she gave me three days, she could do as she pleased afterward, and I promised her amnesty." He laughed coldly. "I also told her I loved her. And I kept repeating it, as though those few silly words were an impenetrable barrier against pain, sorrow, and death."

Handley stared thoughtfully off through the woods. He seemed to have lost his bearings, forgotten where he was.

"What did she say?" Turner finally asked.

"Say?" Handley blinked at him. "She laughed at me. She said she had no idea what I was talking about. She said my brain must be addled from too many years with the CIA. If I didn't know better, I'd have almost believed her. It was the coldest performance I've ever seen, bar none. And at that moment I was as near to burning an entire network to

191

indulge my own feelings as I pray I'll ever be. I was actually
ready to let her get away with it. Then I felt a fear in my
chest, as though the ghosts of those eight people were already
paying me back, and something clicked off." Handley
shrugged, sorrowful and defeated. "I kissed her. I gave her
the champagne. We drank together and I held her until she
was gone. It was faster than you can imagine."

I'm going out of my head, thought Turner dully. I've just
listened to this guy tell me how he killed my wife, and I'll be
damned if I don't feel like consoling him.

"Sometimes I'm sure I'm in the wrong line of work,"
Handley murmured softly. "You said it yourself before. You
stop being human. The smallest dose of pity, of simple humanity, and you're finished. And others are finished along
with you. Love and God become dangerous anachronisms. If
they're not held in check, they can wipe you out."

The path ended in a patch of brambles, and they started
back. At one point, Handley sighed profoundly, as though relieved of a terrible weight. What I should do, thought
Turner, is charge him the standard psychiatrist's dumping
fee. Still, it was he himself, not Handley, who had asked for
the meeting. Whatever his own needs were, he assumed they
had been met. It was about as close to an even swap as he
could get these days.

Almost as an afterthought, he gave Handley the microfilm
that was allegedly the reason for their meeting. He also gave
him the printout, which was in the original Russian and contained the classified Soviet defense material that Jake had
translated.

Handley glanced through the finely printed sheets. "Have
you had it translated?"

"No," Turner lied. "Is it anything important?"

"It's hard to tell at a quick reading."

"What's in it?"

"Details of advanced Soviet missile systems, order of battle
data, tables of equipment for mechanized and infantry divisions. That sort of thing."

"Why would Maria have had classified Russian material lying around?"

"Offhand, I'd guess it was probably just some disinformation she planned to sprinkle about. But I'll have it checked out."

Back at the cars, they shook hands.

"I appreciate your coming down," said Handley. "For more reasons than one. There's no one else alive I could have talked to as I talked to you today."

"Will you let me know about the film when you find out more?"

"You can count on it. It'll give me an excuse to see you again."

"You don't need an excuse."

Handley got into his car and drove off. Turner stood gazing after him. I'm getting to know him, he thought. By the time he left, the sun had disappeared behind a bank of thunderheads, and it had started to shower. Heavy drops spattered the leaves. They dripped down into the grass and glittered like precious stones. Puddles began forming on the path where the two men had walked not long before.

FOURTEEN

The Present

Turner watched it become light as he drove. He had always loved this hour of the day . . . except, of course, when he was in bed, unable to sleep. Now he watched the darkness fade as the sky lightened, and he saw the road, shiny with mist, stretching ahead of him. The trees at the side seemed to form a tunnel, pine trunks so solid and brown that he could almost feel their roughness. Behind him, maintaining a steady hundred-yard interval, were the lights of Lewicki's car. Occasionally, lights passed going in the opposite direction, but this did not happen often, and most of the time there were just the four lights of the two cars moving in tandem.

The road curved and climbed. Then it crested at a scenic rest area, and Turner swung over and parked. Lewicki drew up beside him. "What are you, a goddamned camel? Another minute and I'd have wet my pants."

"Next time sound your horn when you have to stop."

"Sure." Lewicki headed for a rustic comfort station. "You need special toilet training to tail guys like you."

They had a smoke together and watched the sky go from gray to purple to pink. A hawk rose, circled, and dipped behind a line of trees. A crow called and others joined in. Then it was quiet.

"Why don't you just tell me where you're going?" said

Lewicki. "Think how much easier that would make it for me."

Turner smiled.

"What's the difference? You're not going to lose me. Maybe it would even be a good idea to travel in one car. Then we could cut expenses and not have to be alone. Surveillance is such a miserably lonely business. I've always hated it." He inhaled deeply, savoring the smoke. "Besides, you owe me a favor."

"Why? Just because you saved my life?"

Lewicki gazed off at the sky.

Turner said, "Tell me something. You're a cop and should know about these things. Could those two animals really have gotten away with it?"

"Why not? All they would have had to do was fire a pickup gun into a tree, plant it on you, and claim they shot in self-defense. And since you already had your own gun, complete with silencer, that part would have been even easier. Who would know the difference? Then tomorrow they'd be front page heroes, with citations and promotions to follow."

"You make it sound like standard operational procedure."

Lewicki's eyes looked tired. "It happens. Here and there, every so often, it happens. There are good and bad in every line of work, but a bad cop has power enough to be deadly."

"What do you think they'll do now?"

"Come after us. Not only do we know what really happened, but we humiliated them in their own town. Which is a killing offense around here. Imagine two cops being found tied to a tree. It might have been kinder to shoot them."

Turner saw the hawk again. It circled gracefully, a dagger-winged falcon. When it reached a cluster of trees in the valley below, it folded its wings and dropped like a bomb until it disappeared.

Moments later he drove off into the sun, Lewicki following at his established interval. The road was smooth, and the rented Chevrolet responded well, not slipping on the curves and coming up with enough power to take the hills in high.

195

The countryside was almost achingly beautiful, with sudden mountain vistas, sunlit glades, and sparkling white-water streams. Turner could feel it inside him as though he were part of the landscape. *A sharp sword in the heart.* And who had written that? The half-forgotten fragment of poetry teased his memory. *Beauty seen but unshared by your beloved was a sharp sword in the heart.* Was that it? Undoubtedly misquoted, yet he could feel the pain. He glanced at the mirror and saw the blue Ford behind him. Did Lewicki feel such things? Or was the handsome young cop still an innocent in matters of love and their attendant pain? Lewicki, look! Pay attention. There's beauty out there.

Lewicki's response seemed to be three quick blasts of his horn. Turner looked back and saw the detective waving him to the side of the road. It was too soon for another rest stop. He pulled over, and Lewicki parked behind him and trotted forward. "There's a roadblock ahead."

Turner had not even noticed. Now he saw a line-up of cars about half a mile down the road. A revolving light flashed above them. "It might have nothing to do with us."

"Maybe. But we'd better find out."

"How?"

Lewicki kicked at the grass. "I'll call my precinct in New York. If that roadblock is for us, then our two friends had to put out an official story to go with it."

"The last phone was about fifteen miles back."

"You in a rush to get somewhere?"

"Not at all. This is a pleasure trip."

They made a fast U-turn and started back. If I were setting up a roadblock, thought Turner, I'd have a man with binoculars posted to watch for cars doing exactly what we're doing. Apparently the Virginia police were not that resourceful; no one came after them.

The phone was in a food and service stop at a crossroad center. Turner sat smoking in his car while Lewicki made the call. *My partner.* The thought amused him. He had set out to perform what seemed like a relatively simple, straightforward act, and here he was driving all over the Virginia countryside with a New York cop who had already saved his hide once and was in the process of trying to do it again. For all his youth and apparent ingenuousness, Lewicki was a man with vitality who gave off a silent message: *Depend on me.* For the moment, Turner was pleased to do exactly that.

Lewicki stuck his head in the car window. "It's for us all right. We'd better get away from here and talk."

They found an isolated country road a few miles to the west and parked the two cars in a clearing screened by high brush. Lewicki slid into the Chevrolet. "I spoke to my precinct commander, and here's what Richmond is saying: They claim you spotted their two men tailing you, led them into a park, and pulled a gun on them. When they rushed you, you shot to kill. The shot missed, and they disarmed you before you could fire again. The bullet was found in a tree later and dug out as evidence." Lewicki sighed. "I really wish you hadn't taken that shot."

Turner remembered the sergeant's face as the bullet buzzed his ear. "It was worth it."

"Anyway," Lewicki continued, "they're saying that it was at this point that I appeared on the scene, put a gun to Byrd's head, handcuffed him and the lieutenant to a tree, and stole their car. So they want you for attempted murder and me for obstructing two police officers in the performance of their duty and also for grand theft auto." He grinned. "My mother always told me the South was no place for a Polack."

"Or a Jew."

"Who ever heard of a Jewish Turner?"

"My grandfather's name was Turnovsky. My father thought being Turner would make life easier."

"Did it?"

"No. What did your boss say when you told him what really happened?"

"First, he swore. Then he admitted there wasn't much he or anyone else could do until we were picked up and given a hearing. But he thinks we'd be crazy to let these rednecks get

197

their hands on us. And I agree. We're armed and considered dangerous, and those two cops aren't about to give us a chance to tell the truth. They'll blow us away first, then come up with a dozen good reasons for doing it."

They sat together in the rented car. A squirrel chattered from a tree, and they watched it climb down the trunk, stopping along the way to stare back at them, its plumed tail jerking nervously.

"I'm sorry I had to get you into this," said Turner.

"I got myself in."

"I think we should separate. You'll be better off alone. It's really me they want, not you."

The detective laughed. "You don't really think you can shake me that easily, do you?"

Turner had momentarily forgotten about the surveillance. Lewicki obviously had not. A curious young man. There was more to him than you thought. Hell, there was more to everyone than you thought. "I think I should tell you something. I already owe you a lot, and I may yet owe you more. But when the time comes to lose you, you're going to be lost."

Lewicki smiled. It was a warm, open smile. You can trust me, it seemed to say. You can trust your life to me. How can it be that you don't know it?

FIFTEEN

The Past

Turner was at his typewriter, but he was not working on his book. He was making a list of loose ends. There suddenly seemed to be a lot of them, and he felt they were drifting away. It brought him to the edge of panic. Maria had always been the one to establish order out of a confusion of detail, not he. The abstract was more his sphere—broad philosophical concepts he could deal with one at a time. Two together and he was in a sweat. But he had found it helped to make lists, usually numbered ones. The numbers themselves had nothing to do with chronology, order of importance, or anything else, yet they were, somehow, reassuring. He wrote:

1. Maria's network. All six dead. Why were they killed rather than arrested or left in place and used?
2. Microfilm of Russian military information. Is it authentic or not? If it is, why did Maria have it? Jake said it may have been her insurance against KGB power struggles. Was it?
3. Microfilm of Jewish condition in Russia. Ditto above.
4. What about the agent Handley said he exiled to Africa for giving Maria the wrong information at the reception? What was his name? Pretty sure Handley called him Reison ... or Rosen ... or Rawson.

Something like that. Maybe check it . . . him out.
5. President's reaction to Maria's death. Also, why did he grant me security clearance over computer? Keep on with Fran.
6. Be kind to Peggy.
7. If Handley doesn't report on microfilm in a few days, call him. Keep up a good relationship. This is important. He seems to want, even need, it.
8. Use Uncle Herschel where possible. He can save time and effort. Hank won't like it, but what the hell.

He leaned back in his chair and studied the list. It made him feel better to see it all in writing, as if he had nailed down the separate pieces of a puzzle and no longer had to worry about losing them. Yet he still did not know what he had. Maybe a cleverer man, a true investigator, would know, but for him it was like staring into the sun. After awhile you saw nothing. Still, there were things you could feel.

Turnovsky had invited him to Friday night dinner. There were lighted candles and *challa* and chicken noodle soup and sweet red wine and all the proper Hebrew prayers. Turner felt as though his grandfather were still alive, which was the last time he had heard the words *Burach ee, burach shmoi . . .* recited on the Sabbath eve as candles glowed. Except that at his grandfather's house there had been no fancy French chef in the kitchen, no Japanese houseman doing the serving, and no beautiful Episcopalian lawyer acting as hostess. Still, it was a traditional Sabbath dinner with all the trimmings, including *yarmulkahs* and *gemütlichkeit.*

Turnovsky had been to a funeral that afternoon and was in a philosophical mood. He attended a great many funerals, never missing an opportunity to see someone he knew buried . . . whether friend or foe. Dead was dead. "There's nothing like a graveside," he said, "to make you know you're alive, to

200

help you appreciate living. Everyone should go once a week. There'd be less boredom, less whining, less need to *kvetch* to a shrink at sixty bucks an hour. People don't understand. Without the presence of death, life has no real meaning." He looked across the table at Turner. "You fought in a war, Pauly. You lived with it. How did you feel?"

"Scared sick."

"Okay. Sure. But what about the other times?"

"There were no other times."

"What about on leave, away from the fighting?"

"Then I was scared sick about having to go back."

Turnovsky smiled. "It's not nice to make fun of your uncle."

Hank said, "I don't think Paul wants to talk about it, Herschel."

"He's right." Turnovsky waved aside the entire subject with a sweep of his wine glass. "Not on *Shabbes* by *nacht*. Who needs the Angel of Death with Friday night candles? So what should we talk about, Pauly? You pick the topic."

"How about Jews?"

"Better. More fitting. Any special kind?"

"Russian. I'd like to talk about saving Russian Jews from Soviet oppression."

Hank and Turnovsky looked at him. Kieto came in, silently collected their empty plates, and disappeared.

"Jake said some things just before he was shot," Turner went on. "He wasn't your greatest fan, Uncle Herschel, but he said that at least you understood about Jews. He said you'd never turn from one of your own in trouble. He called it the single purity in your blood."

"That was Jake, all right."

Hank said, "I'm beginning to see the whole thing. The saving of Russian Jews is about to lead us straight to Maria."

Turner's eyes swept over and past her. "Have you ever been involved in getting Jews out of Russia, Uncle Herschel?"

"I've dabbled."

"What does that mean?"

"You're a big writer. You don't know what dabbled means? It means it hasn't exactly been my life's work."

"Do you know any people whose life's work it *has* been?"

"People?" Turnovsky shook his head. "Not people. But one person, I might know."

"Who's that?"

"Chaim Spitzer. A long-nosed rabbi. He's crazy, same as you. Only one thing on his mind. Except with him it's not a dead wife. It's Jews. He eats, sleeps, and breathes Jews. Anything happens with Russian Jews, he knows about it. And he runs the whole *shmeer* himself from an old downtown *shul.*"

"Do you think I could talk to him?"

"You've got a mouth. Why not?" Turnovsky placed two muscular hands, like meat cleavers, flat on the table. He clucked softly. "And here I thought you came just for Jean Pierre's chicken soup and *tsimmes.*"

Hank walked Turner to the door as he was leaving. "I must admit this whole thing is beginning to fascinate me," she said. "It's the first chance I've ever had to watch a perfectly normal man evolve into a fanatic."

He could think of nothing to say, so he smiled.

"Your wife must have been an extraordinary woman. I wish I had known her."

Descending in one of the Waldorf's private elevators, Turner wished he had known her, too. His uncle had said that without the presence of death life had no real meaning, and maybe he was right. But could death also give meaning to a life you had somehow missed?

He found Rabbi Chaim Spitzer in the office of an ancient orthodox synagogue that huddled in the shadow of the Williamsburg Bridge. When Turner was six or seven, his grandfather had once taken him to a similar *shul* on the Lower East Side to visit some old cronies, and he recalled the smell almost instantly. It was a unique odor, coat upon coat of assorted aromas built up over nearly a century . . . molding prayer books, old men's bodies, polished wood benches, dampness, and dust. For years he had believed it to be the odor of God. Maybe it was.

Spitzer was exactly as Turnovsky had described him—long-nosed; he was a thin, shrunken scholar in a black, ash-dusted suit and a *yarmulkah,* who squinted narrowly at Turner through thick glasses and the smoke of a cigarette clamped between yellowed teeth. It was only after Turner had been with him for several minutes that he realized the rabbi was no older than he. The aging of sanctity. Spitzer's initial act of greeting was to give him a *yarmulkah* to cover his bare head. Then, settled in his gloomy cave of an office, he asked, "Are you a big shot gangster like your uncle?"

Turner shook his head.

"So what then do you do?"

I look for hidden signs of my wife, thought Turner. But he said, "I write."

"About the Jewish condition?"

"No."

"Why not?"

Turner lit a cigarette and added to the room's already thick layer of smoke. "It's not my subject."

"If you're a Jew, it's your subject." Spitzer's eyes pecked at him from behind his glasses. "I'll be honest, Turnovsky. I have little patience for assimilated Yid writers. They're invariably rootless, ethnic ciphers. I've never read anything worthwhile by any of them."

Turner said nothing and didn't even bother to correct Spitzer's assumption that his name was the same as his uncle's. He was here for a favor, not to defend his writing. These professional *Yidlach* were all alike. They didn't discuss. They attacked.

"You're not going to argue with me?"

"That's not what I'm here for."

The rabbi looked disappointed. "Your uncle said you wanted to talk to me, but he never said about what. Evidently it's not my literary judgment you want." He showed his yel-

203

low teeth. "So what can I do for you, Turnovsky? Any up-town Jew who comes to the Lower East Side these days has to want something badly."

"I've been told you're very much involved with Russian Jewry . . . helping them get out of the Soviet Union, that sort of thing."

"So?"

"I wondered if you had perhaps known or heard about my wife in all this."

"Your wife is a Russian Jew?"

"No. She's no longer alive, but she was American. Her name was Maria Monroe."

Spitzer's face was blank.

"She had her own radio show for years." Turner suddenly felt tired. "You never heard of her?"

"I don't listen to the radio."

Turner gazed at the wall above the rabbi's head, a faded monument to Russian Jewry. Photographs of imprisoned and rescued Jews were arranged in rows. Yellowed clippings told of trials, persecution, and daring escapes to Israel and the United States. "I have reason to believe my wife was active in this cause. Could she have worked with someone other than you?"

"It's possible."

"But not likely?"

A half-inch of ash dribbled down Spitzer's chest. "We make a lot of noise, but we're only a small group. Whatever action we take is tightly coordinated and under my control. I'd know if your wife had been active. I don't understand. Had she told you she was involved?"

"No. But after she died I came across some material that seemed to connect her with what you're doing."

"What sort of material?"

"Some Russian-language microfilm."

"You understand Russian?"

"No. Jake Holtzman translated it for me. I guess you knew Jake."

204

"Of course. His death was a great loss for us." The rabbi's face looked no different than it had a moment before, but his body seemed to have suddenly grown alert. "Do you happen to have a printout with you?"

Turner took out several folded sheets and gave them to Spitzer. Then he sat looking at the gallery of Russian Jews as the rabbi read. The air of centuries seemed to float off the collection . . . dim ghetto rooms in forgotten cities, precarious *shtetls* awaiting the next Cossack pogrom. Yet this was the year 1980. Czarist oppression was long gone, and the revolution was supposed to have brought hope, freedom, and equality for all, Jews included.

Spitzer finished reading. "How long has your wife been dead?"

"Just a few months."

"Aaah . . ." The sigh carried a flicker of pain. "Such a young woman. How is it possible? An accident?"

"A heart attack."

"She never spoke to you about this film?"

"Never. Is it important to you?"

"To many more than just me. Didn't Jake tell you?"

"Yes. But I needed confirmation."

"What I don't understand is why Jake himself didn't tell me about this after you brought it to him."

"He never had the chance. He was killed that same night."

"How do you know?"

"I was there. I shot the man who killed him."

The rabbi straightened once more. "The newspapers said they shot one another."

"I thought it best to make it look that way."

"Turnovsky, you seem to be a man of unsuspected depths." Spitzer's eyes, newly respectful, remained wary. "You're not CIA, are you?"

"Christ, no!"

"Lovely talk. Some Jew."

"I have a Jewish heart."

"We need more than your heart, Turnovsky. If Jewish writers don't write about the Jewish condition, who will? Moslems and Christians?" Spitzer took off his glasses, rubbed his eyes, and squinted through swollen lids. "Now leave me alone for a minute. I have to get something to show you."

Turner left the rabbi to rummage through his secret cache. For Spitzer's sake, he hoped it was fireproof. This was exactly the kind of place that was torched by anti-Semitic vandals. He moved among the polished benches and stared up at the Ark of the Convenant, crowned with two mystical hands, thumbs and index fingers touching. Below it, enclosed in a maroon-curtained cabinet, lay the Holy Scrolls. Turner touched the dry, velvet fabric. How many thousands of years? The Scrolls were a continuum. His grandfather and countless Turnovskys before him had been part of it. His father, becoming Turner and dreaming his own American dream, had been less so. And he himself, probably not at all. Never mind what he had told Spitzer about his Jewish heart. Never mind his silently whispered, *Shmah . . . yisroyail . . .* before closing his eyes each night. If there had been Jews like him only, the five thousand years of continuing tradition would have been dead a long time ago. Yet he felt no guilt.

"Turnovsky!" Spitzer called out his grandfather's name, and he returned to the office.

The rabbi showed him a stack of papers in a metal box. They were microfilm printouts and were all in Russian. Turner glanced blankly through them. Then Spitzer placed another metal box in front of him, this one containing several dozen strips and rolls of microfilm. Turner picked a few up and put them down again. "I don't understand."

"I'll explain," said Spitzer. "One day, about eight years ago, I received a phone call from a woman I didn't know. She said she was interested in helping Jews who wanted to leave Russia and told me where I could find some microfilm that might prove useful to that end. I thought it was probably a crank call, but followed it up anyway. The film was there and contained information about Soviet dissidents that I'd never seen before. After that, I received two or three calls a year telling me where to find additional pieces of microfilm, all of which were invaluable to me and all consistently beyond my usual sources. Everything is in these two boxes."

Turner fumbled for a cigarette and dropped the pack. "It was always the same woman?"

"Yes."

"And she never identified herself? Never said anything more?"

"All she ever told me was the location and timing of a new drop. Which was never the same twice. She also warned me never to share my source of information with anyone or it would end. And until this moment I never have. Not even with Jake. If I had, he would have been able to recognize the pattern when you brought him your wife's film."

Spitzer sat staring at the two tin boxes. He looked weary, a shrunken, aging scholar full of doubts and premonitions. "So she's gone. Ah, I can't tell you how sorry I am. A terrible loss . . . for you, for me, for many more than anyone can imagine. What did you say her name was?"

"Maria. Maria Monroe."

"And she had a radio program?"

"It was a talk show. A good one. 'Maria at Noon.' "

"Imagine," Spitzer said distantly. "If I had listened even one time, I might have recognized her voice." He looked at Turner. "But how in heaven's name was she ever able to pick up such highly classified information?"

"She was an agent for the KGB."

The rabbi sat in silence. His face, having a will of its own, rejected outright what he had just heard.

"You don't believe me?"

"No."

"Why would I lie to you about something like that?"

"I haven't the vaguest idea."

"And if I told you she didn't die of a heart attack, that she was murdered as a KGB agent by the CIA? Would you believe that?"

Spitzer considered the question gravely. "Yes."

"But you still wouldn't believe she was actually working for the Russians?"

"No."

"Why not?"

Spitzer picked up the box of microfilm. "Because of this."

"And that's enough?"

"Enough? For eight years I've blessed this woman in my prayers without knowing who she was. If we went in for such things and if I possessed the power, I'd canonize her. Yes, Turnovsky, I'd say that's enough."

Turner found himself grinning like an idiot. He was afraid that if he didn't, he might start crying and not be able to stop.

He was writing.

The assault came as a surprise because they had learned not to expect to be attacked by such numbers and with such weapons and tactics. They were in a line of deep, solid hilltop bunkers that had reinforced concrete on top and seemed impossible to take. Yet sometime during the night, the North Vietnamese came and took them. They started with a six-round-a-minute artillery barrage, then followed up with light tanks and satchel charges, bangalore torpedoes, tear gas, and napalm, squeezing everything down into the machine-gun slits and air vents and whatever other holes they were able to find or blow. Inside, there was no place to hide, nowhere to go. They couldn't see, they couldn't breathe. Whatever minds they had were fading out. The gas was in their eyes, ripping and burning. They inhaled fire and tried to block it out, but their lungs kicked their throats open. Deaf and blind, they stampeded and crashed into one another. The dead lay in growing piles, flesh upon flesh. The hands of the living clawed. The fire reached for their bodies and ate their skin. They tried to cover their faces with their arms, but the fire was everywhere. They fell, rolled, and leaped up. Grenades exploded, and scraps of flesh flew. They looked for the enemy, but saw nothing. He was everywhere, yet invisible. They scuttled about like mice looking for holes. They pressed their faces into the earth. Blood oozed. They were dead, overrun, wiped out.

Division headquarters reported that the bunkers had only been bait, a minor diversionary position, and were not considered important.

He had worked late and afterward slept fitfully. Now he was awoken by the telephone. He groped for the receiver and grunted.

"Why haven't you called me?" asked Fran Woodruff.

He smiled at the ceiling.

"Stop grinning, and answer my question."

"Because I hate smart-alecky women."

"You know you don't hate me."

He stuck a cigarette in his mouth and struggled to light it.

"Do you?" she said with less certainty.

"No."

"I was afraid I had scared you off."

"Heroes of the Republic don't scare."

"I have preview tickets for the new Robert Redford movie tonight. Will you go with me?"

"Why not? I like bleached blonds, too."

"Do you really think he bleaches it?"

"Name one forty-year-old blond who doesn't."

She couldn't. Another illusion shattered. They arranged to meet at eight.

When the phone rang again a moment later, he expected it to be Fran with the name of a true, unbleached, forty-year-old blond.

"Paul?" said a man's voice.

"Yes."

"Wendell Handley. How are you?"

My buddy, thought Turner, and was instantly alert.

"Great. And yourself?"

"Fine. I have a report on that film you gave me. A rather surprising one."

Turner waited.

"I'm in town until tomorrow. I thought we might get together sometime tonight."

"Midnight in the graveyard?"

Handley laughed. "Does one-thirty in front of your apartment sound too insane?"

"I'm worried. I'm starting to think it's normal."

"See you then," said Handley and hung up.

Since this seemed to be his morning for the telephone, Turner called Peggy at her office and set up a dinner date for the following evening. He made no effort to fool himself. It was nothing but guilt. God, was he getting Jewish.

He did his usual morning body-straightening routine, checked the by now well-advanced healing of the bullet wound in his arm, showered, put on jeans and a sweater, and went into the kitchen for breakfast. It was after eleven, an unheard-of time for him to be starting his day. He had not gotten to bed until almost five, but the lateness still bothered him. There was no way he could change. He would die compulsive.

He was halfway through his coffee when the downstairs bell rang. "Yes?" he said into the intercom.

"It's Hank."

He thought he had heard incorrectly. "Who?"

"Hank Adams."

He pressed the buzzer and waited on the stairway landing until she appeared, cheeks flushed from the climb, her expression slightly apologetic and uncertain. It made her look young, almost girlish. "Sorry to barge in like this. Am I interrupting anything?"

"Just my regular orgy-of-the-month. But it was beginning to bore me, anyway."

She smiled politely at the poor joke. It was her first visit, and she made a proper fuss over the apartment, using words

210

like *charming* and *warm* and asking about particular pieces of furniture. She might have been any well-bred Boston lady at a literary tea in one of those federalist houses on Beacon Hill. Except that Turner served her coffee rather than tea and decided that no ass like hers could ever have looked truly at home in those passionless, early-American surroundings.

"All right," he finally said, "what is it?"

They were in the living room, and she settled into a straight chair, carefully balancing her coffee and not leaning back, as though any such concession to comfort might be mistaken for weakness. "I just thought it time I spoke to you alone, outside of Herschel's dominion. He can be overpowering. I tend to fade out around him."

"Not really."

She shrugged off the compliment. "You're important to Herschel so you're important to me. I want you to know that."

He said nothing.

"The fact is, I'm probably just jealous of what I've called your fanaticism. I'm certain no man is ever going to feel anything close to that way about me." She sat unmoving, and her face had the stillness of a portrait. "But now I really think you should drop it. Please, Paul, leave it alone while you still can."

"Why now?"

"Because you suddenly seem to be getting close to something."

"That doesn't make sense."

"A lot of people have been killed just to keep some undetermined thing buried. Why should you be allowed to dig it up? You're in areas you know nothing about. If you don't care about your own life, at least consider Herschel's."

"That's unfair."

"Is it? You've involved him. He knows what you know. Don't you think they're aware of that?"

"I'm sure he can take care of himself."

"Really?" Hank put down her coffee and rubbed her

hands on her arms as if suddenly cold. "Well, let me offer a few pertinent facts about Herschel Turnovsky. He's mortal. He's vulnerable. He lives from minute to minute on a high wire. His life is a balancing act over a snakepit. It looks easy and pleasant enough from the ground, but every breeze is an earthquake. In the past five years alone, they've tried to blow his brains out seven times. His bodyguards go everywhere but to bed with us, yet we both know that one day he's going to be killed anyway. I'm not complaining. I can live with all that because it's what Herschel chose a long time ago and it comes with the territory. What I can't accept is his now having to be exposed to forces that don't concern him, that he knows nothing about, and that none of us can even see. And all for no better reason than a lovely but futile obsession that, even if it succeeds, can never resurrect the dead. You still won't have your wife back, Paul."

Turner let it wash coldly over him. "I take it Herschel doesn't know you're here."

"No, and I'd appreciate your keeping it that way. He would consider it an affront to his macho image. Incredible. At his age." She stood up and walked to a window. Outlined by the sunlight, she looked delicate and gilded. "I don't suppose I've budged you one inch."

"That's not so. I never thought of Herschel's exposure. From now on I'll keep him out of it."

"But not yourself?"

He shrugged.

"Then there's no point in trying to keep Herschel out. As long as you're still poking around, he'll be considered part of it. The connection between you has been made. If you're burned, he'll go up with you. I know that from personal experience. It works that way in our business, too."

He had almost forgotten. She was a very tough lady. A gangster's moll. "I'll keep Herschel out anyway."

"No. If you're still involved, that would only make it worse for him. He would never know what to expect, when to expect it, or from which direction it might come. Just go on keeping him informed, and let him help where he can. That way he might have a chance when the sky falls."

"You seem so sure it will."

"I am." She came close and kissed his cheek. "Thanks for listening. And please. Not a word to Herschel."

He breathed her perfume. Even her sisterly peck carried overtones of sex. At the door he wanted to say something warm and hopeful, something that would show he cared about what she had tried to do and that he was not unmoved. But before he could speak, she was already part way down the stairs, her perfume trailing faintly behind her. She did not glance back.

It was only later that a thought occurred to him: If his uncle was indeed endangered by his involvement with him, so was Hank.

Robert Redford smiled his fantastic smile, looked irresistibly boyish despite encroaching middle age, and proved equal to whatever crises his script writers provided for him. I should only do as well, thought Turner.

Afterward, with Tony and Frank in tow, they had a light supper at a Greek restaurant on East Eighty-sixth Street and went back to Fran's apartment for a drink. This time Frank established a beachhead outside the elevator, while Tony took a back-up position in the adjacent suite. Just the logistics of Fran's security were intriguing. The simplest thing was no longer simple. Every move had to be thought out in advance. Nothing was taken for granted. Ogres lurked.

When they were alone, Fran automatically turned up the stereo to smother possible microphones. "I think we should kiss right now and get that part over with," she said. "Otherwise I'm just going to be tense and nervous, wondering when it's going to happen, and I won't be able to enjoy myself."

He laughed. "You are too much."

"Come on, Paul."

"No."

213

"Don't you want to kiss me?"

"Not at this particular moment. And certainly not on command."

"Would you like a brandy while we wait for the right moment?"

"Now you're making me feel foolish."

"It's just that I hate everything moving according to a predetermined mating ritual. It embarrasses me to make believe I don't know what's going to happen."

In the soft lamplight, her face was shadowy and elusive. He was finding a new directness in women these days, and he was not sure he liked it. They were a different breed . . . first Peggy and now this one. Everybody insisted upon being so honest and open that all the mystery was gone. He almost smiled. What in God's name did he want with more mystery?

She said, "I don't exactly turn you on, do I?"

"Don't think that."

"What else can I think? I even had to be the one to call this morning."

"Well, you were the one who had the tickets."

"I made that up. I only got them after you said okay."

He had to smile. But there was suddenly something so sad and vulnerable about the way she looked, that he held her as he would a child. Then he felt her body, and there was nothing childlike about any part of it.

"Do you think this might be the right moment?" she said.

Her lips were warm and seemed to taste of candy. She twisted her face away and spoke into his shoulder. "I know how I'm coming across, but please don't think I'm easy. I've loved only one man. He was married and wouldn't leave his wife and was probably a little crazy, but I loved him for three years."

"Not anymore?"

"He was one of those lunatic skydivers and died doing it. It took a while, but I finally buried him."

It seemed reasonable. Bury your dead. But when would *he?*

214

The Past

Making love with her for the first time was easier than it had been with Peggy. Still, they came together less as lovers than as chance acquaintances meeting in the proper mood. It was love almost without preliminary. Not five minutes had gone by before he slipped easily into her. She had great energy, which made her more athletic than sensual. Joyous in the act, she had no idea there was a difference. Gently, he quieted her. First times were touchy. You had to absorb each other. Yet they fit together well, as equals. The sum of her life and body at that moment added up to the sum of his. Yet her flesh was so young. Which in itself made it exquisite. And him, immortal. He floated through violet shadows. With all the passion, there was coolness in the mood. Beginning the long final slide, he felt it impossible for either of them to make a mistake.

She hid her face in the warmth at the side of his neck. "Oh my."

He had kept the room dark to avoid having her see his body. The music, following them protectively, covered them like a blanket. He thought of Frank outside in the vestibule, Tony in the next apartment, and the possible microphones everywhere. He touched her breast and felt it rise and fall with her breathing.

She said, "I think I've been waiting for this ever since I talked to you at the reception that night. I didn't care a bit that you were married. I didn't understand it then, and I don't now. And it was more than simply lust. I've felt that before, too. It was never like this."

Her skin was so lovely, so soft and smooth. This was how the species insured its survival. They were all sexually interchangeable.

"Even my father sensed what I felt. I never talked about you that much, but he knew. He must be more intuitive than I realized."

"Does that mean I'm going to have to marry you?"

"Only if he needs the Jewish vote. But I think he might like to talk to you when he's next in town."

215

"About what? A possible cabinet appointment?"

She laughed, and it sounded good in the dark. "I think he'd just like a few words with you."

"Did he tell you that?"

"Sort of. Would you object?"

"Hell, he's your daddy, isn't he?" It took effort to keep the excitement from his voice.

He arrived in front of his house at 1:20 A.M., ten minutes early for his appointment with Handley. He was early for everything. Maria had suffered the same affliction. She once said they were lucky to have found one another, that no one else could have lived with either of them. Without warning, the thought brought tears pressing against his eyelids. Terrific. He shook his head in disgust. The urge to weep came often and easily these days. With no effort, he could become an outstanding crier, a true master of the hot, palpable tear. An absolutely worthless talent. What good were tears? They meant little, affected nothing, were not even a dependable sign of compassion. Murderers wept too, loved their children, grieved for their dead wives. At moments, he was ashamed of being human. The species did not enjoy a great history of benevolence. It gorged on its own. Yet where did you go to resign?

Wendell Handley's car appeared at 1:35. Turner saw no other cars behind him. He got in and shook the deputy director's hand.

This time they drove west to Madison Avenue, then north. Handley was again wearing dinner clothes, as on their first meeting. He seemed in a good mood, and Turner caught a faint whiff of liquor along with his pipe tobacco. They were like two old friends, he thought, out for a late drive, talking, making easy conversation. These days he could get his mouth to say just about anything.

Handley gazed through the windshield at Madison Avenue. "That Russian-language film of Maria's turned out to be authentic. Every detail checked out. To be honest, I never expected it."

"What does it mean?"

"There are several possibilities. She might have expected some sort of problem with the KGB and was holding it for extra bargaining power. Or she may even have been looking ahead to trouble with us and a possible deal. Either way, the film would have carried weight."

Night had erased all color and life from Madison Avenue. Closed shops and dark gray buildings slid past Turner's eyes. He was beginning to feel a vague hint of something. "Enough weight to get her what she wanted?"

"Maybe not in itself. But if you found this, there was probably much more. She had been active for many years."

Turner carefully lit a cigarette, making the most of the small ritual. If he ever gave up smoking, what would he do with his hands? What would he hide behind?

"You haven't found any additional material, have you, Paul?"

"If I had, don't you think I'd have told you?"

Handley shrugged exquisitely tailored shoulders. Turner was sure the cost of his dinner suit alone would feed, house, and clothe a family of four in India for a year. "I don't know," said the deputy director.

"What reason would I have not to?"

"I don't know that either."

"Then why would you ask a question like that?"

"Because I'm in a business were it's considered pro forma to ask any kind of question about anything."

Turner didn't believe him.

"I live and work in a metaphysical whorehouse of suspicion, Paul. I've told you before. Truth, trust, honor, friendship, and love are rarely tolerated and then only at grave personal risk. But if I ever felt I could trust anyone, it's you. Good Lord, some of the things I've shared. In the wrong

217

hands they could finish me."

"It was I who came to you with what I found. I didn't have to."

Handley drove west on Eighty-sixth Street, then downtown on Fifth Avenue, the dark, no man's land of Central Park on one side and high-rise luxury on the other. "Yes. But you came with candy in one hand and a club in the other because you wanted information. And I gave it to you."

"That was the first time."

"The second time, too. If I was anxious to talk, you were no less anxious to listen. But neither of us is a fool. We both know the best way to get something is to have something to offer. I never really believed you just found that last bit of film. I think you had it all along with the rest and kept it back until the right moment. Just as I also think you're holding a lot more in reserve right now. Which is fine with me. I'm always willing to deal."

Turner tapped ash into an ash tray. Wonderful. Handley's mind was so convoluted that he was beginning to think circles around himself.

They headed west on Fifty-seventh Street, then turned downtown beside the Hudson and under the elevated highway. The QEII was at her pier, and Turner stared up at her gracefully soaring prow. He had always been fascinated by the self-contained world of a great liner and had once tried to get Maria to take a cruise with him. But along with her usual time problem, her feeling about ships was that they were the only prisons on earth in which you stood an excellent chance of drowning.

"Allen Dulles was directing The Company when I started," said Handley, "and I remember something he said to us as recruits. He said that the only principle of political ethics worth holding onto was that the end justifies the means. He claimed that anything else was just water flowing through a sieve. It may sound overly simplistic to you, but it works. I mention this only so . . . ."

The rattle of gunfire cut him short. The shots went off in a quick, short burst. A car sped past on the right. Turner barely glimpsed it before he was thrown against the door. Handley spun the wheel, fought for control, glanced off a steel pillar, and slammed into another. There was the sound of rending metal and breaking glass. Handley turned off the ignition to prevent fire. Then everything was quiet.

"Are you all right?" said the deputy director.

Turner nodded. The window beside him and the windshield were shattered, and there was broken glass everywhere. He glanced at Handley. His pipe was still in his mouth, and, other than for a sprinkling of glass particles on his lap, he looked no different.

They got out. Cars stopped around them, and people came running. Three police cars were there in minutes. Handley identified himself and spoke to a gold-braided sergeant who did everything but snap to attention and salute. The car was left to await a tow truck, and they were driven to a midtown precinct station and given the use of an unmarked police vehicle. Twenty minutes after the shots went off, Handley was driving crosstown with Turner beside him.

"Does this sort of thing happen to you often?" Turner said.

"It wasn't me they wanted. It was you."

"You've got to be kidding."

"They came up on the right. My window wasn't even touched. Besides, I haven't had anyone take a shot at me in fifteen years. Why, suddenly, now?"

"But why *me?*"

"Because you're Maria's husband and you're out driving with the deputy director of the CIA. The KGB probably figures you've found something and are passing it on to us."

Turner dug for a match and found a tiny fragment of glass in his pocket. No. He was not buying it. If the KGB had wanted him, they could have had him, they could have had him a long time ago. And with far less commotion. Still, they had obviously been shooting at him, not at Handley. Christ,

219

at a distance of less than four feet how could trained profes-
sionals have missed? Unless, he thought dimly, missing was
what they had intended.

"I'm sorry it had to come to this," said Handley. "But I
can arrange protection for you."

"Forget it. I couldn't live like that."

Handley stopped for a light at Park Avenue. "It may be
the only way you *can* live. If they tried once, they'll try again.
Don't be foolish, Paul. I can give you solid coverage around
the clock."

Turner could feel everything simplifying, all the separate
parts beginning to slide together. There was even a beautiful
kind of symmetry in it. Of course the gunmen intended to
miss. They were probably Handley's own men. The concept
was clear. Create a sudden threat from a common enemy and
draw him into a new round of confidences. God only knew
what kind of high level, classified material Handley thought
he still had squirreled away. Great. Let him keep thinking it.
The more he thought he had, the better.

"I'm willing to take my chances," he said.

"But I'm not willing to let you. Not with the kind of information you may have hidden. If you go, that goes. I can't
let that happen."

"It's not up to you." Turner lit a fresh cigarette and
stretched the silence. "If you put anyone on my back for even
five minutes, I'll burn everything. And don't bother waving
the flag at me. I've had that."

Handley stopped in front of Turner's house. They had
traveled in a big circle. "What do you want, Paul? What is it
you're after?"

"I don't know. But when I do, you'll hear from me."

"Don't wait too long."

Turner had no such intention.

SIXTEEN

The Present

Moonlight made the room a silvery blue, and he lay staring at the shadows on the ceiling and listening to Lewicki snore in the other bed. They were in one of a group of crumbling, rustic cabins off a two-lane blacktop halfway between Charlottesville and Fredericksburg, an end cabin with forest at its side and back and their cars parked on the grass in front. There had been nothing on the radio about them so Lewicki figured no all-points bulletin had been issued and they could still consider themselves safe as far as the general public was concerned. It was also his theory that Lieutenant Taylor and Sergeant Byrd would be handling things pretty much on their own, calling in surrounding locals only for occasional roadblocks. With that breed, it was all a matter of saving face. They wanted two nontalking bodies brought in. Nothing more.

Lying on a lumpy mattress that smelled of mildew and worse, Turner found such a concept far easier to believe now than he would have even a month ago. Now he was ready to believe almost anything. And if any faint doubts happened to remain, Lewicki fed him statistics to remove these as well. The prime cause of death for the young, after accidents, was murder. It was replacing baseball as the national pastime. And those not actually participating were avid spectators. Hourly newscasts dripped blood, while Hollywood gave it to you as the latest art form, in full color, and sometimes even in slow motion so you could better appreciate its beauty. A billion knives and guns hanging loose, more being sold every day, and the country was at peace, for God sake! Murder, mutilation, and rape. The big three. And as American as apple pie. So declared Lewicki.

Maria had also told him something about it. It was the first time he had talked with her about marriage. "I can't have children," she had said. "Not ever."

It came as a shock. "Who cares?"

"I don't want to be unfair to you."

"You won't be. Unless you don't marry me."

"You might feel differently if I told you the whole story."

"Try me."

She tested him with her eyes. "All right," she said in a low voice. "When I was fifteen, I was raped in the back seat of a Buick convertible by four of our school's football heroes. They had just won the county championship and decided to make me part of the victory celebration. They were drunk but not that drunk. I was too ashamed to tell anyone. Then I found out I was pregnant and told my parents because abortions weren't legal then and I didn't know what to do."

She looked at him to see how he was taking it. He must have passed this test, too, because she continued. "Back in Russia, my father would have simply loaded his rifle and shot all four of them. As it was, he made a concession to America's more advanced culture. He waited for them one at a time and just put each in the hospital for a few weeks. Then he took me over to the Bronx for a botched abortion that almost killed me and ended forever any chance of future pregnancies."

"Listen . . ." he said thickly, "I hate babies anyway. They cry and are too dumb to talk and are always pissing in their pants."

She smiled brightly at him. "A charming bit of Americana. Football players. I know it could have happened anywhere, but I was sure it happened here, to me, because my parents were Ukrainian immigrants. I was also sure it happened here because violence is as much a part of America as its addiction to football. Sometimes I'm still sure."

Now, so was he.

Lewicki rolled over, and his snoring gave way to the regular breathing of deep sleep. I could drive off with his keys and lose him right here, thought Turner, but knew he was not going to.

Their not having children had never really bothered him. He had felt no lack in his life, no void that required filling. There had always been the two of them, and with his work he had felt complete. But she still believed she had cheated him and never stopped carrying the burden of that belief. Which was odd, in retrospect, considering everything else she had done. To the end, she had not been able to look at a child without a quick, searching glance at him to see what he might be feeling. "It's so *unjust*," she once said, despising injustice as she despised nothing else, reacting each time as though she personally was the only one conscious of its existence. And football? Sanctioned savagery, performed by barbarians, appealing to the most bestial of instincts. She was unforgiving.

He slept.

When he opened his eyes, he had no idea where he was or what had wakened him. Then he saw a shape silhouetted against the silver glass of a window, and he reached for the gun under his pillow. He released the safety, took careful aim at the center of the figure, and realized he was about to shoot Lewicki. "Jesus," he whispered, "what's going on?"

The detective motioned with an arm, and Turner slid out of bed and joined him at the window. He saw their cars in the moonlight, the blackness of the surrounding woods, and the outline of another car parked about fifty yards back. The third car had not been there when they went to bed.

"I heard it pull up a few minutes ago," Lewicki said softly. "No one has gotten out yet."

Turner saw the revolver in his hand. "Relax. There's little

chance it's them."

A single light was on in front of the cabin that doubled as an office. Up on the road, a neon sign hung between two posts, the effect of the flickering red tubes suddenly tragic and forboding. They knelt at the window, silently watching the car. Moments passed. Then both car doors opened and two men got out. In the glow of the dome light, Turner recognized Lieutenant Taylor and Sergeant Byrd.

"It figures," said Lewicki.

"How the devil could they have found us?"

"They must have stuck a beeper in your car back in Richmond. With a long range receiver they can pick up a signal from quite a way off. Or else it was just dumb luck." He spoke in a whisper. His eyes never left the two men. "We'll let them come in, then take them from behind. Okay?"

Turner nodded, wondering what had happened to Lewicki's bumbling uncertainty. He had not started out this confident and resourceful.

The two detectives were approaching the cabin with drawn revolvers. The moon shone full on them in a blue wash, softening their features, lengthening their shadows on the grass. They came slowly, bodies slightly bent forward, reminding Turner of pictures he had seen of World War I infantrymen advancing across no man's land. Lewicki was right. These two wanted him all to themselves. And at this point they also had to want Lewicki. What they clearly did not want were prisoners.

Lewicki flattened himself against the front wall of the cabin.

Turner did the same. There was the faint, metallic click of the door latch being tried. It was followed by movement at the window. Lewicki pointed to the door. This was where they would enter. It was an old, thin, plywood door with a cheap lock. One solid kick would do it. Guns in hands, they pressed against the wall and waited.

Wood splintered, and the door burst inward with a *whump.* The two police officers followed, one behind the other, their

224

momentum carrying them halfway across the cabin before they saw the two empty beds. By that time, there were gun muzzles at their heads.

"Drop them," said Lewicki.

Two service revolvers fell. Turner picked them up and tossed them on a bed.

"Face down on the floor," Lewicki ordered.

"Hey, listen . . ." Byrd began.

Lewicki clubbed him to his knees. "Just do it."

Awkwardly, they lay down. Turner stood off to one side, feeling the tension run up into his neck. He and Lewicki were both in their underwear. Lewicki's body was slender, very young, undeveloped in the arms and legs. His thick layered hair made him appear almost girlish from the back. But the pistol in his hand looked no less menacing because of that.

"Cuff their hands behind them," he said.

Once more, using their own handcuffs, Turner did it. Lewicki squatted over them. "Okay. How did you know where we were?"

Neither man answered. Lewicki rapped their heads with his gunbutt, first Byrd, then Taylor. It sounded like melons being thumped.

The lieutenant said, "We planted a long range beeper in Turner's car."

"Where?"

"Inside the lip of the rear bumper. To the left."

"My car, too?"

Taylor hesitated. "Yeah."

Lewicki nodded to Turner. "Take a look."

Turner found the tiny, magnetized transistors and brought them in. He had never even known such things existed. The world was getting away from him.

Lewicki said, "Do any others besides you two have receivers for them?"

"No," said Taylor.

"Why not?"

"Go fuck yourself," said Byrd.

Lewicki hit him. "Why not?"

Byrd spat on the floor. At least he could still spit, thought Turner.

"Why not?" Lewicki repeated.

"Shit, we wanted you all to ourselves."

"Sure," said Lewicki. "Like we want you." Moving swiftly, he gagged the two men with washcloths, then slipped pillowcases over their heads as blindfolds. "Let's get our clothes on," he told Turner.

"Are we going to just leave them here?"

"I have a better idea."

"What?"

"Don't worry about it. It'll be okay."

The new Lewicki.

Dressed, they led the two gagged, manacled, blindfolded cops to their own car and stretched them out in back. The other cabins were empty and dark. The light was still on in front of the office, but no one was there.

"I'll drive their car," said Lewicki. "Follow me in yours."

"What about your car?"

"We'll come back for it."

It was after four, and there was no traffic. The road climbed, twisting between narrow dirt shoulders backed by tall stands of pine. They had been driving less than ten minutes when Lewicki pulled off the road and parked on dirt. Turner stopped behind him. The shoulder edged a deep ravine. A line of boulders served as a guardrail. In the distance, mountains arched darkly against the moonlit sky. It was a still, breezeless night. Not a leaf stirred. It seemed a dead place.

Turner walked over to the other car. Lewicki was maneuvering the two Richmond police officers into the front seat—Byrd behind the wheel and Taylor close beside him. With the pillowcases over their heads they looked like Klansmen out for a night ride. Exactly the type, thought Turner. Lethargically, almost feeling himself a disinterested spectator, he watched Lewicki fussing about the car. The detective was in the back seat now, a busy stage manager setting up a key scene on opening night. Reaching forward, he placed both his hands on one of the hooded heads—right hand on top, left hand where the chin would be. Then he abruptly swung the invisible head counterclockwise. There was a dry, cracking sound, and the cop went limp against the steering wheel. Lewicki pressed the second hooded head forward and down, and in a hard cutting blow drove the edge of his hand against the exposed neck area. The body slid sideways. The entire process had taken no more than seven or eight seconds.

"My God," said Turner. "Have you gone crazy? You've killed them."

Lewicki seemed to discover him for the first time. "Save the shock for later. Right now we've got things to do. And fast. I don't think any cars will be passing, but you never can tell."

Turner took a deep breath. His lethargy was gone. He was through being a spectator.

They removed the hoods, gags, and handcuffs from the two bodies, placed the handcuffs and keys back in the pockets where they had been found, and wiped all fingerprints from the car and everything in it. Lewicki had remembered to bring along the cops' guns, and he slipped these back into their holsters. Using a fallen branch for leverage, they pried aside two of the rocks that served as a guardrail, eased the detectives' car through to the edge of the ravine, and rolled the rocks back into place behind it. Lewicki did the rest alone. He started the engine, put it into gear, and sent it down into the ravine. Picking up speed, it flew over a ledge, soared free for a moment, and crashed into a ball of orange and blue flame. They stood watching it burn. Surrounded by rocks, the fire did not seem to be spreading. There was another explosion, then a third. They got into Turner's car and drove back toward the cabin.

Lewicki gave Turner a cigarette, took one for himself, and lit them both as Turner drove. "All right. What would *you* have done with them?"

Turner did not answer.

227

"If we tied them up and left them, they'd only have come after us again. And given the chance, you know they'd have treated us no differently."

"Yes. But I'd like to think we're supposed to be just the slightest bit better."

"We are. But that doesn't mean we have to be suicidal idiots."

Turner felt the sweat turning cold against his back. He had no right to act superior. Without Lewicki, he would have been killed by these two back in Richmond. And, to be honest about it, he must have had a fair idea of what the detective was planning. Yet he had stood back, keeping his hands clean while Lewicki did what had to be done. "When did you get to be such a killer?"

"When I was eleven."

Turner glanced at Lewicki's face in silhouette. It was flat, unsmiling. The question had been strictly rhetorical, a small attempt at humor, but Lewicki had answered it straight. "Are you kidding?"

"No."

"What happened?"

"My old man took me for a walk one hot night and was stabbed to death by a mugger, a hopped-up creep who just decided he didn't like his face. I spotted him in some pictures the cops showed me, but I never said anything about it. I wanted to take care of him myself."

"Christ, at the age of *eleven?*"

"There was no reason for my father to die. He had already given the guy his wallet. Then the sonofabitch just says, 'I don't like your fucking face,' and sticks a six-inch blade in him. He would have finished me too, but I ran. I waited six months, but I finally got him when he was pissing drunk and cut out his throat in an alley. I never knew there was so much blood in a person." Lewicki stared off at the road. "I guess you could never understand that kind of craziness, could you?"

Turner just drove.

The Present

At the cabin, they put the pillowcases back on the pillows, the washcloths in the sink, and checked to see that everything else was in order. They had paid for the cabin on arrival, so they just walked out and closed the door. Their cars were parked side-by-side, and they stood between them.

"So where are you taking me now?" said Lewicki.

"I'm not taking you anyplace. You're taking yourself."

"No. You're taking me."

Turner opened his car door. "Tell me something. That whole scene on the plane, when you played the ingenuous, bumbling, rookie cop. You actually wanted me to spot you, right?"

Lewicki grinned.

"But why?"

"I figured we should get to know each other. Besides, fallibility makes a person more lovable."

"Why the hell don't you go to Hollywood? They'd really love you there."

"And leave you all alone?" Lewicki's eyes were wide. "How would you ever manage?"

SEVENTEEN

The Past

"Are you nervous?" asked Peggy.

They had eaten dinner at a Chinese restaurant and were back at her apartment, sipping Drambuie and watching Greta Garbo in a late movie on Channel Thirteen, a woman so exquisite that even in fifty-five-year-old black-and-white she appeared luminescent.

"I guess so," he said.

She seemed far more nervous than he. She kept looking at her watch, then at him. "Isn't it about time for you to leave?"

"In a few minutes." He was studying the way Garbo's deep, arched eyes gazed tragically at John Gilbert through half-closed lids.

The president was in New York to address a fund-raising dinner at the Waldorf and, through his daughter, had invited Turner to meet with him in his Towers suite immediately afterward.

"What do you suppose he wants to see you about?"

It was the third time she had asked him that question. "I have no idea."

"I think he wants to talk to you about his daughter."

Turner stared at the century's early dream of beauty and passion. Garbo had begun to remind him of Maria . . . the long, pale face, the wide mouth and eyes, all reflecting pain and deep Northern melancholy; Garbo, from Sweden, Maria,

230

one generation removed from Russia, and both apparently having wanted to be alone. Except that Garbo was still alive somewhere, an old woman behind dark glasses, occasionally recognized by an alert photographer. *Maruschka*, at least, had been spared the blessings of creeping senescence.

"I think you two are beginning to worry him a little," Peggy said.

"I doubt it."

"Well, you're beginning to worry *me*."

Turner guessed that much was true.

"Is she at least a good lay?"

He had never admitted having gone to bed with Fran.

"Well? Is she?"

Turner stood up. Peggy and Garbo were beginning to depress him. "Not as good as you."

Being careful not to look at her eyes, he kissed her and prepared to leave.

"Do you know something? There are times, if you try hard enough, when you can be a real bastard."

He turned to take a final look at Garbo, languishing in John Gilbert's arms, her face tear-stained but still irresistibly beautiful.

There were barricades set up as far away as Lexington Avenue. He had to abandon his cab and show a police captain the special pass Fran had gotten for him. The captain passed him on to a sergeant who got with him into a patrol car and drove to the Waldorf's Fiftieth Street entrance. Long black limousines were parked all the way up the block, and squads of motorcycle police stood about in shining leather. Inside, crowding the hotel's lobby, was a small army of Secret Service men, one of whom examined his pass and made a call on a house phone. Then he went over Turner for weapons and took him upstairs in a private elevator, past the level where Turnovsky lived, to the presidential suite on the thirty-sixth floor.

He was left alone in an elegant, high-ceilinged room decorated in period French, with crystal chandeliers and gold-leafed carvings of cupids and nymphs. If he had not been especially nervous before, he was now. He was beginning to feel as though he was at what might prove to be the great terminus of his life. Too dramatic. It could also turn out to be nothing.

The door opened, and Turner stood up as the president came forward to greet him. Woodruff was in dinner clothes, but his shirt collar was open, his tie hung loose, and he looked like a tired, aging business man who wanted nothing so much as to get off alone in the sun somewhere. The amenities dispensed with, Turner waited, fidgeting with his cigarette. He was sitting face to face with the president of the United States, just the two of them in a room, and the full weight of it had settled on him like a mountain. The president looked at him across the coffee table.

"I'm sure you're as tired as I am, Paul, so I'll get straight to the point. Frances indicated you knew of your wife's work for the KGB. Is that true?"

"Yes, Mr. President."

"May I ask how you found out?"

"It was after Maria had died. I came across some suspicious-looking material in a wall safe and brought it to Wendell Handley. He told me."

"It must have been a terrible shock for you."

Turner said nothing.

In the light of a pair of wall sconces, Woodruff's face was bleached wood. "Were you aware that Maria and I knew one another many years ago, long before I became president?"

"No, sir."

"We first met when I was chairman of the Federal Communications Commission. She headed a reform panel for me. She was extraordinary even then. A tremendous help. In time, we became extremely close friends."

Christ. Not *him*, too.

Woodruff seemed to read his mind. "It was all innocent enough. Besides enjoying an excellent marriage, I was too po-

232

litically ambitious to risk any hint of impropriety. But good friends we were, and we remained so until her untimely death." He shook his head. "Incredible. A coronary at the age of thirty-four. A woman like that."

Turner was watching the president's face. He meant it. He didn't know. It was a disappointment. He had been depending upon the fabled magic of the presidency to somehow conjure up a miracle. Instead, Woodruff apparently knew less than he did about Maria's death.

"I don't know if you're familiar with my personal history, Paul, but after leaving the FCC I was made director of the Central Intelligence Agency. The Company was in trouble in those days, and the president wanted an outsider to help clean up its image. It was no easy job. My appointment caused great resentment among the careerists. So, not knowing whom I could trust inside, I sometimes went outside the agency for my people. And one of those I went to was Maria."

Woodruff paused, and in the following silence Turner felt a trickle of sweat slide down his back.

"Consider Maria's background: Her parents were Ukrainian émigrés, she spoke Russian fluently, she had been raised in an insulated Ukrainian enclave steeped in old country traditions, and she had many relatives still living in Russia. All of which, together with her work in the media, made her a very appealing candidate for KGB recruitment."

"Then it was they who made the original approach?"

"Yes. But not without a little subtle prodding. I let word filter through about her potential, and they swallowed it whole." Woodruff smiled somewhat wistfully. "In a year's time, Maria was the most productive agent the KGB had operating in this country. And there was not a piece of information or disinformation that she passed to them that was not carefully selected by us. Maria was the best we had, Paul. When Frances told me you had somehow discovered the mask she wore all those years . . . when I realized what it must be doing to you, I felt I had to tell you the truth."

Ah, God. Curiously, Turner felt no joy, no exhilaration. If

233

he felt anything at all, it was a bottomless sorrow. "Why in God's name didn't Handley tell me all this?"

"Because he didn't know."

Turner showed his disbelief.

"It's the truth, Paul. Only the present director of the CIA and I ever knew Maria was our own. It's the only way she could have survived as long as she did. Every intelligence service has leaks. Even the best."

Something exploded in Turner's brain. There was no reason for Maria to have died. If Handley had known she was ours, he would have realized his people were never really threatened. It was the most bitter irony imaginable. Rage stifled his breath. He wanted to scream. He wanted to stand up before this tired-looking, decent man who was the president of the United States and shout, *She didn't have to die. There was no need, no need.* Then he breathed deeply and retrieved a fine edge of sanity. From a long way off, he heard Woodruff talking.

"Maria was more valuable to me than I could ever explain. Not only when I headed the CIA, but when I became president. Perhaps more so then. Because the higher you go, the fewer there are to trust. You're constantly surrounded by predatory, self-serving political animals. Maria's single loyalty was to me, and I never had reason to doubt her."

"I was her husband," Turner said flatly. "What about her loyalty to me?"

"That was my fault. I ordered her not to share this even with you. It was never an easy order for her to obey. But when she said she wanted to get married, I left her no choice."

Of course. Woodruff had been sleeping with her, too. Never mind his earlier disclaimer. It was patently impossible for him to have worked for so long and in such close association with a woman like Maria and not end up in bed with her. Her legs had opened and closed as easily as a pair of scissors. Okay. So his wife had been a whore. Or did a whore do it only for money? What the hell. At least she hadn't sold out her country. Only her poor *shmuck* of a husband.

"I know none of this can be easy," said Woodruff quietly, "but I thought you might feel better knowing the truth."

He was tempted to reciprocate with another truth. He was tempted to tell the president that Maria had been needlessly murdered because of his idiotic secrecy. God almighty. A pack of killer paranoiacs playing their own lunatic version of blindman's-buff. But he held back. It was not out of kindness. It was just that he still wanted to keep something in reserve. So all he said was, "I appreciate it, Mr. President."

Descending in the elevator, a string of appropriate homilies passed through him in a cynical parade. *The husband is the last to know. Love is blind. Never give all the heart to love, for everything that is lovely is but a brief, dreamy kind of delight.* He kept adding to the litany, piling stone upon stone as though building a memorial whose weight would finally crush him. But the worst was still that she had died for nothing. This, above all, remained beyond acceptance.

It had often seemed lovely during the search-and-destroys in the rice fields, where sudden death was everywhere, but so, also, was the gold haze under a late sun, and the cranes hovering lightly as mocking-birds, and the bamboo huts reflecting in the water. It was all so peaceful, so beatific. Until the first shots went off and the water slowly turned red.

There was not even the muted joy of vindication. The senselessness of her death had robbed him of even that. He felt cheated. He had not given up. He had stayed with it against all evidence, all logic. He had believed when there was no reason to believe. His rage, his despair, his hurt, his clinging to her memory had made him an instrument of truth, and all he had dug up was a wasted corpse. He felt worse than before. He felt a nostalgia for death, almost wishing he were back in Vietnam with lightning in his hands and power

235

enough to blow holes in sky and earth. He was in mourning all over again. How many times could she die? He floated between fury and frustration. He laughed wildly, then dissolved into tears. And, perhaps most frightening of all, he was suddenly without a goal. His strength, his support, his greatest crutch had been his obsession. Like a madman he had set out to prove that black could be white, had proven it, and found himself impaled on the result.

Still, he put a decent face on it. He was not about to indulge himself further. So that telling Peggy, his eyes were bright, his manner cool, his voice crisp. He could feel himself projecting victory. He had showed them all. And against impossible odds. His wife, by God, had been a martyred patriot, not a traitor. Hallelujah!

Peggy listened, not quite looking at him, her face shadowed by a lock of falling hair. She had a habit of fooling with her hair when she was tense, of nervously pulling and teasing it, and her fingers had not stopped. She was frowning. Three fine lines plucked at her brows. When he had finished, she said, "What is it now, Paul?"

"What's what?"

"You're having a quiet nervous breakdown."

He sighed. "And I thought I was carrying it off pretty well."

"Sure, darling."

"Those crazy sons-of-bitches killed her for nothing. One end eats and the other shits without knowing it. From top to bottom there's no coordination, no trust. She didn't have to die at all."

"Okay. What else?"

He hesitated. "I'm sure Woodruff was fucking her, too."

"And that bothers you?"

"What the hell do you mean bothers me? Jesus Christ! My wife is turning out to have been a goddamned CIA groupie."

"Fine. Then stop eating your heart out. If you feel that way about it you can always tell yourself she got pretty much what she deserved."

He glared at her.

"It's what we in the literary field enjoy calling poetic justice."

"Damn you! Don't do that to me."

She smiled benignly.

It was different with Fran. She was, after all, the president's daughter. He was not about to tell her he was sure her father had been involved in a long-term, adulterous relationship with his late wife. Nor could he mention the tragic irony of Maria's having been unwittingly destroyed by one of her own. Not even Woodruff was aware of that. So all that remained for him to share of his meeting with her father was the discovery that his wife had been a patriot rather than a traitor. Admittedly, no small thing. . . yet suddenly so affected by what had to remain unstated that it had turned sour for him.

But not for Fran. She beamed. She hugged him. She danced her own small dance of joy. "I'm so happy for you, Paul."

"It was really you who did it."

She looked at him.

"If you hadn't complained to your father about my not getting clearance, I'd never have found out."

The thought sobered her. "How awful. I can't think of anything worse."

Turner could.

He had saved his uncle and Hank for last. These two would be judgmental, and he had needed time to prepare himself. He had made a discovery. It was not within him to live without others. Having found this out only after losing

237

the one who was closest to him, he was left with an almost desperate need to communicate, to make contact, to reach for and share knowledge with those of his own species. It was a way of soothing the ache of loneliness. He had never known it could go this deep. He knew now.

He also felt a certain pleasure in the responses of Turnovsky and his lady. They admired him. They displayed wonder at what he had achieved. Having known what he faced, having tried to discourage him from the beginning, they were that much more responsive to what his faith had revealed. Worldly and cynical, they were still willing to pay ungrudging homage to the believer in their midst. Which did not mean the bitterness was lost on them . . . or, indeed, the irony. They were familiar with both, were longtime experts on the double-edged sword that cut both ways. So that their understanding, their sympathy, and their anger were as real as their other responses.

But perhaps most of all, they were moved. Turnovsky, because it was his way, put on his *tallis*, bent his head like an orthodox Jew before the Wailing Wall, and chanted a prayer for his nephew's martyred wife. The gangster and God, thought Turner. Yet he was touched. Who else was there to chant, to intercede for her? Maybe it changed nothing, but how could it hurt? Indeed, he found a curious comfort in it, as if these ancient Hebrew words that he did not even understand, which were being recited by a man whose life, in the eyes of God, was surely less than exemplary, would somehow get through and make a difference. As for Hank, this often hostile New England lady gazed warmly at him, and in her thickly lashed eyes he seemed to have achieved something of lasting importance. She made him feel this. See what you have done for love, said her eyes . . . see where your faith has taken you. Where, indeed. Still, after months of turmoil, he allowed himself to be lulled into a deceptive calm.

Turnovsky had finished his chanting. In his *tallis* and *yarmulkah* and with his solid build, he had the bearing of a Maccabean general. He looked at Turner; all communion with

238

God had fled his face. That part, the mourning, was through. He was already in the next phase. "Something bothers me, Pauly. Since it now turns out your Maria was working for the president, don't you think she would have told this to Handley at the reception?"

"She hadn't told him for ten years. Why, suddenly, then?"

Turnovsky lit up one of his Cubans. "To keep from dying."

Hank cut in. "Come on, Herschel. Do you really think the woman knew she was about to be poisoned?"

"Obviously not. But she had to know the danger of her position. To Handley, she was KGB, a loaded gun at the heads of eight of his people. She had to know he was not about to just write them off."

"What are you getting at, Uncle Herschel?"

"I think we've been fools. We've talked, we've figured, we've added up, and finally we know only what was put there for us to know."

"Stop that," said Hank. She sounded angry. "You're imagining things. It's finished. Even Paul finally knows that."

"Not really," said Turner.

She turned on him. "You came here tonight riding a cloud. You had scrubbed your Maria clean. Don't let Herschel spoil it for you."

"It's not just Uncle Herschel. I must have had my own doubts. If I didn't, I'd have told Woodruff Maria was murdered."

No one spoke, and the room closed in on them. Even the paintings seemed diminished, their colors somehow faded. Hank appeared ready to attack them both. "All right," she said. "If you two are still so hot about this, why hasn't anyone even mentioned the one person besides Handley who knows Maria was murdered? What was the name of the agent who blundered that night and actually caused the whole thing?" She looked at Turner. "Did Handley ever say?"

"Yes. I think he said his name was Rieson . . . or Rosen . . . or maybe Rorrson. Something like that."

239

Hank dug out a copy of the reception guest list that Mutsie had stolen and studied it. "There's a Herbert Rawson here . . . with a New York address and the title of vice president of production for the Spartacus Oil Company."

"That's the name. Except that Handley said he had buried him in Africa. I'll make a call tomorrow and find out exactly where."

Turnovsky chewed at his cigar. "And when you do find out?"

"I'll probably go over and have a little talk with him."

"Talking to you isn't something he's going to be very happy to do."

Turner smiled. "I'll make him a proposition he can't refuse."

"Don't be so smart. I can contact people and make things easier."

"Thanks, but I think I can manage, Uncle Herschel."

"And if it turns out you thought wrong?"

"Then I'll yell."

"With a mouthful of dirt?"

Hank did not look happy. "I know this was my idea, Paul, but I'm still not very sure how productive it can be. Would Handley really have been stupid enough to mention Rawson by name, unless he knew his version of what happened would corroborate his own?"

"Not if he considered it coldly. But I'm hoping he may have been upset enough at that moment to have just let it slip out."

Hank seemed to regret having brought up Rawson at all. She's afraid . . . she doesn't want anything to happen to me, thought Turner, and somehow he found such a possibility more appealing than he was prepared to admit or understand at that moment.

He called the Spartacus Oil Company early the next morning and was told that Herbert Rawson had been transferred to the firm's installation in Lagos, Nigeria, where he could be contacted by mail, cable, or telephone.

EIGHTEEN

The Present

The last time Turner had been in a place anything like this had been thirteen years ago, in Saigon, where he was suffering the gnawing, indiscriminate lust of a soldier on leave. The tiny, doll-like Vietnamese dancers had shaken and jiggled what little extra flesh they had, and the crowd of hungry grunts in the stifling bar had shouted obscenities in three languages over their beers. It had all been less than noble, less than joyous, and, in its own way, as wantonly dehumanizing as the war itself. Yet he had gone home afterward with one of the dancers, a child, it seemed, although as practiced in her sexuality as any whore, and finally it was he who had felt like the child.

But the Jet Lounge, the topless bar in which he and Lewicki sat drinking tonight, was near Hagerstown, Maryland, rather than in Saigon; the girl dancing was tall and blonde and had heroic breasts; and most of the patrons were workers from nearby industrial plants. Bathed in a shimmering blue spot, the girl worked on a small stage at the rear of the lounge, bumping and grinding to the blare of a recorded rock beat that wiped out all other sound. Lewicki's head bobbed in time with the music. Huddled over the remains of his fourth whiskey, he licked at the dancer's flesh with glassy eyes. A half-naked waitress brought fresh drinks, and Lewicki patted

241

her behind fondly as Turner paid.

"Terrific." Lewicki drank and bobbed his head. "I'm loving every minute. You just keep buying and I'll keep drinking."

Turner seemed equally pleased with the arrangement.

"But I'm warning you. It won't work. Who ever heard of a Yid outdrinking a Polack?"

"We're learning."

"Hell, all I'm getting here is a hard-on."

"I'm sure that can be taken care of, too."

"Only if we're all in the same bed."

"You're on your own there, buddy."

"You mean you couldn't go for a nice friendly little orgy?"

"I'm Jewish. Remember?"

"Who do you think set up Sodom and Gomorrah?"

"That was a bit before my time."

Lewicki considered him over his whiskey. "Maybe so. But Vietnam wasn't. And I understand you were a real big hero over there . . . medals and everything. So don't try to impress me with any special claims to virtue."

The crowd whistled and stomped as the dancer did something wild with her pelvis. Turner nursed his whiskey. He could feel it moving from his stomach to his limbs "What's that supposed to mean?"

"It means I happen to have had a big hero brother over there. Third Marine Division. He came back with medals, too. He also came back with a fine collection of ears, noses, fingers, balls, and tits. So I know exactly what kind of action you hotshot heroes had going for yourselves."

Lewicki had to be drunker than he looked. And he was not turning out to be one of those happy, mindless drunks. "Well, we tried to take our small pleasures where we could."

"What kind of collection did *you* come back with?"

"Cocks. Best damned assortment of gook cocks this side of Saigon. Took the division title. Remind me to show them to you sometime."

"Stick 'em up your ass."

"That's for fags like you." Turner smiled sweetly. He had been pressing all day, pushing for long, hard stretches of driving with very few stops because he had wanted Lewicki to drink on an empty stomach tonight. But the detective's alcoholic belligerence seemed oddly out of character. Yet what did he really know about Lewicki's character? The man was perpetually on stage, a consummate performer. "You don't seem to care much for your brother."

"Care much? I hate his guts."

"Is he a cop, too?"

"Hell, he's nothing . . . a psycho at Kingsbridge General. I visit him once in while just for laughs. I like to make sudden noises and watch him hit the floor and shake. It's how I get my kicks. The dumb Polack had to be a fucking Marine. I mean, he *volunteered*, for Christ's sake. Couldn't wait to get out of school and join up. Well, he joined up all right. For life." Lewicki stared blankly at the dancer. "All crap aside, Turner, what did you guys think you were doing over there? I know war is hell and all that, but my brother told me things. . . . I swear to Christ I couldn't believe him at first. I thought he'd flipped even before he really did. Then he showed me his goddamned gook collection."

Turner said nothing.

"I'm talking to you, goddamn it!"

"I hear you."

The eyes were suddenly cold. "This is actually a big treat for me. I've never talked to a real live Jewish war hero before. I didn't even know there were any. I thought you Yids were too smart for that. I thought you left all that garbage for us *goyim*. What happened? Where did *you* go wrong?"

Turner put down his drink and lit a cigarette. This, too? His mother had said scratch any Christian deep enough, even the decent ones. . . . Still, it was a disappointment. It always was. Yet he had married one, and she had been a better Jew than he. "I guess I was just dumb, like your brother."

The blonde finished her number to cheers and applause

243

and disappeared behind a purple curtain. She was replaced almost immediately by an equally big-breasted redhead with a Caesarean-scarred stomach. Her nipples were small and pink, dainty rosettes, and her flesh glistened and shook. Turner glanced around. Every face seemed lost in its own fantasy. Heat rose in waves.

"Would you believe he's cut his goddamned wrists four times so far?" Back to his brother, Lewicki leaned across the table, his face tight and close. "The scars look like fucking bracelets. He can't even get *that* right. Sometimes he laughs about it. 'Hey, I'm some marine, huh? Can't even waste *myself.*' Other times he just sits there, hugging himself, rocking back and forth. Shit. My brother, the hero." He gripped Turner's wrist hard, painfully. "How come you're not like that?"

"There were times I think I could have been."

"Yeah, but you're not."

Turner waited until the hand on his wrist relaxed. "Some are luckier than others. I can at least write about it, burn it off that way. But never entirely. So there are still moments. Mostly, it's the waste. You keep taking the same hills, killing and dying . . . giving them back, killing and dying . . . taking them again, killing and dying. The thing is, it just goes on. There's no time to care, to cry, to mourn. You find you're an animal. And that's just the way it is. You fall home to death. Until finally there's just the blood and the dead, and you're still right there on the same lousy hill." He looked at the two bouncing breasts in front of him. "I'm sorry about your brother."

"Aah, fuck him. The asshole did it to himself. He had to be John Wayne with real bullets." Lewicki laughed. "He used to take me to all those idiot war movies on Saturday afternoons. Hollywood. Kill and be a big man. It was like your balls would grow with your body count."

"Don't kid yourself. It was true. That was one of the worst parts. The killing did make you feel real macho. There was a terrible kind of exhilaration in it. You were twenty feet

244

tall. A giant. An avenging God with lightning in your hands. It was grass, coke, and horse all in one. It was the worst of addictions, but its high was the absolute top. What could equal it? Christ, you were the Angel of Death. Then they sent you home, took away your lovely shooters, and made you quit cold turkey. Only not everyone was able to. So an awful lot of us ended up dead, in jail, or off the wall like your brother."

"How about in the cops?"

Turner gulped more whiskey than he had intended and felt it burn going down. "That too, I suppose." He thought of Taylor and Byrd, broken-necked and incinerated somewhere in the Virginia hills. "I must admit you did pretty well yourself back there this morning. How did *you* feel?"

"Like I had the balls of a bull." Lewicki made a loud sucking sound at the redhead, who grinned and tossed all she owned at him. A cornucopia of gifts. "Hey, what do you say, Turner? It's been a long, hard couple of days. You can have the blonde. I'll take little old scarbelly here."

It was the ultimate adolescent fantasy—eager hands moving softly over your flesh, a wealth of orifices, clinging and moist, primed with lust, insatiable. The bodies themselves were warm and anonymous, the breathing heavy, gasping, lascivious; and hanging over everything, like the smell of cordite over a battle in progress, were the combined odors of carnality, of nubile animals in rut, of cheap perfume and expensive whiskey.

I'm in a goddamned dirty movie, thought Turner. But he made no move to leave. Why should he? Was he in such a great rush to die? The *Malachamuvous* could wait. There would always be time to meet the Big Angel.

They were on the redhead's bed, in her room two floors above the Jet Lounge. It had not been especially difficult to get there. Lewicki had simply smiled his irresistible Polish smile, and all doors seemed to have opened for him. Turner, with some prodding, had done little more than follow. With a

245

smile and face like that, Lewicki was wasting himself in the cops. In six-months' time, he could out-Redford them all. Turner marveled at the results. The past several hours had been a wild, knowing, drowning experience, a sensual journey to the moon, a flood of lust that had swept away all the days of twisting and turning, all thought of what lay immediately ahead, all memory of the past months of anguish and searching. It was as if everything that had taken place before this moment had vanished on this bed, among these bodies, in the moonlit room. Yet nothing was loving here. There was no sign of tenderness. Four people were present, two men and two women, and each seemed to be alone. Whiskey and fatigue made Turner feel he had no brain left, but something bright and fierce was loose, bearing gifts of the circus. If Lewicki was ringmaster, Turner was surely a stallion, the two women at least star aerialists. Yet they were all hot, mean, greedy, and without glory. It was a battle, no, a street fight, full of the slum, to which they had brought their own weapons.

Still, nearing the end, there was a reluctant reaching out. If every coming carried its own small death, who, after all, wanted to die alone? So, finally, there was an instant of joining. Briefly, they were no longer apart. *Hold me. Love me, I'm dying.* Who wasn't?

Turner had dozed. Now he lay half awake, half in stupor. There was an open window opposite the bed, and the curtains moved in a light breeze. A pale haze of moonlight softened the outlines of a bureau, a dressing table, and a few chairs with small piles of clothing scattered over them. He felt a weight on his stomach. Shifting his eyes, he saw the blonde's head. The rest of her angled away. The feet on the pillow beside him belonged to the redhead, who lay clutching Lewicki with both arms, a child with her favorite stuffed animal. The two girls had names. They were not just random collections of soft curves and moist places in which to find pleasure

246

and take refuge. One was Marie, the other, Lucy. But which was which? It made him sad that he could not remember. They deserved better. *He* deserved better than a pair of anonymous bodies as his last sexual memory. Assuming, of course, that there was memory after death. Assuming, too, that he was going to die sometime during the next few days. There was no certainty of anything, but the odds did favor it. Even more so than during the war. He was surely more alone in this than he had ever been in combat. Or had he already forgotten how alone you could be in that? Still, this had to be different. There was not even anyone to talk to in this. In Nam there had at least been a commonality of purpose and fear. You had buddies, warm bodies close around you. You talked. You made ghoulish jokes. You screamed the same screams. The only person he had now was Lewicki, who was turning out to be full of surprises. An enigma. Not at all the same thing. And he was about to get rid of even him.

He looked across the bed at the detective. Lewicki's face was pressed against the redhead's breast, his lips were parted, he was breathing softly, and he seemed as innocent and content as a nursing infant. How vulnerable he looked in sleep, how gentle, how nonthreatening. Everyone did. We should be forced to look upon one another's sleeping faces. It might ease the distrust, soothe the general paranoia. Lewicki stirred, sighed, and snuggled against his pillow of flesh, sleeping his human sleep.

All right. Let's get on with it.

Moving slowly and carefully, Turner eased himself out from under the fair, slumbering head on his stomach, past the other two unconscious bodies, and off the bed. It took several moments to sift through the piles of scattered clothing (abandoned in so wild a rush two hours before) and pick out his own. Even so, one shoe remained missing. He crawled about on his hands and knees until he discovered it under the bureau and finally dressed in silence. Then he went through Lewicki's pockets and took his car keys. Not far away, a train whistle blew, its almost archaic sound still strangely moving in the night. He paused at the door and looked back. The three naked bodies had not stirred. They appeared pale and fragile in the moonlight, drained of life, fallen statues in a trampled garden. On Lewicki's face, Turner imagined he saw a sly, sensual smile of satisfaction. He stepped past the door and closed it softly behind him.

A rear stairway let him out among piles of garbage behind the kitchen. He checked his watch. It was not quite five o'clock. The lounge was shut down, quiet, dark except for security lights in back, where half a dozen cars remained scattered about the parking area. Turner huddled against the chill, lit a cigarette, and crossed the graveled lot to his car. He got in and turned on the ignition. The starter came alive, shattering the stillness and echoing off the nearby mountains, but the engine failed to catch. Turner depressed the gas pedal, released it slowly, and tried again. The engine still refused to start. Nor was it any better the next three times. He checked the gas gauge. It read more than half full, so it was probably dampness in the ignition wires. The windows and windshield dripped moisture. He swore softly and glanced back at the roadhouse, wondering if the cranking had awoken Lewicki. The place was still dark and quiet. Then, remembering he had both sets of keys, he hurried over to the detective's car, turned on the ignition, and eased down on the accelerator. It was the same thing all over again. The starter cranked all right, but the engine refused to catch. He got out and lifted the hood. But after checking for a possible loose battery cable, he had no idea what else to look for. He was back in his own car, trying again there, when Lewicki slid in beside him.

"What's the matter? Trouble starting?"

Turner inhaled deeply. His cigarette flared, lighting Lewicki's face. A night of drink and debauchery and the bastard still had the glow of a milk-fed choir boy.

"You disappoint me," said the detective. "I thought we'd become such good buddies. And you weren't even going to say goodbye."

The Present

Turner felt cold, tired, hungover, and utterly frustrated. What he did not feel very much like at that particular moment was playing straight man to Lewicki's cuteness.

"It's the rotor. The modern internal combustion engine absolutely refuses to function without the rotor. So I took the liberty of removing them. Just as a precaution, you understand."

"You mean you removed them from *both* cars?"

"They're easy enough to put back."

"I'm proud of you. I'm sure you'll go far."

The mountains were a black wall around them. Far off, Turner thought he heard the train whistle again. It seemed to be moving west. Lewicki held out his hand for a cigarette, and Turner gave him the pack. They sat smoking.

"All I'm trying to do is take care of you, Paul."

Another one trying to take care of him. They were evolving into a new religious order. Missionaries—Turner's Saviors. "Just put my goddamned rotor back where it belongs."

"First tell me why you're in such a big rush to drive off and get yourself killed."

"What are you talking about?"

"Don't you think it's time to start playing it straight with me? What do I have to do to prove I'm on your side, for Christ's sake?"

"Attach my rotor, kiss me goodbye, and go back to bed with the Dolly Sisters. Then you can have breakfast and start all over again."

Lewicki sighed. "Listen, I'm no cockeyed genius, but neither am I an idiot. It all adds up. You're chasing around with a loaded handgun and silencer in your pocket, a federal agency is worried enough to want you under twenty-four hour surveillance, and now you're trying to lose *me*, whom I know you love dearly. Which can only mean you're planning to quietly shoot somebody important. Except that with so many alerted, it can't possibly be quiet. All it can be is suicidal."

"You think I want to die?"

"Of course. You and my poor dumb brother. All you bloody heroes are alike. That's why you're heroes."

"Or smartass cops."

"I have no death wish."

"Keep following me much longer and we'll see."

Lewicki looked at him curiously. "Would you really kill me?"

"Only if you finally leave me no choice."

"There's always a choice."

"You know better than that."

Lewicki said nothing. He seemed to be thinking about it. When he finished his cigarette, he asked Turner for his keys and took the two rotors out of the trunk of his car. He reinstalled his own first, then Turner's. They left just as the sky was beginning to lighten over a humpbacked mountain to the east. Turner's Chevrolet was in front. Lewicki followed at his usual hundred-yard distance.

He did not know Lewicki's brother, but he knew the suicidals well. There had been three from Charley Company and four from his own outfit who had not fooled around, who had simply blown away substantial portions of their brains on their first tries. There had also been a lot of the others, those who had messed up and merely damaged themselves once or twice before they finally got it right. Unfortunately, no one in either group had ever learned the important thing, which was that ordinary life went on, that under the grace of daily routine, of getting up and going to the bathroom, of eating and working and dealing with small pleasures and anxieties, it was impossible to despise yourself at all times, to be continuously frightened, or to neverendingly flay yourself with remembered horrors. And because they had never learned this, they stared off with their hundred-mile stares and carried their pain like a skin disease on the surface, sensitive to the slightest touch, and scratched and tore at it until at last there was nothing left, only the dying.

250

NINETEEN

The Past

The guidebook had described Lagos as the biggest disaster area ever to pass for a city, and after being there less than three days, Turner was beginning to understand why. He was also beginning to understand the nature of Herbert Rawson's exile. Handley had not merely banished the agent to Africa for his fatal blunder, but seemed to have turned him into a kind of expatriate pariah. Solitary and friendless, Rawson appeared to be a joyless man who worked, ate, walked, drank, and slept almost entirely alone. But whether his seclusiveness had evolved through choice or necessity, Turner still had no way of judging. He had not even talked to the CIA agent as yet. He had just been observing him. The talking would come later that evening.

A great deal of time and effort had gone into simply arriving at this point. First, there had been the matter of his travel documents. Since no one other than Hank and his uncle were to know where he was going, he had to get a passport and visa under a false name. Turnovsky had offered to help, but he had turned him down because his uncle might be tainted by their past association and his efforts traced. So Turner had gone to Mutsie who, with his usual finesse, had arranged for a superb forgery by a cousin who was an artist at such things. Then, because a logical explanation for his absence seemed

251

provident, he invented a story about having to go back to Saigon (now called Ho Chi Minh City) to do some research for his novel . . . an idea inspired by Peggy's criticism that several of his more recent Vietnamese passages lacked convincing detail. Even so, when he admitted she was right and said he was going back to refresh his memory, she was immediately suspicious. "Why now?"

"You said there wasn't enough description and mood in the narrative passages."

"I've said the same things a dozen times before."

"This time I think you're right. I'm faking."

She brooded over it. "Maybe I can go with you. I'd love that."

"Could you get away?"

"No, darn it. I'm way behind on two deadlines now."

He let himself breathe again.

Fran was no problem. To her, writers were basically strange people who tended to behave in odd, unpredictable ways. So if Turner said he had to travel most of the way around the world in order to write more convincingly of fictional characters and events that might never have existed or happened at all, she saw no reason to doubt him. Her single concern seemed to be the doll-like Vietnamese women, whom she was certain Turner would find irresistible. "I resisted them before," he said.

"Yes, but then you were young, inexperienced, and a soldier. Now you're none of these things and therefore vulnerable."

He thought she probably had that backward, but he played his assigned part and reassured her. Pursuing the ghost of a dead woman, he seemed to be attracting a growing number of live women. Which surprised him since he had never really considered himself especially appealing to the opposite sex. What was it? His stubborn air of mourning, the wistful aura of lost love that seemed to cling to the recently bereaved? Even Hank had lately begun to signal a curious hint of warmth and feeling. Still, his primary concern remained a dead woman. These others all wanted to preserve him, to bring comfort, order, and happiness to his life, and his life remained elsewhere.

To Wendell Handley, along with his travel story, he had tossed a fresh bone—another section of Russian microfilm from Maria's cache. The deputy director was almost smug in his satisfaction at having figured it out correctly, at having deduced that Turner had a great deal more of his wife's material hoarded away for release at propitious moments. What he was still unable to resolve in his mind, and what seemed to be increasingly disturbing to him, was what Turner was finally going to want in return. In a world of dealing, there was no such thing as a free lunch. So he brought it up again. "I'm still waiting for some kind of bill, Paul."

"Can't I just be a patriot?"

"You once told me not to wave the flag at you."

"You're not. I'm the one waving it."

"And that makes such a difference?"

"This way it's my own choice."

"What about the rest of the material? You're going on a long trip. What if something happens to you?"

"My God, you're a worrier. How have you ever lasted so long in this business?"

"By being a worrier."

Turnovsky remained disapproving but philosophical about the whole concept of the trip. Wasn't everybody free to choose their own sacrifices, free to carve their will out of the void? Life was little more than one long argument with death anyway, and who could finally win it? If you were reasonable, all you could hope to do was postpone the decision. If you were less than reasonable, you closed your eyes, jumped up in the air, clicked your heels, and rushed blindly toward it. Turnovsky smiled, but it came out a sigh. "So what can you do, Pauly? You're not so different from me. We're both blind rushers."

Hank showed little love for such philosophy. It sounded negative to her. She was more interested in life's pleasures

253

than in its endings. She was a lawyer and therefore practical, a gangster's lady and therefore tough, but she also knew the value of joy, the bliss of food, the comfort of sleep, and the uses of the flesh and the spirit within the flesh. Still, those who spoke of joy often had sad eyes. Hank's eyes seemed especially so to Turner. They also seemed to expect more from him than he was able to understand or to offer. She kissed him goodbye with warm, scented lips. "Don't be more foolish than you absolutely have to." He looked into her face and saw familiar loneliness and unreasonable hope. But she was still a stranger.

He flew away from them all.

The trip was uneventful. Using his own passport, he took a TWA 747 to Rome and remained there for twenty-four hours to be certain he had not been followed. Then he boarded an early morning Alitalia flight under the forged documents of an imaginary Arthur Sonking. And after five intermediate stops, two plane changes, and fourteen hours, he landed in Lagos, Nigeria, along with thirty-two blacks and seven whites, none of whom so much as smiled, nodded, or said a word to him. Leaving the plane, he walked into a brilliant red and purple sunset that he could only have described as the ultimate cliché.

Downtown Lagos had a great many old houses built in the Brazilian baroque style brought back by repatriated slaves and a handful of high-rise commercial buildings in which the foreign oil companies responsible for most of Nigeria's recent wealth had their offices. The Spartacus Oil Company had its African headquarters in one of these buildings, on Yakubu Gowon Street, and Turner sat at a sidewalk café directly across the road, sipping a tall gin and tonic and watching the building's entrance. It was after 7:00 P.M., and almost everyone who worked in the building was long gone, but Turner knew that Rawson would not be coming out for close to another twenty minutes. He also knew that when the CIA agent did finally appear, he would walk up the block to another café, sit himself at an end table, have two drinks and a leisurely dinner, and take a taxi home at about ten o'clock. All of which he would do alone. At least this had been his pattern during the two evenings that Turner had spent observing him. And judging from the methodical, self-absorbed way Rawson moved and functioned, it seemed unlikely that the routine would be varied tonight.

The evening was warm despite a sea breeze, but Turner had on a seersucker jacket and a wide-brimmed cocoa straw hat that he kept tilted low over his eyes. He had reasons for wearing both. The jacket was to hide the revolver in his belt, the hat, to cover as much as possible of his face. He had no way of knowing whether Rawson would recognize him even if he did see his face, but he thought it best to play it safe. His attention was focused on the building across the street, yet he missed little of Lagos's colorful bustle. Barefoot mothers with babies slung over their backs walked side by side elegantly dressed Europeans. Donkeys raced with Mercedes. Beggars and robed tribesmen jostled oil millionaires. Horns honked, and drivers shouted and swore in four tribal and three European languages and English. Turner sat drinking his gin.

At exactly 7:45, Rawson appeared. He was a tall, thin, slightly stooped man with sandy hair, a man slow in movement and locked in himself, whose wrinkled tropicals looked as though they had not been taken off in a week. Gazing straight ahead, he seemed to float through the crowd, his head a full six inches above everyone else's. He sat down at his usual table at the café up the street, keeping his back toward Turner. A waiter brought his drink. Fifteen minutes later, the waiter brought him another drink. And half an hour after that, he was served his dinner. Turner ordered also. Following his guidebook's advice to avoid European dishes in favor of Nigerian, he had *egusi* soup, which was made from ground melon seeds, and pepper chicken. Surprisingly, he found he was enjoying the native food. Never an adventurous eater, he even avoided such popular bottom crawlers as crab, lobster, and the like. *Feh!* his mother had said, and *feh!* his stomach still responded. In Lagos, however, he seemed to have suspended his prejudices.

At 10:17, Rawson paid his check, hailed a taxi, and drove off. Turner lit a fresh cigarette to have with his coffee. There was no need to follow immediately. He knew where Rawson lived. It would be better, in fact, to allow him time to settle in. Half an hour later, he waved down his own cab and told the driver to take him to Victoria Island.

The city of Lagos was made up of four islands and the mainland. Lagos Island, which Turner was now leaving, was the commercial center, and most of it was covered with office buildings, shops, and restaurants. In the northwest section of the island, the residential area, the population density was higher than in a Manhattan slum, and even at this hour the streets were jammed with children and animals. They crossed by causeway to a more pastoral island, Ikoyi, then drove south to Victoria, a racially mixed oasis of the richer Lagosians and expatriates. This was where Herbert Rawson lived.

Turner had the driver let him out a quarter of a mile from the agent's villa, and he walked the rest of the way. The house itself was set well back from the road, at the end of a sweeping lawn and behind heavy tropical shrubbery, but was modest in size, a white, single-story bungalow with dark shutters and screened-in porches on two sides. It was well lit inside and out, perhaps a bit too well lit for a man living alone. It said he was lonely, frightened, or both. Turner walked up to the door and rang the bell. He waited beneath a wrought-iron lantern that shone down on his wide-brimmed straw hat and kept his face in shadow. He had planned it so, and he congratulated himself.

He felt metal against the flesh at the back of his neck. "Put your hands up." The voice was quiet, cool, relaxed to the point of boredom, and distinctly New England. "Slowly, please. No sudden moves."

He did as he was told. Congratulations, *shmuck*.

A hand came around and moved lightly over his body. He could see long, slender fingers and overgrown nails. The pistol in his belt was removed. It occurred to him that he should

256

say something. "Is this typical Lagosian hospitality?"

"Open the door and go inside please, Mr. Turner."

He entered the house. More than anything, he felt outclassed.

"Sit down in that chair to the right. And you may as well take off that ridiculous hat."

Seated, he had his first close look at Rawson's face, which was as long and spare as his body, with tight skin, sharp bones, and eyes so pale they looked blind when the light caught them. It was a face that reminded one of blue fiords, ice, and trackless snow, and in five thousand years, thought Turner, the Jews had never produced anything even remotely like it. "How did I give myself away? I thought I was careful."

Rawson sat halfway across the room. A .38-caliber revolver looked like a toy in his hand. "Your procedures weren't bad. It's just that I always expect the worst and never stop looking for it. Besides, I knew your face."

"I didn't know yours."

"Mine isn't on book jackets. I also had long-term dealings with your wife. In such cases, I like to know about any close family." He seemed to settle inside his clothes. "Now suppose you tell me why you've traveled six thousand miles to my doorstep with a loaded gun in your belt and the name of Sonking on your passport."

"I think I could use a drink."

"There's gin in that cabinet. Please pour two. Carefully. Put mine on the coffee table."

Turner fixed the drinks and returned to his chair, which was wicker. As was the rest of the furniture. Very tropical. The walls, however, were covered with nineteenth-century American genre paintings, as weirdly out of place in that setting as their owner.

"All right, Mr. Turner, I'm listening."

He hesitated. He was still off balance. This was not how he had planned it. "I came to talk to you."

"Six thousand miles? I'm not that brilliant a conversationalist."

257

"I've found out how my wife died."

The pale eyes measured him. "Who told you?"

"Wendell Handley."

"Fine. Then what did you want from me?"

"Corroboration."

"And you planned on getting it with a gun?"

"I wasn't sure how cooperative you'd be."

Rawson laughed. It had the sound of breaking glass. "You could be a dangerous man, Mr. Turner. But since you've come all this way, why don't you let me hear exactly what the deputy director told you. Then, perhaps, we'll have something to talk about."

It was not, of course, his first telling, and the gin did help, but it was still not easy for him. It still came out as a gothic tale that iced his veins. Rawson listened in silence, his eyes flat, his face drained of expression. When Turner had finished, he just sat looking at him for several moments. Then he said, "So Handley implied it was my careless blunder that actually caused your wife's death?"

"Yes."

"Then what you really came down here for was to shoot me in reprisal."

"No. I came down to ask you if it was true."

Rawson sat holding the .38 in one hand and his drink in the other. He might have been at a cocktail party. Still, even his silence exerted a deadly force. "Tell me, Mr. Turner, from what you've observed of me and my modus operandi so far, do I really strike you as the kind of man who would do anything as foolish, as criminally irresponsible, as the kind of blunder Mr. Handley described?"

"Anyone can make a mistake."

"Not like that. I've worked covertly for The Company for more than twenty years, Mr. Turner. Two decades in a pressure cooker. You don't seek public credit for these things. You choose your path and you follow it. I'm not a political animal like Mr. Handley. I'm not interested in having my picture in *Time* or climbing the power ladder. I'm content to work quietly for what I consider a basically decent cause. Though I admit it can be very cold and lonely." He stared vaguely at Turner as though forgetting for the moment who he was talking to and why. "But the point is, in all this time I've never been careless enough to make any sort of mistake that resulted in the loss of a single human life. I take life too seriously to squander it. Nor do I take pride or joy even in the death of an enemy. When I've had to kill, I've killed sparingly, remorsefully, and with deep sorrow. So perhaps you can understand my resentment at being made the fool of Mr. Handley's personal passion play."

"Are you telling me it was all a lie?"

"To begin with, there's something about Maria you should know. She was not really working for the KGB. She was actually an American double agent." Something must have shown in Turner's face. "You knew this?"

"Yes."

"How? I'm sure neither Maria nor Mr. Handley ever told you."

"The president did." Turner felt choked, as though his lungs had begun filling with blood. "He also told me he and the CIA director were the only ones who knew."

"That's what he believed."

"Then if you knew, Handley knew too."

"Naturally. So you can see my alleged blunder was just part of the story you forced him to create for your benefit."

Turner saw, yet he did not see. Handley had known Maria was really no threat, and he had killed her anyway? There was a bitter taste in his mouth that the gin was unable to wash away.

"It was Maria herself who told Mr. Handley of her arrangement with the president." Rawson seemed mildly amused. "By any standards, Mr. Turner, your wife was a most unusual woman."

"Why would she risk her security by telling him?"

"She obviously didn't consider it a risk. There was, after all, considerable feeling between them."

Turner sat holding himself together. "And the president never even knew she had told him?"

"No. In a way, Maria was really in business for herself. She had her own needs and made her own rules. There are no pure altruists in this world, Mr. Turner, not even on the side of the angels. Maria's addiction was intrigue. She loved to outfox the foxes. Machiavelli would have adored her. The Borgias would have kissed her feet. She could balance all the subtle intricacies of six lives and never lose control of one. The only reason she failed at the end was because she broke one of her own cardinal rules and allowed sentiment to cloud her usually clear judgement. It was such a foolish waste."

Turner sat staring dimly at the .38. There was a high-pitched animal sound somewhere out in the bush, and he listened thoughtfully to it. "How do I know you're not just playing games with me like everyone else?"

"You don't. But why would I lie to you?"

"You people don't need a reason. You lie by instinct."

"Through necessity would be more accurate. But I have the gun, Mr. Turner, so I can allow myself the unusual indulgence of telling the truth."

"Even about Maria's death?"

"Even that. If I thought it might serve some purpose."

"How about if it kept me from killing you?"

Rawson laughed, and this time there was genuine amusement in it. "I must say you're an extraordinary man, Mr. Turner. I don't know anyone else who would say that while looking into a gun muzzle."

"You have just two ways of keeping me from blowing your head off. You can either shoot me right now or tell me the truth about Maria's death. I've had enough bullshit. I'm up to my fucking ears in it. So take your choice. Pull the goddamned trigger or start talking."

Rawson looked at him for a long, icy moment. "I believe you. There are those of us who do sometimes lose our normal sensitivity to fear. It may mean we're temporarily insane, but that only makes us more dangerous." A flush of excitement came off him, and he suddenly seemed like a big, unchained animal. "All right, Mr. Turner. I'll tell you the truth. In a way, I suppose you deserve it. Anyone who wants something that badly has a right, finally, not to be thwarted. But I doubt that it will make you very happy."

Turner sat silent and unmoving, afraid to upset the delicate point of balance upon which this curious man's intentions seemed to rest.

"Do you know what a mole is?" said Rawson. "And I don't mean the fur-bearing kind."

Turner had a fair idea, but shook his head.

"In trade jargon, the term refers to an agent who is secretly working for an enemy intelligence service. In the case at hand, Mr. Handley was himself running his own extremely valuable mole. In fact, his mole was actually inside the KGB's Moscow headquarters, a man so well placed that he all but gave us our own listening post in the Kremlin. That is, until a power struggle within the KGB itself threatened his position and, consequently, our own. To keep this from happening, Mr. Handley conceived of a unique plan to bolster his man's weakening status in the KGB. The method he chose was cold and hard but absolutely ingenious. It called for him to sacrifice two of his own undercover networks in Poland and Czechoslovakia, to actually reveal his agent's identities to the mole, so the Russian would appear to have carried out the coup himself and consequently would achieve new strength and favor."

Turner suddenly thought he sensed movement, a presence, through the porch screening behind Rawson's back. Then it was gone. Or had he imagined it, a vague dark shape against a lesser darkness? "Are you saying his own people would be killed?"

"Precisely. Eight Poles and Czechs would be sacrificed in the hope of saving many more than that number of American lives sometime in the future."

"And, of course, those would be the same eight Poles and Czechs Handley had supposedly saved by killing Maria?"

There was almost a terrible kind of symmetry beginning to take shape in it all.

"Now you're getting the idea."

"Jesus Christ!"

"In any event, Mr. Handley was justifiably proud of his little scheme. So proud, in fact, that he foolishly violated a basic tenet of intelligence tradecraft that declares unequivocally that no one is to be told anything about a top-secret operation such as this except on a need-to-know basis." The pale eyes seemed to be smiling. "Where women are concerned, some men, regardless of how mature and brilliant they may otherwise be, somehow remain little boys doing handsprings to impress the girl next door. So on the night of the British reception, with perhaps a bit too much champagne in him, with Maria as beautiful and mercurially beguiling as only she could be at such times, Mr. Handley did his own series of handsprings and boasted to her of his cleverness."

"He told her about the plan?"

"Unfortunately, yes. And it exploded in his face. Maria surprised him. She again demonstrated her incredible unpredictability. Instead of admiring the idea, she was horrified by it. She blasted it as barbaric, inhuman, and God only knows what else. To waste one's own, for whatever the purpose, was unthinkable. She was so furious that she threatened to expose the entire plan to the president that night if Mr. Handley did not promise to abandon it."

A devil's messenger reached Turner's brain. He lit a cigarette, and in the flare of the match he was again dimly aware of an amorphous presence behind the porch screen.

"Maria's threat was a big mistake." Rawson gazed abstractedly at his pistol, then at Turner, as though confirming an earlier commitment. "If you intend to do something, you do it. You don't talk about it. A threat only acts as a warning. In this instance, Mr. Handley agreed to Maria's request. Then he went ahead and did what had to be done."

"Just like that?"

"No. Not just like that. These things always seem simpler and colder in the telling than they ever really are. In all fairness, Mr. Handley cared deeply for your wife. He had to make a terrible choice. He knew the president would have wiped out the plan. Mr. Woodruff is a politician and a humanist. That's why he once failed so miserably as CIA director. He's not qualified to make such judgments. So Mr. Handley was forced to do the only thing possible under the circumstances."

"Are you saying you agree with what he did?"

"Agree? It was I who gave him the cyanide."

Turner wanted to pick up a lamp, an ashtray, a bottle, a chair, anything at all and beat out his brains. Some part of this feeling must have showed because Rawson's hand tightened perceptibly on the gun. "Control your emotions, Mr. Turner. There were no practical alternatives. Maria was a professional. She should have known that."

This time Turner could actually make out a shape. Someone had been out on the porch listening all the while. "And Handley's eight Poles and Czechs are as dead as she?"

"The plan has already more than justified its cost." His eyes locked into Turner's. Then he shrugged. "I told you it wouldn't make you happy."

"What's the difference? You're going to shoot me anyway."

Rawson smiled the ironic smile of a final arbiter. "I wish it were safe to let you loose."

"Safe for whom?"

"For Mr. Handley, of course."

"I've never tried to do him damage before."

"Ah, but you didn't know the truth before."

Turner could not think of a single argument. It would have changed nothing anyway. To Rawson, he had been as good as dead from the moment he threatened him. Perhaps even from the moment he stepped off the plane in Lagos. Rawson's eyes were startlingly candid. All was settled.

The agent put down his drink, stood up, took a silencer

from his pocket, and fitted it to the .38. "I'm genuinely sorry about this. But as a writer you're probably more aware than most of the mortality of our passions, of the compromises and disillusionments worked by time. So dying young isn't always the terrible tragedy it seems."

"Save your two-bit philosophy. I have something a lot more comforting."

"What's that?"

"Someone on the porch with a gun on your back."

Rawson's smile was faintly superior. "Such a tired old dodge. It's really unworthy of you, Mr. Turner."

"Don't dismiss it. The moment you raise and aim that gun, you're going to take a bullet in the back of your head."

The agent started to lift his arm. Then he laughed and let it fall of its own weight. "It's an odd thing. I know there's no one back there. I know you're just making a last, desperate stab at one of the most obvious tricks in the book. I know for certain that no one came to Lagos with you because I keep a constant check on all airport arrivals. Yet I must admit I'm still tempted to glance around."

"He didn't come with me. He flew into Accra and came overland."

"You're handling this well. It's beginning to interest me." Rawson slowly sat down. The color in his face had deepened. "It makes what I have to do a bit more bearable." He studied Turner as though seeking hidden signs, perhaps a reason for delay. He found it. "I'd like to ask a personal question. I respect you. You're clearly a very straight, very principled, very moral man. How have you been able to accept your wife's infidelity so well?"

"Who said I've accepted it?"

"You've come a long way for Maria. You're near to dying for her. Yet I've heard no recrimination."

"She's dead. I don't have to go home tonight and look at her face. I don't have to go on living with her."

Rawson was staring curiously at him. "My wife was unfaithful, too. The day I found out, I left the house and never saw her again. That was twenty-three years ago, and I love her as much today as I ever did. I've never loved another woman. I don't suppose you can really afford that luxury in this business. Mr. Handley's experience with Maria is a perfect case in point. And he's one of our best. Which is why I'm being forced to take this unhappy action. It's just your bad luck that he happens to be less expendable than you."

"Less expendable to whom?"

The agent looked mildly surprised. "Why to the country, of course. I thought you understood that."

"Forgive me. Sometimes I'm a little slow."

The irony was wasted. Rawson was somewhere else. "Which is too bad. Because in many ways you're far more admirable a representative of our less than noble species than Mr. Handley. It's just that he happens to be precisely what The Company needs during our current crises of faith and national confusion. So it's important that he be preserved."

"How about preserving me, too?"

"Your primitive vision of justice wouldn't permit it."

The man was right. Turner considered diving for the gun, but knew he would never make it. He stared hard at the shadowy form behind the screen. Whose friend was it? Not his. He had no friends here. But probably not Rawson's either. No friend would lurk in the darkness of a man's porch.

The agent rose once more. "Stand up please, Mr. Turner."

"I don't think so."

"Don't make it harder than it is."

"I'm not making it anything. I'm just sitting here. If you want to shoot me this way, go ahead and try. But I'm telling you again—you'll never make it."

The room and the night were silent. The .38 with its long silencer hung loosely at Rawson's side. Turner sat looking up at the agent's eyes. Whatever the odds, he had to dive at the first movement of the gun. His legs were water, and his stomach felt sucked out of him. Who said you finally stopped being afraid? Even Rawson was no longer enjoying it. There

265

was a new emptiness in his face that Turner sensed he could enter.

"One last time, Mr. Turner. I'd rather not do it this way. But if I have to, I will."

Turner stared into the void. He had looked into it before, but it was never the same. *Maruschka.* His eyes filled helplessly with her. Why have you brought me here?

Then a breath came out of the darkness, a faint whisper, nothing more. It was so soft it was barely audible, but Rawson whirled at the sound, firing twice as he spun—*whoosh . . . whoosh.* A single unsilenced shot followed. Turner saw the gun-flash behind the screening. Rawson fell backward, wearing a crown of blood. He lay silent and unmoving at Turner's feet. His pale eyes stared at the ceiling. He seemed terribly tired, as if he had been carrying an impossible weight for too long.

Turner looked out at the porch, but saw only dark gray and black. He took the gun from Rawson's hand and went outside. No one was there. He searched until he found three bullet holes in the screening. Far off in the African night, an animal wailed. It was sad, like a siren in Harlem.

He left Lagos on the afternoon flight to Rome. He studied the faces of the other passengers, looking for possible hints. There were none. At thirty thousand feet he began to wonder why, if Rawson had made no blunder that last night, Handley had banished him to Africa.

TWENTY

The Present

He drove straight to Washington on Interstate 76 without a break. Then he turned southwest and headed for Arlington. The cemetery gates opened at 6:00 A.M. At exactly 6:20, he pulled up at an approach road, parked the Chevrolet, and walked in. None of the living were in sight.

Lewicki caught up with him on one of the footpaths. He asked no questions, and Turner offered no answers. It was daylight, but a heavy ground fog rose from the grass and cut off the sun and the tops of trees. White headstones stretched off into the gray mists. Turner set the pace, and they walked slowly, almost casually. The only sound was their footsteps on the path. They passed the eternal flame of John Fitzgerald Kennedy and the statues of three Union generals on horseback. Farther up a long, gentle slope were the Civil War dead. They were followed by acre after acre of the Spanish-American War dead, the World War I dead, the World War II dead, the Korean War dead, and finally, spilling out over the most recently developed acreage across Arlington Ridge Road and seeming to stretch to infinity, were the markers of those who had died in Vietnam.

Shivering in the early morning chill, Turner lit a cigarette. He suddenly stopped walking and stood among the white crosses and scattered Stars of David. He slowly turned and looked about him as if, staring through the mist, he was being given a glimpse into a future he did not especially like, but did not dare to miss.

"You're almost there, aren't you?" said Lewicki.

"Where?"

"Where you've been heading all this time."

Turner huddled inside his raincoat, moving his feet in the wet grass, still turning.

"What are you doing? Picking out a good spot for yourself?"

Turner did not seem to hear him. "Even dead we're different from the rest." He stretched out an arm, circling, to embrace the Vietnam section. "They've given us no statues, no memorials, no noble sentiments etched in stone. I used to come here when I was convalescing at Walter Reed. It was the only place I could feel comfortable. My friends were here. No one else seemed to understand what it was all about."

He started to walk once more, moving slowly among the markers, Lewicki beside him. "With all the killing and blood, maybe even because of it, I swear we had a very real kind of love going. All those crazy, death-spaced grunts, saying all those godawful, heartbreaking things they always said and making believe they were so nonchalant about it. Then I'd hear the politicians and protestors on the radio. I'd read what they were saying in the newspapers about it being an immoral, cruel, useless war, and I'd want to beat my head and weep. Not because what they said wasn't true. What war finally isn't all those things? But because we were the ones doing the bleeding and dying, and no one seemed to give a damn about that. It was as if our blood didn't count, only Charley's."

He stopped in front of a white Star of David. "Samuel Ellman . . . Private . . . U. S. Army. There's another of your smart Yids, Lewicki. There's another of us who wasn't smart enough to leave all that stupid garbage to the *goyim.*"

"Listen . . ." The detective looked embarrassed. "I was drinking pretty good last night. I didn't mean . . ."

"Sure. Don't worry about it. I'm not that wild about you Polacks either. I mean you people were burning Jews three hundred years before the Germans were even dreaming of their final solution."

"Hey, give me a break. We all get drunk once in a while and say what we don't really mean."

Turner stared reflectively at the Jewish star. "Let me tell you about Private Ellman . . ."

"You mean you actually knew him?"

"The guy was in my platoon for more than a year. Worst goddamn soldier I ever saw. Used to make me ashamed he was Jewish. A skinny kid with round shoulders and a walk like a duck. Looked like Woody Allen, only not as handsome. He even had ulcers, for Christ's sake."

"How could they take him with ulcers?"

"He never told them. I only found out myself when I spotted him doubled up one day in the bushes. He put a gun to my head and said he'd kill me if I ever told. He couldn't kill a cockroach, but it was important for him to stay in, so I kept quiet. He had this thing about Jews fighting for their country. He felt we owed a debt that had to be paid." Turner smiled. "Maybe he once heard some anti-Semitic prick shooting off his mouth in a bar somewhere. I don't know. He was very intellectual about it. He had all these theories about Jews proving their physical courage. He proved his, all right. He finally ran straight at a machine gun, yelling like a fucking Texan till it cut him in two. Private Samuel Ellman. Hell, I never should have listened to him. I should have had him thrown out. He could have been proving his physical courage on some well-tended fairway on Long Island this morning."

Turner walked on, threading his way among the markers. Lewicki grabbed his arm. "Listen, you superior sonofabitch, I'm no anti-Semitic prick in a bar."

"No. Now you're an anti-Semitic prick in a cemetery."

Turner never saw it coming, a clean right hand that Lewicki started low and brought up and across with his shoulder behind it. Turner fell backward between two crosses. He felt wet grass against his neck and stared up at two Lewickis. He shook his head, reduced the two to one, and came up swinging . . . right, left, then right again with everything he had. He hit nothing. Somehow, the detective's head was never where it seemed.

"Okay," said Lewicki. "That's enough."

"Not for me."

He swung again, but Lewicki ducked under it and pushed him away. "I said that's enough. Leave it alone."

"Like hell."

"Then for Christ's sake hit me and get it over with." He stood waiting, hands loose at his sides.

Turner suddenly felt ridiculous, like a kid being taught a lesson by an older brother. Except that Lewicki was probably ten years his junior and half his size.

"Damn you, Turner!" Even now, Lewicki was furious. "Nobody calls me an anti-Semitic prick. That's pure shit."

Turner swallowed and tasted blood. Somehow the detective's anger gave him enormous satisfaction. "It's been in you so long you don't even know it's there anymore. But get you drunk or angry enough and out it pops like pus from a boil."

He watched Lewicki fight for control and nail a cover over his rage. They stood facing one another between the crosses in the soft, rising mist. Somewhere in the gray, Turner heard the beating of wings and crows calling. "Why are you so worked up? We all have our dirty little prejudices. It just depends on where we're coming from. Me? I'm Jewish so I'm not so wild about Poles and Germans." He tried to smile, but his jaw ached too much and it came out crooked. "Also Russians, French, Hungarians, Rumanians, English, Argentines, and Arabs."

"I don't need any lectures on prejudice. I'm a Polack, remember? What do you think it was like for me, growing up smack in the middle of all you smartass New York Yids? I wasn't a kid like other kids. I was a walking Polack joke. Even the spics and niggers did a job on me."

"Okay. So along with us Yids, you also don't care much

270

for Hispanics and Blacks. Now I know why you joined the cops. You can beat on all our heads and get paid for it."

Lewicki stood chewing his lip. "What are you trying to do, Turner?"

"Find out how much you really love me."

"Like I love eating shit."

"Is that why you're working so hard to keep me in one piece?"

"I'd do the same for a squirrel."

"I appreciate it anyway. I want you to know that." Turner gazed thoughtfully at the detective. "Funny thing. The only time I can remember not thinking, feeling, and reacting as a Jew, the only time I can remember responding without history or prejudice, was during a firefight. Then there were just our guys and Charley, and it was as simple as that." He shrugged. "I guess the point of all this, with me talking and you standing there glaring, is that I want you to know that your being an anti-Semitic prick doesn't make me care about you any less . . . that I understand it . . . that we're all pretty much anti-something pricks until it gets down to the bottom line." He laughed because he was embarrassed. "Then, I guess, we're finally just scared."

Lewicki's face dripped mist. "That had the sound of a farewell speech. You thinking of leaving me?"

"I have all along."

"Yes, but now I think you're ready."

"I've also been ready before."

"I can't let you, Paul."

It was the first time Lewicki has used his given name. It was not unlike a clasping of hands. Turner heard the crows again in the distance. The fog, instead of lightening with the day, seemed to be getting heavier. The grave markers disappeared at forty feet. Beyond that distance everything wore a shroud. "Forget it. This has nothing to do with you."

"You'd better give me your gun."

It was only then that Turner saw the snub-nosed revolver

271

in his hand. He had no idea when Lewicki had taken it out. Somehow, lately, he always seemed to be staring into gun muzzles. "Are you willing to shoot me to get it?"

"I wouldn't like to."

"That's not what I asked."

"I guess not." Lewicki put away his revolver. "Which just means I'll have to take it from you."

"You can try."

"Don't make me do it."

"I'm not making you do anything. I've never really understood your part in this, and I understand it even less now. What is it you want?"

"Only your gun."

"Not while I'm standing."

Lewicki moved toward him.

"All right." Turner put up his hand, and there was such authority in it that Lewicki stopped in his tracks. "But before you have your little go at me, I'd like you to know there are no hard feelings from my end. What about you?"

"Hey, I'm on your side. Remember?"

"Sure," said Turner. Was the fog rising or was he falling? He saw dead men's markers. He felt mist on his face, sweat on his back, and the remains of the night's whiskey in his stomach. "Until now, anyway."

"Not so. This is going to be my best present to you yet."

Turner again held out his hand, this time in friendship, and Lewicki grasped it. As he did, Turner yanked him forward and drove a knee into his groin. Lewicki doubled over with a grunt, and Turner clubbed him in the neck with both hands. The detective fell face down. Turner bent and rolled him onto his back. His eyes were closed, and his dark lashes, curled over the high flush of his cheeks, gave his face an almost girlish look. He was breathing heavily but regularly. Turner felt the pulse in his neck and found it strong.

How young he looked.

Helplessly, feeling as though he had betrayed the last friend he would ever have, Turner walked away through the

272

mist. He glanced back once. But the fog had already closed in behind him, and all he saw were the white markers.

Walking among the country's dead, he seemed to sense he had forgotten something important. He could feel his heart beating very fast, and he heard his own breathing and the same or different crows still cawing through the fog. He did not really expect to see Lewicki again, and he suddenly wished he had said more to him, wished he had somehow been better able to let him know that he understood what he had tried to do, and that, everything considered, he was not ungrateful. Still, who ever really managed to say such things? You risked your brother and yourself and never made proper accommodation. Or if you did, it was usually too late.

He reached the Chevrolet and saw Lewicki's Ford parked a short distance away. There were no other cars in sight. He stood there for a moment, considering Lewicki's car. Smiling faintly, he lifted the Ford's hood, took out the rotor, and tossed it behind some bushes. He had once read somewhere that the moment you stopped learning, you started to die. He was still learning, all right, but he would die anyway. Then he got into his car and drove across the Potomac to Washington.

TWENTY-ONE

The Past

He was back in New York. Night covered what he could see of Central Park from Peggy's bedroom.

His flight from Rome had landed at Kennedy three hours late, and it had been after midnight before he cleared customs and got a cab to take him into the city. He was in a curious mood. Rawson and Lagos echoed in his brain, death still chilled his blood, and Maria sat like a rock on his heart. He did not want to be alone tonight. He did not want to go to his apartment. So he went to Peggy.

In her bed, she exorcized his ghosts. She reminded him about her flesh. He had been away for eleven days and nights, and it seemed a year. Her lips were warm. Her breasts nestled against his palms. And, like the friendliest of garden gates, her body opened to receive him. Welcome home, darling.

He lay enclosed, enjoying the abstract unity of sex. He was committed to danger, to obsession, to insecurity and action, but not here. He smiled in the dark. The true opiate of the people. But you had to be open to it, not crippled by the past, not haunted by the dead.

"My God, I've missed you," she said.

His own hunger was greater than he would have guessed. He snipped, bit, and nibbled at the feast, wanting it all. It was better than thinking, better than brooding, infinitely better

274

than dying. She lulled him, carried him away.

But eventually it was over, and they returned to where they had been before. "So how did it feel to be back in Vietnam?"

"That's not where I was," he said and told her about Lagos, Rawson, and the rest of it. From the moment he started, he could feel her drifting away. When he finished, they were about as far apart as two people in the same bed can get. "I'm sorry I had to lie to you."

"No you're not. I think you've begun to enjoy lying. It's become a natural extension of this whole new subculture of yours. It must even be sexually stimulating. You bastard. You've never been better in me."

He lit a cigarette and blew smoke at the ceiling.

"All right," she said. "So now you've got it all. Are you happy?"

"Happy isn't exactly the word for it."

"What are you going to do now?"

"I don't know."

"You're lying again."

Other than for the glow of his cigarette, the room was dark. He reached over and touched her face with the tips of his fingers. She pushed his hand away.

"Can't you be honest even now?"

"I thought I was."

"Then you're getting sicker by the minute. You should be quarantined before you start an epidemic."

He studied the orange ember at the tip of his cigarette. It might have been a crystal ball.

"It's all suddenly so clear." It was her editor's voice— quiet, omniscient, coldly reasonable. "It's like a subtle, beautifully crafted novel. Out of confusion, out of seemingly unrelated bits and pieces, everything has fallen into place. You've finally gotten what you wanted, haven't you?"

"What have I wanted?"

Peggy leaned toward him in the darkness. Even her body seemed accusing. "A bona fide ogre. A cold blooded, Machiavellian type who can at last make you feel morally justified in wreaking your deadly vengeance."

"You sound like something out of *Macbeth*. Nobody wreaks deadly vengeance these days."

"Except for you. You're a throwback, a walking anachronism."

"You romanticize me, Peggy."

"You romanticize yourself. Just as you romanticize Maria. But I've told you that before," she said tiredly, "haven't I?"

He thought he heard an animal howl. Was he still in Africa? Then it became the inescapable siren, the death rattle of urban America.

"Still, we do have something different here now," she said. "You've learned things about Maria. She's not the innocent you once thought. Yet you seem to have lost your anger. At least as far as Maria is concerned. What happened?"

He could make out the shadows of her eyes in the paler oval of her face. "I've had time to think, so I've thought. Alive, she never gave me anything but love. When she did hurt me, it was from the grave, and that wasn't anything she could control. So I can't really fault her on intention."

"How about faulting her on Handley and Woodruff? Do you think you can manage that?"

It was so openly malicious, so unabashedly catty that he had to smile. "I came late to the feast. Those two were well into her life before she even met me. Yet I was the one she chose to marry. And it could hardly have been easy for her. So there had to be love. Which is still a reasonable thing to settle for."

"My God, you've done a selling job on yourself. That must have been some trip home you just had."

He laughed. "I thought you were her friend."

"I was. When she was alive. Now all she can do is get you killed, and I hate her for it." Her lips, a dark blur, trembled. "She was worse than a whore. At least a whore is open about what she is. Maria was apparently never open about anything."

"Peggy . . ."

"Don't Peggy me." She was suddenly so furious she began to weep. "And don't you dare talk to me about what she did for the country. Whatever she did was for herself. Sweet Jesus, spare us from the blessed patriots of the world. They not only end up killing one another, but sooner or later ask us to die for them, too."

"Nobody is asking anyone to die for anything."

"Liar," she wept. "Right this minute, straight from the grave, that whore is asking you to die for her."

Her hurt reached him. He had never known she carried so much spleen. He held her, feeling the bones beneath her flesh. She pressed his face between her breasts. Her body shook. He felt her pain.

At last she was asleep, and he lit a fresh cigarette, cupping the match to shield her face from the flare of light. This decent women who offered him asylum from the dead. If only he wanted it. She had said Maria was worse than a whore, that she hated her, and who could blame her? Yet to him, his wife had never been a hateful woman. Nor, apparently, to others. To Spitzer the rabbi she had in fact been worthy of canonization. To a humanist president, she had been the best by every standard. And finally, to eight unknowing strangers whom she had futilely tried to save, she had died a martyr. *Maruschka.* In so many years, how could she not have given him a sign?

Or had she?

"What's wrong with us?" she had once asked. "Why are we so hard, so selfish, so comfort- and pleasure-loving? I look at plays, movies, television. I read books. I sit in restaurants. I see endless automobiles. I watch sporting events cheered by millions. And do you know what I want to do? I want to weep with shame. More than half the people on earth are bleeding or starving, and all we seem to care about are our silly, childish indulgences."

He had considered her angst, her *Weltschmerz,* just a generalized concern for the state of the world and not to be taken seriously or personally.

"What about you?" she asked. "Don't you ever feel you'd like to try to do something about it?"

"Christ, no. And if I did, I'd bang my head with a hammer until any such dangerous notions were knocked loose."

They had not been married long, and his reply had made her angrier than he had yet seen her. "You're not a fool," she said, "and I know how deeply you care about people. How can you say something like that?"

"It's easy. I just remember the fifty-seven thousand we shipped home from Nam in boxes. And if that's not enough, then I remind myself of the couple of million Vietnamese, North and South, men, women, and children, who were buried over there."

"I don't believe you."

"Believe me."

"Then why did you bother fighting?"

"I was drafted."

"You could have gone to Canada or Sweden."

"Not my style. Besides, I started out believing as you do. I was a lucky American. I had all the best of it. So, of course, I had to share it with the less fortunate. Even if they didn't want it."

"Paul . . ."

"I'll tell you about us lucky Americans. We're no better than the lucky Russians. And they're about as bad as you can get. We're all equally dangerous. Neither side, neither one of us, can stand the idea that anyone anywhere else shouldn't want what we want. Our better way of life. Our one true faith. Whether it be democracy or communism. And God help those who refuse to accept what we offer. We'll shove it down their throats at the end of a bayonet, like a shish kebab."

Had she been trying to give him a sign then? If she had, he had chosen not to see it.

In bed beside another woman, this one asleep rather than dead, he wondered how many other hints he might have rejected. Had he unknowingly asked, even required, her to keep this part of her life hidden from him? People lied for many different reasons. Never mind that Woodruff had ordered her to keep silent. If she had really wanted to share, if she had believed his response would be positive, she would have shared. But he had been especially full of pain in those days, his psyche as deeply scarred as his body. His youthful enthusiasm, his commitment, and his belief had all exploded in a nightmare of death, disillusionment, and national turmoil. Sudden noises made him jump. A friendly tap on the back whirled him about, crouched and ready to attack. He was writing his second novel then and having to bury his dead all over again. And a vast majority of those good Americans whose laws had sent him to kill and be killed, having later decided they opposed the war on moral grounds, now regarded him and other returnees with contempt and hostility. It was not a time when he was able to take kindly to suggestions about easing the pain of others. He was still hurting too much himself. Inevitably, the suggestions had stopped.

So she had died with cyanide and the lessons of history implanted in her body. There were those who killed and always those who believed they killed for good reason. Still, she had not been afraid to play out her fate, thought Turner. After all the anguish, all the confusion, all the degraded clowning you went through from birth to death, she had evidently felt she knew what was important. And so few did. She had at least fulfilled her obligations, been loyal to her own beliefs. What did he want of her?

They shared a cab in the morning and rode downtown in strained silence. Peggy seemed unable to meet his eyes. Was she angry or just ashamed? Still, getting out in front of her office, she leaned back and kissed him goodbye. Poor Peggy. He felt guilty at the thought. Sympathy was not what she wanted from him.

It was not quite nine when he reached his house. Tense,

emotionally spent, he stood on the sidewalk beside his valise and fought an impulse to jump back into the cab. And go where? People brushed past him, hurrying to work, and he envied them their air of purpose, their commitment to routine. Reluctantly, he picked up his valise, carried it up the three flights of stairs to his apartment, and let himself in.

With his first breath, an effluvium attacked his nose, his throat, burned its way down, and settled in his lungs. He opened his valise and took out the revolver that had traveled to Africa and back between layers of shirts and underwear. A trench coat lay draped over a hall chair. It was not his. He walked silently through the living room and into the bedroom. A gray suit and a blue oxford shirt hung from hangers on the closet door, and these were not his either. The bed was unmade, and he was sure he had not left it so. He heard water running in the master bath. He opened the door just as Wendell Handley stepped from the shower, naked and dripping.

"Welcome home," said the deputy director.

Turner stared at him from behind the revolver. He passed a hand across his forehead as though shading his eyes from the sun. Something seemed to stir in the room, although the water was no longer running and neither man had moved. There he was, delivered up to him by a considerate Providence. Those cornflower blue eyes and dark lashes, the sharp Indian cheekbones, and a pleasant, oddly cheerful expression that seemed to say, "If you're going to shoot me, this is surely as good a time as any and better than most." Turner's hand tightened on the gun, and there was something almost galvanic in the trigger. Then he looked at the deputy director's eyes once more, and it was as if someone had thrown a switch and cut off the current. Not like this, he thought. This icy *momzer* could, but I can't. He abruptly left the room.

He lit a cigarette and put on coffee. That was it. Keep the mouth and hands busy. When Handley at last appeared, fully dressed and sucking his pipe like a pacifier, Turner was waiting in the library.

The Past

They sat facing one another across a stripped oak table that Maria had bought in a New England antique barn and carried home on the roof of her car. Handley touched its surface appreciatively. "Beautiful grain. I remember how excited she was when she found this piece. Somewhere up in Connecticut, wasn't it?"

Turner said nothing.

"I expected you back last night. When you didn't show, I took the liberty of staying over." Handley's glance embraced the paneled library, the foyer, and what he could see of the living room through open double doors. "It was strange being here. As long as I've known Maria, I've never seen this place, never spent a moment where she lived. It used to bother me. I felt cheated."

Turner stared full into the deputy director's face. "You said you expected me back last night. You knew where I was coming from, what flight I was on?"

"For some reason, you persist in underestimating me." Handley sighed an old man's sigh. "I assume Rawson told you everything before you shot him."

Turner did not bother to deny the killing. "You sonofabitch. You'd have let me believe she was really KGB, that she was cold and vicious enough to have pulled the plug on those eight people."

"So what? You couldn't have loved her that way? I could have. Besides, I didn't think you were ready to handle the truth before."

"What makes you think I'll handle it now?"

"You didn't quite pull the trigger when you saw me."

"Why in Christ's name are you here, anyway?"

"I want you to hear my side."

"I've already heard your lies. Be smart. Get out of here before I blow your goddamned head off."

The blood ran darkly through Handley's cheeks. If Turner could have believed such a thing possible, he would have judged it a mark of pain.

"I'm not your enemy," said the deputy director. "If I

281

were, I could have gotten rid of you a long time ago. You must be aware of that."

Turner lit one cigarette from another. Some part of that had to be true. Which was one of the things that bothered him.

"Did Rawson tell you it was he who supplied the cyanide?"

"Yes. But you were the murderer."

"I can't deny that. But I'm still human enough to want to explain, to plead, to try to justify the death of someone I loved very dearly."

"Don't expect absolution from *me*, you bastard."

"We all have to finally tell our dirty little stories to someone, and you're the only one I know who might have a chance of understanding mine."

Turner's face was so rigid it ached. Was there no end to the man's gall? Yet this was where they always seemed to end up—Handley presenting his latest version of the truth, and him, listening.

"Of course, with the brilliance of hindsight," said the deputy director, "it's easy enough to see now that I never should have exposed my plan to Maria in the first place. But there's always that unpredictable human factor, and with all our years of professional experience, Maria and I were as much its victims that night as any two neophytes. I, with an almost adolescent need to demonstrate my brilliance . . . Maria, with a sentimentality that suddenly made her more concerned with the lives of eight expendable foreign agents than with the invaluable strategic advantage their loss could buy."

Handley picked up his coffee, looked broodingly into it, and put it down without drinking. "The result was that she flayed me alive for the whole amoral idea and threatened to go to the president if I didn't promise to scrub it. And since Woodruff's Sunday-school approach to national survival would never have sanctioned any such plan, I knew that would be the end of it."

"Rawson told me all that," Turner said flatly. "So you just decided to kill her."

"No. She was too far into me for that. I tried arguing with her, but it was useless. I'd never seen her so aroused. So I finally said, *okay. You win. You don't have to go to Jesus Christ. The plan is scrubbed.*" He paused. "Did Rawson tell you that part?"

Turner shook his head.

"I didn't think so. Anyway, there lay my brilliant scheme. Dead. Until Herb Rawson began whispering in my ear. My own Iago. He appeared just as Maria was leaving the room, and I told him what had happened. Which turned out to be my second mistake of the night. He was a smart man, a good talker, a brilliant dialectician. He blew bugles. He wrapped us both in Old Glory. He reminded me of all the things I knew as well as he, but which I had carefully blocked out—that in our work, sentiment was the whispering of the Devil . . . that history was a priori amoral . . . that to listen to one's heart and conscience was professional perfidy. And, of course, he was right. There was no way I could answer him."

The deputy director gazed thoughtfully at a patch of sunlight on the floor. "In retrospect, I seem to have moved through the rest of that night in a semi-catatonic state. I felt incapable of carrying out the simplest action. I didn't have to. My trusty Iago took care of everything. Given my tacit approval . . . I swear to God I was barely capable of speech . . . he prepared three glasses of champagne, put the cyanide into one, and went to call Maria back on some pretext or other. While he was gone, I actually considered switching the glasses and giving him the cyanide. But I couldn't generate the necessary motion. Then he was back with Maria, passing out the champagne and proposing a toast to the unannounced news of my appointment as director of The Company. And that was how she died," Handley finished tonelessly, "drinking a toast to my future."

They sat at opposite sides of Maria's table. Turner waited to feel something, but he seemed to have run out of emotion. "So now you're telling me Rawson did the killing, not you."

"No. He just did the dirty work for me. For which I ended up despising him, exiling him to Lagos, and even

283

dropping his name, perhaps hoping subconsciously that you might remember it and put a bullet in him. Which you finally did." His smile was sour. "I do seem to have a knack for getting others to do my dirty work, don't I?"

More flowers for the graveyard. The man confessed, then confessed again, then still again. He had an apparently unlimited supply of fresh disclosures to replace any that turned rotten along the way. "And you weren't worried about my coming after you when I got the good news from Rawson?"

"You're no assassin. You're too much of a Boy Scout. The only reason Herb Rawson is dead is because he shot at you first."

"How could you know that?"

"He was killed instantly. A single bullet to the heart. And his own gun had been fired twice." Handley's teeth bit into his pipe. "I'm glad you made it safely back. And I mean that sincerely."

"Why? Because you love me like a brother?"

The deputy director's expression was flat, a mask behind a mask. "I know how you felt and still feel about Maria, and for that reason alone I can't avoid an affinity for you. But there's also a more practical reason. You still have material of hers, and you're my only hope of getting it."

"Try whistling."

"It may take a while, but you'll give it to me. Do you know why? Because despite everything, you can't quite convince yourself of my villainy. Because deep down you have to ask yourself why I've done this godawful thing. And the single answer you can't avoid is that I did it not for myself, but for a large number of anonymous Americans whose lives have been entrusted to me and who are likely to live a bit longer and more safely because of it."

The plumbing groaned like an old man inside the walls.

"Just one thing," said Handley. "Why did Rawson try to shoot you?"

"To keep me from killing you."

"He should have known better."

284

The Past

At the Waldorf that night, his uncle's bodyguards seemed happy to see him. They grinned at him from beneath flinty eyes, asked where he had been hiding lately, and claimed to have missed seeing him around. Still, being practical men who earned their living as students of the less attractive elements of human nature, they examined him as carefully as ever before letting him into their employer's apartment.

Hank and Turnovsky welcomed him back, embraced him, held him close, let him feel their love and concern. Turner was moved. They had been worried about him. He was surprised at how responsive he was to all this. It was unlike him. Or was it? What did he really know of himself? Increasingly, it seemed, less and less. Yet feeling his uncle's thick arms about him, the wet kiss on the cheek that was his father's all over again, he felt suddenly at home and accounted for. In Hank's arms he felt something else. Women who looked as she looked had to be very careful with their affectionate hugs. Regardless of intent, they gave off erotic signals.

Then, once more, he was telling them his story. It was getting to be an endless serial, he thought. While the two alert, hard-faced men outside kept them safe from predators, they listened patiently, showed deep interest, and sipped their obligatory brandy. Odysseus, returned from his wanderings, could not have had a more sympathetic audience for all he had to tell. Almost as an afterthought, he threw in that morning's meeting with Handley.

Turnovsky nodded when he had finished. "So at least you're back in one piece. Which is the important thing. Which is still what worries me more than anything."

"You don't have to worry about me."

"Sure, Mr. Big Shot. In the meantime they came pretty close to burying you in that beautiful paradise of the *shvartzehs*. Right this minute I could have been sitting *shivah* for you on a wooden box."

"I managed okay."

Turnovksy puffed at one of his long Cubans. "Tell him, Hank. Let him know how okay he managed."

285

"I thought you weren't going to say anything about that."

"I've changed my mind. I think it'll be better if he knows the score."

Hank looked uncomfortable. "Then tell him yourself."

"Tell me what, for God sake?"

"That we had someone covering your back," said Turnovsky. "That if we hadn't, you'd have been a special kosher dinner for the hyenas."

Turner sat looking at them. Somehow, he was not especially surprised.

"Didn't you at least wonder who shot your friend Rawson?" said Turnovsky. "Did you think it was some crazy Zulu?"

He felt a flush of irrational anger. He also felt foolish. "I guess I should be grateful. Thanks."

"That's not why I told you, Pauly. It's just time you realized that not even a *shtarker* like you can handle this alone."

"Then you knew the whole story before I even got here."

"Not about Handley's visit this morning. The rest, we knew."

"You should have shut me up. I feel like an ass."

"Please don't take it that way," said Hank. "Let's just be thankful it worked out as it did."

Turnovsky straightened his *yarmulkah*. "Enough stroking. Too bad if Pauly's delicate feelings are hurt. Better that than dead. And that's just history, anyway. Now it's time for current events." The Tartar eyes glared at Turner. "You going to listen to sense or go on playing Don Quixote till they drop a windmill on you?"

It was a no-win question. Turner left it alone.

"Okay, Pauly. So now I'm doing this my way. Once and for all I'm finishing it. I've already let it go too long. Maybe five times you've almost died of it. Handley was right when he said you were no assassin. The man knows you better than you know yourself. All you'll do is dig on and on until he finally kills you. The only reason he hasn't finished you yet is because he hasn't found what he's looking for and thinks you have it. Incidentally, *do* you?''

Turner shook his head. "I doubt it. I've already given him most of what I've found, and what's left is just more of the same.''

"Which means he either discovers you don't have what he wants and finishes you . . . or finds it himself somewhere and finishes you . . . or just gets tired of waiting and finishes you. So we can assume that unless you're prepared to act first, you're as good as dead.''

"I don't necessarily agree with that assumption.''

"Of course not. It wouldn't be your style. Face it, Pauly. You'll never be ready to get rid of this man. You'll talk and threaten. You'll be shocked by his lies and what he's done. But you'll always keep finding new reasons not to burn him.''

Turner looked at Hank. But she was staring into her drink and refused to meet his eyes. She obviously agreed with his uncle.

"I'm not saying that's bad,'' Turnovsky continued. "Who needs more gangsters and assassins in this world? What we need are more writers. So just leave this to me. It happens to be part of my business. And that's how I'll take care of it. No fuss, no excitement. Everything nice and clean. Then you can stop beating your breast and start leading a normal life again. You're worth a dozen *shmendricks* like Wendell Handley.''

"No. This is mine.''

Turnovsky rose. He measured Turner from under a vast biblical forehead and grizzled hair. "It has stopped being yours, Pauly. You surrendered your exclusive rights when you pointed a gun at Handley's *vercockteh shlang* this morning and didn't shoot it off. If you couldn't do it then, with all you'd just learned from Rawson, you'll never be able to do it. I'm taking it out of your hands.''

"You're going to have him butchered like a gangster in the gutter?''

"You're old fashioned. We don't do much dying in gutters, anymore. That went out a long time ago, with Bugsy Siegal. But you can be sure it'll get done.''

287

"No."

"You think he deserves better?"

Turner had no clear idea of what he thought at that moment. The whole discussion seemed to have taken a surrealist turn. Was he really defending Wendell Handley's right to murder his wife and live on, unpunished? Again, he looked at Hank. Seeking what? This time she gazed back. Her eyes were wide, clear, soft, human. They shone with hidden lights. But they offered nothing.

"Pauly, he's going to kill you the instant he's ready. He has to now. You know too much. Just a whisper from you in the president's ear, just one word about what he's done, and his career is finished. Do you think he's going to let you walk around with that kind of sword over his head?"

"I'll handle it myself."

"You've had your chance."

"I need more time."

"I'm not giving it to you."

"You have no right. It's not yours."

"I have every right," said his uncle, a man who had learned his lessons well, whose eyes signaled regret at the way the world was put together, but who knew how to deal with it without weeping. "I love you. You're my brother's son. I don't want you dying before I die. I'm making it mine."

If I am bereaved of my sons, the original Jacob had said, then am I bereaved. Had he also said something about nephews?

Often with Fran there was an uncomfortable, even a disturbing moment of tightness on entering her. It made him cautious. He was afraid of hurting her. It made it hard for him to revel freely in her fair, slender, flexible body. It was not always the relaxing playground he wanted and needed. That night, in the glow of the small lamp she enjoyed having on when they made love, the light reflected from patches of moisture on her skin in such a way that they set off nightmare images of napalm burns. Which, in turn, made him see the usual bodies emerging from smoke—small, ambulatory fires that ran back and forth and scrambled about like ants on a burning log until they popped and lay still.

Finally, he, too, lay still.

"What's the matter?" she said and automatically turned up the stereo volume control beside the bed.

"Nothing fatal. I was just thinking of the wrong things."

"Was it your going back to Vietnam?"

She was the only one still stuck with the lie of where he had been. He shrugged.

"Do you want to talk about it?"

"No."

She was silent, and he lay feeling the weight of the air. It stuck to the back of his throat like mucous.

"You shut me out of everything," she said. "I sometimes wonder why you see me at all."

"You're a terrific lay."

"I wish I were." Her voice was as heavy as the air, leaden. "I'm human, you're human, and it's no more than that. Even when you're with me, you're off somewhere. I get more of you from reading your books than I do from you."

"Maybe that's all there is."

"No. I couldn't feel this way if that were true. While you were gone I suddenly had the feeling I might never see you again, and it made me physically ill. Isn't that awful?"

Reaching for a cigarette, she leaned across him, and even her body felt stiff, resentful. Still, she laughed. "I guess I should have listened to my father. He was afraid you'd be too much for me. Yet he liked, respected, even admired you. He could even understand my being attracted to you." She inhaled deeply and blew smoke at the ceiling. "And do you know something else? I'm sure he had a thing for your wife, as well."

He felt something dip. A divining rod? "What makes you say that?"

"Ah, the man is suddenly interested. I'd like to see you

come alive like that for me, someday." She was only half teasing.

He waited.

"I spent a weekend with my parents while you were gone. I generally despise the White House, but I was feeling restless and edgy so I went. One night my father and I stayed up drinking and talking. I suppose it was my involvement with you that got him started, but almost all of it had to do with your wife."

She stopped abruptly. "God, I'm a bitch. All I'm really trying to do is punish you."

"For what?"

"Not taking me seriously." She shut her eyes. "I never thought I could be like this. I guess you just have to want something badly enough and not be able to get it."

He kissed her cheek. It felt hot and feverish to his lips. "Okay. So you're slightly less than perfect. Like a few others of us. Now get on with it."

"It will only hurt you."

"No. I've already pushed through that."

She turned and looked at him. A tiny white lamp shone from each iris. "You knew?"

"After I spoke to your father that night, I guessed. So you may as well tell me the rest. You know you're dying to, anyway."

"I am. That's what makes it so awful." But her tone carried more relief than anguish. "Your wife was apparently quite a woman . . . clever, beautiful, charming, heroic. My God, could she really have been that much larger than life?"

"Please. No eulogies. I've had enough of those."

"I was only quoting my father. He called her an extremely precious human being. His exact words. He also said she was the only complete woman he had ever found. And I'll tell you this. My father has never been lazy about looking." She smiled vaguely at the ceiling. "I love my father dearly, and in her own way so does my mother, but neither of us has ever been blind to his need for a continuing parade of adoring women. I can't say whether your wife adored or simply used him, but it was clear enough how he felt about her."

She got out of bed and walked to a window, her body luminous against the outside darkness. Being naked elongated her legs, made them seem incredibly long and slender. "He said she was complete because she had love in her heart. Love for everybody. For Americans, for Russians, for you, for him, even for those she was forced to hurt. And do you know something? Hearing it I felt no love at all, only malice. No one has the right to be that transcendent. It automatically diminishes the rest of us. I'm surprised she died a natural death. If she was such a saint, she should have been properly martyred."

"She was."

"Very funny."

"I'm not joking. My wife didn't die of a heart attack. She was murdered."

Fran turned. Her mouth was open slightly. She came back to the bed and knelt there, studying his face.

"You accused me before of shutting you out," he said. "Well, you're not shut out anymore. I'm letting you in. Though I'm not doing you much of a favor. Maria died of cyanide poisoning. Not even your father knows. And I want your word that you won't tell him. Do I have it?"

Seemingly mute, she nodded.

"I'd also like you to do something for me." His clothes were draped over a chair beside the bed, and he took a sealed, unmarked envelope from the jacket and handed it to her. "Do you have a safe place to keep this?"

She found a kind of voice. "Yes."

"Where?"

"There's a false bottom in that second bureau drawer. I had it made last year when I discovered some of my papers were being read."

"Okay. Please put this there and forget about it. But if anything happens to me during the next few weeks, I want you to give it to your father."

291

"What could happen to you?"

"I don't know. Probably nothing. But if anything does . . . even if it appears to be an accident . . . car, plane, fall, mugging, heart attack, whatever . . . just make sure your dad gets it. No one else. Understand?"

Eyes wide, she held tightly to the envelope. "You know who killed your wife? Is that what's in here?"

"Among other things. I'm sorry I can't tell you more right now. I'm also sorry for the way I've been these past weeks. Whatever it was, it's not what I am."

"Aah, love." Her voice was so soft it seemed to be coming from another room. She lay with her head on his chest. She still held the envelope. It appeared to be enough for her.

TWENTY-TWO

The Present

He had not known how tired he was until he fell asleep at the wheel and drove across the grass in front of the Jefferson Memorial. Luckily, it was still early morning, there was hardly any traffic, and no police had seen him. The fog also offered cover, a thick, rolling blanket, pressing close to the ground and freighted with the smell of spring. It would have been all over if the police had picked him up in Washington. Before he did anything, he had to get some sleep. Suddenly he missed Lewicki.

He drove back across the Potomac to a small motel just outside of Alexandria. It was off Route 28 and had a red neon sign in front that boasted brightly of color TV and low rates, but simply looked pathetic and depressing through the shifting layers of fog. He paid cash in advance for a room and went right to bed with his clothes on and his revolver beneath the pillow.

But with sleep available, his thoughts began racing wildly and all he did was stare up at a cluster of stains on the ceiling. Then someone in the next room switched on the news, and he was treated to that morning's recital of death and disaster. Why was he so manic about what he was doing? Regardless of what he did or didn't do, people would go right on destroying themselves and one another. But the thought offered little

293

comfort. Everyone was still responsible for his or her own behavior, and he was aware of a disturbing anarchy in his. It was as though, having once been set in motion, he was without further control. Yet he was not a raw adolescent. Where was the restraint of age, of deeper experience? Or had he buried that, too, somewhere in Southeast Asia?

Somehow, it always seemed to come back to that. What was he trying to do—establish himself as a lifelong battle casualty? Was everything he finally did—good, bad, or indifferent—going to be blamed on a national trauma that was now only history? He had no right. Or had he? Had not the then president of the United States personally declared, "We are in Vietnam to fulfill one of the most solemn pledges of the American nation. We will stand in Vietnam." And had not he, Paul (Turnovsky) Turner, having been between the ages of eighteen and twenty-six, having been mentally, morally, and physically competent, and having finished with school, received the highest honor that the government can offer its citizens? Had they not made him 1-A? And had that not, in turn, made his father proud and his mother dead?

His mother had died of cancer of the liver. The malignancy had been deep inside, nibbling at her vitals, turning her face yellow. His mother. Ma. She was forty-three, and when he saw her hands in her coffin, they had looked as though they belonged to an old woman. She had been sure it was his uniform that had given her cancer. Never mind what the doctors said. She knew her own sickness better than any doctors. She had felt it take root the instant he raised his right hand to be sworn in as a soldier. She had the day and hour inscribed on her liver. It had grown from there. She had begged him to see a draft counselor, turn conscientious objector, go to Canada or Sweden, go anywhere but into the army. It was not just the inevitable and recurring question of a possibly wrong war. Again, always again, what war was right? It was any war, any army, any uniform. Her Pauly, her son, did not belong in it. So whose son did, Ma? The time had come to once again defeat the enemies of freedom. The time had come to fight for the honor of the country. God, what words. And each and every one spoken without self-consciousness or embarrassment. He was an American. He was a Jew, made constitutionally safe from persecution. It was his duty and privilege to stand up and fight the forces of darkness on the battlefield.

His mother spit blood.

He was given a small red pamphlet. It contained the GI's Code of Conduct. It began, *I am an American fighting man. I serve in the forces which guard my country and our way of life. I am prepared to give my life in their defense.* He carried the pamphlet in his pocket all through basic training. He carried it until it fell apart. He thought it was the most stirring thing he had ever read. Until he went into combat. Then he found it was just bullshit. He found he wasn't fighting the Communists. He wasn't fighting the VC. He wasn't fighting for liberty or America or unpersecuted Jews or the girl up the block. What he really was fighting for was the only true GI code of conduct, the only one that could stand up under an actual fire-fight. It was called staying alive. And what it involved, mostly, was killing people. In theory, it seemed simple enough. In practice, it took some getting used to. In time, he became very good at it. One of the best, he was told. They even gave him a very highly regarded medal for it. At first he dismissed his staying alive as just dumb luck, but later he knew better. It was a total concentration of the senses on trusting nobody and nothing . . . not the sky, not the earth, not the country-side, not the people. It went further. If your right hand was stupid enough to trust your left hand, it would kill you. Many couldn't accept this and died. He accepted it and lived.

He, Paul (Turnovsky) Turner, who had been a skinny kid with blond, silky girl's hair and a disturbing habit of throwing up his breakfast on the way to school in the morning. He had a red Columbia bicycle with fat tires and a scooter made of scrap wood and old skate wheels. His father took him for Sunday walks along Riverside Drive, and he carried a cap pistol to defend them both against Indian attacks. There were no Indians, just blacks and Puerto Ricans, and none of these ever attacked them. He lived and grew up in a three-room apartment in a city of eight million strangers who passed him on the streets without recognition. And the only thing he ever really wanted was to live in a private house, with a lawn, in a small town where everyone would know his name and say "Hi, Paul" when they met him on the street. He wanted to be friendly. He wanted to have friends. He discovered that people were the most marvelous of all God's creatures. He made this discovery entirely alone, all by himself, as if no one before him had ever thought of such an idea. He did not understand such words as love or trust or goodness, but they somehow became his familiars, and he lived with them in the imaginary small-town house he never had. He read and heard about wars and killing, but these were things that would never have anything to do with him. He lived in New York, the center of life, the capital of the universe. He looked into people's eyes and saw only joy, affection, the hopes of all his days and years to come. Or so he enjoyed believing.

Still, he had lived. And living, he had discovered important bits of information. Among them was the fact that jungle did not really burn, not even with napalm. What it did was smolder. It sent smoke drifting along the vines like fog. If you stayed around long enough to breathe, the smell was something like gasoline and charred wood. Except for the roasting flesh, which was more like the tail end of a hamburger joint. He also discovered that an eighty-year-old woman or a ten-year-old kid could kill you just as dead as a hard-faced, fully equipped North Vietnamese regular . . . that if he was captured, his nuts would be cut off and stuffed in his mouth . . . that if he waved at even his own planes he was likely to be machine-gunned because American pilots had been told that if it was in the jungle and it moved, you shot at it . . . that he was a soldier, not a thinker, and that it was up to his elected representatives in the government to tell him what he should and shouldn't do and what was right and what was wrong. Thinking, he had discovered, had gotten more grunts killed

296

than stupidity had.

But now he could think. He was no longer a soldier. (Then why did he have this loaded gun under his pillow?) He was an American civilian, a member in good standing of the best damned democratic society in the history of western civilization. He did not have to swallow the Communists' assertion that this was a century of war, calamity, and revolution. He was free to believe in peace, and weekend tennis, and movies, and two-car garages, and everything pleasant. He was allowed to be against distrust, evil, and unending menace. He could turn away from the utterly frightful. He could once more be permitted the luxury of thinking that most people were worthy of trust and did not intend him and those close to him harm. He was essentially like that. Which did not mean he was still childishly naïve, still blind to the existence of immorality, cruelty, and the loathsome. He knew only too well that they were there. But he also insisted upon his right to hope they might one day end.

He stared at the ceiling with tired eyes. All that fine, humanist sentiment, all those decent instincts. Yet he was in this place for only one purpose—to prepare himself for a killing. It was almost laughable, if one could laugh at the prospect of murder. If Lewicki were here, Turner was sure he could have managed it. The detective had demonstrated an unfailing appreciation for the ludicrous. Which he would probably need when he came to among Arlington's armies of the dead. Thinking about Lewicki, the litany of large and small disasters still drifting in from the next room, Turner smiled faintly as he sank toward sleep.

TWENTY-THREE

The Past

Mutsie showed himself to be as solidly dependable as ever. Less than an hour after Turner called, he was there with his little black satchel. In a time of growing mediocrity and falling standards, the small, elegant burglar remained a bulwark of elitist philosophy and performance. Over coffee, eyes darkly alive in his lean, bald head, he mourned the absence of professionalism in his field, bitterly decried the invasion of junkies, punks, and wanton killers into a line of work where skill and sensitivity had once stood for something. "Suddenly every *putz* with the price of a crowbar and a Saturday Night Special is breaking and entering. There's no finesse anymore, no proper research. They haven't the mentality. They only know how to do damage. They go into occupied premises. They hurt, rape, and murder. I can't listen to the news anymore. It's like hearing a recital of the police blotter. It makes me ashamed. If I played better gin rummy, I swear I'd quit once and for all and go to Miami."

He sighed and shot his cuffs so that the proper one and a half inches of shirt showed below his jacket sleeves. "But I'm sure you didn't call me over here just to hear my *kvetching*. What can I do for you, Pauly?"

"More of the same. Something my wife may have hidden. Except that this time I don't even know what I'm looking for.

298

In fact, there might not even be anything. But someone else seems to think there is, so I guess it's worth a try."

"This someone else . . . he gave you no background, no time element, no description?"

Turner shook his head.

"And I take it you can't ask him."

"He thinks I already have it."

"And you want him to go on thinking it?"

"It may be what's keeping me alive."

As Mutsie searched, he once again asked Turner to tell him about his wife and her habits. And once again Turner found himself struggling for a clearer perspective of a woman he had lived with for eight years and never truly seen. Maybe it was the passion that had blinded him. But that was long gone now, and he still saw little that was different. Physically, the apartment itself was still home to him, still the same, yet it seemed more like a once well-tended garden gone to seed. Talking about it, Maria, them, even his body felt purged, emptied of its juices. Nevertheless, concentrating on Maria, trying to give this good, hard-working thief some small grasp of what she might have been, he caused a tear in her death through which small details pushed loose—the precise, absorbed way she put on her lipstick, the automatic humming when she walked, the sucking of her pen while reconciling a bank balance, a favorite dress she wore (red with a tiny white print) even when it became old, threadbare, and out-of-style. For himself, he tried to picture how she would move soundlessly from one room to another in her bare feet, like an Indian, and he remembered her frequent frenzied searches for suddenly missing gloves, keys, credit cards, and wallets. How had she survived as long as she did in so complex and dangerous an existence? She seemed to be forever losing things.

Mutsie picked up on this. "She was that careless?"

"It often seemed so. Yet she wasn't really. Not when it counted. Then her mind would grow teeth. I don't think she ever once forgot anything she really wanted to remember. Not in her whole life."

299

It was late afternoon, and they were in the living room. Mutsie was just about through. He had searched for eight hours and found nothing. Which meant that in all likelihood there was nothing to find. But he still wanted to talk. "What about you? Do you ever forget things you really want to remember?"

"All the time. If I don't make lists and leave myself reminders, I'm finished."

"Do you think you might have forgotten something important about your wife?"

Turner shrugged. Tired and depressed, he poured a glass of white wine for Mutsie and a strong shot of bourbon for himself. "Probably," he said.

"Maybe we've been going about this one all wrong. What if your wife didn't really want to hide this from you. What if she wanted you to find it instead?"

Turner looked at him blankly.

"Were you serious before when you said having it could help you stay alive?"

"Not necessarily having it. It's Handley's thinking I have it that could do me some good."

"But wouldn't it be better to actually have it?"

Turner realized, belatedly, that he had mentioned the deputy director by name. Not that it mattered with Mutsie. But how easily a dangerous slip could be made. "Sure it would be better. But the damned thing might not even exist."

"For argument's sake, let's say it does. And let's also say your wife wanted only you and no one else to find it. Where would she have put it then?"

"The whole premise is crazy."

"Why?"

"Because Maria spent the entire eight years of our marriage keeping me from finding things. You saw how carefully she buried those rolls of microfilm. Why would she suddenly want me to find this?"

"Who knows? Your wife was no average *hausfrau*. God bless her memory, she's led you a merry chase." Mutsie

300

paused to savor his wine, delicately fastidious even in this, a man marching through life on egg shells. "But again for argument's sake, let's say she had her reasons for wanting you to find it. Maybe she felt it could be important for you. Maybe she had a premonition of death and wanted to tell you what she couldn't mention while she was alive. Who knows why? Right now the only thing that matters is where she might have put it."

"She would have given something like that to her lawyer, with her will."

"Not if she wanted it to be for your eyes alone. She was playing hard ball with pros. That would have been the first place they'd have looked. With or without license."

Turner hunched broodingly over his bourbon. He had little patience for such hypotheses. Still, Mutsie was only trying to help. "You're just wasting your time with that kind of thinking. It's a dead end."

"Your wife never left you notes?"

"Sure. On my typewriter. In my underwear drawer. On my pillow." He smiled crookedly. "But not since she died."

"May I ask a very personal question?"

"I don't have many secrets from you, Mutsie."

"Do you believe your wife loved you?"

It was like walking into a door he had thought was open. "While she was alive, I never doubted it."

"And now?"

"I guess I still don't doubt it. I wouldn't be carrying on like this if I did. I'd have laid her to rest long ago."

Mutsie's narrow face was calm, candid, his complexion very pale, an indoor, nighttime color. "And loving you, do you really think she would have left without a word, without a proper goodbye?"

"I doubt that Maria expected to die that night."

"How do you know? People die all the time in her line of work. If not one night, then another. Don't you think she was aware of that? And don't you think she would have done something about it?"

Turner felt as though they were waltzing in circles. He suddenly wished Mutsie would leave him alone.

"It's not so unusual," said the thief. "Big-shot lawyers hire me all the time. Like you, they want me to make quiet searches. People are funny. They die leaving all sorts of things squirreled away—wills, notes, cash, and diamonds and other jewelry. You'd be amazed at the places I find things. Not only that, they leave these crazy messages that sometimes take days to figure out. Believe me, Pauly, people can be wild. Even from the grave, they try to protect themselves. And you wonder, from what? You said before that your wife left a will?"

"Yes. But there was nothing mysterious or unusual about it. Her lawyer was the executor."

"There was nothing addressed to you?"

"Just a letter of instructions."

"Where is it?"

"In a safe deposit box with a lot of other papers and junk. There was nothing personal in it. In fact, it read like a goddamned business form. Which bothered me when I saw it. I wasn't in such great shape at the time, anyway, and the stiff formality only made me feel worse."

"And you haven't read it since?"

"Why would I? So I could feel lousy all over again?"

"Time has passed. You know things now that you didn't know before. It might read differently a second time."

"Sure. Worse."

"It can't hurt."

"Like hell it can't."

Mutsie's pale face was vividly warm, sympathetic. He rose, adjusted his tie in a mirror and collected his things. "I'm sorry I couldn't give you what you wanted."

"It probably doesn't exist. I appreciate your trying."

The thief paused at the door. "For whatever it's worth, I don't really think you'll be getting much trouble from your friend Handley. He's due to be hit. There's a contract out on him. Which should pretty well take care of things for you."

A platoon of ants marched up Turner's spine. "How do you know?"

"I know."

"For when?"

Mutsie hesitated. "He'll be in town tonight. He's speaking at the Hilton."

Turner stood there, looking at him.

"I shouldn't be saying anything. It could cost me. But I thought it might give you a lift."

"Thanks." Turner's voice was flat. "Was it my uncle?"

Mutsie was silent, but his eyes said it was about as stupid a question as he had heard in a long time. Turner shook his hand. How small it was, a child's. Some child. He suddenly felt five years old next to him. Next to anybody.

The hotel was ablaze with light, and the usual limousines were lined up in front. There were no uniformed police, but Turner was able to pick out at least half a dozen men, standing and sitting around the lobby, who looked as though they might be working security. According to a bulletin board, the International Press Club was holding its annual awards dinner in the main ballroom at eight o'clock. It was now almost nine. Turner had worn his dinner suit so as to be less conspicuous. Yet its net effect was to make him feel exactly the opposite. A matador's suit of lights, last worn the night of the British reception. Earlier, he had tried to contact Wendell Handley by phone, but the deputy director had either not yet arrived at the hotel or was not taking calls.

The main ballroom was at the terminus of a wide, carpeted corridor. Turner looked in. Banquet tables reached to the walls. Dinner was still being served, and the place was loud with the clatter of china, the drone of conversation, and the forced laughter of a great many people making an effort to be congenial. There was a long speakers' table on a dais at the far end of the room, and this was where Handley was seated. Turner stared at him with a mixture of relief and re-

303

sentment. At least the *momzer* was still alive. But why should this matter so much to him?

Three tall men with the faces of overaged linebackers stood to one side of the door. Turner walked up to the one nearest him. "I'd like to get a message to someone at the speakers' table."

"Who's that?"

"Wendell Handley."

The man's eyes took him apart and put him together again. "What's the message?"

"Just say Paul wants to talk to him."

"Paul who?"

"He'll know."

"You're Paul?"

"Yes."

Turner watched him work his way among the tables to the dais. Then he saw Handley glance toward the ballroom entrance where he was standing. When the man returned, he handed Turner a sealed envelope. Turner went out into the corridor to open it. A note and a Hilton room key were inside. The note said, *See you upstairs.*

It was a large, elegant suite on the eighteenth floor—living room, bedroom, and bath—and the lights were burning in every room. If one were to make judgments from such things, it would appear that top Company people lived exceedingly well, were deathly afraid of entering dark rooms, and suffered no concern for the energy shortage.

Turner picked a chair facing the door and sat down to wait. His neck and back literally ached with tension. He understood the deputy director's reluctance to be seen with him, but he wished he might have delivered his warning immediately. He had a sudden vision of himself sitting here waiting, while Handley was neatly picked-off in the elevator. He half listened for a commotion in the hall and the wail of sirens. He felt a depressing responsibility. Had the anonymous hit man seen him come in, recognized him, and guessed he was here to deliver a warning? If so, Handley would never make it upstairs. Turner glanced at the time. He had been sitting for almost a quarter of an hour. Then the door opened, and the deputy director came in.

He seemed amused by Turner's dinner clothes. "If all that elegance is just for me, I appreciate it. Sometimes I'm sure I spend less time in my office than at these infernal rubber chicken and roast beef banquets. Do you know the title of my talk tonight? 'Democracy's Survival in a Hostile World.' And its sole purpose is to convince the American public that Central Intelligence Agency isn't just another name for Gestapo." He took out his pipe and filled it. "I hope your being here means you have something for me."

"It means you may get blown away tonight. There's a contract out on you. I just learned about it a few hours ago. I thought you should know."

"Are you serious?" Handley frowned at him. "Of course you are. You're not one to make jokes about such things."

Turner watched him light his pipe. It might have been the most fascinating act in the world. He had become curiously absorbed in the deputy director—pale eyes; thick, smooth hair; tanned face; the soft, even quality of his breathing. The full human spectrum of Wendell Handley was suddenly being presented to him as a potential corpse, and he found it intriguing.

"I'm certain any number of people would be happy to see me dead, but who's planning it for tonight?"

"I don't know that. I'm not even sure it's set for tonight. But I saw no point in taking chances."

Handley sat down facing him. "Thanks for telling me. It only enforces my feelings about you."

"Can your security people handle this?"

"That's what they're around for."

"I must say, you don't seem very concerned."

"Oh, I'm concerned, all right. I'm no more anxious to die than anyone else. But all reasonable security measures have already been taken. As they are for every public appearance I make. And unless I'm willing to cancel my talk, there's nothing much I can do about it. You're sure you can't tell me more?"

"I don't know any more. It was only by accident that I found out this much."

"From whom?"

"I can't tell you that."

"But you did say it was a contract."

Turner nodded.

"Well, that's a lot better than some nut who just wants to save the world and doesn't care whether or not he's killed with me. There's no way to stop that kind of fanatic. At least a professional wants to get away afterward. So there are limitations to what he can do."

The deputy director picked up the phone and dialed. "Hello, Tommy. I've just been told someone may go for the brass ring tonight. Tighten up wherever possible. No. It seems to be a cash job. I'll be up here for awhile. Call me when you've finished checking." He hung up. "That's about all I can do."

"When are you scheduled to speak?"

"Not for half an hour." Handley worked at his pipe. "I'm disappointed. When I got your message, I was sure you had something of Maria's for me. I don't understand why you would come up here to save my life, yet hold back on that."

"I'll let you know when I figure it out myself."

There was a knock at the door, and Turner half started out of his seat.

Handley smiled. "Relax. I ordered some champagne sent up. Who is it?" he called.

"Room service, sir."

Turner said, "I thought you might have had enough champagne for one lifetime."

"I'm sorry." Handley's face flushed. "That was very thoughtless, very insensitive of me."

He opened the door, and a white-jacketed waiter came in carrying an ice bucket of champagne and glasses. He set the tray down on a coffee table. He was a short, compact man with the pleasant, almost deferential manner of someone who took satisfaction, even pride, in performing a service well. Handley signed the check. He seemed abstracted, apparently still brooding over his lapse in ordering the champagne. Glancing up, he saw part of the waiter's skull lift off and spatter against the wall. The shot had been soundless, except for the usual soft *whoosh* of a silenced bullet. The waiter fell backward onto the carpet. A revolver was in his hand. It was still partly covered by a large napkin. He lay unmoving.

Handley stared down at the man's face, at the spreading red stain on the carpeting. He appeared to be more puzzled than frightened. "How did you know?"

"I was more nervous than you, so I was watching carefully." Turner pocketed his revolver. "Then he didn't ask if you wanted the champagne opened. Finally, I spotted part of the gun under the napkin."

Handley went through the man's pockets. He removed a wallet, a handkerchief, and some keys and put them in a bureau drawer. "Do you always walk around with a silenced revolver in your pocket?"

"It was a last minute thought."

"We're both lucky you had it."

Turner looked at him.

"Do you think he would have just let you walk out of here?"

The thought had not even occurred to him. By trying to protect him, by doing his best to save his life, his uncle had almost managed to bury him.

"I owe you a big one," said Handley. "Now you'd better get out of here. I've got to have this mess cleaned up, and I don't want even a hint of you involved."

He went straight home and began drinking seriously. It was a curious progression. From wanting to kill the man, he had ended up saving his life. Why? Because they had both loved the same woman? Did it really work like an axiom in-plane geometry? Did it have to follow that those enmeshed with the same love were irrevocably entangled with each other? In some vaguely mystical way had killing Handley come to mean wiping out significant parts of himself? Or, even more insanely, and for a second time, Maria?

But this was all too simple and orderly, and he distrusted such neat explanations in much the same way that he distrusted psychological ones. Maria had been his wife, he had been her husband, and that was how it had been for as long as they were together. He had been bewitched, utterly gone, from the first time he saw her, this beautiful and already famous lady who, incredibly, appeared to have discovered something of equal value in him. She had made him feel young and whole despite his damaged body and years of turmoil. She had offered her flesh to console him for his pain. She had laughed at his terrible jokes. She had helped him climb out of the void. She had become his unfailing answer to the horrors of loneliness. She had made him want to leap into the future. She had presented him with the gifts of love and hope. And what had all or any of this to do with Wendell Handley?

Sitting there, still dressed in his suit of lights, his killing clothes, he felt her lips against his neck and proceeded to look for her at the bottom of the bottle.

The early sun angled in without warmth and woke him in the same chair. A battle was going on inside his head. Its dead lay unburied in his mouth. He came out of it feeling sick and stumbled to the bathroom just in time. Everything came up. It rose from the cellar of his feet, all the worst of it, all the bile of old fears, of confusion, of actions taken and not taken. It was not the night's bourbon that had gone sour in him, but everything else. Far from mourning Maria at that moment, he longed to be rid of her.

The phone was ringing as he came out of the shower. It was Hank. They were just leaving to catch the Concorde for London, and Turnovsky wanted to stop by and see him. Would it be all right? He made one of his poor jokes about allowing him time to hide the women in the closets and carefully measured her laugh for mood. It and she sounded fine.

His uncle arrived fifteen minutes later. He was alone and puffing from the stairs. "What's the matter? A big, important writer can't afford a house with an elevator?"

"Where's Hank?"

"Waiting in the car. There's no reason for both of us to have heart attacks." He sat down heavily in the living room and looked around. "Nice. A little on the high class gentile side, but very nice. It's too bad your mother and father never lived to see where you landed. They'd have *kvelled.*"

"Do you have time for coffee? It's ready."

"Why not?"

Turner brought in two cups. It occurred to him that this was the first time he was seeing his uncle without Hank present. He did not think it was an accident.

Turnovsky lit a cigar and peered at Turner through the smoke. "You look terrible. Pale green. You don't feel so good?"

"Too much bourbon last night. I'm okay."

"Sure."

Turnovsky sipped the coffee and nodded approval. He said nothing more, and Turner began to feel uncomfortable with the silence. "Will you be away long?"

"A week. Maybe ten days."

"Where are you going, besides London?"

"Paris, Rome, Brussels. I should stop in Berlin, too, but I can't get myself to set foot in any part of that Hansel and Gretel slaughterhouse. Not even to spit. If I died this morning, Pauly, there's only one thing I'd regret—that I never personally got to kill any Germans."

"You can hate that much?"

"In that, I'm unforgiving."

Once more, they sat in silence. Turnovsky glanced at his watch and sighed. "I've been waiting, but it looks like you're not going to tell me, eh, Pauly?"

"Tell you what?"

"About last night."

Turner absorbed himself in lighting a fresh cigarette. His uncle watched him with faint amusement. Tartar eyes, ruddy complexion, arched lids. The morning sunlight revealed networks of tiny lines in the stubborn face. Turnovsky suddenly looked his age.

"You were seen arriving at the Hilton last night at around nine and leaving close to an hour later. This morning a friend in the coronor's office told me that one of our better, hard-working *pistoleros* had a very important part of his head blown off in that same hotel during that same time period. I was just wondering whether it was all coincidence."

"No. It wasn't coincidence."

"Then you had something to do with Selwyn's death?"

Selwyn, thought Turner. Some name for a hired gun. "I found out Handley was going to be hit and went to warn him. I was in his room when your man came in. I got off a lucky shot."

"Selwyn was the best around. You're the one the coronor's office might have been calling me about this morning. Don't you know that?"

"I told you I didn't want Handley hit. You wouldn't listen to me."

"So you fixed it. Fine. And I almost ended up getting *you* hit. Are you out of your head, Pauly?"

"It's beginning to seem that way."

"Who told you about the hit?"

"Nobody."

Turnovsky sought answers in his coffee cup. A Jewish gypsy. "It had to be Mutsie. You didn't know anyone else."

"I figured it out myself."

"You couldn't figure shit out yourself." The old man showed his anger for the first time. "I don't know where you ever got the sense to write books. You're a goddamned amateur. And a moral one, besides. Which is what makes you so dangerous. You don't follow the rules. You're unpredictable. You spread mayhem like manure and don't even know what

310

you're doing. But Mutsie did know. He's a lifetime member of the order. He's the one I blame for this whole mess.''

"It wasn't his fault. He had the idea I wanted Handley dead. He was just trying to let me know it was set to happen. Don't take it out on poor Mutsie.''

"You're worried about poor Mutsie? That's nice of you. It happens you just killed his brother-in-law.''

"Selwyn? . . .''

"Exactly.''

"Oh, Christ!''

"Like I said, Pauly, there are rules in this like in everything else. If you don't know them, you can't follow them. Then everyone is in trouble." Turnovsky's old man's flesh seemed tired. "But I blame myself, too. Maybe more than you and Mutsie. If you said no, I should have let it be no. You can't help a man who doesn't want to be helped. You've got plenty of *shtiks,* but they're yours and I guess you're entitled to them. I'm not as smart as I like to think. I made a very serious mistake this time, and I'm afraid it could cost me.''

"What do you mean, cost you?''

"Come on, Pauly. Pay attention. I have a plane to catch and it's getting late. Who do you think your friend Handley is going to tie in to Selwyn? The Prince of Wales? And when he does make the connection, what do you think he's going to do? Let me keep trying until I get it right? The man should have been dead this morning. Now he has to protect himself. And there's only one practical way for him to do that.''

Turner sat there, unmoving. Emotion silenced him. Hank had once come to warn him of something like this, but he had failed to listen. "Is that why you're suddenly going to Europe?''

"I had to go soon, anyway. So I'm going a little sooner.''

"I had no idea, Uncle Herschel.''

"Of course you had no idea. You think I don't know that? The trouble is we're not used to such high, moral types. You're too straight for us. It throws everyone and everything off.''

311

Turner felt a dry, burning sensation behind his eyes. "I'm sorry. I never should have come to you in the first place."

"Now you're talking crazy. So who else should you have come to? I'm your father's brother. We bleed the same blood."

"That has nothing to do with it."

"No? So what has to do with it?"

Turner rose and walked to a window. He felt a disturbing urge to weep. But for whom? In the street below, his uncle's long black limousine was double-parked in front of the house, backing up traffic. A bodyguard leaned against the hood. The second bodyguard and Hank were not visible.

"Let me tell you about blood," said Turnovsky. "It has everything to do with it. Your father, may he rest in peace, didn't know that. He was ashamed of me. I was a disgrace, not a brother. You'd think brothers grew on trees. I didn't behave, I didn't act as he would have liked me to act, so I was finished. Me? I don't judge those I love. I just do what I can for them. Maybe it's not always right, but at least. I try."

Turner left the window. "I'm turning out to be the worst thing that ever happened to you."

"Stop talking nonsense. Six months ago there was only one person in this world I cared anything about—Hank. Now I have two. You've doubled my *gemütlichkeit.* And that's a lot for an old *gonif* like me. Remember the book *The Godfather?* A literary phenomenon. Why? Because the author was able to take a bunch of thieves and killers and make millions of decent, law-abiding readers care about them. And how did he do it? By showing how those *gonifs* looked after their own. Without compromise. No matter what." He laughed. "It even makes a kind of practical sense. How else can the damned pick up a few crumbs of grace?"

Turnovksy stood up and embraced his nephew. "Don't look so unhappy, Pauly. We do what we can. For better or worse. We take our own risks."

Turner went down to the limousine with him. Hank was sitting in back. Turnovsky told her, "You could die climbing

312

those steps. Better he should visit us."

Hank lowered a window. "Please take care, Pauly."

Turner leaned in and kissed her cheek. If she condemned him, it did not show. But for the first time he noticed dark rings under her eyes, and the bones of her face seemed to be pushing out of her skin. What had he done to these people?

He stood on the sidewalk, watching the glossy, armored limousine glide away from the curb like an ocean liner leaving its pier. He wished he had confetti. The two bodyguards were in front. Hank and Turnovsky sat behind a glass partition in the rear. He watched until the car turned a corner and disappeared.

Back in his apartment, he thought about calling Mutsie. But what could he say? I'm sorry I shot your wife's brother in the head? Instead, and almost as if by way of atonement, he decided to take the thief's advice and go over Maria's final letter of instructions. The whole idea was depressing. But maybe, as Mutsie had said, it couldn't hurt.

Mutsie turned out to be wrong. It hurt.

In the tiny, bank cubicle, he sat among faded bits and pieces of their lives and forced his way through Maria's letter for the second time. She had evidently dictated it to her secretary, who had then typed it in standard business form beneath the broadcasting network's official letterhead.

Dear Paul,

This is just a brief addendum to my formal will, which, in its present form, should effectively detail my wishes concerning my estate proper. Since I have never been especially interested in the accumulation of possessions per se, I doubt that you shall be burdened with the need to dispose of too great an amount of clothing, jewelry, and other such personal items. But whatever does exist in this category, please feel free to handle in whatever way you deem fitting.

Most importantly, do not feel constrained to keep anything you do not truly want. Neither of us has ever been sentimental about the inanimate. To this end, the old adage "If it doesn't bleed, don't cry over it" more than ever holds true. You would do well to act

313

accordingly under whatever conditions may exist at the moment you are reading this letter.

Perhaps if you had ever given me something as a gift, I might have felt differently. But you were never big on presents, which is just as well because I could never abide having to make a fuss over token gestures of endearment. I place such things in the same category as hearts carved on trees along with their accompanying messages. Both are for the very young or the very foolish, and it has been a while since we fit into either category. Or perhaps you have even forgotten that once we did.

Your wife,
Maria Monroe

He sat staring at the signature: *Your wife, Maria Monroe.* Her last four words of personal communication. Followed by her secretary's and her own initials. The letter had scraped him raw when he read it immediately after her death, and it was just as irritating now. The thing was, it did not even sound like her. It was as if she had deliberately tried, in this, in what could well prove to be her final message to him, to come across as someone else. When had she ever signed anything addressed to him as Maria Monroe? In fact, the entire letter suddenly struck him as unnecessary. It told him nothing he did not already know. His wife had been a busy, precise, efficient woman who never wasted an instant of time or a modicum of effort. Why in heaven's name would she have taken the trouble to dictate to her secretary a stuffy, stilted letter that served absolutely no purpose?

Jesus Christ, he thought.

Once glimpsed, it seemed so obvious that he could only wonder how he had managed not to see it before. It was simple. She would never in a million years have written such a letter unless it was meant deliberately to tell him something that only he would be able to understand. Again, he had been blind and stupid. No. Not really. During his original reading, he had simply had his mind on other things. Or, more likely, he had still been in shock. In any case, he had not been looking. Now, silently blessing Mutsie for having pushed him into it, he looked. And in something less than two minutes, he saw what he felt certain she had wanted him to see.

He left the bank and walked east. He was headed for the garage where he kept his car. It was one of those sunny, brilliantly clear days of early spring, and everyone seemed to have shed his or her dark clothes in celebration. He found himself hurrying and deliberately slowed his pace. It was too beautiful a day to rush. A lie. He simply did not want to get there too quickly. He might discover he was wrong.

Ten minutes later he was in the Mustang. He drove north along the East River toward the approach to the George Washington Bridge. Again, he kept his speed down. He checked his rear view mirror, saw nothing suspicious, and forgot about his back. He was beginning to feel almost euphoric. An odd sensation for him. Particularly at this stage. What did he expect to find?

Everything.

In memory, each outing had been a kind of idyll, a lovely pastoral indulgence, a welcome break in their busy urban lives, a few hours of sunlight and trees, sparkling stream water, the warmth and fragrance of summer grass. They usually went on Sundays, starting early to beat the traffic and carrying elaborate lunches of cold chicken or turkey or duck and always plenty of wine. They had stumbled over the place by accident their first time out and never went anywhere else. They just kept going back. They did not want to risk changing a single ingredient.

The place itself was an hour and a half drive north of the city, in Putnam County, a tiny green glade about a mile from the Taconic Parkway, reached, finally, by a winding dirt trail that seemed to go nowhere. The surrounding trees were tall and old and the undergrowth thick, especially in late summer. But there was always plenty of sunlight breaking through, and the shadows were cool and edged in purple. There were no houses, no traffic noises, and New York and the rest of the world were light years away. Only birds, squirrels, and rabbits intruded. And occasionally a curious deer. Otherwise, the place was wholly theirs . . . to talk, to make love, to doze, or simply to watch the sky.

Then, of course, there was the tree. Some kind of oak, Turner thought. Although being a city type, he was never too certain of such things. But it was very tall and old and partially dead, with great, twisting, agonized limbs that reached far out and carried their years with stubborn grace. The ground beneath was soft and sweet-smelling, and this was where they would make love.

"I'd like to die here," Maria had once sighed.

Passion spent, they lay holding one another.

"Not yet," he said. "I'm still enjoying you too much."

"Do you think there's sex after death?"

"Ask Woody Allen."

"What about spirit communication? Do you believe in any of that?"

"No. That's why I'm writing as fast as I can. So if you have any really important messages for me, better not wait."

"It's not always that simple. Maybe we ought to arrange something."

"Like what? An intercelestial message drop?"

"Why not?"

"What did you have in mind?"

Maria gazed up through the oak's arthritic branches. She pointed to a hole in the trunk. "How about that small, hollow place there?"

"You mean our spiritual messages are going to be inscribed on paper?"

"Or sheets of sunlight. It doesn't matter. As long as we have a place to leave them."

He laughed and kissed her. "You're positively poetic."

She rose, slender and naked in the sun, picked up a paring knife, and begun cutting at the tree trunk.

"What are you doing?"

"You'll see."

It was not easy going. The bark was tough and had to be painstakingly scraped away. But when she was finished,

316

The Past

Turner saw two hearts with the words *Intercelestial Drop* carved beneath them.

"Don't you dare laugh," she warned.

He had no such intention.

"But you have to remember to look," she said.

"You're the one who will have to remember. Statistics favor your outlasting me by at least five years."

"No. I'll die first."

"You haven't looked at my body lately."

She shook her head. "Promise me you'll remember to look."

"Okay, okay. I promise."

"Seriously."

"I promise seriously."

"That you'll remember to look," she insisted, wanting everything neatly spelled out.

"That I'll remember to look," he repeated gravely.

But, of course, he had not remembered. In truth, he had never been especially big on that sort of whimsy. Nor, for that matter, had Maria. Still, viewed within the context of recent events, what else could she have been referring to?

It was a bit past noon when he left the Taconic Parkway, drove west for several miles on a two-lane blacktop, and found the dirt trail leading off to the right.

He got out of the car and pushed through pale, spring growth until he came to the clearing. It was smaller than he remembered and covered with dead weeds and last year's grass. He heard the stream, running fast with recent rains, and saw patches of light where the water caught and reflected the sun. A rabbit dashed out of the brush almost at his feet, startling him and making him brace for an attack. Birds sang. He stopped at the edge of the clearing, looked up, and saw the oak.

It towered above the surrounding trees, an ailing black giant with a massive trunk and crawling roots. A great many dead branches had fallen, but the rest were in bud and carried the beginnings of leaves. This one would not die easy, would not go gently into any sweet night. He moved closer, circling to the right until he saw the hole in the trunk, narrow and dark and about five feet from the ground.

He stopped, caught in sudden fear. What if he had figured wrong? He wanted this so badly that it infuriated him. He felt shamed by the depth of his need. Then he saw the faint outlines of the two hearts and the words *Intercelestial Drop* and knew there was no way he could have figured this one wrong.

He stepped forward, reached deep into the hole, and took out what his wife had left there for him.

It was a small package, wrapped in plastic and tin foil to protect it from the weather. When this was removed, Turner found an oblong metal box with a key taped to the top. Squirrels. She had even remembered to guard it against the squirrels, he thought. He tried to open the box, but his hands were shaking so badly that he finally gave up in disgust, sat down on the dead grass, and lit a cigarette.

When he felt calmer, he fit the tiny key into the lock, opened the box, and found a sheaf of folded papers wrapped in a plastic bag. He smoothed them out and counted them. There were fifteen sheets of plain, unlined typing paper. There was no letterhead or date. All were covered with Maria's neat, evenly spaced writing. He read:

My Darling,

I'm so very sorry. Because if you are reading this, then I am gone and won't be seeing you again. And this, in considering it even now, makes me inexpressibly sad. For myself, because I love you and despise having to say goodbye. And for you, because I know what my death is going to do to you. This alone is enough to break my heart. My poor, dear, love . . .

He had to stop. Tears poured out and blinded him. Salt ran down his face and into his mouth. He never knew he had so much water in his head. How in God's name was he going to read this? He bit his lip until blood ran with the salt. He swallowed both. Then he took hold and went on.

The Past

There's so much to tell you, so much to explain, so much to beg forgiveness for, so much to justify, that I'm almost afraid to start. The truth is, I've always prayed it would never come to this. I was foolish. I should have known that one day it finally would. You don't do what I've spent most of my life doing and expect to die of old age, in a comfortable bed, surrounded by your loved ones. It just doesn't work that way. But, of course, at this point you don't even know what I'm talking about, so I'd better begin at the beginning, which isn't going to be easy for either of us. Not for me, writing, and especially not for you, reading. You may even loathe me by the time we're through. If you do, I can't help it. But please, please darling, try not to.

This is going to be a very long story, so I hope you have plenty of cigarettes. In my mind, I can almost see you sitting and reading this under our tree. And if I know you at all, you probably started to break up before even getting through the first paragraph. You're really such a lovely crier. I'm sure I fell in love with you the first time I saw you quietly crying in the movies and licking away the tears so I wouldn't notice. What I'm less sure of is how long it will finally take you to figure out my rather oblique reference to *hearts carved on trees with their accompanying messages.* You have one of the most sensitively imaginative minds I've ever known, but also one of the most foggy and abstracted. Still, I know you'll eventually get my message. In fact, I'm counting on it. Because this may well be the most important communication I've ever written. And this is why I was so subtle in pointing you to it. I couldn't risk its falling into any hands but yours. You'll soon understand why. That is, if I ever stop stalling with all these little asides and really start.

My God, I never knew I was such a coward. I'm so scared I can actually feel my stomach turning over. I'm afraid you'll think harshly of me. I'm afraid you'll hate my memory. I'm afraid all that loveliness we shared will turn ugly. Now isn't that crazy? What difference should it make? If you're reading this, I'm already beyond any possible mortal damage. What can it do to me? Ah, I suppose what I'm really afraid of is what it might do to you. All right, darling. For better or worse, for richer or poorer, in sickness and in health, till death do us part. Oh God, listen to me run on, will you. Anyway, here goes, love.

If this is going to make any sense at all, I suppose it has to start with my parents. Because whatever I eventually became originated

319

with them. To begin with, my mother and father were never really the bitter, angry émigrés that you and everyone else believed them to be. They did not detest Russia, they loved Russia. They were not random victims of the war, of the German invasion, cruelly driven out of their home and into the camps. It was all deliberately arranged by Moscow. They did not come to this country because they longed to share in the American dream. They came because it was their assigned duty. What I'm trying to tell you, darling, is that for as long as my mother and father were in this country, they were never anything but loyal Russians, members of the Communist Party working for the Soviet Committee for State Security. That is, the KGB. But don't be misled. They were actually very small potatoes. They passed on no highly classified security information to the Kremlin. They never knew any. What they did mostly was keep an eye on the Russian émigré community here, report on ties to dissidents at home, and occasionally provide back-up support and information to more highly placed agents. But they believed with all their hearts in what they were doing and died whispering devout prayers for the future of world revolution.

In retrospect, I suppose their single major contribution to the Soviet intelligence effort was really me. I'm sorry, darling. I know this is going to go off in your head like a thousand-pound bomb. But from the day I was born, and perhaps even from the day I was conceived, my path, my calling, was chosen for me. I was born to two Soviet agents. I lived my entire adult life as a Soviet agent. And now, finally, since you are reading this letter, I have evidently died as a Soviet agent. These are the simple, irreducible facts. Everything else is either elaboration. . . .

He stopped reading. She was wrong. She had made some sort of wild mistake. She had everything backward. He sat numbly in his patch of sunlight and stared up at the tree. It was like trying to walk on water. You sank deeper with every step. When would he learn not to try? Was there no end to his foolishness? "Everything else is either elaboration," he read again,

or explanation. Although these are important, too. Because later in this confessional I'm going to have to ask you to do something for me. And since I can no longer ask you to do anything on trust alone, there's a lot I'll have to explain. But first, a little background, darling. For as Mr. Freud himself once said, the adult is never far from the child. And I came early to this particular feast. No apologies here. Just facts. Whatever apologies I have will come later and for different reasons.

You know, of course, how much I loved, respected, even revered my parents. It was actually more of an old world attitude than an American one. What they told me, I accepted without question. What they cared about, I cared about. What they believed, I believed. And since they were convinced in their hearts that communism was the one true faith, the world's single hope of salvation before Armageddon, I, too, was convinced. I know there are those who would simply dismiss us all as traitors, and even you are undoubtedly among them, darling. But my mother and father used to talk to me about world communism as a higher call, a duty to humanity that transcended and was far loftier than any narrow loyalty to one's country. Not that I was a mere robot, mouthing simplistic Party dogma. I very quickly learned that even Russia was no Valhalla, that it wasn't really a land of happily singing workers and peasants, that Pravda printed as many lies and half-truths as our newspapers, that people were often exiled, imprisoned, and killed for holding the wrong views. But I did honestly believe that if there was ever going to be any hope at all for the earth's millions of poor, neglected, beat-up, and deprived, it had far less chance of coming from the dog-eat-dog philosophy of western capitalism than from communism's basically humanistic doctrine of sharing.

All right, love. So much for how I got into this and the purity of my motives, which you're probably still shocked and angry enough not to give a damn about anyway, but which is nevertheless important to my image. (Joke.) Suffice it to say, I was in it up to my eyeballs at a time when other girls my age had little more on their minds than the size and shape of their breasts and how far to let their boyfriends go on the fourth date. Although it did make me feel rather superior. As any true calling does. While others simply drifted without purpose, I moved with single-minded dedication straight toward my goal. And my goal, with typical childish immodesty, was to be nothing less than the greatest covert female agent since Mata Hari. No fooling, darling. In my solitary, virgin's bed, this was the dream I dreamed. Never mind the alleged altruism and

321

justice of the cause. Forget the sociological and political theories involved. When it comes right down to it, it's the ego that is the real driving force. That soaring feeling of "Hey, gang, look what I'm doing" without which few of us would ever want to get out of bed in the morning. So I really adored the whole idea. And from the age of fourteen on, when my parents and their KGB superiors judged me mature enough to begin my actual indoctrination and training, this took precedence over everything else in my life.

Anyway, darling, I happen to have done incredibly well. Not that I expect you (my poor betrayed patriot) to be thrilled by my success. But my parents were secretly honored with no less a tribute than the Order of Lenin for having contributed such a hotshot to the cause of world revolution. And they died happily and pridefully because of it. But don't worry. I'm not going to afflict you with any recitation of details. I'm not that insensitive to what you must be feeling at this moment. Yet for you to understand what I'm going to ask you to do later, you do have to know certain things. So please bear with me, love, and try not to despise me too much. At least, not until I'm through.

He put down the letter and lit a fresh cigarette. He needed the break. It was impossible to read and absorb this all in one stretch. Besides, he wanted to make it last as long as possible. How could she have thought he'd despise her? It was as if he was actually hearing her speak. What she said was almost secondary. As long as he was reading, she was here, sitting with him. Like a miser, he wanted to count the remaining pages to see how much treasure he had left. When he could hold off no longer, he began reading once more.

My going into broadcasting was no accident. What it did was give me ready access to the top people in every significant area of government, industry, and international politics. Everyone was available to me. I could go anywhere and ask anything without arousing suspicion. And because of this, I was even able to enter the orbit of the man who would one day become president. Of course Tom Woodruff was still a long way from the Oval Office when I met him. But all you had to do was spend a few hours with the man to know he was headed for big things. At least that was my early impression of him, and it obviously turned out to be correct. I mention this only because Woodruff was and still is far and away the most important element in everything I've been trying to achieve for the past eleven years. In fact, he happens to be the one who inadvertantly made it possible for me to accomplish what might well be one of the most dramatic intelligence coups of the decade. And that's what I want to tell you about next.

We first met when he was chairman of the Federal Communications Commission and I was a bright-eyed young broadcaster with both of my big, bright eyes on the main chance. And to me, Tom was so clearly and emphatically it that I went after him with everything I had, as well as with a few things I only made believe I had. I must admit it was not really that difficult. Regardless of his considerable abilities and strengths, the man was incredibly vulnerable in certain areas. With the result that in a year's time I had impressed him so strongly, had so thoroughly convinced him I was one of the few people around whom he could really trust, that when he was appointed director of the CIA, I had exactly the inside track I wanted. A few months later, believe it or not, it was actually Woodruff himself who approached *me*, with the idea of working undercover for the Central Intelligence Agency. As a good American, I naturally had no choice but to accept.

God, I hope I don't sound too smartass and facetious about this. Because that's certainly not the way I feel. In fact, the reverse is true. This is all really so desperately solemn that I suppose I'm unconsciously trying to lighten it up a bit. I'm also self-conscious about how I must be coming across. Cynical and devious. And that is not how I wanted you to remember me. Unfortunately, I'm in a cynical, devious business, and no one has yet figured out any other way to survive in it.

Okay. So there I was, an honest-to-God Soviet spy who had miraculously managed to get herself hired as a high level United States agent by no less a personage than the CIA director himself. Honestly, love, it dazzled even me. And my intended function? To be recruited by the Russians so I could feed them disinformation carefully selected by the CIA. This was, of course, easy enough to arrange and ultimately gave me an invaluable inside line to much of the CIA's strategic planning. And when Tom moved on to become president, my connections went even higher.

So we now come to the third and final member of our little

troika, which is very much how I've come to think of us over the years. A team of three seemingly unrelated components irrevocably joined by mutual deception. You already know about Woodruff and me. Our third partner is a man you may never even have heard of, but who, for current purposes, may well be the most significant of all. His name is Wendell Handley, and he is the deputy director of the CIA. Their number two man. But more importantly, he also happens to be the highest ranking KGB agent in this country.

Turner stared at the last sentence so long and hard that his·eyes blurred. He blinked to clear them and read it twice more. It was a waste of time. It said the same thing. He looked up at the sky. He was beginning to feel like a prisoner in a Chinese puzzle—a man within a box, within a box, within a box. Whre in God's name did the progression end? He forced his eyes back to the letter and read on.

Let me tell you about Handley. Unlike me, he is not of Russian descent—recent or otherwise. In fact, his forebears were among the founding fathers of this country. In their day, revolutionaries of a more generally respected sort. Handley is strictly an ideological Communist, which is usually the most rabid kind. Very zealous, very intense, very uncompromising, very straight and humorless about the whole thing. Devoid of Russian blood, he feels compelled to out-Russian the Russians in his devotion to the Revolution. But he is smart, too handsome to be real, and an absolute charmer. For more than twelve years I've known him as well as it's possible to know anyone, and we've worked together for most of this time. Through necessity, we've lived similarly unnatural lives. We've both had good marriages, yet neither of us has been able to share much of our lives with our respective mates. So, in a vital area of my daily existence, the only person I was ever really able to relax and discuss things with was Wendell Handley, and vice versa for him. Yet at this moment, if I was asked for my single overriding reaction to Wendell Handley as a man, as a fellow KGB agent and disciple of world communism, and as deputy director of the CIA, my answer would have to be that he scares the absolute hell out of me. I know this sounds crazy. But I'm going to explain why it's so.

Mostly, I suppose, my reaction has to do with what I've learned during all these years of schizophrenic living, of peering closely into the best and worst of our two conflicting worlds and ideologies, of seeing what happens when the two greatest intelligence networks on the planet, Russian and American, struggle to outwit, penetrate, and immobilize one another. And do you know what I've found happens? Very little. Almost nothing. Oh, we have plenty of action and movement, all right. There's no scarcity in that area. Billions of rubles and dollars are spent worldwide every year on manpower and equipment, and something does have to be shown for that kind of money. So we have all these intricate, marvelously sophisticated listening devices, and spy planes, and satellites in the sky, and millions of feet of recording tape, and offices and buildings full of overt and covert agents functioning in every major city of every continent on earth, and news reports about dangerous breaches of security, and intelligence breakthroughs, and dirty traitors, and even, from time to time, dramatic spy trials like that of the poor Rosenbergs, which was all really a tragic mistake because the times were bad and somebody went crazy and broke the rules. But, generally, the end result is that nothing much really happens. At least, not on any sort of cataclysmic scale. Russia remains Russia, America remains America, and the good citizens of both countries go on with their daily living, working, aging, and dying without being dramatically affected by what happens in Moscow and Washington.

Why? Because ritual propaganda to the contrary, there really aren't any madmen or criminals in the Kremlin and White House. What we have there generally, despite any ideological differences, are people of fair good will who realize that nobody is going to win any all-out nuclear war and that they'd damn well better not try. So as I see it, our greatest danger lies not so much in our doctrinal squabbles as in the outside chance that someone of less than fair good will may reach a strong enough position, in either capitol, to tip the balance of power. And that's why Wendell Handley frightens me. He's not only the kind of uncompromising zealot who could sacrifice any number of lives (Russian and/or American) for principle without blinking an eye, but he's very near to being named chief of the Central Intelligence Agency. And when you add to this the fact that he is also a force in the KGB, God only knows what cries of havoc may be loosed along with his bloody dogs of war.

I hope you're following me, love, because this is important. The point is, I know Handley too well. I'm the only one functioning in this country who does know him. Despite much of what I've said, however, we're close friends. So close, that I feel I can keep a reasonable rein on him. In my own way, I suppose I always have. And he also knows that if he crosses a particular line, I can blow the whistle on him. It has been many years since I stopped being as rabid and doctrinaire a revolutionary as he. I still do my work for the KGB, but more on my own terms than I would admit to either Wendell or Moscow. Believe it or not, love, I've even managed to do a bit of good for our more repressed and unhappy Jews over there. I don't know. Maybe I've actually become a burnt-out case. All I seem interested in doing these days is keeping the possible damage on both sides to a minimum and maintaining a peaceful status quo. I'm like the old time roulette player who starts betting both red and black because he needs the money and just wants to break even.

I suppose you could consider this letter as a kind of insurance policy. And I'm naming the citizens of this essentially decent country as its chief beneficiaries. Writing it, I have no way of knowing whether or not I'm going to die any time in the near future. But if you are reading it, I obviously have. So know this, love: Regardless of what anyone tells you, you can be sure I did not die of natural causes. This prospect does not especially upset me. Abrupt ends are an occupational hazard I've become well acquainted with over the years. And, in the final analysis, it beats dying in a nursing home in a 'puddle of urine. Though I guess there might have been more pleasant alternatives somewhere in-between.

All right, darling. We now come to what this entire letter has been leading up to. That is, your part in my little insurance metaphor. What I want you to do is hand deliver these pages to President Woodruff. I want you to give them to him when no one else is present. I want you to sit there with him while he reads every word. And when he is finished reading, I want you to answer whatever questions he has as to how and where I left the letter for you. He won't question its authenticity. He knows my handwriting, and most of the enclosed facts speak for themselves. Since there was no practical way for me to write this after my death (at least none that I now know about), I had to go through this convoluted procedure of writing it before and leaving it in the only place I could think of that neither crowd, American or Russian, would be swarming over the instant my death became known. I simply can't conceive of leaving Wendell behind me, unattended, unchecked, uncompromising, as the Kremlin's personal director of the CIA. The power distortions inherent in so monstrous a political freak are just too frightening for me to accept. And when I remember that it was not too long ago that Tom Woodruff himself used this very same position as a springboard to the presidency, my fear becomes that much greater.

I ask only one favor of the president. Regardless of how harshly I may judge Wendell politically, he is still a longtime friend and collaborator. I don't want anything to happen to him. I don't want him terminated or imprisoned. Let him be sent to Russia. With or without his family. Despite all his inspired talk of a communist utopia, I'm sure he will find that punishment enough.

A thought strikes me. If you're reading this, love, and I am, indeed, dead, I wonder how I died. I wonder how, why, and by whom I was finally done in. I must admit I have sometimes had the feeling it could be Wendell. I know he cares deeply for me, but this would never stop him if he ever considered me a threat to our cause. Interesting, isn't it? Ah, I'm beginning to ramble, which means I've finished telling you everything of importance, but don't want to say goodbye. How sad that I was never able to tell you any of this face to face, in person. But neither of us could have come close to living with it. There is so much for me to apologize for, darling, so much I hated to do. I hated shutting you out. I hated deceiving you. I hated your not being a part of everything I was doing. Still, it was either that or not having you at all, and God how I did want you. It was clearly insane for me to marry at all. I'm sure you can understand that now. But this was one time I refused to be sane. You are the only major indulgence I have allowed myself since I was fourteen and beginning my first lessons in politics, pragmatism, and survival. I guess I felt I was owed. I horrified everyone when I said I was marrying. Both sides—Moscow and Washington. But I was too valuable for anything to be done about it. You were the romantic dream I had never had. So lovely, so noble, so brave, so monumentally innocent (at one point I almost thought stupid), that at first I couldn't believe you were real. My God, you had everything but a white horse. And I'll tell you this, love. In all our years together, you never proved to be less than I expected you to be. I never regretted any part of it. The only thing that ever hurt me about you was that I couldn't give you more.

Turner's Wife

Damn it, I don't want to wrap this up. It appalls me to have to say goodbye. Especially like this. Apart from everything else, it's so ridiculously unnatural. Here I am, sitting here, very much alive and well, in my office, writing to you as though I were already dead. Then I'm going to drive up to Putnam County, leave this in our tree, and go home and have dinner with you tonight. And perhaps, with luck, a few thousand nights after that. Maybe we'll even grow old and decrepit together. Who knows? I've lasted this long, haven't I? But I obviously don't believe that or I wouldn't be taking the time and trouble to tell you all this.

The fact is, things have been happening lately that I don't like. Nothing big or overt. Just small subtle intimations. And I don't doubt that much of it has to do with the deterioration in my attitude. And for a functioning agent in place, I'm afraid it is a deterioration. I've become much too humanist in my judgments. People have become more important to me than predetermined, doctrinaire goals. As I've already told you, I just don't believe that most of what we're doing matters that much anymore. And this means I no longer have the single-mindedness and dedication so necessary to this kind of work. Truthfully, I should have gotten out a long time ago, but there's just no practical way. I'm not complaining, love. I've always known the rules. This is simply by way of explanation.

I'm beginning to feel I've opened a floodgate I can't close. But I keep thinking of things to tell you, dead, that I'm unable to say alive. Crazy, isn't it? There's almost a sense of panic. What if I forget to mention something really important and have to drift through eternity, trying futilely to reach you? If there is an eternity (something else I've been considering lately). No. It's more than lately. I think that was why I converted to Judaism when we married. The conversion actually mattered far less to you than it did to me. I suppose I needed some sort of cosmic protection. Judaism was, after all, the oldest continuing conduit to God currently available. You people had survived with it for five thousand years against some pretty tough going. I figured you must know something. Until then, communism was the only religion I had room for. But it was, after all, less than seventy years old. It was also struggling, imperfect, subject to review without warning, and able to offer no promises about getting me into any next place. And that had suddenly become important. The thing was, love, if I couldn't share everything with you here and now, I thought it best to hedge my bets about our being together at some future time and place.

So much for God and the hereafter. I guess I should have made myself a checklist. Final statements are too important to handle in this sort of catch-as-catch-can style. Still, I think I've touched on all the truly significant areas. And since I don't expect to be leaving you immediately, I can always come back and add whatever I happen to think of later.

Ah, immediately there is something else. I lied to you about not being able to have children. The rape and abortion were true, but not the other. It just was not feasible for me. Besides, it would have been unfair for all concerned. I never really cared that much about not having children, but you would have made such a marvelous father. You have so much to offer a child. Maybe you can find someone nice and young and start a family now. I'm sure it's far from too late. But talking of finding someone, did you know that Peggy has had a thing for you for years? You probably never even noticed. You're the absolute last of a vanishing breed. A true one-woman man. It's foolish to swear for anyone's fidelity, darling, but I'd swear for yours in a minute. No matter. The moment you're alone, they'll be coming at you in droves. You'll need a club to beat them away. Just choose more carefully next time, love. Someone nice and young and uncomplicated. And maybe even wide in the hips for proper childbearing. Which lets poor Peggy out on all counts. I think you've known her too long, anyway. She would be too entangled in your mind with me and with our past. She couldn't give you the fresh start you're going to need. Sorry, Peggy. But watch out for her. She's clever and aggressive. She knows men. She'll be in your pants before the first rain has dried on my grave. So don't mistake her needs for yours.

Without knowing precisely how, when, or why I'm finally going to be terminated, I can't prepare you for what may follow. But I am sure of at least two things. My office and the apartment are going to be thoroughly picked apart, and Wendell will be doing a lot of sniffing around. All I can hope for is that you'll find this letter quickly and bring it to the president at once. From there, he should be able to take care of everything. Tom Woodruff is a good man. Trust him.

I'm going to end this now, darling. If I don't, I'm sure I'll only get maudlin and that's not going to do either of us any good. Forgive me if you can, love. If you can't, who could blame you? But please, please remember this. Regardless of everything—regardless of whatever I've told you and regardless of what you may read into it or hear afterward—one thing has remained constant for me. And that's my feeling for you. I've loved you from beginning to end.

Forever and always,
Your Maruschka

And that was it.

He read the fifteen pages again, pausing here and there to absorb particular passages. Then he just sat there in the clearing and watched the sun sink slowly behind a ridge. When it was not quite dark, he carefully folded the letter along its original lines, smoothed the cluster of pages flat, slid them into an inside jacket pocket, and drove back to New York.

TWENTY-FOUR

The Past

He garaged the Mustang and was in his apartment slightly before eight o'clock. Five minutes later, the phone rang. Letting it ring, he poured some bourbon. He felt the letter in his pocket, pressing against his chest, but he did not take it out. Ten minutes later the phone rang again. This time he picked it up.

"I've been trying to get you for hours," said Peggy. "Where have you been?"

The question irritated him. Her tone made it sound like an accusation. "Nowhere. For a drive in the country."

"Are you all right?" She clearly did not believe him.

"Why shouldn't I be all right? It's spring. Or is it my driving that worries you?"

The line was silent.

"What's the matter?" he said.

"I'll be over in fifteen minutes. Don't you dare move until I get there."

It actually took her twenty minutes. Breathless from the stairs, she kissed him and poured herself a generous drink. They sat down in the study.

"What's the matter?" he asked again. "Why have you been trying to get me for hours? What's all the urgency?"

"I guess you haven't been listening to the news."

"You know I never listen to the news. What's happened, damn it?"

"There was some sort of explosion. Your uncle's car went up. The reports said it happened near Kennedy Airport."

Turner sat holding his drink. He felt as though he was waiting for death. His body was tensed to receive it.

"Your uncle was killed." Her voice was soft, toneless. She did not quite look at him as she spoke. "So were two other men in the car. His bodyguards, they said."

His vision seemed to be tinged black. His color. He blinked to clear his eyes. Goodbye, Uncle Herschel. He sat, mute.

"I'm sorry, Paul."

"What about Hank?"

"I don't know. I don't remember hearing anything about her." She drank without pleasure. "The police seem to think it was linked to some sort of crime syndicate war."

"The police are full of shit."

"I know how you feel. But that was how he lived, Paul. That was why he never moved without bodyguards."

"Sure."

They sat with it.

"Please. Do me a favor," he said. "Call the *Times* and see what they know about Hank."

"She may not even have been in the car."

"She was," he said flatly. "They stopped here this morning on the way to Kennedy."

Peggy put through the call, and Turner went to refill their glasses. He did not want to sit there, listening. Not her, too, he said silently. It was as close to a prayer as he could come.

Peggy hung up the receiver as he returned. "She's in Queens General Hospital. That's all they know."

"I'm going out there."

"I'll go with you."

"Thanks, but no."

"Paul . . ."

"I appreciate your not telling me on the phone. That was

kind. Now just forget the whole thing."

"How do I do that?"

"I don't know. But please try."

He took a taxi and forty minutes later was out at the hos-pital, an aging pile of brick on Queens Boulevard. There were three patrol cars in front and uniformed cops in the lobby. He asked for Henrietta Adams's room number at the reception desk and found a gold-braided police lieutenant standing beside him.

"Who are you, mister?"

"Paul Turner."

"What's your business with Miss Adams?"

"I'm Herschel Turnovsky's nephew."

"Any identification?"

Turner gave him his driver's license and credit cards. The lieutenant examined and kept them. "You'll have to be searched."

Turner extended his arms and one of the policemen went over him. "What's that in your jacket?"

Maria's letter bulged against an inside pocket. "Just some papers."

"Please take them out."

Turner froze. "They're papers, not a deadly weapon."

"We have to see nothing's concealed in them."

"They're confidential."

"Nobody's gonna read them."

Turner handed him the folded papers and did not breathe until the policeman had squeezed, bent, probed, and given them back.

"Sign your name here," said the lieutenant.

When Turner had complied, the officer compared the sig-nature with those on his driver's license and credit cards and returned them to him. "Okay. Come with me."

In the elevator, Turner said, "How bad is she?"

"I don't know. But you should have seen the goddamned

333

car. It's a wonder she's still alive."

Two more uniformed policemen and a detective were at the fourth floor nurses' station opposite the intensive care unit.

"This is Paul Turner," said the lieutenant. "He says he's Turnovsky's nephew." He left him with the detective, a dark, middle-aged man whose mouth was set in a meaningless expression of pleasantness.

"I'm Captain Vincencie. Too bad about your uncle." He shook Turner's hand. "I've known him since I was a rookie. We were good friends. It was Herschel who offered me my first bribe."

"Did you take it?"

"How do you think we got to be good friends?"

Turner stared past him and saw Hank. Tubes connected to plastic bottles and monitoring devices were attached to her wrists, arms, and body. Fluids ran in and out of her flesh. Colored lights blinked, sending out messages. Her head and part of her face were hidden by bandages, but the tip of her nose was unmistakable. Her eyes were closed, and her skin was the color of brick dust. He felt weak and utterly helpless.

"She's not as pretty as she was," said Vincencie, "but she's alive."

Turner walked into the room and stood by the bed. Obviously under heavy sedation, Hank lay very still. But there seemed to be faint signs of movement behind her eyelids. She appeared strangely young, almost childish, and Turner remembered that the wounded had always looked the same way when the morphine first took hold and they lost consciousness.

He went back to Captain Vincencie. "Does she know my uncle is dead?"

"Yeah. She knows. She was conscious the whole damn time. Like she was afraid she might miss something. They had to finally put her out."

"How did it happen?" He felt a curious stiffness throughout his body. Even his tongue felt stiff. It moved all right, but someone else seemed to be moving it.

"Some sort of remote control device. Very sophisticated. It was probably set off from a following car at just the right moment. For which we should be grateful, I suppose. If that much stuff had gone off in a heavily trafficked area, we'd still be collecting bodies. This was controlled. They picked a nice empty spot on a back approach to the airport. Very considerate. Very public spirited."

Turner looked at the cops sitting on either side of Hank's door. One was picking his nails with a knife blade. The other stared at a pretty nurse. "You expect them to come up here to finish the job?"

"It's been known to happen," said Vincencie. "But I don't really know what I expect. This whole deal was a surprise. Things have been quiet for Herschel lately. Or so I thought." At this moment he looked more like an old gangster himself than a captain of detectives. Twenty years of close association appeared to have seeped into his genes and altered his flesh. "Do you know anything I don't?"

"I've never been part of my uncle's business dealings."

"Sure. I didn't even think Herschel had a relative left. When did you last see him?"

"This morning."

"Did he have anything special to say?"

"Just goodbye. He was going to Europe."

"He didn't seemed worried?"

Turner shook his head. The stiffness had passed. It had been replaced by an emptiness in his chest and stomach. But there was also the cold calm, almost an apathy, that sometimes took over before a firefight, when you had already made a reluctant kind of peace with death and knew that all you had to do was more or less go through the now close to automatic motions of what you had been trained to do. "Were you able to question Hank at all?"

"Some. She just looked at me as if I was crazy. It's their fucking religion. They like to keep it personal. In the family, so to speak."

335

Of course, thought Turner.

Vincencie left after awhile, and Turner went in and sat with her. The two policemen were still outside in the corridor. They were talking softly now. A nurse came in and checked the tubes and flickering lights. "Are you a relative?"

"Her only brother."

The nurse was young but looked old. "No one should be in here now."

"If you don't tell anyone, I won't either."

"It's really against the rules," she said, but let him stay.

He sat for an hour, staring at the sheet that covered her body, listening to her breathe, his lungs filled with hospital air. Well, no more Uncle Herschel. One more part of him taken away. The last true Turnovsky. *Did he have anything to say,* Vincencie had asked. *Just goodbye.* Turner had converted to their religion. He, too, was keeping it in the family.

He glanced up and found her eyes looking at him.

"Pauly . . ."

He pressed her hand where it lay on the sheet. It felt warm, feverish. He tried a smile to reassure her and failed miserably.

"I'm afraid we didn't quite make it," she whispered.

Each word was a needle in his chest.

"Are the police still outside?"

He nodded.

"Vincencie?"

"He left. Hank I . . ."

"Shhh . . ." She whispered, "Come closer."

He leaned toward her.

"I'm bugged." She barely breathed it into his ear. "They thought I was asleep, but I saw them. They put a mike in the radiator grill. Vincencie is right down the hall, listening."

Turner covered the grill with an extra pillow and blanket. He came back and sat pressing her hand. The coldness inside him suddenly felt like hemorrhaging. "I killed my Uncle Herschel and almost killed you."

"Pauly . . ."

336

"You warned me and I wouldn't listen."

She closed her eyes briefly. Pain came in flurries.

"You should have locked me away," he whispered. "I'm a walking plague. I'm worse than Typhoid Mary."

"Herschel never blamed you. He understood."

"And you?"

"It took me a while. But Herschel saw it early. No addict sets out to be an addict. I finally learned that. You couldn't help yourself."

"It's so damned unfair."

She managed a kind of smile. "So what else is new?"

Her eyes clouded as she fought the drugs. Then they closed. He sat watching her sleep. A fat doctor with a head of wild, curly hair, straight out of the late sixties, came in to examine her. Turner waited for him in the corridor. "How is she?"

"Are you family?"

"Yes."

"There's concussion and severe lacerations, but nothing really life threatening. Her heart is strong, and her general condition is excellent."

"She'll be all right?"

"Just give her a little time."

"What about her face?"

"They work wonders with plastic surgery these days."

Turner shook the doctor's hand. The simple act was deceptive. It took conscious effort to let go.

He was in Fran Woodruff's apartment forty minutes later. He had called first from the hospital to find out if she was home and then had taken a cab directly there.

Fran hugged him with her usual energy. She consoled him on the death of Turnovsky. The papers and news reports were apparently full of it. She knew of their relationship, not of their involvement. "They said his girlfriend was the only survivor. How is she?"

"Surviving."

He took her into the bedroom, closed the door, and turned up the music. "Do you have a large envelope?"

"Why? What is it now?"

"Just give me the envelope."

When she brought it to him, he sealed Maria's letter inside and handed it back to her. "Please. Put this with the first envelope I gave you."

"Right this second?"

He nodded.

"I'm beginning to feel like a dead-letter drop." She knelt before her bureau's hidden compartment. "Do the same instructions go with this as with the other?"

"If anything happens to me, give them both to your father."

"I wish I knew what was going on."

"I'd tell you if I could."

"Don't you trust me?"

"If I didn't trust you, why would I leave you with two obviously important envelopes you could open the minute I walked out of here?"

She considered this. "Will you answer one question?"

"If I can."

"Did your uncle's death have anything to do with all this?"

He lit a cigarette. Not wanting to lie to her, he chose to say nothing.

"Lordy, lordy," she breathed.

"Nothing will happen to you."

"It's not me I'm worried about, dummy. I'm the president's daughter. I'm untouchable."

She came close and held him. He breathed her perfume. "You don't feel untouchable."

"Okay," she said.

"Okay, what?"

"Can we go to bed now?"

"I can't stay."

"That's not what I asked."

"Is there something about me that turns women sexually aggressive?"

"Since you ask, yes."

"What? My perfect body?"

"That can't be overlooked, of course. But I think it's more your air of bemused indifference."

"What does that do?"

"It makes a woman feel that unless she strips naked and grabs you, nothing is ever going to happen."

As he thought about this, she began removing her clothes. He smiled and reached for her, and they pressed and touched and fumbled and unzipped, and she was all sweet flesh beneath his hands, a soft, snowy land of dips and rises that he had passed through before, but which he still felt he was entering for the first time. He thighs parted easily. She was not fooling. She wanted him. And he, suddenly, wanted her. That incredible source of continuing wonder. Here in the midst of personal loss and grief, of accelerating intrigue and violent death, of security threats at the highest level, everything ground to a halt while he had an erection.

Later, he began the always self-conscious sorting out of his things from hers, this time even more so because he felt pressed.

She lay watching from the bed. "It's not polite to love and run."

"I told you I couldn't stay."

"Simple good breeding calls for at least a twenty-two minute interval."

He walked over to the bed and kissed her. "I guess I'll have to owe you seven minutes."

"It's almost midnight. Where are you rushing to at this hour?"

"There's someone waiting at my apartment."

"Bastard."

He sat on the edge of the bed and saw his reflection in a wavy, antique mirror. His body looked confused and erratic in the cloudy glass, reminding him of all the wounded men he had ever seen who were tired, depressed, and hurting and who sat on the edges of their bunks wondering how they were going to get through not only the rest of their lives but the next twenty-four hours. "It's a man," he said.

"If he's someone I should worry about, please tell me so I can start now."

"He's no one to worry about."

He stood up and began to dress. The windows were open, and a faint breeze came off Central Park and stirred the curtains. The antique mirror reflected splinters of gold on the ceiling, on the carpet, on the two watercolors hanging over the bureau, on the smooth ivory of Fran's breasts. Turner dressed in silence. He had the feeling he would never see this pleasant room again, never see this lovely, girlish woman who was young enough, and whose hips were probably wide enough to satisfy Maria's carefully considered specifications for the as yet unchosen mother of his unborn children.

He went into the bathroom to comb his hair and put on his tie. In the clearer glass of the medicine cabinet mirror, he looked less damaged than he had in the bedroom. Testing, he smiled crookedly at himself. Not too bad. With a little effort, a man could get his face to do just about anything.

Fran was unconvinced. "I don't think I like what's happening."

He bent over and smoothed her hair as he would a child's. "Go to sleep. You'll like it better in the morning."

"From the way things seem to be going, you could be dead in the morning."

"Don't be so melodramatic."

She gazed up at him, unsmiling, dark eyes shiningly solemn. "I love you," she said. "If it means anything at all."

To his surprise, it did.

There turned out to be a kind of perverse pleasure in finding Wendell Handley exactly where he had expected him to be, the satisfaction, even the magic, of knowing he was finally beginning to understand the man well enough to figure

340

out how he was likely to behave next. And he looked so right, so totally at ease, waiting in the study with his pipe and cognac. I've started to study him like the Talmud, thought Turner.

"I had no alternative, Paul. I hope you understand that. Your uncle did. It was why he was leaving the country."

Turner poured himself some Courvoisier from the bottle that Handley had out on the table. He drank, feeling the warmth enter his chest. But the cognac in no way affected the cold, almost apathetic calm he had settled into earlier, at the hospital, and which he still found reassuring. "It must be nice to be right as often as you. I keep making one mistake after the other. And my biggest mistake was not letting that turkey shoot you last night."

"If you had, he would have shot you, too. I told you that. Turnovsky was the one who made the mistake. He never should have tried something like that without your approval." The deputy director tapped out his pipe in a glass ashtray. "And you're much too moral for cold-blooded murder."

"Why aren't you?"

"I am. Come on, Paul. You know very well that if I hadn't had your uncle put away, I'd have been dead soon myself. It was as pure an act of self-defense as you're likely to find. But I'm sure Turnovsky explained all that to you when he stopped up here this morning."

"What about Hank Adams?"

"What about her?"

"She's going to recover."

"I know."

"Are you going to let her stay recovered?"

Handley put down his glass and began refilling his pipe. "There's no point in lying to you. Hank Adams is about as close to an alter ego as Turnovsky could have had. She knows everything and everyone he knew and carries as much weight. In fact, she was generally considered to be the tougher of the two. And I don't think she's going to be very forgiving of his death."

341

"So you again have no alternative?"

Handley took a moment to relight his pipe. He looked gravely and a bit sadly at Turner. He sighed. He had any number of ways to offer an unpleasant answer without having to say a word.

"Marvelous," said Turner. "Not having alternatives must be very comforting. It spares you from having to make all sorts of difficult and possibly painful decisions. But in this particular case I'm going to offer you a choice. Would you like to hear what it is?"

"Yes. Certainly."

"Yes. Certainly," Turner repeated, mimicking the deputy director's polite, soft-spoken manner. "Christ, you've got class, Wendell. Breeding really does pay off, doesn't it? I wish I had some of that beautiful Anglo-Saxon cool of yours. Under pressure, I always seem to revert to my sweaty, heavy-breathing Mediterranean origins."

"What's my choice?"

"Letting Hank live. Protecting her from the threat of various and sundry accidents. Personally guaranteeing that when she does finally die, it will be in a warm, clean bed, of natural causes."

"And why would I do that?"

"To prevent my offering the president documented evidence that his soon-to-be director of the CIA is actually a hard-working member of the Soviet Union's Committee for State Security."

Handley nodded. Then he kept on nodding, his head going slowly up and down, up and down like one of those toy dogs on springs that motorists sometimes keep in the rear windows of their cars. Meanwhile his face and the hard blue shells of his eyes did not change. He seemed neither surprised nor especially concerned. "So you've finally found it, have you?"

Turner sipped his Courvoisier and said nothing.

"I wondered how long it would take. I knew Maria had to have left you something, somewhere. When did you find it?"

"What's the difference? I've got it. Are you ready to make a deal?"

"You mean Hank Adams's guaranteed safety for your silence?"

Turner nodded.

"Of course. I know when I'm outgunned. It's just hard for me to believe you would be able to accept something like this under any conditions."

"Believe it."

"You're a genuine hero of the Republic. You almost gave your life for this country. Yet you would betray it now?"

"You're the one doing the betraying."

"Then you would be sanctioning it."

"Herschel Turnovsky was killed only because he tried to help me. Hank came very close to dying for the same reason. I can't do anything for my uncle anymore, but I can for Hank. The country can somehow survive without further help from me. Hank can't. So it's simply a question of priorities."

Handley's face still showed nothing, but a vein had started to pulse in his forehead and there were tiny beads of perspiration on his upper lip. "I suppose it's not really out of character. You've already proven yourself a man of deep personal loyalty. But I'm curious. How did you reconcile your feeling for Maria with the fact of her turning out to have been a Soviet agent?"

"I didn't have to. She was gone when I found out. Living with it might have been something else." Turner ground out his cigarette and lit a fresh one. "What about your wife? How do you think she would react if she ever learned the truth about you?"

"I'm not sure. I've thought about it, of course. I can only hope she would love me enough to react as well as you."

"And if she didn't? Would you feed her cyanide, too?"

Handley turned his head to one side, as if not wanting to see him. His profile, sharp nose and lean, angular jaw, outlined by a lamp, might have been that of an early Greek statue. "Didn't I tell you I loved Maria more than any woman I've ever known?"

"Yes. But you also told me a lot of other things that obviously no longer hold true. Like the reason for Maria's death that night."

"That still essentially holds."

"How could it? At the last telling, you were both allegedly CIA. Now it turns out you were both KGB. Or are you saying it's all nothing more than just switching a few initials around? That everything else can remain the same?"

"I know it sounds insane, yet it happens to be so. Because regardless of whether our allegiance was American or Russian, our conflict that night was still basically between Maria's sentimental humanism on the one hand and my pragmatism on the other. To me, it was still essential that the same eight agents in Poland and Czechoslovakia be sacrificed. The one big difference being that instead of using their deaths to strengthen the position of any alleged mole, I was actually using them to prop up the faltering career of the single KGB officer whom Maria and I could really trust, the one man who has been our control and safeguard all these years."

"But could Maria have exposed what you were planning to the president without also exposing your positions?"

"Probably not."

"Yet she threatened to do it anyway?"

"That was exactly the essence of it." He looked almost entreatingly at Turner. "Much of it was my own fault. I had seen what was happening to her for some time. She just had no heart for it anymore. The pressure can finally be terrible. Unrelieved. It can get to even the best. And there was no one better than Maria. I'm not always as cold as I should be. If I was, it would never have reached the point it did at the reception. I just kept closing my eyes, trying to postpone the inevitable. So the inevitable happened that night. She started making those wild threats about going to the president."

"And Rawson's part?"

"That was also pretty much as you heard it. Except, of

344

course, that Herb Rawson believed my plan to sacrifice the eight agents involved building up my fictitious mole in the KGB, rather than the man running Maria and me in the Kremlin."

They sat smoking and drinking. The air was as heavy as the silence. It was like the vacuum that often follows an explosion in a confined area. The deputy director watched Turner expectantly, as if waiting for more questions. He almost seemed eager for them. "Weird as it seems," he said quietly, "you now know more about me, are probably closer to where I live, than anyone else alive. Deny it as much as you want. No two people could be joined by stronger ties. You actually sacrificed your uncle's life by coming to warn me of his plan. How do you explain that?"

"Extreme stupidity."

"You're not a stupid man, Paul."

"That's getting harder and harder to prove."

The phone went off with the shock and stridency of an alarm. Turner went over to his desk and picked it up.

"It's me," said Fran.

Turner's back was to Handley. He smiled at the wall. "I know."

"Is the man still there?"

"Yes."

"I can't seem to fall asleep."

Turner was silent.

"I never have trouble falling asleep," she said. "All my life I've been an absolutely sensational sleeper."

"I can't tell you how pleased I am to hear that."

"Do you see what you've done to me?"

"Very clearly."

"He's sitting right there, isn't he?"

"Yes."

"And although you're absolutely thrilled that I called, would like to talk to me for hours, and love me madly, you'd be very grateful if I hung up this second."

"You're wise beyond your years."

345

"Will you call the instant he leaves?"

"No."

"That's cruel and unusual punishment. But in case you're worried, I still love you," she said and hung up.

Turner poured some more cognac for them both, returned to his chair, and waited for his new calm to settle in and take hold. When it did, he said, "It's not really very hard to understand Maria's reasons for all this. A thousand years of Russian blood. Her parents brainwashing her since childhood. It even makes a sad, twisted kind of sense. But what the devil pushed *you* into it?"

"Something a lot more sensible than either blood or brainwashing. Namely, conviction. I simply happen to believe that world communism will ultimately prove itself to be the only political system rational enough to keep mankind from destroying itself." The deputy director smiled dimly. "Or does that sound too grand and pompous to you? I must confess it sometimes does to me. Just the word *mankind* is so awesome it embarrasses me. But I suppose I need something awesome to justify some of the less than joyous things I'm forced to do in its name."

"Such as?"

Handley shrugged. "Unfortunately, you already know too many of them. Such as doing everything possible to damage a country that has never been anything but generous and decent to my family for two hundred years and to me since the day I was born. Such as lying day after day and year after year to those who love and trust me. Such as destroying the careers and often the lives of those whose only offense is that they don't happen to believe as I do. And finally, of course, such as being forced to bury someone without whom the rest of my days will have lost most of their glitter. So as you can see, I need something larger than life to hold onto. Not only to justify what I'm doing, but to preserve my sanity."

He paused and waited, as though for an attack. But Turner remained silent and he went on, his voice low and oddly toneless in the comfortable, book-lined room. "I'm

truly sorry about your uncle," he said, seemingly out of nowhere. "I know how you must have felt about him. I also had
an uncle who was very close to me. My mother's older
brother. A real old-time, dyed-in-the-wool Red, out of the
Depression and probably a little crazy besides. Although I
never thought so. My father hated him. He wouldn't even let
him into the house after my mother died, so I used to visit
him secretly. He lived in one room, down near the factories,
in the black part of town. The walls were covered with all
these old newspaper clippings about Sacco and Vanzetti, the
Palmer raids, the Scottsboro boys, the defense of Stalingrad,
and God only knows what else. I think I really learned to
read from my Uncle Mike's walls. He used to tell me there
was only one thing that mattered in the world, and that was
knowing what value to set upon a human life. All the rest was
crap. He also talked a lot about mankind. Except that the way
he said the word it didn't sound grand or pompous or awesome. It sounded like just us, him and me."

The deputy director sucked at his pipe. It had gone out as
he spoke, but he did not bother to relight it. "I guess my
uncle couldn't have been any more than in his early forties
then, but he always seemed like an old man to me. His hair
was completely gray, he was lean and stringy, and he walked
with a heavy limp and sometimes used a cane. His legs had
been broken in four places by pick handles and were never
set right. He had been trying to organize some kind of mill
down south, and a platoon of company goons worked him
over. Before that, he had lost an eye and a kidney because the
San Francisco police didn't want any dirty Commies hanging
around their docks, trying to get longshoremen a living wage
and job security. So mankind hadn't really been too great to
him. Still, he loved everybody, the whole goddamned world.
As though everyone in it was precious. Not precious as Christians or Jews or Moslems, or as Americans or Russians or English. But precious as human beings. And somewhere along
the line—from his reading, from his personal experience,
from those he knew—he had become convinced that that was

347

what the Communists stood for.

"Please understand," said Handley, "my uncle was by no means a highly educated man. I don't think he ever finished high school. Nor was he an especially deep or original thinker. He knew *Das Kapital* backward, forward, and inside out, but Karl Marx was never really the major source of his convictions. I suppose it was mostly the Party attitude toward blacks and Chinese and Mexicans and Jews, and enough money to live on for migrant workers and the sick and the aged, and not letting all those millions and millions of dollars simply pile up, generation after generation, in the safe-deposit boxes and bank and brokerage accounts of people who had never done an honest day's work in their lives. It was also seeing that the Party wasn't just a lot of talk and cheap dialectics, that when it came down to it they actually went off and got themselves shot to pieces in Spain. And he saw they knew what they were talking about in that, too. They had tried to sound the alarm about fascism, but the world refused to hear and ended up paying with twenty million dead. So apart from the rest, my uncle felt they understood the nature of our beast and how best to deal with it."

"That was a lot of years ago," Turner said quietly. "How do you think he'd feel about communism's record today?"

"Mike was a realist. He never expected perfection. He knew we all had faults. But what he did look for from the Party was the kind of universalism that was impossible within the narrow economic and sociological strictures of western democracy. And he didn't just mean its slogans. Workers of the world . . . Peace for all . . . To each according to his need . . . Brotherhood . . . and so on, and so on were all very nice for Party rallies and parades. But he knew they signified nothing when it came right down to the practicalities of survival in a nuclear age. He also knew we had been incredibly lucky so far. We were divided into two opposing camps, each with the capability of destroying every vestige of life as we know it on this planet today. Only a fine, delicately balanced thread of sanity has so far kept this from happening. But as things now

348

stand, it has finally and inescapably got to happen. Because no weapon has ever been conceived—from our first sharpened stick to our first atomic bomb—that hasn't eventually been put to use. And our only practical hope of its not happening this time is to merge our two opposing camps into one."

"Under the Red flag, of course."

Handley shrugged. "My uncle felt it was the most logical choice. It was at least a single flag with a single political philosophy of harmony and equality. The alternative would have had to have been a dozen squabbling, narrowly nationalistic, capitalist camps that would instantly start lining up and taking sides. In any case, that was how Mike felt about it more than thirty years ago and how he taught me to feel. And nothing has happened since to make me feel differently. I admit there have been disappointments and disillusionments. There are no supermen in the Kremlin. Mistakes have been made, many of them grievous, painful, and cruel. But by and large they've been more human error than mistakes inherent in the system. And the basic goals have remained the same."

The deputy director stared thoughtfully at Turner. He seemed to be measuring the degree of acceptance or rejection he was receiving. "So that poor little room with its yellowed clippings pasted to the walls was my second womb. Whatever I became was to a large degree nurtured there. No one knew what was going on. Certainly not my father. Had he ever found out, I think he'd have shot both Mike and me and then blown out his own brains for having spawned such a viper. But my uncle was too smart to let that happen. Though he was unfailingly modest. The only grand things in his entire life were his love for humankind and his plans for me. Although I didn't know it until many years later, Maria's path and mine took almost parallel courses. Each of us was being secretly prepared to lead two very separate lives. I'm certain Maria has fully explained hers in whatever documentation she left you. My own path moved from Yale, to the practice of law in Washington, to recruitment by the CIA on the overt level. While covertly, of course, I was already functioning for the KGB. Mike made the necessary contact for that when I was sixteen."

"And how many more little time bombs like you has the CIA been lucky enough to recruit?"

Handley studied him. "Thank God you're able to keep a hint of humor. It could be a saving grace for us both."

"I don't really feel much like laughing."

"Who does?" The deputy director's eyes were sunken and deep, and his skin looked yellow in the lamplight. "You suddenly have in your hands the power to destroy everything I've been trying to accomplish for thirty years. Now all I can do is pray that Hank Adams's life continues to remain as important to you as it is at this moment."

"You mean you really pray?"

"Yes. And when I'm cut, I bleed."

Turner had intended no sarcasm. He had been truly surprised. He said nothing.

"Despite anything Maria may have written, Paul, I'm not really a creature from outer space."

"I know. Nobody is really a monster, anymore. Nobody is a true villain. Nobody is pure evil. Nobody is ever anything but just another poor, faulted human being with basically decent aspirations. Yet somehow more and more bodies keep piling up." Turner finished his Courvoisier in a single harsh gulp and put down the glass. "Just out of curiosity. One of the first things I found was a list of four men and two women. I discovered they had all been killed within twenty-four hours after Maria's death. I've wondered why."

"Unfortunately, they were part of a red herring, a fake network Maria was allegedly running for the KGB. She was supposed to be feeding them disinformation for the Central Intelligence Agency. With her gone, they became potentially dangerous loose ends."

"I see."

"No you don't. You have that superior, judgmental look on your face that's supposed to make me feel like Attila the Hun. As it happens, that particular job was carried out by

American agents, not Russian. Although even that means nothing because the Russians would have handled it the same way. None of us, neither side, can afford the luxury of lofty moral positions in something like this. As a soldier, you should be able to understand that. How many VC did you blow away before they even saw you? How many of your own grunts were wasted the same way? And don't tell me that was war. What do you think this is?"

Turner saw that he had scraped a nerve. But anger was not what he was looking for from the deputy director tonight. "Well, at least your uncle must be proud of you. Is he still alive?"

"Mike died about eleven years ago. He was out demonstrating against the Vietnam War and some of Mayor Daley's bully boys got him alone in an alley and did a job on him. Busted his skull like an egg." He smiled wearily. "Still, someone took pictures of what was left of him and they made the Walter Cronkite show and the cover of *Life* magazine. Who knows? Maybe it helped shorten your war by a few days."

"It wasn't my war."

"Any war you fight in is yours."

"Now who's being superior and judgmental?"

"You're right. I suppose it's just that I was in the unique position of being able to watch that particular disaster from both sides. Which made it doubly tragic. I apologize. I know you only did what you had to."

Turner waited for him to add the inevitable *as we all did, or do, or whatever*. But if the temptation to self-justify was there, this time the deputy director did not give in to it.

Handley tapped out his pipe and slowly got up, wincing slightly as he straightened his back. Tiredness made his shoulders droop, and he looked older and more vulnerable than he ever had before. "It's odd when you think of it. I would never have considered you a serious threat in all this, and look where you've managed to get to. You've turned out to be the single knife at my throat."

"Yet you always knew Maria had left me the weapon."

"Not really. I never actually knew. I only suspected. And I felt that if she had, I'd be able to get to it before you did. Not that it matters now, but when did you find it?"

"This afternoon."

Handley stared at him. "Good God. Then up until a few hours ago you still believed Maria and me to be straight CIA?"

Turner nodded. Which also meant, he thought, reading the deputy director's mind, that up until a few hours ago you'd have been able to bury both Hank and me with absolute impunity. No, not quite. There would still have been the first envelope for Fran to deliver to her father if he had died. But that would have simply accused the deputy director of having sacrificed Maria and the eight European agents for the greater glory of the CIA and the country. A far cry from being indicted as a Soviet agent who was about to take over the directorship of the Central Intelligence Agency.

"When did Maria write the letter?" Handley asked.

"I don't know. It was undated."

"Christ, how I wish I could see it."

"I'll bet."

Handley shook his head. "Not for the reason you think. You know now how close, how involved, Maria and I were. I just wondered when she suspected it would end for her. At least tell me this. Did she have any idea at all that it might be me who would do it?"

"Yes."

"Aah . . ."

It was so soft it was barely audible. Yet it was the kind of sound, thought Turner, that a man might make as a spike was being driven through his hand.

The deputy director stood staring off somewhere. He seemed lost in his reveries, a gaunt, middle-aged man suddenly low on energy, full of doubts and premonitions. "We'll be all right," he said. "In a sense, it's a stalemate. So there's no real joy here for either of us. But it will be a lot easier for me to live with than for you. I've lived with varying shades of compromise all my life. You haven't. Good lord, you still believe in the forces of light and darkness. And I must admit that still worries me a little."

"I've made the deal, and I'll stick with it. Hank's safety is what matters most to me. I've told you that."

"I know what you've told me." Handley made an impatient gesture with his arm. "Hell, we're locked into it, anyway. Just be sure to tell Hank exactly what the situation is and that she'll be watched and held accountable for any attempts to follow through on your uncle's failed contractual arrangements." He paused. "But what I started to say was that it may not really be that terrible for you to accept the situation as it now stands. I care as much for the people of this country as anyone. More. I've been risking my life, freedom, and sanity for them since I was sixteen years old. I feel responsible for them. I don't want them to die in senseless wars and final mushroom clouds. And maybe they'll stand me in front of a firing squad for it in the end, but I swear to God it won't be because I ever wished a single one of them any harm."

Turner was silent. They stood there, not quite looking at each other. Neither of them seemed to have anything more to say.

"Well . . ." Handley said, and Turner could see that he was trying to smile. But there was also something baffled and pleading in the usually controlled, handsome face. "Goodbye, Paul."

"Goodbye."

They did not shake hands, and the deputy director left the apartment. Turner stood on the landing and watched him walk slowly down the stairs. Handley had his hands in his pockets, his shoulders were hunched, and he seemed almost too tired to move. But halfway to the floor below he suddenly paused, straightened his back, and went down the rest of the stairs quickly, with the easy arrogant step that Turner had come to know so well. Then he opened the vestibule door

353

and went out into the early morning darkness.

Herschel Turnovsky lay in his coffin in a large, flower-filled room in a popular funeral chapel on New York's Upper West Side. The services were supposed to have been private, for family only, but other than for Turner the deceased had no family, and the place was crowded instead with curiosity seekers, the media, past and present business associates, and representatives of the police department and district attorney's office, the latter two groups being there in the hope of picking up possible leads to Turnovsky's killer. The coffin was open. For despite the violence of the old gangster's death, his face had miraculously escaped damage.

Turner had arrived early and gone over to the coffin to pay his last respects. A soft, pink light filtered down from electrified candles and fell on his uncle's face, on the strong, fierce nose, the curved nostrils, the deep eyesockets with their no longer visible Tartar eyes, the high, noble brow, and the thick iron gray hair. Handling the arrangements, Turner had instructed the funeral director to bury his uncle in his *yarmulkah* and *tallis*. But he had neglected to tell the man not to use any cosmetics, and Herschel Turnovsky lay rouged, powdered, and lipsticked in his coffin, a gaudy biblical prophet headed for his final journey to the Sinai. Impulsively, Turner kissed his uncle's cheek. It felt cold as stone, yet Turner half expected Herschel to open his eyes, look at him, and smile, as he had never failed to do the moment he saw him walk into a room. The thing was, the old man had really cared about him.

The officiating rabbi, having been engaged for the occasion by the funeral chapel, had never met Herschel Turnovsky and had asked Turner what his uncle had been like. The question was pure formality. The rabbi read the newspapers. Turner had shrugged. He wanted no platitudes. "What was Herschel Turnovsky like?" he repeated. "He was a good Jew. He prayed morning and night. He cared for his own without compromise."

For a moment, he had been half-tempted to tell the rabbi that his uncle had been killed only because he had tried to keep him from harm. But he did not think the rabbi would be especially comfortable with this piece of information or even find it very enlightening. Also, he saw no point in complicating what was otherwise a basically straightforward, unsentimental ceremony for a man who had, after all, been a lifelong thief and gangster. "Just make it as short and simple as possible," he said.

The rabbi did as he was told. His prayers and speeches, at the gravesite as well as at the chapel, were about as brief and unemotional as such things could be. Nevertheless, leaving the cemetery afterward, with the sky clear, the air warm, and the forsythia blazing its brilliant yellow, Turner thought . . . That was some goddamned *gonif* . . . and wept.

He had the driver of the limousine let him off at the hospital. Captain Vincencie was nowhere in sight, but another shift of uniformed officers was on duty in the corridor outside Hank's room. Her eyes were closed, the same lights blinked, and the same fluids ran in and out of her body through their plastic tubes. But she was not asleep.

"How was it?" she said softly.

He pressed his lips to a small piece of unbandaged forehead. "The usual theatre. Very brisk, very efficient, very meaningless."

"Still, you wept." She had seen his eyes.

"What can I do? I happen to be an old-time crier."

"So was Herschel. He had an unlimited supply of tears. For every occasion."

"Jews," said Turner. "We've been in training for more than five thousand years. We've developed the act of weeping into a major art form."

Silently, she began to cry. Her tears ran from concentric,

blue-black circles and disappeared into her bandages. He sat beside the bed, holding her hand. His uncle's lovely, high-class Boston lady.

"Please, Pauly." She reduced her voice to a whisper. "Smother that silly microphone."

He used the same pillow and blanket he had used the last time.

"I don't suppose Handley was at the funeral," she said.

"No."

"Have you seen him since all this happened?"

"Sure. We had dinner and went to a show together."

"You're going to have to promise me something."

He waited, knowing, of course, what it was.

"I want your word that you won't try anything stupid and futile."

He nodded. "Whatever you want."

"I want you to swear to me."

"I swear to you."

Her eyes, wet and searching, did not believe him for an instant. "For God sake, Pauly, don't waste Herschel's death."

"I promise you," he said and took her bandaged face in his hands, delicately, barely touching her, that poor, fragile, broken vessel. "I promise you I won't waste a thing."

Leaving, he saw Captain Vincencie in the downstairs lobby. He went over, grabbed the detective by the shoulder, and swung him around. "Take care of her," he said fiercely. "If anything happens to that woman, I promise you I will personally blow your head off."

He left before the startled man could speak.

Turner went to bed early that night, before ten, and fell asleep at once.

Sometime later, he awoke in a cold sweat. An invisible beast rode his chest. It was more than just a nightmare. Something lay on him like a ton of weight . . . the ghost of a conversation, a gnawing fragment of dialogue.

The Past

In the dark, his body moved on the bed, arching upward as if twitched by an inner pain. He groaned aloud, a fish hooked deep, in the heart. He turned on a bedside lamp. The light attacked his eyes, but he did blink. A clock said it was near midnight. He picked up the phone and dialed Fran Woodruff's number.

"Don't be frightened," he said. "It's only me."

"Why should I be frightened?" But her voice was instantly tense. "What's happened? What's wrong?"

Hearing her voice, he felt foolish. "Probably nothing. Sorry to call so late."

"Ah, you couldn't bear another minute of not talking to me."

"Exactly." He cradled the receiver in the crook of his neck and lit a cigarette. "But as long as I've got you on the phone, would you do me a favor?"

"What is it, you miserable faker?"

He smiled, imagining her face, feeling calmer by the second. "That material I gave you to hold?"

"Yes."

"Would you just take a quick look and see if it's okay."

"Why shouldn't it be okay?"

"Please. Just look."

"All right." Her voice was again tense.

He waited.

"Paul?"

"Yes."

He heard her take a deep breath.

"It's gone."

Naturally, he thought.

"I don't understand," she whispered. "How could something like that happen? Who could have known? God, I feel awful. What are we going to do?"

Coldly, his composure settled in. *We.* What a lovely word. "We're not going to do anything. And don't be upset. It's no great loss." And then, in case either phone was bugged, "I have copies of everything."

357

"I feel as though I've failed you."

"That's ridiculous. Besides, it's not that important. Now please forget it."

"Is there anything you want me to tell my father?"

"No. Nothing."

"When will I see you?"

"I'm not sure. I have to go out of town for a few days."

"Is it because of this?"

"No." This, at least, was true. He had decided even before the discovery of the loss. "I'll call you when I get back."

"Just remember," she said a trifle desperately.

"What?"

"Who loves you."

The magic incantation against death, disaster, and irreplacable loss.

Slowly, thoughtfully, he hung up. What bothered him as much as anything was how easily he had been outwitted. *Not that it matters now, but when did you find it?* He should have known. Wendell Handley was simply not a man to ask a question, any question, out of pure curiosity. So that, having established the fact that Maria's letter had been discovered just that afternoon and having undoubtedly been keeping him under at least partial surveillance for some time, it would have been a comparatively easy matter for the deputy director to check out the few places he had been immediately afterward. Namely, his own apartment, the hospital, and Fran's place. What's the use of kidding myself, he thought tiredly. I'm just no match for the guy.

He turned off the lamp because the light was hurting his eyes and the sight of even his own bedroom was suddenly an intrusion. Wearing the darkness like a robe, he lay there smoking. The night itself seemed almost obtrusively quiet. There were not even the usual traffic noises. He tried to think of Maria, but found her farther away than ever. He felt oddly disoriented. At one point, he actually imagined himself back in the jungle, with the silence screaming in his ears, invisible eyes peering at him from the shadows, and death lurking beside each path. It seemed that whatever he did it somehow turned out to be wrong. All he was looking for was the truth, but the truth was forever changing. And what was so damned sacred about the truth? How was it supposed to help Maria? She had finally left it for him in a letter, yet this in itself had failed to resurrect her. And in the end, he had even lost the letter. That, along with everything else. No. Not everything. He still had tomorrow.

TWENTY-FIVE

The Present

He sat parked in his rented Chevrolet in Langley, Virginia. It was a cool, fragrant, star-filled night, with no clouds or mist, and the shapes of the trees on either side of the road stood out sharply in silhouette. Above them, the lights of a late-arriving plane pointed the way to Washington's National Airport. A world in order. Even his breathing was relaxed, easy, and undisturbed by any thought of what lay ahead. If he was gifted with such a thing as a soul, he decided, tonight it was at peace. Yet he knew in his heart that this was just sentimental nonsense. There was nothing peaceful about the true order of things. The cosmos was violent and wrathful. The human species was tearing itself apart. Death waited, knowing it must finally win. So if you sensed a moment of peace, and you were smart, you kept it carefully hidden.

He had to smile at his instinctive reaction to the ancient Yiddish superstition, the old wives' tale that warned, in letters of fire, that to admit to the possibility of hope was to invite the wrath of the Devil. But he did resist the temptation to spit three times and glance over his shoulder. So a bit of progress toward enlightenment had perhaps been made, after all. Turner, the enlightened Jew. Although considering how he had spent the past sixteen hours, any such concept might seem questionable.

He had started at seven that morning, parked a short distance up the block from Wendell Handley's red-brick Georgetown house. It was much too early for any activity, but he had no way of knowing when the deputy director might leave for his office, and he did not want to risk missing him. At 7:45 a large black woman and two little blonde girls came out of the house, walked to the corner, and stood there waiting. The girls were dressed alike and looked to be the same size, and Turner remembered that Handley had been described, in an early report, as having six-year-old twin daughters. A school bus picked up the girls five minutes later, and the woman returned to the house. Handley himself came out soon after. He opened the garage doors and drove off in the same gray Pontiac sedan with the high, two-way radio antenna that he had been driving on the two occasions that Turner had met him in the Washington area. At a distance of two blocks, Turner followed him. He checked his rear-view mirror. No other cars were going in his direction.

It proved to be a fast-paced day for the deputy director. But then Turner assumed that all Handley's days were hectic. Considering the nature of his involvements, how could they be otherwise? He went first to Central Intelligence headquarters in Langley, left it an hour later for the State Department's four-square-block building back in Washington, and came out of there after half an hour with two men. They entered an official, black, chauffeur-driven limousine and were taken to the Senate office building on Capitol Hill where, Turner guessed, they must have had a working lunch. When Handley appeared again, alone, it was almost two o'clock, and Turner was beginning to hear rumblings of complaint from his own stomach. From here, another official limousine drove the deputy director to the White House, and Turner chanced going off for a few minutes to pick up a container of coffee and a couple of hamburgers. An hour later the same limousine took Handley to the National Press building on Fourteenth and F streets. He remained there until four-thirty and then was chauffeured back to the State Department building, where he picked up his own car and drove in the general direction of Georgetown. Here, Turner actually lost him in the rush hour traffic. But assuming he was headed home, Turner passed in front of his house in time to see the gray sedan pull into his driveway.

It was seven o'clock when the deputy director appeared again. This time he was dressed in dinner clothes and accompanied by a tall woman who Turner assumed was his wife. They drove directly to the French Embassy on Kalorama Road, and Turner had to park almost out of sight of the palatial, brilliantly lit building because of the security in the immediate area. But by using a pair of high-powered night glasses that he had bought earlier for just such an emergency, he had a clear enough view of the embassy's driveway and entrance to be able to see anyone entering or leaving the building.

At 9:35 Handley came out alone. He stood smoking his pipe until an attendant brought his car around. Then he drove off, apparently leaving his wife to be escorted home by someone else. Following at a safe distance, Turner trailed him across the Potomac, northwest on the George Washington Memorial Parkway, and back to CIA headquarters in Langley. When the deputy director entered the compound, Turner continued on past the huge office complex, made a sharp U turn a quarter of a mile down the road, drove past the entrance once more, and parked off a narrow, tree-lined side road. From here he would have no problem spotting the deputy director when he left.

Sixteen hours. He had put nothing in his stomach since the hamburgers and coffee at two o'clock, but he felt no desire for food. What he did want was a cigarette. But even a tiny glow could be visible for a mile in the wooded dark, and he was not about to take the chance.

A cloud floated by, soiling the purity of the sky. He looked at his hands, dimly luminescent in the darkness—tough, muscular, heavily veined. Not the hands of a writer but of a fighter or manual laborer. Even (may God forgive him) a killer. Which he had been. Which he still was. Which he would continue to be. Never mind his sensitivity, his creative talent, his alleged soul. When it became necessary to kill, whether out of national or historical or personal necessity, he killed. It was as simple as that. As if to emphasize, even prove, his point, as if to physically demonstrate the harshness of his nature, he took out his .38, broke open the breech, checked to see that the cylinder was fully loaded (as if he didn't know), snapped the revolver shut, released the safety, and placed the gun on the seat beside him. Yet some part of him remained unconvinced. If he was really tough, he would have bought himself a high-powered rifle with scope sights days ago and done his killing from an impersonal, sensibly safe distance.

At midnight, he started to watch the CIA entrance through his glasses. Twenty minutes later, he saw the deputy director's gray sedan drive out of the main gate, head in his direction, and pass within fifty yards of where he was parked. He pulled out from among the trees, switched on his lights only after passing a crossroad, and followed. There were very few cars on the road at this hour, and he was able to maintain a full quarter-mile interval without having to be concerned about losing sight of the sedan's tail lights.

At Kirby Road, Handley left the parkway and drove southwest, away from Washington. Turner accelerated and began closing the gap. The road narrowed to two lanes here and stretched off into the darkness. There were fields and forests on both sides. No houses were visible. In the distance, a barn and silo loomed against the sky. Turner felt the power of the car's engine, the remains of the hamburgers in his stomach, the cold sweat on his back, the solid reassurance of the revolver on the seat. He also felt everything reduced to a manageable size. The unessentials had been eliminated, burned away. Finally, there was just the two of them. Turner had never seen this road before, but he sensed he had been moving toward it for a long time. As the gap between the cars closed to about a hundred yards, he lowered the window on the passenger's side and picked up the revolver.

A truck suddenly loomed, looking like the side of a house. It was a tractor-trailer, one of the big eighteen-wheelers, which seemed to have come from nowhere. It had actually come out of a break in the trees and stopped dead across the road. Turner slammed on his brakes. At fifty miles an hour, his tires screamed like dying animals. His wheels locked, and the car spun around twice. He dropped the revolver and gripped the steering wheel with both hands to keep from going through the windshield. The car shuddered to a stop. It was about six feet from the side of the truck.

"You crazy sonofabitch!"

He was furious, shaking. He did not yet understand. He still thought he was dealing with a wildly reckless truck driver. Then he saw the men.

There were three of them. Two revolvers pointed at his head, one through each door. The third man lay straight across the hood, aiming at him through the windshield. They seemed young and were dressed in conservative business suits. The boys from Yale, Turner thought, and was pulled out from behind the wheel.

His hands were cuffed behind his back, and he was gagged. One of the men swung the Chevrolet off the road and into the break in the trees out of which the tractor-trailer had appeared. The truck itself had also been backed off the road and was now out of sight. The entire operation had taken no more than three or four minutes. Not a car had passed.

Now, however, as though it had been waiting in the wings for its cue, the gray sedan came back. Handley parked alongside the Chevrolet, got out of his car, and paused deliberately to light his pipe. Turner stared at him, fascinated. The deputy director wore no topcoat, but had a white silk scarf draped loosely about his neck. As always, his dinner clothes were faultless. His scarf and shirtfront seemed to throw off an inner light in the surrounding darkness. His air of insouciance, thought Turner, was straight out of F. Scott Fitzgerald. What a Marxist.

"Tie his legs and stretch him out on the back seat of his car," said the deputy director.

These were the first words Turner had heard spoken since he was stopped. If Handley's four agents were capable of speech, they had so far given no sign of it. One of them now bound his ankles together with a precut length of rope, two others carefully aimed their revolvers at his head, and a fourth man held open the rear door of the Chevrolet in preparation for his entrance. A textbook study in time and motion.

Bound, gagged, thoroughly immobilized, Turner was placed in the back of the Chevrolet. He lay on his side, facing front. The gag nauseated him. He breathed slowly and deeply through his nose until he felt better.

Handley slid behind the wheel and started the motor. "Follow in my car at about two hundred yards," he told his men. When they had moved away, he leaned back and pulled the handkerchief out of Turner's mouth. "Sorry about the gag. They do that automatically." His voice was quiet, relaxed, without any theatricality. It was the voice of a man who no longer had to bother with pretense.

The car moved out onto the road. From where Turner lay, all he could see was the well-shaped, beautifully layered back of the deputy director's head and some sky and trees. He noticed they were not moving very quickly. Wherever they were going, Handley was evidently in no great rush to get there.

Turner licked the dryness from his lips. "Aren't you afraid I'll tell them about you?"

"They would never believe you. They're used to hearing that sort of wild accusation from people in trouble. Besides, if you'll forgive the irony, I've already told them you're the one who is KGB."

"And they believed that?"

"I'm the number two man in The Company. Why would I lie to them? They're flattered to be chosen for so sensitive an operation. I've sworn them to silence. They understand how

365

important it could be to our national pride and image that one of the few genuine heroes we have from our sad little Vietnam debacle not be publicly tried as a traitor. They realize that a timely accident would be simpler and to the advantage of all concerned."

Turner breathed the sweet aroma of Handley's tobacco. So that was it. He was scheduled to exit in a Lewicki Special, a carefully staged auto crash. Which was evidently a far more popular termination technique than the general public was ever likely to suspect.

"I'm sorry, Paul, but I suppose it did finally have to be one of us. I knew that, yet I made a near fatal mistake. Instead of going after you the instant I found Maria's letter, I waited to see whether you would come after me. Because you did save my life, because I felt I owed you one, I held back. It could have cost me."

"It can still cost you. The moment I'm gone, a photocopy of the letter will automatically be sent to the president."

"You missed your chance there. I know everyplace you stopped the day you found that letter. You were never anywhere near a copying machine."

Turner could feel the car slowing and swinging to the right. Curiously, he was aware of no specific fear. Maybe it was just that he had been close to death so many times that the expected sense of tragedy was finally lost. Even his anger was gone. If he felt anything at all, it was disgust. He had bungled everything right down to the end. Whatever was about to happen to him, he deserved. Death was the single unavoidable moment of sentimentality in every life, and he had managed to turn his own into pure soap opera. He felt worse for Hank than for himself. With him gone and the letter in the deputy director's hands, she would very quickly be next.

"We all have the same quarrel with death," said Handley, "and none of us ever resolves it. All we do is stumble around, waiting to fall into the common hole. So wherever you go,

366

Paul, I won't be far behind.''

Whatever the deputy director's intentions, his words were less than reassuring.

Moments later, the car stopped. Handley cut off the motor and got out without glancing back. He had already said his goodbye.

The four agents were casual and almost pleasant about it. The brisk, no-nonsense efficiency of the ambush seemed to have disappeared. They were a short distance off the road now, screened by several layers of brush and trees, and no longer had to worry about the possibility of a car passing. Two of the men helped Turner out of the Chevrolet and onto his feet. A third man untied the rope from around his ankles. The fourth agent stood holding a revolver pointed at his chest. Handley was about twenty feet away, strolling through the high grass and not even looking at what was going on. His back was to them, and he seemed to be studying the stars. Turner saw that they were in a clearing that ran from a sharp bend in the road on one side to what appeared to be a deep ravine on the other. The sound of running water came from far below. Trees and heavy growth threw black, irregular shadows on the blue-purple of the grass. There were no lights anywhere. The world ended at the edge of the clearing.

"Listen to me." Turner spoke softly and quickly. "He lied to you. I'm not what he told you I am. I've fought, killed, and almost died for this country. He's the traitor, not I. That's why he has to get rid of me. I know the truth about him. He's been KGB for years. He's the highest ranking mole the Russians have ever had in this country."

He said all this not because he expected to be believed, but in the hope of achieving a momentary distraction. He did not get even that. Their faces, in the darkness, were as smoothly complacent and uninvolved as before. They went right on doing what they were doing. He might as well have been speaking a foreign language. But his legs were free now,

367

and one of the agents was digging into a jacket pocket for what Turner hoped would be the key to his handcuffs. It was. He felt it being worked behind his back, first sliding against the metal in search of the keyhole, then clicking against the edge and glancing off, the simple operation made suddenly difficult by the darkness and the position of his hands. Come on. He felt the sweat along his back. There were three guns on him now, but to hell with that. They were going to break his head or his neck, not shoot him. A bullet wound would ruin any chance of his death appearing to be an accident. Besides, they were so relaxed they were actually standing around him in a loose circle. If they started to shoot, they would shoot each other.

The key went in, turned once, twice, and the cuffs came loose. He felt his stomach sucking out of him as though he were about to take a long fall. Then he dived, throwing himself sideways at the two men directly in front. They came down on top of him and he chopped one in the groin, the other in the throat. He rolled free in the grass and took a glancing kick in the head from a foot he never saw. Had it landed solidly, it would have cracked his skull. He staggered to his feet, lowered his head, and prepared to charge. The four agents surrounded him again. This time they were in a wider, more cautious circle. The tallest of them aimed his revolver at Turner's chest. Turner saw his eyes, narrow, black, set in angry circles. This one was not going to fool around anymore.

"Put down that gun, you fool," said Handley. "I told you we can't have any bullets in him." He spoke from about thirty feet away, his voice sharp enough to carry above the sound of the water in the ravine. "Or don't you think the four of you can manage to handle him?"

Two came at him together, front and back—the tall one who had now holstered his gun, and a second agent whom Turner sensed rather than saw. He kicked backward and felt his heel drive up between the man's legs, grinding into the softness, into those mother-loving Anglo-Saxon balls dangling

368

in their smooth-fitting Brooks Brothers trousers. The man cried out, a high, almost musical yelp, as though he had already made the necessary transition and did not really find it all that bad. Sing, you sonofabitch. Turner felt something warm starting to run wild in his chest. He met the tall agent head-on, ducked under a furious backhand chop, and stabbed four stiff fingers straight up into his windpipe. The man went down, choking, clutching his throat. The other two agents came at him in tandem, one getting in the way of the other in their eagerness to close, a pair of vicious attack dogs set loose by their master but blind without instructions. Turner hooked a leg under the first, a lean whippet, as he rushed forward, then cold-chopped him on the back of the neck, not getting him squarely or he would have killed him, but still managing enough force to drive him to his knees. His partner, close behind, overran him, lurched forward into Turner's fist, and found himself spitting blood and teeth.

"Beautiful," said Handley. There was a mixture of amusement and disgust in his voice—a Roman emperor at the Coliseum watching an overmatched slave making cream cheese out of his champion gladiators. "Maybe I should have brought an even dozen of you."

Turner started to break for the nearest bushes. But they were alert now and waiting, and he was tackled before he had gone six feet. He came down hard, flat out, and they were on him. The pressure behind his neck eased up and exploded in flashes of light. They fought to get at him. It was personal now. They needed to tear him apart. He was the fox, caught in a bog by hounds. He waited for the first teeth at his throat. They grunted and swore as they went at him. A whispering came out of the trees and joined with their animal sounds. He fought wildly, as much animal as they. He tore, gouged, kicked, punched, bit. Whatever he could reach, he damaged. He felt himself soar out on the beating of his heart, and it was better than waiting for it. He was reaching, flying out to meet it. The four men started to take on different colors—red, green, blue, yellow—and he wondered if he were close to

369

passing out. He was aware of being struck and struck again, but he felt no pain. A bad sign. The colored faces glared furiously at him. They were no longer smoothly complacent, no longer uninvolved. They were tasting him now, and they loved his flavor. All those straight-lipped mouths with their fine Protestant rectitude. Go ahead, he thought, drink my Turnovksy blood, you dumb Company bastards. You're killing the wrong man. But as long as you're killing *somebody* what's the difference?

Dimly, he saw the tall agent raise the butt of his revolver, hold it over his head, and wait for an opening. Then he heard the sharp crack of a pistol shot (or a dead branch breaking somewhere in the forest) and watched the agent's arm come down. It came down slowly, as though the agent had considered the situation more carefully, changed his mind, and decided not to bludgeon him to death after all. When the arm was fully extended at his side, he dropped the revolver and fell forward on his face.

All action instantly stopped. It might have been the frozen frame ending of an arty movie. The stillness was that complete. Everyone turned and stared at Wendell Handley. They were looking to see whether he had become annoyed enough with his men to actually start shooting them. But as the deputy director slowly approached the group, the only thing visible in his hand was his pipe.

"Marvelous," he said. "Which idiot left his safety off?"

There was another shot. A second man spun in a tight, half-circle, landed on his back, and lay still. This time, however, everyone exploded into action. Turner grabbed the tall man's revolver and dove into the brush. Handley broke for a line of trees. His two surviving agents followed close behind. There was a third shot and the last man stumbled, fell, crawled for a few more feet, then collapsed and flattened out.

Turner felt for the revolver's safety, found it beside the cylinder, and flicked it off. He crawled through the brush, moving in a wide circle to his right, heading in the direction in which Handley and his one remaining agent had gone.

370

The Present

There was no point in trying to run. Wherever he ran, they would find him. The fact was, he did not even want to run. The warmth, the exhilaration that had started earlier in his chest, was still running wild. This was his turf, his métier. It was for this that they had trained him, sent him off to fight, and awarded him their highest decoration. If he couldn't handle himself here, with a loaded gun in his hand, he would send back their damned medal.

He crawled another twenty-five yards and stopped to listen. He heard the water running off to the right and the soft crackling of dead leaves and branches straight ahead. He was deep in the forest now, and less of the starlight broke through. The ground was soft. He felt the give of pine needles under his hands and knees and the wetness of the dew. Slowly, more carefully now, he started to move once more, wondering how many he would have to shoot before he could reasonably expect to walk out of there. The deputy director and his man were only two. But how many others were scattered about this crazy, blacked-out shooting gallery? Although three shots had very neatly accounted for three agents, there was no way of judging how many men had actually done the firing. In retrospect, the shots seemed to have come from different directions, but there was no absolute certainty about this, either. The only sure thing was the fact of its having been exceptionally fine shooting. Also, of course, that it could not possibly have turned out better for him. Not that he had any illusions about this being its intention. That, he felt, was pure dumb luck. He could easily have been picked off along with the others. A man was a man in the darkness. As to who had done the shooting and for what purpose, well, in the violent, convoluted world in which Wendell Handley functioned, how could anything close to a rational judgment be made as to who was trying to kill whom and for what reason?

A pistol shot shattered the quiet. It was followed by another, then three more in rapid succession. The sounds echoed and died, and there was quiet once more. Turner had seen no muzzle flashes, but the firing seemed to have come

371

from a short distance ahead and to the right. Silently, feeling his way through the brush, keeping his head as low as possible, he moved in that direction.

He heard the faint sound of movement to his left, and he dropped flat and pointed his revolver. But he decided it was probably just a rabbit and continued on. He could feel his heart going very fast. His brain was also racing. He wondered who had done the latest firing and whether anyone had been hit. Were Handley and/or his man dead? Were the anonymous marksmen dead? Was some unlucky rabbit dead? Easy, he thought. Relax. Concentrate on what you're doing or you won't ever have to worry about relaxing again. Just make believe you're back in Nam, he told himself and for a moment could feel himself looking back into that bloody glitter of past death and could almost hear its song. Except that what he really heard was a twig snapping.

No more than ten feet ahead of him he saw a dark shape, and he fired straight into it, firing once and rolling, then firing again as he saw the black form start to flatten out and go down. He rolled twice more to the left and stopped behind a tree. He lay there, waiting. Everything was quiet. When several minutes had passed and he still heard nothing, he crawled forward to see what he had.

The man lay face down in the pine needles, and he had to turn him over to look at him. It was Handley's agent. One shot had caught him in the throat, the other, in the chest, and he was dead. Turner took the revolver from his hand and slid back behind the tree. He broke open the gun, a .38, and took out the six cartridges. None had been fired. He ejected the two spent cartridges from his own revolver, which was the same caliber, replaced them with two live ones, and put the four remaining bullets in his pocket as reserve. Then he began creeping through the brush once again, this time following a tight arc to the left.

He moved more and more slowly and stopped every few seconds to listen. In his mind, he had marked the silhouette of a tall pine as the approximate point at which the deputy director had disappeared into the woods. If he had figured correctly, his own line of movement would bring him to that area from the rear. Crawling, he breathed as though there was hardly any air remaining in the state of Virginia and what was left carried some awful stench. Which somehow brought a premonition of disaster. He found this strange, since he was infinitely better off at this moment than he had been less than twenty minutes ago. Yet some icy hint of intelligence presented him with a vision of Wendell Handley sitting quietly somewhere ahead in the darkness, waiting, his revolver aimed at the exact spot where Turner would appear. And with that image a chill went through him, as though his own death had passed by in the night air. Or was it some other silly, simplistic hero being blown away somewhere else at this instant, in some other wood or war or planned accident? Was another poor, foolish bungler about to breathe his last, his cry unheard in the dark yet somehow reaching Turner's ears? And was one more especially clever murderer about to go unpunished and soar on to greater glory?

Turner absolutely did not see the man until he almost crawled over him. He lay on his back beside a maple and looked to be little more than a bundle of old clothes that some careless camper had left behind. Turner thought at first he was dead. But then he heard his breathing, a harsh rasping that sounded as though there was a tear somewhere and air and blood were leaking out. The man lay in shadow, his head turned slightly away. There was a gun in his hand, one of those short-barreled revolvers that city police forces often carried. Turner knelt there, staring at it.

Then, being careful to move very gently, he turned Lewicki's head so that he could see him. He looked at the boyish, movie star face with the mass of thick hair curling above it. A thin trail of blood ran from his temple down the side of his face. The bullet had apparently just grazed him, but his breathing sounded as though something more had happened. He pulled open his clothing and saw that he had also been hit in the chest. He was bleeding more heavily here.

373

Turner almost yelled for a corpsman. He pressed a handkerchief to the wound and tied it on with his belt. He crouched
there, listening to Lewicki's breathing, letting what he saw
sink into his brain. Christ! He took the revolver from his hand
and broke it open. All six cartridges had been fired. Three of
the bullets had accounted for the three agents, so the remaining three had probably been fired at Handley. Turner remembered hearing five shots go off. Two of them had hit
Lewicki. Had the detective's shots also been on target?

Turner put the gun in his jacket pocket and knelt there,
trying to hear something other than Lewicki's breathing. The
man had to be gotten to a hospital, but if Handley was still
alive out there, he would shoot them both before Turner was
able to carry the detective twenty feet. It was too bad, but
Lewicki was going to have to stay where he was for a while.
Turner again crawled through the darkness.

He moved, if possible, with even more care than before.
Dead or alive, the deputy director was not likely to be very
far from where he had found Lewicki. Turner felt his brain
working with difficulty, but it did seem logical that unless
Handley was dead or too badly wounded to move, he would
have heard him approaching and picked him off as he attended to Lewicki. Except that the reverse might also be true.
Maybe Handley had not been hit at all, and finding himself
without support and hunted by an armed adversary, he had
simply taken off. Why face Turner alone in the darkness
when he could safely get away and send a small army after
him in the morning? It made sense. Yet Turner had heard no
automobile starting up, and it seemed unlikely that the deputy director would try to leave on foot.

A twig suddenly cracked under Turner's weight, and the
sound carried like a rifle shot. He froze.

"Is . . . that you . . . Paul?"

The words floated up out of the darkness to the left. The
articulation was garbled, as though the speaker was either
drunk, very sleepy, or had a mouthful of food. The voice itself bore no resemblance to Handley's, yet who else's could it

374

be? He knelt there, silent, unmoving. Waiting for what?

"I'm . . . done," said the voice weakly. "Took three bad . . . hits. Can't move . . . my legs. Think I got him . . . though. Who was he?"

Turner slid slightly to the left and peered through the undergrowth. The voice seemed to be very close, no more than twenty feet away, but he could see nothing. He sniffed the air as though seeking with his nose what his eyes failed to find. A sweetly poisonous fire seemed to be burning somewhere, giving heated promise of the Devil, of wizards and fiends. The forest had stopped being a forest. It was a black cave, spiced with damp and rot, fenced in with gargoyles' horns.

There was a sudden spasm of coughing, and Turner moved closer. He was able to see Handley now. The deputy director lay half propped against a tree trunk, legs spread crookedly, like those of a broken doll. In the muted starlight, his face seemed as white as those few parts of his shirtfront that were not now dark with blood. When he stopped coughing, his head drooped forward as though it had grown too heavy for his neck to support. One hand held his scarf to his stomach in an obviously futile attempt to stop the bleeding. The other hand hung limply at his side. His gun lay several feet away in the grass.

Turner rose and came forward. Even now he was watchful, his revolver aimed and ready. He knelt, picked up Handley's gun and stuck it in his belt. With some struggle, the deputy director lifted his head and looked at him. Turner stared back. Old lights moved between them.

"Who was . . . he?" It was hard for him to talk, but the question was important.

"A cop. He's been tailing me since I left New York. I was sure I had lost him."

"Name . . ."

"Lewicki."

"Jesus . . . a Polack." He seemed to smile with a clown's deep gloom. A bubble of blood formed at the corner of his mouth, broke, and dribbled down his chin. "I'm glad I'm not yet . . . dead. I need . . . a favor.''

Turner knelt beside him in the grass. Was it possible? He had a sudden horror of being forced, against all logic, will, and sanity, to do whatever this dying man asked him to do. Had they been joined in blood by some devil's pact?

The bloodied mouth worked, struggled, came up with its oddly garbled message. "Please. Don't tell about . . . me. I'm dead. It won't matter. Just . . . to my family. My wife . . . my daughters. Mark them for . . . life. Why punish them because . . . of me?''

A fresh spasm of coughing rushed blood from his mouth. Turner tasted a sickness of his own. He saw the carnage and wanted to look away. But somehow he didn't.

"Please . . .'' The word made a gurgling sound. "Promise . . . me.''

Turner stared at him. The *chutzpa* of the man. He had the nerve to ask *him* for promises. As if merely his dying was in itself enough to settle up all accounts.

"A deal . . .'' Handley whispered. "I'll give you names. Proof. A high cabinet . . . official. Three senators. All . . . KGB. They don't know . . . about me. But I know about . . . them. I have tapes . . . film. You can . . . do the country a service. Just . . . promise me . . .''

Turner was reached. "You would do this?''

"Only for my . . . family.''

"Where's the material?''

"Your . . . word?''

"Yes.''

"I trust . . . you. As no one else.'' Handley sighed from a long way off. "I have a cabin . . . on the Rappahannock. Two miles . . . south of Route 17. Near Kelly's . . . Ford. Turn right at . . . water tower. A mile and a . . . half. It's on the river.'' Blood ran from his mouth and cut him off. He closed his eyes. When he was able to speak again, he said, "There's a fireplace. The hearthstone . . . lifts up. It's all in a . . . tin box.''

"Are there any keys?''

"Only for the . . . door. It's in the porch lantern. The . . . base screws off."

Bubbles of blood damaged the words. The talking seemed to have exhausted him, used up the last of his strength. His head drooped.

Turner sat there in the wet grass. The deputy director's face was ashen and there was blood on his chin, but the real carnage was below. With everything, thought Turner, it was not I who did it to him. Nor was he able, finally, to finish me. In some far corner of his brain, a tiny piece of the symmetry seemed lost.

"Paul . . .?"

Turner looked at him. It was all there in his fast-fading eyes, colorless now in the starry night. He actually seemed impatient for what would come next.

"I'm . . . sorry . . ." The red bubbles did odd things to his words. Or was it some vague, final regret? Still staring at Turner, the light went from his eyes. He was hemorrhaging badly now. It took him only minutes to die.

On an apology, thought Turner.

He sat for a moment, imagining his heart had slowed down. He was sure he could feel it, a delicate change in the beat, an adjustment to its newly altered state. Something had been pressing it and suddenly was no longer there. Did he miss it or was he just a little crazy? There was increasing evidence for the latter.

He got up and walked away. It took some effort, but he did not glance back.

Lewicki looked neither better nor worse than when he had left him. The improvised bandage seemed to have stopped the bleeding, but he was still unconscious and his breath sputtered like a faulty pump. Kneeling, Turner lifted him in his arms as he would a child and carried him back toward the clearing. How thin he was, how incredibly small and light. But so was a bayonet.

He lay the detective on the back seat of the Chevrolet, handling the damaged body as he would something delicate and precious. He took off his jacket and put it across Lewicki's chest. He wished he had a blanket. Then he took a deep breath and looked about the small, grassy place where he had most recently come near to dying. Now for God sake think, he told himself.

The three agents Lewicki had shot seemed to be lying exactly as they had fallen. The first two were near the center of the clearing. The third man lay at the edge of the woods he had never quite reached. Turner went to examine them. Those in the clearing were dead. The man who had been shot while running was unconscious, but still had a faint heartbeat. Turner had seen enough battlefield wounds to know that in all probability he would be dead within the hour. He also knew there was an outside chance he might be found alive. In which case he would repeat Handley's story identifying him, Turner, as a KGB agent who, together with his confederates, had murdered the deputy director and his men.

Turner stepped back, aimed carefully, and fired a single round into the back of the CIA man's head. A month ago, he thought dully, I'd have put him in the car without even thinking twice about it, and taken him to the hospital with Lewicki. He in no way mistook the change for an improvement.

He drove back toward Washington at a steady seventy miles per hour. It was nearly 3:00 A.M. and no one else was on the road. Crossing a high bridge, he stopped in the middle and tossed three revolvers into the river below. Two of the guns had belonged to Handley and Lewicki. The third was the pistol he had taken from the dead agent and used himself. Then he remembered his own revolver, which he had dropped when the truck suddenly appeared and which he had never had a chance to pick up. He found it now under the dashboard and threw it into the water after the others.

He was driving once more when Lewicki said, "Who wrapped this damned belt around my chest?" The voice was raspy, but recognizable and surprisingly strong.

"How do you feel?"

"How do you think I feel, you *shmuck?* Like I've been shot in the fucking head and chest." Lewicki swore softly. "How bad am I?"

Turner slowed a bit and glanced back. Lewicki lay on the seat, staring at him. His hair, matted in blood, had dried in ringlets around his face, making him look even younger. "The head wound is what put you out, but it's nothing. Just a crease. I don't know about the other. Do you feel cold inside?"

"Not very. It just hurts like hell."

"Then maybe the hemorrhaging has stopped. At least you're not in shock."

"Where are you taking me?"

"Washington. The first hospital I come to."

"No. Get me to Georgetown Medical. They've got the best emergency facility around. Do you know where it is?"

"Yes, I've passed it a couple of times."

Lewicki breathed deeply and swore at the pain. "I thought I got Handley before I conked out. Did I?"

"He died a few minutes after I found him."

"What about the fourth man?"

"I shot him."

"Dead?"

"Yes. And I checked the other three before I left. They were also dead." He did not feel it necessary to go into details.

"Did you get rid of the guns?"

"I threw them in a river."

"You're learning."

Turner drove for a moment in silence. "I was sure I had lost you in Arlington. I guess Hank must have told you where I was eventually heading."

"Who's Hank?"

"Hank Adams."

"You mean Herschel Turnovsky's girlfriend? Never met the lady. Why should she tell me anything?"

"Are you kidding?"

Lewicki's breath gurgled in his chest. "Christ, do I sound like I'm in the mood for jokes?"

"Then it wasn't Hank who sent you to watch my back?"

"Hell no. You were just a routine surveillance job to me when I left New York."

"And my uncle never sent you to Africa, either?"

"Don't know any uncles. Never been to Africa." Lewicki's voice missed a few beats. "Hey . . . what is it with you?"

Turner peered blankly at the road ahead. "Then how did you find me after I dumped you in Arlington?"

"I've had a beeper planted in your car since Richmond."

"You said you didn't."

"Never trust a cop."

"But why?" Turner shook his head. Was everyone in the world suddenly insane? "Why in the name of God did you do it? What the hell am I to you?"

Lewicki did not answer, and Turner began to think he might have lost consciousness again. But when he glanced back, the detective was staring at him out of that bloody sweet face, that young, Polish beauty of a face with eyes so blue they seemed to go all the way back to Jesus Christ. At least that was how Turner had once heard such eyes described by a Mississippi grunt in his original platoon. "I once told you what you are to me," Lewicki said in his bullet-scraped voice. "You're exactly the same kind of horse's ass as my brother. Real prime. Which is to say you need looking after."

Turner's knuckles showed white on the wheel. Were there really such people?

"I still have no idea why you needed so desperately to shoot the deputy director of the CIA," said Lewicki. "But I'd be willing to swear my idiot brother would have done the same thing."

"Handley murdered my wife." Which, thought Turner, was about as succinct an oversimplification as it was possible to manage.

"Aaah . . ." sighed Lewicki, and he was either content to

leave it at that or too weak and hurting to press it further.

But crossing the Potomac into Washington, he said quietly, "Here's the story we tell. I was mugged and you were driving by and found me. You were just a good Samaritan. And don't hang around. Leave the hospital at once, before any cops come. I don't want you having to identify yourself. Wait. Stop here."

Turner pulled over to the curb.

"Take my wallet and shield out of my pocket. If I was mugged, they would have grabbed everything. My revolver is gone anyway."

Turner did as instructed and started to drive once more. "How will you identify yourself?"

"The police can call my precinct in New York."

Turner suddenly remembered. "Damn it! Your car is still back there. They'll be able to trace it to you."

"No they won't. I used a fake credit card at the Richmond Airport. The card is in my wallet. Burn it with everything else."

He was silent then, and Turner mentally timed his breathing. It seemed faster and more labored than before. His lasting this long and regaining consciousness were good signs, but Turner had seen men joking one moment and lying dead of shock the next.

They entered the hospital's emergency driveway. There were two ambulances parked outside. Turner drove between them and stopped a few feet from the entrance ramp. "We're here."

Lewicki had begun to shiver. "Remember," he said between chattering teeth, "the minute they take me in, you beat it."

Turner did not like the shivering. How could he deliver him like a package and drive off? "I'll just check with a doctor."

"No!" Lewicki's teeth clicked like castanets. He was furious. "I want none of that shit. Do you think I shot four men and took two slugs myself so you can blow it all now? They'll grab

381

you as a material witness. You'll be identified. And once that happens, you'll be tied in with me, then with Handley, and we'll both be finished."

It made sense. How many times did this man have to pluck him from the fire? Still, Turner hesitated. He felt as though his chest was breaking up, as though large, important pieces of it were floating away and melting.

"You goddamned horse's ass!" swore Lewicki.

Turner went inside.

A team of four came out with a wheeled stretcher and plasma. They moved fast and efficiently. Turner had never seen any corpsmen move better. He watched them ease Lewicki out of the car, onto the stretcher, and up the ramp. The detective's face looked pained and pale blue, but his eyes, meeting Turner's, were still fierce. Beat it, they ordered. Turner continued to stand there. His last glimpse of Lewicki was of a frail, fair-haired young man, shivering and in pain, glaring furiously at him as he disappeared behind the light green doors of Georgetown Medical. He got into his car and drove off before someone remembered him and came out looking for him.

He drove south for close to an hour on Route 95, then west for another twenty minutes on 17. When he reached Kelly's Ford, he looked for the water tower that Handley had described. He found it, a solid, circular mass, black against the sky. He turned right onto a narrow, unpaved road. Watching his speedometer, he counted off a mile and a half and stopped. He heard the Rappahannock River rushing by on his left, but saw no sign of any cabin, only dark clusters of trees and foliage. Between branches, he caught a glimpse of stars reflecting on water and saw a rowboat tied up at a small wooden dock. Then he made out an opening in the trees almost dead ahead, drove into and through it, and parked on a flat, grassy area between a single story log cabin and what seemed to be a tool shed.

The Present

He got out and looked around. The place was totally isolated and very rustic, with not even a power line visible. Trees and bushes crowded close against the cabin on three sides. But a grouping of redwood garden furniture was set up on a graveled oval, facing the Rappahannock, which was less than fifty yards away. Soft night sounds came from the forest and the water.

Turner got a flashlight out of the car and walked slowly toward the house. There was something about the place that seemed to preclude moving quickly. He looked for the lantern that Handley had mentioned and saw it hanging from a porch post at the right of the steps. He unscrewed the base, reached inside, and took out a large key. It fit the front door, and he entered the cabin.

He was in a large central room. There were two doors opening off it, one, straight ahead, and the other, off to the right. On the left, was the fireplace. It was made of stone and covered almost half the wall. Deliberately, he turned his back on it. He walked around the room, following the beam of his flashlight. There were no curtains on the windows, and the furniture was simple, rough and mostly of unfinished pine. Kerosene lamps stood on two tables. A gun rack holding a bolt-action rifle and two over-and-under shotguns was nailed to the wall. Three fishing rods and a pair of hip-length wading boots stood in a corner. *Goyish naches*, his mother would have called such things. Christian pleasures. Hunting and fishing. As long as they were killing something, they were happy. But better fish, animals, and things that flew than Jews. His mother had taken an overly simplified view of the problem. One was not necessarily a substitute for the other. For two thousand years they had managed to do both.

A fleet of model sailing ships stood on a wall of shelves. They were the type that a young boy would make, and Turner had no doubt that Wendell Handley had made them as a child. There were also old baseball gloves, a Louisville Slugger, a pair of hockey skates, and two warped, wooden tennis rackets with half their strings missing. Other memora-

383

bilia was scattered about the walls, tables, and shelves—photographs of hunting and fishing parties, old high school and college pictures, yellowed newspaper stories of long-forgotten athletic victories, loving cups and trophies, racks filled with pipes of every size, shape, and type. The place was a Wendell Handley Museum, a totally male sanctuary into which neither girl nor woman had ever been invited or welcomed. There was not a photograph, not even so much as a snapshot, of the man's wife and daughters.

He finally turned and shone his flashlight on the hearth. The move was almost reluctant, as if what lay under the hearthstone was not actually the reason for his presence here, but something he was being forced to consider against his will and better judgment. Handley had said a cabinet member and three senators. Four more lives about to slide to hell in a basket. There had been so many lately. He felt vaguely troubled. Something was disturbing him. Was this it?

He looked at the stone. It was long and rectangular in shape, made of some sort of blue-gray slate, and looked to be about an inch thick. It was surrounded on three sides by rough, plank flooring and on the fourth by fieldstone. There appeared to be enough room between the slate and the righthand flooring to get a grip with his fingers. He put down the flashlight and angled its beam toward the fireplace. Then he dug in with both hands, strained against the solid weight, and slowly lifted and slid the hearthstone to one side. Under it, nestled into a hole scraped from the dirt, was a large, nail-studded, metal box. It measured about one by two feet and had no lock. There was a handle on top, and it apparently opened upward. Buried treasure. For once, Handley had not been lying.

Turner rewarded himself with a cigarette. He settled wearily into one of the pine chairs and sat there for a moment, smoking. Strangely, he was still less than anxious to expose himself to whatever damning information the box contained. Was this how Pandora had felt on her mission for Zeus? But she had opened her little bundle anyway, and the species was still reeling from its ills. Yet Wendell Handley had been far from a mythic god and was dead besides. What damage could he do now? This was simply his posthumous offering, his guarantee of protection for his family. What he had never been in life, what he had, indeed, never failed to attack in others, he had ironically managed to become in death—a humanist, a man suddenly willing to sacrifice a lifetime of doctrinaire belief for the sake of his wife and daughters.

Then, having thought this, he once more walked about the deputy director's rustic little museum. Here he was, thought Turner, boy and man. And he felt his heart pounding, his blood rising, and the colors of everything in the room starting to heighten. He had never even felt tempted to try LSD, but from everything he had read about the drug, he had the feeling that its effects might not be very different from the sensations he was experiencing now. But whether what he felt was good or bad, elation or depression, he was utterly unprepared to judge.

He crushed out his cigarette and looked about the cabin. He approached the fishing gear in the corner and picked up one of the rods. He had never fished in his life, but it took him only a moment to figure out how the reel worked. Anchoring the attached hook around a table leg, he backed out of the cabin, reeling out line as he went. When he had gone about fifty yards, he leaned the rod against a tree and went back inside the house. He disengaged the hook from the table leg and tied it around the handle of the tin box, which was still sitting in its neat excavation in front of the fireplace. He did it gently, being careful not to disturb either the handle or the box itself. His fingers felt thick and clumsy on the fine fishing line, and his palms were cold and sweaty. Easy, he told himself. You've been consistently wrong about this man in the past, and you're probably going to be wrong about him again. But he knew it was not that simple, and there was the taste of pennies in his mouth and a cold breath of the tomb seemed to come up out of the box. With the line at last secure on the handle, he went outside once more and picked up the fishing rod.

He turned the reel slowly. He heard the metallic, whirring sound it made as it revolved and the slack was taken up. Turner the dry-land fisherman. He was some fisherman all right. His mother should see the kind of fisherman her son had become.

> Simple Simon went afishing,
> Fishing for a whale.
> But all the water he could find
> Was in his mother's pail.

The last of the slack was reeled in, and the line felt taut. He put down the rod, grasped the line with both hands, took a few turns around his wrist, and dug in his heels for leverage. But at the last moment he held back, as though even now he was afraid to know for sure. Was there really hope hidden somewhere in uncertainty? And if there was, what was it that he was hoping for? That he might be proven right or wrong? Did he have a whale on his hook, a sardine, or only an old shoe? Feeling his lungs swelling against his chest, he yanked as hard as he could on the line.

For an instant there seemed to be nothing, just pure, airless, soundless vacuum. Then there was a sharp, cracking roar and whole sections of the roof shot straight up into the air. Turner felt the blast from the explosion push back against him, and he flattened out, face down, behind a tree. He breathed the familiar stench of cordite as the smoke rolled over him, and he heard it start to rain pieces of wood and stone. He felt some fragments fly past like shrapnel, while others drifted down through the trees, snapping branches and tearing leaves.

When things had stopped falling, he raised his head and looked at what remained. There was not much to see. A few small fires glowed, but they were scattered and quickly extinguished themselves. There had been explosives enough in the booby-trapped box to bring down a ten-story building. Nothing was left.

He pushed himself to his feet. The fishing line was still wrapped around his wrist, and he stood there, slowly unwinding it. Some small part of him must have known all along. There had been too exquisite a consistency to the man. The act of dying was not about to suddenly change him. Still, it was the contents of the cabin itself that had finally weighted whatever doubts he might have had. And this was what had saved him. Christ, not even a snapshot of his wife and kids. They were simply not that important to him.

He got into the car and drove quickly away before anyone came to investigate the explosion.

Well, Maruschka . . .

She had started him going, but how long ago was it that he had left her behind? It was impossible to pretend otherwise. This strange organism that was Paul (Turnovsky) Turner. Some people were just more bone-headed and stubborn than others. But did it mean anything? Did it in some way make him better, or did it make him worse? He had followed it to the end and maybe even achieved a kind of rudimentary, less than poetic justice. But dear, sweet God, at what cost. Somehow there were always more lessons to be learned. Yet who could survive the learning?

Turner was on his way home. He should have been drained, utterly exhausted, yet his body and brain swarmed with bubbling pools of energy. He should have taken a plane, yet he had taken the car. Driving, he rode into an orange sun. He looked at verdant trees. He watched a cloud, shaped like an eagle, drift low over a mountain. He saw white church steeples pointing in the general direction of God. He opened the car's windows and breathed the kind of air that was said to be the final resting place of the soul. Which he admitted to knowing absolutely nothing about, but which was still just about as much as anyone else knew.

Approaching Baltimore, he stopped and called Georgetown Hospital. He said he was Detective James Lewicki's precinct commander in New York and was told that the detective's vital signs were stable and were, in fact, slightly improved. Maybe not everything, yet infinitely more than dead. Which was nothing.

Near Aberdeen, the hills lost the sun on one side and took on a more purple color. On the other side, they were still a pale, muted green. There seemed to be a lot of geese flying. Patches of red flowers grew wild along both sides of the road. Yellow school buses droned along like giant bees and picked up small groups of black and white children.

Not a single snapshot.

He started to think about them, this woman he had helped make into a widow and her two fatherless little girls. But he put a lid on it fast. He was not about to push himself into that particular trap. Once in, there was no reasonable way of climbing out. Jesus. Widows and orphans. Still, he wondered if they had known they were not that important. He, at least, would carry out his part of the bargain. He would say nothing. With Maria's letter gone, who would believe him, anyway?

An alarm went off. Old dreads returned. They all came back at once, like swallows to Capistrano. *Who would believe him?* Obviously nobody. Which Handley had to have known. And which he himself should have known, but which, characteristically, he had not thought of in time for it to have done him any good. The bastard had simply wanted him dead. And to what end? For what substantive purpose? It was just pure maliciousness. I'm dying, so why not you? Turner could almost see him smiling, a sweet smile, the loveliest he owned. Checkmate, old buddy. We may just as well go together.

He suddenly felt sick, struck down, as if something of him were passing through unseen disasters. Yet what had he expected? Why was he continually being shocked, horror-struck, rendered almost physically ill by his entry into each new level of human darkness? Why was he always feeling betrayed, even by alleged enemies? Life on this earth was no Sunday School outing. Humankind survived mainly from devouring its own.

The Present

Even dead, it kept eating. Its skeletons grew fat bones.

He drove into a tunnel. It was long. He could not see even a tiny patch of light at the end. Only more and deeper darkness. Breathing the reek of murders past, present, and still to be committed, he was abruptly grateful to Maria for not leaving him with a child. Never mind her reasons. They no longer mattered. He had his own. The kid was better off unborn. It was missing nothing—only disappointments, goodbyes, people telling you one thing and meaning something else, anguish and fighting and confusion, and more and more killing each day, and there was no good reason for any of it. And the way things were moving, the whole bloody planet was going to be blown up soon anyway, with everyone left to rot in the ruins, the lucky ones dead fast, and all their bones sending radioactive signals to Mars. Maria had done both him and the kid a favor.

He left the tunnel and drove into sparkling sunlight. There was a lake with sailboats angled gracefully in the breeze. Three kites flew above a hill—two red and one yellow. A white farmhouse slept in the sun. Four cows stood like brown statues with white spots. The sky, now cloudless, was an incredible cerulean blue. The clarity of the air was almost palpable. Turner's breathing became slower and deeper. He felt himself moved by this springtime wealth. His heart was stirred by its gentleness. What was wrong with him? There were still miracles. Something pure always survived. They were a race of perennials. For every Handley, there had to be a Lewicki. And like it or not, even Handley had to be awarded a measure of grace for the unblemished piety and consistency of his belief. Unseen lives recited their poems. He was involved with them all. He had to be. He was a Jew and by history alone proven inextinguishable.

At Havre de Grace he pulled into a service area, asked for a pocketful of change, and called Fran Woodruff.

He heard her early morning voice—soft, warm, appealingly husky—and found himself grinning like an idiot. Somewhere inside, a familiar knot—solid, cold, hard as concrete—had begun to dissolve. "Just as a point of general information," he said, "what's your feeling about kids?"

It proved to be a reasonably good call. During a full ten minutes of conversation, he managed not to think of his wife for more than half the time.

Still, driving once more, with the sun warm through the windshield and the fields as shiny as the coat of a fox, he listened to a country singer lament *And loving her was easier than anything I'll ever do again* and found he had to turn off the radio. Which did not especially worry him. He knew he'd be able to handle that part all right. He just had to be a bit more careful about the love songs he listened to. At least for a little while. Like maybe about fifty years, he thought.